C000284423

THE WYLD HUNT

Gunnar Roxen

To Hannah: You are my muse.
Special thanks to Marjorie, David & Zeke and to the City of
Asheville, NC: You provided me safe harbour to write.

Revised Edition Thanks: To the eagle-eyed readers who spotted the
typos and grammatical errors I missed. Thank you :)

Legal Information & Copyright

The Wyld Hunt
First published in 2012, Revised 2013 by
Delta14 Publishing, Swindon UK

Paperback ISBN: 978-0-9572423-0-2
Ebook ISBN: 978-0-9572423-1-9

Email: hq@delta14.com
Web: www.delta14.com
Twitter: @Delta14HQ
Facebook: www.facebook.com/Delta14Publishing

Cover design by Richard Ward & Associates, Design Consultant,
Email: richard@rickward.co.uk

More Gunnar Roxen from Delta14 Publishing

DEAD ANGELS
(Agency Case Files Novella)
Paperback ISBN: 978-0-9572423-2-6
Ebook ISBN: 978-0-9572423-3-3

THE FIRESTORM CONSPIRACY
(Agency Case Files #2)
Available Summer 2013
Paperback ISBN: 978-0-9572423-4-0
Ebook ISBN: 978-0-9572423-5-7

Praise for The Wyld Hunt by Gunnar Roxen:
"I really enjoyed The Wyld Hunt. It's a bit of a challenge to find a genre that satisfies; cyberpunk meets noir? That's close but there's almost Dune like sci-fi in the background and elements of horror, even Lovecraft inspired horror, just lurking in the background..."
- GeekNative.com

"He has done everything right in a sci-fi noir novel and you want only one thing: even more of him." - FictionFantasy.de

"Widescreen, high-definition sci-fi thriller with full surround sound."
- Incrediblue

Visit

www.delta14.com

To read more about our books, download more samples and to buy them in paperback or ebook.

Science Fiction, Fantasy, Horror and The Weird

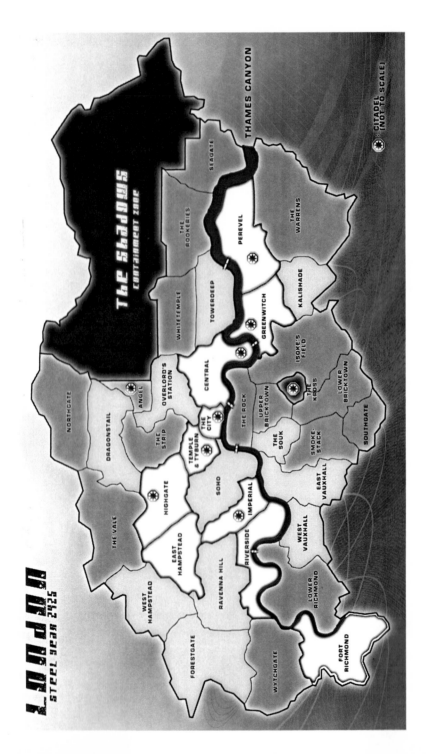

LONDON

STEEL YEAR 2425

THE SHADOWS
CONTAINMENT ZONE

THAMES CANYON

✴ CITADEL
(NOT TO SCALE)

SEAGATE

THE ROOKERIES

PEREVEL ✴

THE WARRENS

WHITETEMPLE

TOWERDEEP

GREENWITCH ✴

KALISHADE

NORTHGATE

ANGEL ✴

OVERLORD'S STATION

CENTRAL

✴

ISOKE'S FIELD

DRAGONSTAIL

THE STRIP

THE CITY ✴

THE ROCK

UPPER BRICKTOWN

✴ THE KROSS

LOWER BRICKTOWN

TEMPLE & TYBURN ✴

THE SOUK

SMOKE STACK

SOUTHGATE

THE VALE

HIGHGATE ✴

SOHO

IMPERIAL ✴

EAST VAUXHALL

EAST HAMPSTEAD

RIVERSIDE

WEST VAUXHALL

WEST HAMPSTEAD

RAVENNA HILL

LOWER RICHMOND

FORESTGATE

WYTCHGATE

FORT RICHMOND

Prologue

Steel Year 2425, Day Zero, Night

It was time to die.

A mournful howl echoed around the empty London streets, it reverberated off the hard brick and steel surfaces — given an otherworldly edge by the dank fog that rolled in from the river.

Out of the darkness of a rubbish-strewn alley emerged a man, running for his life, incongruous to this decaying locale in his finely tailored pin-stripe suit. When he hit the pavement's edge he stumbled and fell into the gutter, spraying filth over himself and tearing his beautifully tailored trousers. He cried out in pain as he twisted his ankle – blood stains blossoming on his scraped knees.

He groaned and climbed to his knees, wiping a hand across his face and smearing a line of stinking dirt as he did so. His breath came in short gulps, his chest heaved and his lungs ached. Pain, real physical visceral pain was new to him and he did not like it.

Never had he cause to run before this evening and it showed. Muscles unused to exertion were strained and weak. Though he – like all of his class – was genetically tailored to live a life measured in centuries, his hands shook like those of an old man. He peered around in the gloom with unfocused eyes. His expression slack, he appeared dazed. It was no good, he could not get his bearings. Even if he could have read a street sign it would not have helped.

The brutal truth was that people like him — people of *breeding* — just did not come to places like this. Sweat and tears poured down his soft face, matting his grey hair and stinging his eyes. With unsteady hands he reached into his jacket pocket and pulled out his personal communicator — his comm — and tried to work it.

"Come on, come on!"

It defied him and stubbornly refused to connect. It was as if he had lost many of his higher-cognitive functions. Rendered useless, the sophisticated device slipped from his sweat-slicked fingers and landed in the gutter with a dull thud.

The man looked at his hands as if he did not recognise them. Normally finely manicured, now chipped nails, ground-in dirt mixed with scratches and caked blood marked them. His whole mouth was full of the taste of his friend's blood. He spat, but the bloody taste would not go. He knew he had swallowed some and revulsion caused him to shudder violently.

Pulling himself together he lifted his gaze up above the nearby rooftops — some twenty stories above. There, in the distance, he could make out an impossibly-tall shining spire, that punched a ragged hole into the storm clouds. It shone like the blade of a sword. Clean, pure.

The tiniest sliver of hope flickered, and — with his mind briefly calmed — he slowly stood and began to hobble off once more. The forgotten comm finally connected. A regal woman's face appeared on it. Her lips moved, but her voice was silenced. She was speaking to no one.

The man stumbled into a busy street given a dreamlike quality by the fog. People hurried to and from work, or shopping, or just stood, chatting. The man was unable to process the scene's normality. He ran without heed and slammed heavily into the side of a car. He held his hands up in apology and pushed past the car, running across two lanes of traffic. Behind him the driver shouted obscenities, but the man could not hear them above the pounding of his own heart.

Spotting an extremely tall, bald man wrapped in an iridescent white coat who was talking on a comm, he ran up and grabbed the man by his arm.

"Please. You've. Got. To help me." he rasped. His voice was raw and hoarse.

The bald man slowly turned to look at him. His face was heavily tattooed and his eyes were yellow, like a wolf's. The bald man's gaze narrowed. Gasping in fear, the suited man mouthed the world '*no*' and staggered back, before turning and fleeing. The bald man shook his head, muttered a simple "Uptown tosser." and went back to his conversation as if nothing had happened.

He ran down the foggy slick streets. Muffled navigation horns and the slap of water against piers told him he was near the docks. Somehow he turned around in the fog and had lost sight of the glowing spire. A renewed wave of hopelessness hit him physically and he staggered once more. His whole body shook uncontrollably. He leaned against the corner of a warehouse and tried to catch his breath. Sweat drenched his shirt and clothes. He knew the chase was almost over, his ankle swollen and raw.

"Think! Think… must be a way!" He tried to examined his situation. He peeled off his jacket and held it in his hand. From a pocket he withdraw a nasty, serrated, silver knife which he held up in the light. Blood flecked the blade. "Yes, yes. Perhaps there is. Perhaps there can be an exchange." With a look of grim determination he gripped it tight with his other hand and looked around. "Who can I can use?"

Then, from out of the darkness behind him came the mournful howl once more. Eyes wide with terror, he glanced back the way he had come. In the darkness of the fog opened a mass of baleful yellow eyes. A foetid stench filled the air. He had one chance to survive. Holding the knife tight, he fled down the street, away from his pursuit. But there was nowhere to run.

1

Steel Year 2425.10.01 (S-Time). Day One, Morning

Agent John Aries looked up at the broken window high above him –
ignoring the heavy raindrops splashing on his upturned face. Though
– chronologically – he was almost fifty years old, his face was barely
lined, his features classically proportioned and unworn. He appeared
to be in his mid-30s and was moderately tall with a strong athletic
physique. His hair was brown, cut short to stay out of his piercing,
but weary, blue eyes. A tattoo of a grey star surrounded his left eye.
He projected an air of reserve, as if trying not to attract attention from
the world around him and wore his dark blue greatcoat pulled tight
against the rain.

Up above him, just visible through the swirling rain, light poured
out of the shattered window. It was at least a hundred metres above
him in the the dark slab-sided corporate tower. A few wet sheets of
paper gusted out and slowly floated down to the street. *A long way to
fall,* he thought to himself. Gargoyles grinned down at him, laughing
at the corpse lying in the rain in front of him.

Aries imagined the victim tumbling over and over, his descent
abruptly halted when he impaled himself with bone shattering force
on the spikes of the iron fence. He glanced over at the body and ran
a hand through his wet hair. Multiple spikes from the railing had
punched through the victim's back and emerged bloody from his
chest. His head and legs hung lifelessly back. The rain was doing a
good job of cleaning the blood from the street, but there had been an
incredible quantity of it, and even now the odd droplet of blood mixed
with rain water trickled down the victim's face.

It was messy, and given the distance from the building, some
twenty-odd metres, the victim either took a running leap or was
thrown. Aries' money was on the leap, though why the victim took
the plunge was still to be determined. He adjusted his high-collared
navy blue greatcoat tighter against the rain, but it did no good. Up this
high in the city, on the elevated roadway, the rain came at him from all
directions like a mischievous djinn.

Aries stifled a yawn. It was too early in the morning, and he wanted
a coffee. *No chance of that until I get this logged.* He also needed to
find out why the Metropolice had called in the Agency. After all, to
all intent it looked like a regular suicide or, possibly, murder. Nothing
screamed "Agency" at him from the scene. At least not yet.

Time to find out why I have been called in.

Aries walked over to the body, ignoring the miserable policeman shivering in the rain. Snapping on some clean forensic gloves Aries gently took the victim's head in his hands and examined it. A brilliant, slightly luminescent grey eight-pointed star tattoo surrounded the victim's left eye, the twin of his own star. *Ah. Of course. Well that is one mystery solved. Echo. At least I know I got the right call.*

John absent-mindedly scratched his own tattoo. It felt warm to the touch, as it always did. *So if the victim was an Echo, maybe he could fly?* The tattoo meant he was Registered, so his abilities should be on record – though still carefully restricted. *Something to look up.* Next, Aries considered the victim's clothes, the pinstripe suit was very expensive, apparently tailored by Xi Volker the exclusive fashion designer.

Even now it was shrugging off the rain and dirt as if, even in death, the victim was too refined to be bothered by such trifles. A large gold signet ring on the victim's left little finger caught John's eye. It was a graduation ring of some sort, though off-hand Aries didn't recognise where it was from. He leaned forward and examined it in more detail. Fine calligraphic Elysian Script surrounded an emerald. The tiny Elysian word characters on it translated to "The Honourable Brotherhood, Chapter of The Divine Imperial Commonwealth University of Victoria. May the Overlord's Hand Guide Us All."

I guess the Overlord was looking the other way today, thought Aries, then caught himself. That kind of thinking would get him in trouble. Behind him he heard the fussing of an approaching forensics team. He ignored them, and scanned the victim with his comm. Obligingly the corpse's identification flashed up:

[Name: Nigel Phillip Volaire Massey de Sargon; REGISTERED ECHO X920398/A3244; Sex: Male; Age 38; Race: Human (Elysian); Occupation: Senior Financial Analyst TMD Financial Services, London, Earth; Medical Cover: Platinum, Nova Response; No outstanding warrants.]

Platinum medical cover? he thought *Then where is the medical team?* Platinum cover should have summoned emergency assistance within seconds. Even these terrible wounds and trauma were not necessarily fatal if they had arrived here fast enough, but, aside from the Metropolice and himself, there was no sign of any emergency response. He was going to have to get the forensics team to find out why Massey de Sargon was lying here dead and not in a regentank being expensively rebuilt. *Another mystery. Intriguing.*

The loud clearing of a forensic tech's throat interrupted his thought process. "Excuse me Agent Aries? Could we take the body now?" Aries nodded and stepped away. He ignored the usual *soto-voce* grumbling about 'Agency trampling all over police investigations'. His mind was analysing the pieces. He fastened the gold buttons down one side of his greatcoat to keep out the cold.

Dead Echo, no medical response, probable suicide. Leapt or was pushed from up there. No other obvious traumas. What led you to have such a bad day, Mr Massey de Sargon?

He frowned, as he knew he did not have enough information to come to any kind of conclusion yet. Best go to the source, as after all this was patently not the crime scene. Whatever happened, happened up *there*. Leaving the forensic techs to finish up, Aries walked through the wrought iron gates and across the pavement to the tower's glass entrance. The doors, detecting his Agency badge, slid open with a hiss and he entered the offices of TMD Financial Services.

He crossed the atrium's marble floor quickly, the heels of his field boots echoing around the room. All around him the videos of TransMael Drive's corporate activities covered the walls. Gigantic ship yards relentlessly churned out warships and merchant spacecraft without pause. Mighty geoengineering machines rewrote the environment of whole planets. Cyclopean mining vessels cracked open planets unsuitable for colonisation to extract all the metals at their core. TMD was about big business. Planetary big. Either side of the reception desk stood ten-meter tall angel statues. They stood vigil with swords upraised and faces twisted by feral snarls. The lobby was intended to intimidate, that was a given, but what Aries took away was that it revealed the corporation's insatiable grasping hunger.

The receptionist looked up, as if only half aware of his presence. Aries knew it was all part of the act to leave him feeling unsettled. "How can I help you, sir?" she asked.

He flashed his Agency badge at her and held her gaze steadily. "Agent Aries. Nigel Massey de Sargon's office. Where is it?" He noticed the small, almost imperceptible start from her when she saw the badge. John fought back a grin. *She thought I was going to be Metropolice.*

Her eyes closed briefly and a holographic cherubim appeared in the air between Aries and the desk. "If you will follow the guide, it will take you to Mr Massey de Sargon's office." Without another word Aries started off after the apparition as it led him toward one of the many columns in the atrium. A lift door silently slid open in the column and Aries stepped in. No destination were required – the lift knew where he was going. It simply started upward, literally toward the painted firmament in the ceiling.

*   *   *

The hallway to Massey de Sargon's office was a plethora of gilt. Everything that could be gilt-edged, was. Aries passed paintings by some of London's most famed artists, now nothing more than ostentatious corridor ornamentation. The holographic cherubim stopped ahead and hovered in front of a door, then vanished. Aries flashed his badge at the door and it dutifully unlocked and swung inward. Inside a mini tornado was destroying the room. Aries shook his head then strode across the room and slammed his fist against a glowing storm shutter button. Instantly steel shutters snapped shut over the broken window and the storm died.

Turning around, Aries surveyed the room. It was a mess. The pressure differential up at this altitude had sucked everything lighter than the furniture across the room, like a demented burglar or wild animal.

By his feet Aries saw a heavy pistol casually discarded. *An Aralyte Terminator, just like mine.* He gave an exasperated look. *A suit like Massey de Sargon would barely have been able to lift a pistol like that, much less fire it with any accuracy.* Aries had received extensive training and had the strength to handle the 14.5mm cannon, but from the look of him Massey de Sargon had not. Therefore, it was, without doubt, a show piece, something to occasionally reveal when Massey de Sargon had felt the need to assert his non-existent street credentials. Still, given that, it was obvious that it had been fired recently, the vents along the slide had slightly singed the carpet.

Mentally filing that information away, John turned his attention to the rest of the room. A large offworld Elysian Mahogany table filled most of the space, with a grand executive chair on one side and a pair of simpler, smaller, chairs on the other. *The Alpha male ego strikes again. It all feels so familiar.* Aries had a momentary flash back to his own past. *Concentrate,* he thought to himself. Aries might have been roused unexpectedly from his sleep to deal with this death, but he was a professional. *Just get the job done John, the move on. Nothing flashy, nothing unprofessional.* Aries sat in Massey de Sargon's chair. A dull rectangular glow appeared at the table's edge, and he waved his hand over it, instantly bringing the holographic display to life in the air above the table. John checked the recent messages and memos. There was one from barely an hour ago. He played it.

The terrified face of Nigel Phillip Volaire Massey de Sargon appeared in the air like a ghost. He appeared to have trouble focusing his eyes, his pupils were hugely dilated. He gave every indication of being on strong hallucinogens. "We should never have started down this road. I thought we could control it, but I — we — can't. He didn't know what he unleashed when we began the hunt." The last was said through clenched teeth. "And now *it* is coming for me. Well, I won't let it! I won't." In a smaller voice "I can't." then back once more to a more even tone "That damned plan, that damned Book. I never should have gone, we should never have used it." With his right hand, Massey de Sargon raised into view the pistol, it wobbled unsteadily in his hand. "But I am not going to go out on *its* terms. It thought it could outsmart me? Outsmart me? Samael's blade take them all!" With the final dramatic utterance, raised the pistol to his head and pulled the trigger. Nothing happened, the gun's inbuilt sensor preventing an accidental discharge against the wielder. Massey de Sargon swore, turned and shot the window. It exploded outward.

Massey de Sargon dropped the pistol and climbed up onto the sill, and turned to face the desk once more. He peered towards the door, his expression suddenly one of curiosity, but – as if realisation had dawned – it became contorted in terror. He was hit by a sharp gust of wind, appeared as if he was thrown out of the window, so suddenly was he pushed. The video ended shortly afterwards. The last thing that Aries noted was that as his fell from view, Massey de Sargon's eyes and Echo tattoo were burning brightly. *Whatever Echo abilities he had, did not save him.*

Aries checked the rest of the room visually. The only other noticeable feature was a large painting of a nightmarish landscape positioned directly across from the desk. Aries walked round to it. The painting was by the famously reclusive artist Simon Ulialias Nuan. Massey de Sargon must have stared at it every day. It gave John the shivers. Surrounding it were various certificates, proclamations and licenses. The summation of everything Massey de Sargon was. *And ever will be...* There was even the Aegis Foundation's feared black scroll proclaiming Nigel Massey de Sargon as a Registered Echo authorised to live, and to be bound for a period of ten years to the TMD corporation. The embossed Star of the Overlord overlaid it, slightly luminescent.

Just for a moment Aries closed his eyes, Aries heard the screams from his own shuttered memories of that dark period of training. For every Echo that survived the training, many did not. There were no second chances. Either you passed and lived, or... His hand brushed the Overlord's Star on the Proclamation. He could feel dull pain of the star branded on his own face, a feeling that caused him intense pride, fear and even a touch of revulsion.

Echoes were the elite of society, gifted — or cursed, depending on your viewpoint — with the ability to reshape reality by force of will, channelling the energies of the chaotic dimension known as the Wyld. As with all power there was a price. The Wyld Cancer was the bane of all Echoes. Every use of their abilities slowly grew the cancer that would eventually kill them. It was incurable. The universe demanded its dues and it was something all Echoes knew and understood. Their lot was short, but they burned brightly, with few Echoes surviving into old age. Only those who learned to minimise their ability use survived. It sounded easy, but the power was intoxicating and always there.

Echo abilities were the bedrock of the interstellar Steel Alliance of humanity. So much of society and technology was built on the blood of Echoes. But Echoes were also a massive threat to society, all Echoes, regardless of how trained, occasionally lost control of the titanic energies they summoned, unleashing what was colloquially — and rather confusingly — known as a Wyld. An unfocused detonation of destructive energies that would destroy everything around the Echo. *Except* the Echo themselves. In an attempt to control this, only the strongest Echoes were allowed to live. It was a cruel, but necessary, requirement, learned through a period of tremendous pain and suffering, known as The Chaos, that almost spelt the end for humanity.

Like every surviving Echo, every millimetre of that pain was burned into Aries' soul.

A knock at the door startled him out of his remembrance. Without even realising it, his hand had gone to the shoulder holster inside his coat. His head snapped around and he fastened his gaze on the intruder.

"What?!" He demanded.

A deep gravelly voice replied "A bit jumpy today aren't we, Agent Aries?" John's gun hand relaxed.

Standing in the doorway, more filling it, was a huge figure. It was Aries' new partner Lovelace. Aged somewhere in his mid-30s he stood just under seven feet tall and was built like a brick shit-house. Real name Tarus Arken Karazhja, he was more commonly known by the nickname 'Lovelace'. Lovelace was one of the human subspecies known as 'Pures'. Like all Pures, who formed a sizeable minority of London's population, his eyes were all black, lacking whites, and stood in contrast to his white skin, grey lips and grey eyelids. Short spiked black dreadlocks stood out from his head. The left-hand side of his face had a vertical line of tattoos in the Pures' script, *Kapaethjan*.

It proclaimed him to be Warrior Caste of the Truthsayer Kindred to any who could read that obscure language.

The tattoos told a story of his life to anyone who could read them. Luckily, Aries could. There: the ritual scars of three mortal duels, fought to the death over disagreements of honour, something central to the life of every Pure, fought as a Truthsayer. Here: the tattoos that told of birth on London but with ascension to adulthood on the homeworld of Kapaethja. The tattoos would continue down his body, each further adding to the tale of his life story.

Lovelace stood there in a black suit, shirt and tie with a massive well-worn sword incongruously strapped over his back. Silver hoops pierced his eyebrows, ears and nose and his white hands with black nails were replete with many silver rings. Despite his relaxed posture, Lovelace always appeared primed for violence.

Of course, these were secondary features about Pures. What most humans noticed first was the mouth full of sharp, pointed teeth evolved for tearing. What Aries noticed however, was that he looked hurried.

"Lovelace where have you been? I have been here for at least twenty minutes." He was annoyed at the Pure's late arrival. This was only their second case together, and Aries still did not have a handle on Lovelace or their partnership yet. *We are so different, we come from such different places.*

The Pure shrugged. "Traffic. Some cock crashed into the Tyburn Rise and I had to drive round to the Highgate. Anyway, what've we got? I saw the body outside."

"A city gentleman, an Echo, by the name of Nigel Massey de Sargon, decided to take a dive. Check out the comm recording on the desk, I left it running."

Lovelace stepped across the room and went to check the vid.

"Isoke's balls! What chems was he taking?"

"I'm not sure, but he was terrified about something. That reminds me. Lovelace, could you check out why Nova Response weren't called in? He had platinum insurance and yet no one attended."

"You thinking it was some kind of corporate hit?"

"The thought had crossed my mind, but my intuition tells me no. Still it is a very loose end, and I do not like loose ends."

"Sure, no problem. I'll get Crypt to run a back-trace on him. Anyway, John, you want to let the forensics guys in now?" Aries nodded, and Lovelace waved in the two white-suited technicians who had quietly been standing in the door way. "You can come in now, boys. We don't bite." said Lovelace whilst flashing them his shark-like grin.

*   *   *

Aries' journey back to Central was contemplative. Lovelace had taken his own bike, leaving Aries alone to fly back. The tiered man-hive that was London surrounded his grav car on all sides, with the vast and majestic Citadels punching up through the clouds. Aries gently lifted off from the landing pad outside the TMD tower, the comm system on-board doing most of the flying. He glanced to the left at the sealed storm shutters of Massey de Sargon's office as he rose past.

Why would a man like that commit suicide. Over a book? He had seemed to be talking about a real, physical book. Although rare they were still used, mostly by the aristocracy and powerful to denote learning. *But this was not 'a' book, it was 'The' Book.* He had heard the enunciation clearly in Massey de Sargon's voice. Something – *it* – had terrified him enough to kill himself rather than face… something. Whatever it was, it was terrifying. Terrifying enough that suicide appeared to be the easier way out. The problem was it was a suicide, the vid proved it, and that meant that the case would be closed up almost as soon as it was opened. The Agency would not care *why* he killed himself, just that he *had*. After all it was not unusual for Echoes to top themselves, regardless of social class or status in society. Walking around as a living bomb of sorts could grind anyone's nerves down, something Aries knew only too well.

That reminded him: while he flew he put in a formal request to the Aegis Foundation to find out what Echo abilities Nigel Massey de Sargon had. Of course, the request would probably take weeks to be processed. The Aegis Foundation was intentionally opaque about such things. It would not do to have all Echoes be open books. Still these formalities had to be followed.

Aries shook his head and concentrated on where he was going. He piloted the grav car through the sheeting rain and the canyons between the nine mighty towers known as 'Citadels'. His grav car soared above the deserted raised roadways of Uptown and the rumbling gauss trains of the Upper Tube's transport lines. The rain came from all directions by the chaotic wind turbulence patterns from the heat and hard surfaces that made up every tower. Above him boiled the semi-permanent storm clouds generated by the heat and humidity. London had its own distinct micro climate, one that could make it a grim place to live. The Citadels did not care, they simply punched through into the sunlight above.

He flew past verdigrised, copper-plated gargoyles and statues of the holy, the famous and the notorious, their dripping trails of green staining the granite, concrete walls and niches. Steam belched out from huge air conditioning systems shaped like the gullets of giant birds, momentarily obscuring his vision.

Competing with the statues, gigantic screens and projections displayed corporate adverts and news from across the Steel Alliance. The sky tonight was fairly light on grav traffic, which made the flight easier, but glancing down, deep into the canyons of Downtown, he could see the streets packed with vehicles and people rippling in the heat haze generated by so many people crammed in so tightly. The lower you went, the more people there were and the less they had.

Then he banked and turned a corner and saw his destination, the mighty government Citadel known only as Central. The eight-sided building itself was vastly tall, constructed of pitted grey concrete. Banners with the flags of the Governor of Terra, the Agency, the Steel Alliance and the Accord covered much of its surface. Golden statues, ancient gun turrets, once part of London's orbital defence system and now silent, and golden eight-pointed stars of the Overlord dotted the tower. Sitting a-top the citadel of Central just above the clouds was the Golden Pyramid where Commander Sir James Villiers-Cavanaugh, head of the London Agency, had his offices.

Surrounding it like flies were hundreds of large transport grav planes, and the smaller grav cars, and grav bikes jetting off across the city on various tasks or simply patrolling the skies around Central.

Aries set the grav car onto autopilot and let the small craft be guided into one of the many landing bays in its upper level. His grav car floated in between twin rows of green lights disappearing into the darkness.

*   *   *

Aries exited the lift and entered the offices of the Agency's Investigations London division known as 'SO-50'. He walked down the short set of steps onto the main office floor.

The circular bank of lifts were built around the building's inner core. The entire outer edge of the offices was one long tinted panoramic window overlooking London. The light that came in had a dusky quality to it which contrasted with the alabaster white desks, walls and onyx floors. The desks and walls were all illuminated from within, casting everything in a soft white glow.

The lower grade Agents worked at desks in a pool between the lifts and the windows, the senior grade Agents, such as Aries, had their own offices at the edge. Displays around the office showed mixtures of crime stats, news channels or data files on the most wanted. Everything was designed to project a sense of clarity and power. Hanging from the ceiling were the Agency and the Accord's twin flags.

Aries never spent much time here, his career in the Agency to date had not exactly been stellar. He worked hard being neither outstanding, nor under performing. For his own reasons he was happiest to fade into the background. However in the back of his mind he had a niggling sensation that his low-key existence was about to be challenged.

Aries' comm beeped and he activated it. A dispassionate female voice spoke "S.A.C. GR5 Agent Captain Linsbury requests a briefing on the Massey de Sargon case."

The 'SAC' (es-ay-see, never 'sack') was the local division's Strategic Agent-in-Command, and ran one of the local divisions such as SO-50 Investigations or SO-40 Intel, and Grade 5 Agent Paul Linsbury was Grade 4 Lieutenant Aries' and Grade 3 Senior Agent Lovelace's direct superior. This despite the fact that Linsbury was an Analyst not a Field Agent. He had earned himself a full command and not, as usual for analysts, taking on the role of Operational Intelligence Officer or Security Evaluator and Coordinator. Rumour had it that Linsbury was a sharp political player, and knew where the bodies were buried.

Aries went into his office only to throw his greatcoat on the chair and headed straight over to Linsbury's office. Lovelace intercepted him from the lift. He looked flushed. John smiled "That was quick for a ground bike. Linsbury wants to see us."

"I shouldn't have rushed then." Lovelace and Linsbury did not get on. As a veteran street cop-turned-Agent, Lovelace was all about the action, and Linsbury was all about the thinking, so it probably was not surprising. As for Aries, just as with his new partner, Lovelace, he had not made up his mind about Linsbury. Linsbury had only taken on the SAC role a couple of months back and had not stamped his mark on it yet.

Aries and Lovelace walked into Captain Linsbury's office. Linsbury's office was unusual. Aries had him figured for the political type when he first met him, and pictured him with a Spartan office and a big picture of London Agency Commander Sir James Villiers-Cavanaugh and a row of polished citations.

He was completely wrong. Displays, maps, comm gear and strangest of all, in one corner, a curio cupboard of archaeological artifacts and fossils filled Linsbury's office. It felt more like the office of an overworked professor than a strategic commander within the Agency. Of course there was the requisite shrine to his patron Disciple, which in this case was Thoth, Lord of Information. Having a personal shrine in an office was not at all uncommon as all Agency personnel of rank G5 or higher received basic priestly training.

Aries and Lovelace had to step around a holographic reconstruction of what appeared to be a bank robbery. Linsbury had it set up so he could model the customer's movements. In fact it appeared he had taken the robbers themselves *out* of the equation. *Interesting,* thought Aries.

"Take a seat agents, I will be with you momentarily."

Linsbury's voice spoke from behind his desk where he was peering at some detailed screens of equations. He wore reading glasses, an unnecessary affectation, which completed the scholarly air.

Aries sat in an armchair. Lovelace, always slightly twitchy, chose to perch on the edge of a cupboard. Linsbury finally looked up.

"So Aries, fill me in on Mr Massey de Sargon's death."

"My initial view is that it was most likely a suicide, and that Mr Massey de Sargon was involved in something very unpleasant and decided that suicide was the easier choice. We have a vid recording of the suicide itself and I was going to have it analysed to check it was not doctored and then check his bank records and other trails to see if it was part of some corporate attack."

"Do you think it was?"

"Honestly? No. I think he was scared into doing it. Something scared him more than committing suicide."

"Hmm. Good. In which case, I have another investigation for you."

"Captain, with respect, I'd like to investigate the Massey de Sargon situation further. Something about it bothers me."

"I understand that Aries, and normally I would let you get on with it. I don't like loose ends either." Linsbury indicated around the room for emphasis, "But, this comes down from on high. From the Commander's office to be exact, and they asked for you by name. Lovelace can follow-up the Massey de Sargon case."

Lovelace quietly muttered "Oh arse." Aries and Linsbury ignored him.

"Me? What do they want me for?"

"The Commander wants you to investigate his close friend's disappearance. The Director of Terran System Planetary Finance for

Stealth-Albion, Viscount Charles Hamilton-Jones, to be precise."

Lovelace let out a low whistle. Aries felt his shoulders tense up. Though neither of them knew this Charles Hamilton-Jones by name, as a Director of Finance, with remit over an entire solar system, for a major division of the largest 'Charter Corporation' in the Steel Alliance, founded under Divine Mandate by the Overlord Himself, they knew that he was powerful. Aries pondered putting up some objections, but if this came from the Commander himself then there was some serious political clout involved. The decision had been made. *But why me? I have deliberately kept a low profile since I joined the Agency. Nothing too showy. Damn!* Aries felt as if someone had poured ice water down his back. He had to clear his throat before speaking again.

"Disappearance?"

"Yes, his wife Clarice Hamilton-Jones reported he had been missing for over twenty-four hours." Linsbury paused. "Look Aries, I don't know why they want you specifically, and nor do I care. I do know that when the Commander says jump we jump, and yes, I know twenty-four hours is barely any time to be missing, but I am sure they have their reasons. Just head over to their estate in East Hampstead and look into it. Hopefully it is nothing, but frankly, I have no idea. So be prepared for anything."

Taking that as a dismissal Aries and Lovelace stood up to leave. As they reached the door Linsbury, who had returned to his equations, spoke again without looking up "Aries, keep your guard up. Nothing is what it seems with those people, and I dislike orders from 'on high'."

Lovelace clapped Aries on the shoulder, "Hope you brought your poison sensor."

Aries had a sinking feeling. *Oh damn. What have I been pulled into?* thought Aries as they left.

2

Steel Year 2425.10.01 (S-Time). Day One, Afternoon

The flight from Central to East Hampstead took him westward across London. The rain had picked up pace and was now bordering on torrential. Aries had left Lovelace at Central to do some further digging on Massey de Sargon, while Aries conducted the first interview with Clarice Hamilton-Jones. It had seemed like a good idea at the time to leave Lovelace behind, but now John was regretting not having the backup. He did not like mixing with the powerful. It was too close to what he had escaped from, and there was always the risk someone would recognise him, despite the cosmetic changes. The journey of his life was long and wreathed in fire, the memories locked away inside the darkest parts of his mind.

He could feel his thoughts spiralling down into depression, so he distracted himself by turning his attention to the city around him. To his left he passed the mighty Stealth Citadel. Built under Divine Mandate from the Overlord himself over two thousand years previously, it was the tallest building ever to have been constructed on Earth. It dominated the city like the crest of the mightiest mountain. More accurately it should be called a volcano, as it tapped deep into the earth to provide the city with limitless geothermal energy. The outside of the tower was a baroque collection of flying buttresses, huge stained-glass windows and statues hundreds of metres tall. Over the many centuries since it had been built the Tower had gained the patina of age. It was an offering to Lady Albion, Disciple of Progress. Now, many of the windows were broken and birds nested inside, the white trails of their guano streaking down the walls. Gnarled trees and vines grew from the sites of ancient battle damage on fractured towers and broken walls. Yet, despite patches of dereliction, the Tower was very much still alive, but the tens of thousands who worked, lived, fought and occasionally died inside filled but a small corner of its five kilometre-high mass. The Stealth-Albion corporation, powerful descendant of Stealth, now tied in an irrevocable, loveless marriage of convenience with its arch rival the Kalidasa Biocorporation, still kept its headquarters for its operations across the whole of the Accord there.

It was from there that this Charles Hamilton-Jones had overseen his mighty fief that stretched across the entire solar system. But that was not where he was headed.

The rest of the city and Citadels crowded around the Stealth Tower:

to the North stood the Hope Tower, white and gleaming seemingly untarnished but wrapped in mystery; to the North-east, the abandoned and hopeless Angel Tower slowly decaying into the forbidden sectors that formed the Shadows; to the East was Central - his base; South-east stood the massive Perevel spaceport, the lifeline to the stars; the South was home to the Kalidasan Pyramid, a prize arcology and slice of Eden; the South-west held the Tower of the Sun, once the proudest and brightest, now sealed off with every attempt made to remove it from memory, only ghosts lived there now; West stood the Tower of Judgement and its smaller sibling, the Necropolis; to the North-west the Golden Spires of Aralyte, once built by a now-forgotten medical corporation, now home to the massive manufacturer of weaponry, Aralyte. Nine Citadels.

Clinging to the Citadels' sides like polyps on a coral reef, were many smaller towers. Elevated roadways and gauss lines were strung between them in a complex web as if spun by an insane spider.

London was divided into four distinct vertical strata. At the top, above the clouds, in a world of cold, clean air, was Zen. Needless to say only the most powerful even saw this world. Beneath this, deep in the clouds and below, was Uptown. Clean, regimented, secure and inward facing, it was possible to live your entire life here without ever touching the ground. Below that was Downtown that arose from street level. Here was a melting pot, with all races, peoples, ages and classes mixed in the part of the city that would be recognisable to any human from history. But the city did not stop there. In an effort to ease chronic overcrowding, city planners built downward, creating the underground world of Ground Zero, where the true ground level once was. Tightly packed corridors, harsh lighting, squeezed apartments, and a mass of people living in too close confinement marked this murky labyrinth.

And that was were the city stopped, though of course there was the legendary 'Deep Zero' formed from ancient, forgotten tunnels, pits and corridors. Wherever entrances were found they were quickly sealed off in case something from the Shadows of old East London, or the Wytchwoods beyond the walls of London found its way in.

Among all this was the enigma of East Hampstead. Once, it was a hill overlooking London, but during the millennia of its existence the city all around it had thrust upwards, eventually leaving this enclave of power a virtual valley. Security was tight and his grav car was scanned. No one entered the sector without permission. Aries knew all this, but as his grav car passed the last tower and the rain clouds surrounding Hampstead, he had to fight a sudden sense of vertigo as the ground disappeared beneath him and he was momentarily blinded by the bright daylight. Complex environmental engines gave Hampstead its own climate. The wealth required to achieve this was staggering, as was the arrogance. For some of the super rich it was not enough to live above the clouds, the clouds had to bend to their will.

He started his descent, dropping rapidly into the valley. Glancing at his heads-up display, he saw the altitude ticking down, 1200 metres... 1000 metres... 800 metres... 600 metres... 400 metres. Beneath him all he could see was parkland: Hampstead had no roads. The only way in was by air. Deer scattered beneath him as he flew across the tree tops. Eventually he reached the Hamilton-Jones estate. A wrought iron fence surrounded the manse. The architecture was baronial in form, with a central graeco-roman columned portico flanked by two grand wings. Within the grounds were exquisitely manicured gardens and pools filled with koi. In front of the main entrance was an area set aside for vehicles to land in. An alert sounded in the car: A targeting system had locked on to him. Despite the apparent lack of obvious security, that alert was to let him know that unexpected visitors would not be welcome.

Aries brought the car in to land. When he stepped out of the car he breathed deeply the smell of fresh-cut grass with a hint of lavender. Looking at the horizon he was surprised that he could not see the rest of the city. It was as if he were in the midst of some pastoral landscape and not, as he knew he was, standing less than a kilometre from the surrounding towers. A predatory bird of some sort circled lazily overhead on the thermals.

It feels like a dream.

A crunching noise on the gravel behind him made him spin with a start. A scarecrow of a man attired in a white suit with matching white tie and gloves had appeared. His eyes were likewise entirely white, yet he was definitely not blind. His face reminded Aries of the bird of prey above.

"Agent Aries, my name is Six. The Lady of the House is expecting you. If you will kindly follow me, sir?" John took one last deep breath before following the strangely named Six into the house.

Six led Aries into the mansion's grand entrance. A grand pair of staircases rose on either side of the hall and curved round to a landing above. Hanging from the walls above the stairs were portraits of proud, ageless men and haughty women whom Aries presumed to be former scions of the house of Hamilton-Jones. It was obvious the dynasty stretched back many centuries. Above the staircase was a full-length portrait of a man in military dress uniform staring out regally into space from a slightly pudgy face. An Echo tattoo seemed incongruous on his weak face. Beside him, in a long white dress, was a woman who stared directly at the viewer. Her dark hair was piled up high and she was dressed classically without undue ornamentation. Her eyes seemed to burn into John where he stood. Though the painting was about the man, it was she – not he – that dominated the space.

"The Master and Lady of the House." spoke Six unbidden, confirming Aries' deduction. "This way, sir." Six led him across the hall and into a side room. It was a library. Books, mostly ancient, filled the shelves to bulging on three sides of the room. On a whim, and given the Massey de Sargon case, he quickly surveyed the shelves to see if any books were missing. A fireplace dominated the fourth wall. Placed centrally were a couch and two overstuffed high-backed chairs around a coffee table. Six indicated one of the chairs which faced away from the door.

Aries felt an explained cold shiver pass through him. There was *something* about the room that he could not quite put his finger on. The moment passed.

"If you will wait here, the Lady will be with you momentarily." Aries sat down and resisted the urge to try to peer over his shoulder at the door. *So far, as expected.*

*   *   *

Lovelace rolled out of Central on his ground bike. As an Agent, he could easily have had a grav version, but he preferred, where possible, to stay at street level. Maybe it was a hangup from his days as a cop, but he liked to feel the city's mood. Being both a local (born in London) and an outsider (a Pure), he held closely to his sense of belonging to the city while always keeping one eye open for when it might turn on him.

London was unusual for having such a large population of Pures. There were very few cities outside of Kapaethja that could equal it. Many of the human subspecies had moved here because it was the Steel Alliance's birthplace. This is where humanity was bound, almost two and a half thousand years ago, in the sealing of the Steel Alliance with the Overlord and His Disciples: the Tattooed Man, Disciple of Judgement; Albion, Disciple of Progress; Kali, Disciple of Death; Isoke, Disciple of Creation; The Fool, Disciple of Change; Samael, Disciple of Vengeance; Cai Shen, Disciple of Commerce; Thoth, Disciple of Knowledge and the soon-to-be-cursed Baal, Disciple of War and Lokden, Disciple of Entropy. Despite everything that had happened in that time – the fall of Baal, the Overlord's disappearance and the myriad empires, republics and civil wars –

it still held a mystical attraction for the Pures, second only to their claimed homeworld, Kapaethja, where the Tattooed Man, their patron Disciple, now resided.

Being raised in London had always made Lovelace suspect with homeworld Pures. As one of the Truthsayer kindred, he had naturally joined the Metropolice, but even that had not eased the suspicion he received from Pures born on Kapaethja, as if he was not Pure *enough*. That suited Lovelace fine mostly, though as the small scars on his face testified, it was not always possible to turn the other cheek. Each scar represented one mortal duel, where he had fought to the death to defend his, or someone else's, honour. The irony was that as a warrior caste Truthsayer, that was his job, but it seemed the more he had worked at being a good Pure, the more he was mistrusted.

He had found his cultural identity instead in the Metropolice. He had worked his way up through the ranks without patronage, based on a dedication to his job and his colleagues. He tried to keep out of the politics endemic to all big organisations as long as he could, until one day the politics caught up with him. Before he knew it, his career in the police was finished, but an ex-partner got in touch and offered him a second start in the Agency. It had pained him to leave the Metropolice, just as it pained him to have to isolate himself from other Pures, but he was a pragmatist first and took the offer.

Now he was partnered with Aries. Lovelace had spent a lot of time watching his new partner. Aries was good, no question about it, but there was something there, something that didn't quite fit. It wasn't that he was an Echo – Lovelace had worked with them before, and unlike most people who held them in a sense of envy/fear, Lovelace tended to pity them. For every Echo who achieved a high level of power, there were a hundred who didn't make it.

No, instead it was as if Aries had to keep himself in check, like he was putting on a role. Samael! I hope he's not a double agent. Lovelace quite liked Aries, he'd shown himself to be a good partner, thoughtful and diligent, but if he was a traitor, Lovelace wouldn't hesitate to put him down himself if he had to. He had done some background research, off the books, on Aries and had found that, essentially, before he had joined the Agency five years ago he had not existed. Since then his career had been solid, without any serious highs or lows. Almost too solid. Lovelace's gut told him that Aries was always holding back. There was definitely a story there, and Lovelace was determined to find out what it was.

He cleared his head and pondered his next move on the Massey de Sargon case. Aries was right, there was something about the guy that did not add up. A toff like him always had the public face and the private one, and Lovelace needed to find out what he got up to when he thought no one else was looking. Where to start? TMD internal security wouldn't be much help, but they often made use of freelance investigators to keep an eye on their assets. Someone of Massey de Sargon's level would make a juicy corporate extraction target with his intimate knowledge of TMD's financial operations. *Yeah, I know just who I can talk to about that. But first I want to find out why medical response wasn't called, and the best way to do that would be a trip to the morgue in the Necropolis.*

He gunned his engine and powered down the rain-swept streets.

*   *   *

Aries' head snapped forward at the sound of the voice. "Agent Aries, very good of you to come." He had, despite his best intentions, found himself peering over his shoulder back at the door only to have Clarice Hamilton-Jones appear in front of him.

She stood above him, her perfectly manicured right hand extended, and Aries hurriedly got to his feet. They were eye level. Her patrician features were ageless, her skin porcelain white contrasting with her deep blue eyes. Her long, loose curled black hair was tied up high. She wore a low-cut midnight blue, long dress which accentuated her perfect physique. The look was completed with a silver – *platinum?*– necklace with a heart-shaped blue stone. Aries' nostrils filled with the scent of wild flowers.

This close her regal bearing was overwhelming, even intoxicating. He felt his pulse quicken. He shook her hand and waited for her to sit down. *I wonder how old she is? My best guess would put here in her seventies, though she appears to be in her thirties. Much like me.*

"Please do sit down, Agent Aries. Would you care for a drink? Tea? Coffee?" She sat down languidly and indicated to Aries to sit. Clarice brushed an errant hair aside and for a moment in the motion Aries saw Ariadne, his dead wife. The whole world ground to a halt.

Clarice repeated the question and Aries struggled to find his voice. "Uh… coffee. Please Mrs Hamilton-Jones." She nodded. Aries assumed the servants were listening in from somewhere else.

"Thank you for taking the time to come over today. May I call you 'John'? You must call me Clarice." She fastened him with an intense gaze that had Aries feeling flushed. *She is letting me know she has done her research.*

"Of course, Clarice." Struggling to gain some kind of control in the conversation, he pushed on, "Could you explain to me why you think your husband has gone missing?"

"Certainly."

A maid entered bearing a tray with tea and coffee interrupting her. While the maid poured the tea, Clarice sat back and evaluated Aries further. *She is good. The maid's timing was perfect,* he thought. He held her gaze, refusing to back down. Once she was done, the maid retreated back the way she came.

Clarice picked up her tea and Aries his coffee. *She is a master of games and I am betting a very dangerous woman to cross. I am going to have to watch my step here.* Despite that sober assessment he found himself liking her. Her aura of power was definitely attractive. Clarice broke the silence with a smile. Aries found himself smiling back.

"Now, John, where were we?"

"You were about to tell me why you thought your husband had gone missing."

"Ah yes." She paused before continuing, as if collecting her thoughts. "Well, Charles came home later than usual the night before last. At the time, I thought nothing of it, as he is prone to overworking. He often works strange hours at the Stealth Tower. However, sometime during the night he left the house in his car, and since then has failed to answer his comm whenever I have tried to call him. It is most unusual behaviour for him. Charles always lets me know where he is going to be. When I called his office, they had not seen him either. I am rather afraid something terrible might have happened to him."

"I see. Mrs… Clarice, did he exhibit any unusual behaviour before he disappeared?"

"Nothing that I am aware of. Though perhaps, on recollection, he did seem rather more preoccupied than normal."

"Interesting. Preoccupied with what?"

"I don't know."

Aries quickly went through all the usual questions for a missing person: Did Charles have any enemies that might wish to harm him? Had Charles received any threats or reported being followed? Were there any financial or relationship indiscretions that Clarice knew of? Had Charles even disappeared before? Had there been any unusual spending on their financial accounts?

Clarice ruled out all of his questions and possibilities quickly and efficiently. Aries was not surprised, but he had to cover all the basics.

"Are there any places he might go? Any meetings he might have mentioned?"

"Well he is a member of the Fox Hunt Club in Highgate. But I cannot think of anywhere else. Charles didn't mention any other meetings. Actually for the last few weeks he has been strangely laconic. In retrospect, actually I find that a little bit strange. After sex he usually likes to talk about his day. He often seeks my opinion on possible strategies."

The way she had looked at him when she had said '*sex*', again made Aries' heart race. Gathering a modicum of self-control, he finished his coffee and stood.

"Could Charles have been the target of a corporate extraction team?"

"No. Definitely not. He is – both of us are, actually – tied irrevocably to Stealth-Albion."

Aries nodded. *Still... I am sure there is more going on.*

"Any close friends?"

"Yes, several – though the Fox Hunt Club could help you with that. Charles and I kept our social lives separate."

"In which case I think that is all for now, Clarice. I will, of course, keep you fully appraised of any developments, and should you think of anything else, please do not hesitate to contact me." She likewise stood, and crossed over to him until she was close enough for Aries to once again smell her perfume. For a moment he thought she might kiss him, but instead she smiled, and held out her hand. John shook it and turned to leave. She placed a hand gently, but firmly, on his upper arm.

"It fills me with great confidence that you are on the case, John. I have every faith in you finding my husband. I believe what they say about you is true. That was why I requested you." Aries smiled awkwardly at that enigmatic comment and left the mansion as quickly as he could. He paused at the door. Before he left there was one more thing to do. He turned to the butler, Mr Six, who was opening the door for him.

"Mr Six, when was the last time you saw Mr Hamilton-Jones?"

The butler looked slightly uncomfortable and Aries prodded, "Come along now Mr Six, if I am to find your master before it is too late, anything you know might be vital."

"Well, two nights ago Mr Hamilton-Jones asked for me to call him a taxi. As a matter of routine, I checked where the taxi took him for when he later needed collecting, and I must confess to have been somewhat surprised." Aries let him continue as he was obviously having to work up the courage to break a confidence.

"Agent Aries, the taxi took Mr Hamilton-Jones to Lower Bricktown. But the strangest part of it, sir, is that when he left he was dressed as a common corporate drudge. It was most distressing"

"Interesting," is what Aries said, but what he thought was: *What would someone as rich and powerful as Charles Hamilton-Jones be doing alone in one of the roughest, most run down and dangerous areas of the city and why go in disguise?*

Once outside he took a long breath. Clarice was intoxicating, powerful and manipulative. John felt simultaneously turned on and repelled. Clarice had left him feeling very confused. Her final comment bounced around his head, and left him feeling distinctly unnerved. Yet despite all that, despite all the warnings, he found himself wanting to see her again. *This is not going to end well.*

"Samael's blade!" he swore aloud as he walked over to the car. Forcing his mind back onto the case, the first thing he would need to do would be to run a trace on Charles Hamilton-Jones' ID and credit accounts. Stealth-Albion should be fine with that. He would also need to put the word on the street with his contacts, and see what else he could dig up that Stealth-Albion would not want to reveal. *A gentleman like him will want to keep much of what he really does, off the record.* First up though, he would put an alert out on Charles' grav car, and then maybe later a visit to the Fox Hunt Club.

*   *   *

The Necropolis sat on the East side of Tyburn Square, across from the Tower of Judgement with the Temple of the Overlord to the North. It was the religious centre of London and formed the Temple and Tyburn district's heart. The square buzzed with not only robed priests, acolytes and worshippers of the Disciples, but also, today, Lovelace noted a protest march of dockers and stevedores, directed at the civil servants in the Tower of Judgement. Their chants of "No tax rise on off-world imports!" and "Fairer union rates!" clashed with a public sermon on the evils of materialism being given by a radical Redemptionist priest from the splinter sect of the Cult of the Overlord. Passing through the crowd in small bunches were groups of Pures, heading to the Temple of the Tattooed Man at the base of the Tower of Judgement. Hawkers pushed their hotdog, noodle or other fast food stands across the square trying to tempt temple goers, protesters and civil servants alike and more than a few pickpockets and other scam artists moved surreptitiously through the crowd, searching out the distracted. Lovelace noted the high police presence in the square and nodded to himself. *Good, I don't like the look of the things between the Redemptionists and the dockers.*

Lovelace walked around the mourners pouring into and out of the Necropolis and headed for the entrance to the morgue. The domain of the priests and priestesses of Kali, goddess of death and war, the Necropolis processed and housed London's dead. Here the dead were prepared for their next journey. It was the Citadel of the Dead. A giant statue of Kali, over many hundreds of metres tall, dominated the massive entrance hall. The walls were covered with uncountable of alcoves, each with a picture of a departed person in it. Wrapping around those walls were walkways spiralling around the hall. The only lighting was from the myriad of candles placed in the alcoves. Relatives, friends and even sometimes enemies of the dead walked quietly, but with purpose, heading to specific alcoves to pay their respects or to send one last insult to the grave. Between the feet of Kali were two giant silver doors, intricately inscribed with runes and images depicting the passage from the living world to the world of the dead.

It was to a set of much smaller doors contained within the greater doors that Lovelace headed. His breath frosted in the Necropolis' cold air despite the thousands of candles. He passed through a security checkpoint manned by two Metropolice officers and a minor acolyte of Kali, and entered the dark passageway beyond, escorted by a second acolyte. The temperature dropped even further once through the door, and Lovelace had to pull his jacket tighter. Their journey through utterly silent corridors was lit by icy blue lights which cast no warmth.

Eventually they arrived at the city morgue. Here, again, two tactical police officers in full armour stood guard. Lovelace left his guide and passed through a secure airlock. The temperature inside the morgue was a numbing cold, and in the airlock he climbed into a white medical heated suit. Turning to the icon of Kali, he murmured "Kali guard my soul.", place his hand, palm open, over his heart in the sign of Kali, and stepped through.

Lovelace narrowed his eyes to slits in the brightly lit room. He fished out a pair of shades and put them on. The morgue itself was a large, sterile chamber, more utilitarian than baroque. Autopsy tables filled the room's centre, while the walls held the body storage racks. A glance around the room showed there to be ten pathologists and their assistants on duty. He could see at least three autopsies being carried out, but from here, none of them looked like Nigel Massey de Sargon. Eventually, after a minute standing in the room, a technician approached Lovelace.

"Yes?" he asked in a monotone.

"Agent Lovelace," he flashed his ID, "I'm here to see the autopsy results for Nigel Massey de Sargon. Are they ready?"

"One moment Agent. I shall consult with Dr Sutcliffe." The technician walked stiffly away, the heated suit making him ungainly. After consulting with several colleagues, one of the group peeled away and headed over to Lovelace. She looked puzzled.

"Hello, Agent... Lovelace, was it? Caspar said you were here about Mr Massey de Sargon?"

"Yes, that's correct. Can I see the results of his autopsy?"

"I thought you knew, we didn't carry out an autopsy. I contacted your office. We received a court injunction denying permission for an autopsy. His body was collected about an hour ago by agents acting on the family's behalf."

"Oh... Interesting." Lovelace's brow furrowed. Dr Sutcliffe began to turn to leave, and Lovelace raised a finger. "Doctor, I wondered if you'd examined the body at all prior to the injunction?"

"Just a brief examination."

"Good. Did you happen to download his bio-status unit logs?"

"Yes of course, Agent. It is standard procedure, though in this case it was a waste of effort."

"Yes?"

"Yes."

Lovelace growled. "Doctor Sutcliffe, are you deliberately being obstructive? What did the bloody BSU say?"

The doctor huffed, "I'm just doing my job Agent, and frankly I don't appreciate personal visits." she sighed, "The fact was, Agent, that there were no logs. The BSU had been disabled prior to Mr Massey de Sargon's death. I would say about four hours prior to his demise."

"Do you know who disabled it or how?"

"Oh yes. It was disabled by Mr Massey de Sargon himself. For whatever reason, your Mr Massey de Sargon did not want anyone to know where he was, not even the emergency services."

"Bollocks!" Uttered Lovelace, and turned to leave.

*　　*　　*

Linsbury's face appeared in the air above Aries' dashboard. "Hello Captain, I thought you might like a situation report so far. I have been to see Mrs Hamilton-Jones, and she gave me the pertinent facts about the situation."

"So, do you think Charles Hamilton-Jones has disappeared?"

"Yes. She would not have called us in unless she was sure. I am also sure she was not telling me the whole story, but that is not surprising. I've put an alert on his car, and I want to request his files – the usual: comm logs, spending, calendar. Can you pull some favours and get me access to that information? I reckon with the Commander breathing down your neck, command should be willing to help."

"I'll see what I can do, but yes, that should be fine. Anything else?"

"Nothing you want to know about, but my instinct tells me this is going to get sticky."

Linsbury frowned, then nodded. "Understood. I'll get to work on the official stuff. Aries?"

"Yes?"

"Try not hang yourself on this one."

"I will do my best." The grav car flew through the day/night terminus around Hampstead and headed out into the dark of the city. Shadows drifted across the car.

John cut the connection, *Now that that is dealt with, I can concentrate on finding out the things that the Hamilton-Jones' and Stealth do not want me finding out about.*

Unbidden, the image of Clarice Hamilton-Jones came to him. He mentally swatted it away, and turned his mind back to the job at hand. First it was time to call in a personal favour. Then, tomorrow he would go and visit Charles' club.

"Comm, call Lovelace."

Lovelace's face appeared above the dash. He was obviously driving his bike, his hair thrown back by the wind.

"Aries."

"Would you like to meet up for a drink later and swap notes?"

"Sure. Wanker! Where did you learn to drive? You spanner!" Lovelace shouted at someone off-screen. Aries smiled, "Where?"

"Methadrine? Say in a couple of hours?"

"Sounds good. I've a quick question for you: Do you know if Massey de Sargon had any family?"

"None that I know of, why?"

"Thought so, I'll tell you later. Later!" Lovelace cut the connection. Aries banked the grav car to the right and headed for the Rock.

Aries landed the grav car in the Rock in the litter and sludgy puddles. The rain had eased to a drizzle. As the car settled down, he glanced out of the windows with a grimace. *Why does Kari choose to live here?* Outside, the crowd was a mix of drudges, paxers, scavs and zeroes.

The Rock was a huge, interconnected housing estate. Built all the way along the Thames on the south bank just North of the Souk and Isoke's Fields, these squat grey monstrosities housed many thousands of people each, in cramped, depressing flats. They were purpose-built centuries ago to deal with the homeless problem after the Shadow's creation in old East London, when tens of thousands of people had needed to be re-housed. Overnight it was decided to build a 'new urban utopia' and the Rock was built. Originally named the Gladstone Estate it soon became known as the *'Rock'* because of the saying that the residents were "caught between a rock and a hard place", and it stuck. Because they were designed as one massive estate, a myriad of walkways crossed between the buildings, granting easy access to all areas as well as the Rock Market. The ugly building's façades were faced with granite and roughly moulded concrete gargoyles. Inside, the corridors were filled with steam from damaged air conditioning units, pools of water and the Overlord knows what else.

The contrast with Hampstead could not be any more in your face. John pulled on a breather mask, opened the hatch and climbed out. He strapped a gun and sword belt around the waist of his great coat and cinched it tight. He checked the ammo on the Aralyte Terminator. It was a full mag. Stepping around the largest puddles, he headed into the Rock's bowels. The grav car locked down behind him as he climbed into a lift.

Aries stepped out of the piss-smelling lift, and strode down the corridor. A few scavs were sleeping in the corridor, but the sight of the masked Aries in his navy blue military greatcoat, boots and, of course, sword and gun, had most of them scrabbling to get out of his way. Broken heating pipes were venting steam into the corridor, and when combined with the few remaining lights, cast the whole area into a permanent twilight. The graffiti on the walls marked out the territory of some paxers, the urine stains on the wall marked someone else's territories.

Eventually he reached a scarred, rusted and battered looking steel door. He banged on it, loudly. Looking up he gave a little salute to the camera watching the door.

From inside, he heard the grinding of machinery. The door slid open and he stepped into a cramped airlock. Pipes had been welded to the walls. The door slammed shut behind him and gears locked it down. A high pitched hissing sound filled the airlock. The exposed patches of skin on Aries' neck and hands tingled. After about ten seconds or so, the hissing finished and the inner door cycled open. Aries pulled off his mask and stepped through.

The large flat inside was actually a whole row of apartments knocked into one. Big ventilation fans in the ceiling cleaned and conditioned the atmosphere. The rest of the space was so utilitarian that it felt like he'd just stepped on to a spacecraft. Screens displayed data on every wall. Track lighting gave the place a clinical feel, and all the furniture was stainless steel. From among all this functional furniture burst a small, tanned, woman moving at high-speed.

"Johnny!" she shouted as she bounded across the room, leaped into the air and slammed into Aries with a big hug. He staggered back, but managed to keep his footing. She gave him a big kiss on the forehead. "It's so good to see you! I missed you. Zeke missed you too, didn't you Zeke?" at the mention of his name, a huge black dog padded into the room. He curled up on the floor, looking nonplussed. As she squeezed him in a big bear hug, the colourful tassels in her hair whipped around. Finally, John managed to put her down and speak.

"Hey Kari, it is good to see you too." He smiled, "I like the new place. Is it not a bit hard-edged?"

As if noticing her environs for the first time, she looked around and frowned. "Yes. But I only just got here. Everything is so hard and cold in this city." She pouted, then abruptly burst into a smile, "But that's ok. Zeke and I will fix it, won't we Zeke?" The dog had fallen asleep, but his ears perked up briefly at the sound of his own name.

Kari grabbed John's hand and pulled him through the apartment. The apartment's rear was totally transformed with bright fabrics, soft pillows and warm lighting. The screens were still present, though. "Sit!" she commanded, and pushed John into a big pile of pillows. Kari collapsed into a cross-legged pose.

"So what brings you to see me?"

"I need you to do some digging for me, Kari. I need you to see what you can find on one Charles Hamilton-Jones." He pulled his comm out of his pocket and casually threw it over to Kari, who snapped it out of the air. She waved her hand over it with a glazed look on her face, as the data flowed from the device to her, then smiled once more. "Ooh… missing rich man from Stealth-Albion. Should have some interesting skeletons in his closet."

"So you will look into him?"

"For you? Sure. It will be like the old days back on Corsair."

"Thank you. I have one further favour to ask."

"Shoot."

"Can you look into his wife too?" Kari's eyes went wide with excitement. She closed her eyes briefly and the face of Clarice Hamilton-Jones filled all the screens.

"You think she's a crook?"

"No, not yet. But I want to be thorough."

Kari grinned, "Is that what we are calling it now?"

*   *   *

Lovelace pulled up outside Methadrine. The premier venue in London, it sat in the heart of Soho. Crowds filled the square outside, while massive arc-lights lit the sky. Music blared out from the giant screens around the square and dancers cavorted in the air on elevated platforms. And this was just the outside.

Methadrine itself was a black tower with ornate silver filigree and red lights running up the sides. Large red banners hung from the walls with the word "Methadrine" written in an ornate script. Everything about it screamed that it was a temple to entertainment, a fact that was very much intentional.

The face of Denver, the owner of Methadrine and the son of the Governor of London, appeared on the giant screens. He was striking, with ice blue eyes, blond hair and high cheekbones, and an elegant Echo tattoo. Part businessman, part super star, part hero, Denver was already a legend. The crowd roared in appreciation, he raised a hand to silence them.

His voice, when he finally spoke was tone perfect and measured. "My people. I love you all. I command you to have fun! The night is young yet, tomorrow is a lifetime away and the wolves howl. Live now!" On the last words fireworks exploded over the square and the speakers blared with powerful dance music. The crowd went wild.

Lovelace found himself tapping along and smiling. *Got to hand it to him, he is really good at this.* He locked the bike, climbed off and started through the crowd toward the club itself. Lovelace had found it easier to enjoy clubs and the London night-life if he dressed as for battle. He wore black fighting leathers with silver fastenings and combat boots. His Renegade Headhunter pistol in a shoulder holster, his Ascension sword strapped across his back and he wore a combat dagger on his calf. Fine silver chains were wrapped around his forearms.

Before he had come here he had stopped at his local Pure temple in Soho and purged his Rage. Some of the wounds still stung, but he felt clearer of mind and was now ready to party.

As he worked his way through the crowd, his senses took everything in with a freshness that he always got after the purging. He could smell hundreds of scents in the air: perfumes, incense, the dancer's musk and the sharp smells of the fast food vendors. It invigorated him.

He climbed the stairs to the VIP entrance, bypassing the queues. The bouncers, all Hulks, all over three metres tall and clad in black bodysuits with red lighting that outlined their muscle groups, wore faceless silver masks. They let him pass when he flashed his Agency badge. No one else challenged him as he entered the club tower itself.

Inside ten floors had been hollowed out to form one giant atrium with balconies on each floor running around the outside. In the centre of the vast space, over a hundred metres above the ground, flew dancers on giant wings, effortlessly spiralling around in the thermals and diving over one another. The air itself pulsed with the music's energy music, the lighting and the dancers, becoming almost alive.

Lovelace rode up in a glass lift to the tenth floor. As the lift rose he moved to the window and stared out at the club, ignoring the couple making out in the lift. Once at his destination floor, he headed through the crowd of people, most of whom were watching the flying dancers while nodding in time to the music, to the bar and grabbed a stool. In sign language he indicated two beers to the barman and waited for Aries.

He did not have to wait long. Less than ten minutes later Aries joined him at the bar. Lovelace could not help noticing that Aries had not changed his clothes. Aries looked pissed.

"Chakka got your balls?" asked Lovelace

"Some little… git, spray-painted my grav car," said Aries with all seriousness. Lovelace roared with laughter. When he finally stopped, he arched his eyebrows and looked at Aries.

"Where the bloody hells did you park it?"

"The Rock. Anyway I had to go and get it cleaned off before I was able to come here."

"The Rock? What did you expect? You are lucky you still had bloody a grav car when you got back. Those little toe-rags will strip a car faster than a hand-job from a whore on Hypervate!" Aries frowned, then broke into a smile at Lovelace's colourful language.

"Overlord! Lovelace you have a mouth like a toilet!" Lovelace guffawed and slapped John on the back. Lovelace spoke in a mock serious voice.

"It's all part of the rich tapestry of life in London." Aries clinked beer bottles with him and swigged deep.

"It is that." He scratched his left eyebrow, "So how are you getting on with your case?" Lovelace's expression became serious.

"So Massey de Sargon's body nicked from the morgue by agents of his 'family'. Family that he doesn't bloody have. Turns out that he turned off his own medical system. Something is definitely fishy, so my next step is to shake the street contacts and see if I can find out what is really going on."

"Good. I wanted you to also see what you can find out from your contacts on Charles Hamilton-Jones. Can you reach out to any of your old mates in the Met?"

"Sure. What do you want to know?"

"Everything. But especially if he had any connections in Lower Bricktown or Vauxhall."

"Well that'd be easy then!" Lovelace, spun around on his chair to face the crowd rather than the bar. He spotted an elegant woman approaching, her gaze on Aries, though Lovelace did notice she quickly appraised him. "Looks like you've got company. A cute one at that."

"What?" Aries spun around and whispered "Holy… What is *she* doing here?" Approaching him, through the crowd, was Clarice Hamilton-Jones, and she looked stunning.

*   *   *

It shocked Aries to see her here. She moved through the crowd effortlessly as it parted around her. It was as if she were real and everyone else just smoke. Clarice reached him at the bar.

"Hello John."

"Hello Clarice. What are you doing here?"

She smiled, "Me? After the pressure of the last few days I needed some relaxation. Besides, I had a feeling you would be here." Aries felt his face flush.

A troubled mind and body out of alignment can led to your downfall. he reminded himself internally. He was relieved when Lovelace leaned over and spoke.

"John, are you going to introduce me to your friend?" Lovelace took a big swig of beer.

"Sure. Lovelace meet Clarice. Clarice Hamilton-Jones." Aries grinned when he saw Lovelace struggle to stop himself spurting out the mouthful of beer at the revealing Clarice's identity.

"Clarice, meet Lovelace. He works with me." Clarice held out her hand, and Lovelace, now recovered, though casting dagger looks at John, leaned forward, took her hand in his and shook it.

"A pleasure. An *unexpected* pleasure." Clarice smiled,

"Yes indeed." Turning to Aries she continued, "John, if it wouldn't be an imposition, would you take a walk with me? We have things to discuss."

He slid off his chair, "No. Of course. Lovelace – catch up with you later?" Clarice took his arm.

"Yes." As they walked away, John looked over his shoulder. Lovelace was watching them closely with his eyebrow arched as if to say *watch yourself.*

Once they were clear of Lovelace, Clarice steered him toward the balcony.

"I realise that this is unusual. But after our meeting earlier I wanted to see you again."

"Mrs… Clarice. If you want to know about the ongoing investigation, you must know I cannot talk about it."

"Of course I do," she said peevishly. Clarice let go of his arm and leaned on the railing looking out at the fliers effortlessly gliding past. She took a deep breath.

"I just wanted company. I didn't want to be alone."

The look on her face was almost haunted, and for a second Aries glimpsed a very much younger Clarice, lacking in the self-confidence and effortless power she exuded. She reminded him of himself. Despite himself, and despite knowing that he was breaking a whole bunch of rules, he stepped over to her and put his hand on hers.

"I am sorry. I did not mean to be rude." She turned and smiled at him, and locked onto him with her blue eyes.

"It's ok John. I don't want to get you in trouble." *Too late.* Thought Aries. She looked at him, "Do you always speak so formally, John?"

"What do you mean?"

"You speak with such care and deliberation, as if you were holding something back." John frowned. *What do you know about me, Clarice?*

The music changed, and her smile became impish. "Do you dance, John?" And before he could respond, she grabbed his arm and pulled him over to the dance floor.

The music was powerful, even overwhelming, with the beats vibrating through their bodies as they danced. The crowd around them were cast into an ever changing set of still tableaux as the lights flashed. Clarice danced close to him, and despite himself and his reservations, Aries found his resistance crumbling away as he was forced to live in the moment. His attention focused on her, he found more and more that his gaze travelled all over her body. Her figure was athletic and the exquisitely tailored dress drew full attention to it. It was pale blue, almost white, and glowed in the darkness. She wore long white gloves and a matching white choker.

Several times during the dance their bodies touched and John felt the heat rising up inside him. Her movements were hypnotic, and the longer the dance went on, the more John felt himself losing control.

I have not been this close to another woman since Ariadne...

Then suddenly it was over. The music stopped, the crowd roared, and the dancers bowed to each other. Clarice looked like she was about to speak, when the crowd around them broke into applause.

Striding across the dance floor in a floor-length blue coat fringed with long fur was Denver. The coat hung open wide revealing his impressively sculpted torso. With a shock Aries realised that Denver was wearing nothing other than a pair of white shorts underneath. The crowd parted for him, though many of the club-goers leaned in to touch him. He tolerated the groping like some incubus-like prophet.

Denver stopped in front of Clarice, bowed low and exclaimed "Clarice! I heard you were here, but I refused to believe it until I saw it for myself. How are you, you old demon?"

Clarice, in turn stepped forward and ran her nails down Denver's chest, leaving red marks. John felt an unexpected twinge of jealousy. Clarice replied "Denver, my dear boy. Still ripped I see. How delightful to see you." She turned to Aries. "Allow me to introduce John Aries, Agent John Aries."

Denver turned his gaze on John. He smiled, displaying a dazzlingly white smile. "Hello there, sweetie." His eyes checked out Aries in exactly the same way they had done Clarice. He reached out his hand and they shook. Denver gave his hand a little squeeze.

"Lovely to meet you. Now, if you don't mind, I must steal Clarice away for a moment. We need to talk."

Clarice leaned forward and whispered in John's ear "Be careful. *They* are watching you now."

She kissed him gently on the cheek and turned to Denver, who held out his arm which Clarice took, and led her away.

Aries had trouble calming himself from the whirlwind of emotions that surged through him. He tried to focus on the calming techniques he had been taught, but he was unable to grab them. Running his hand through his hair, he swore, then pushed his way back through the crowd and headed home. *Who are they? And why are they watching me?*

* * *

Later, in the quietness of his flat, Aries lit the candles below the pictures of his wife and baby son. He made the sign of the Overlord's Star and whispered a quiet prayer. A prayer he hadn't spoken for too long.

"Overlord be the road for you to walk; Kali guide you through the lands of the dead; Isoke show you the way to rebirth; Albion be your shield; Samael be your sword; Tattooed Man give you wisdom, and the Fool keep you smiling in all the dark places you must travel." The words sounded hollow to him, the words learned by rote, but it was the accepted form and he did not know what else to do.

He reached out and touched the picture of his wife.

"I miss you both, but Ariadne I miss you the most. I'm sorry I couldn't save you. I'm sorry I couldn't save either of you." His eyes closed, and though he felt like crying, no tears came. Too much had changed. It was like another age ago, an age that he had all-but erased.

* * *

Steel Year 2389.08.14 (S-Time)

Aurelian looked out at the great crowd in the square below. All around the square stood giant towers that soared into the sky. Immense banners flapped in the breeze all around Hammer Square. The suns shone brightly in the pale blue sky. The smaller of the two suns, Hektor, was barely visible next to the giant, Ajax.

Giant airships floated past, along with silver aerospace fighters, flying in formation and releasing bright coloured smoke in intricate trails.

He felt the excitement in his belly. His father and mother stood to his right. They wore beautiful clothes and the air around them seemed to glow. They radiated regal bearing, and to him seemed giant. His mother held the small form of Isabella, his sister. The image was repeated from a hundred thousand projections. She held the daughter up for the crowd to see, and the crowd below roared their approval.

Aurelian found himself smiling.

His older brother Darius was silent, standing slightly apart in his formal military uniform. Though still under twenty-five, he had already achieved the rank of Under-Colonel in the 2nd Royal Hussars. Like Aurelian, and his entire family, he was an Echo, and already a decorated combat veteran. He had just returned from campaign on Bashkir. *Bashkir, Hussar,* it sounded so exotic. All Aurelian had seen so far in the fourteen years of his life was the Ducal palace here on Metropolis, and the Hunting palace on Kyriakos, a world private, held aside for the Duke and his family.

Darius, by comparison got to travel so far. Aurelian wanted to be just like him and see different worlds. A dark cloud passed in front of the suns and he unconsciously shivered.

3

Steel Year 2425.10.02 (S-Time). Day Two, Morning

The shower cleansed John as he leant on the wall. It was still too early for him. He had never been good with mornings, and his body demanded more sleep, but he wanted to make some headway on the case as soon as possible. Besides, his sleep had been restless. Last night's appearance of Clarice had really thrown him, and he knew Lovelace was going to give him a hard time about it later. He hoped his partner would not tell Captain Linsbury. Aries did not fancy being chewed out by the Captain for breaking the rules.

His sleep had been plagued by dreams of faceless figures watching him, mixed with strongly sexual dreams of Clarice, and of being chased down endless corridors.

He revelled in the shower's pounding action as it drove the night terrors away. Finally after a good twenty minutes, he climbed out and left the bathroom, drying himself. His apartment was on the edge of Uptown in Soho and Victory. The hazy sun shone in through the windows as it managed to cut through the clouds, casting the apartment in a warm yellow light. Walking across the open plan living area while wrapped in a towel, he idly strummed the strings on his guitar mounted on the wall as he passed. Playing classical guitar – or any of a number of instruments – was a secret passion for him. He could lose himself in the music.

Aries made himself a coffee and sat at the kitchen bar. He spoke aloud "Comm, local news." and the news feeds appeared in air above the bar.

The news was dominated by the upcoming election for the Governorship of Terra. After ruling for twenty-eight years Governor Sagacious was stepping down. The position of Governor was incredibly powerful, probably the single most powerful Governorship in the Accord, the region that formed the buffer state between the Federate Combine and the Imperial Commonwealth of Elysia. The Governor not only ruled Terra, but the entire solar system and the neighbouring systems of Gateway and Ravenna. It was also one of the few political positions that dated all the way back to the Steel Alliance's founding, and that meant it was empowered by Divine Mandate from the Overlord himself. Even in these troubled days that still meant something.

There were many potential candidates for Governor, none of whom had officially made any announcements yet, but the ones that stood out the most to Aries were the London Agency Commander, Sir James Villiers-Cavanaugh, his ultimate boss; Commissioner Tanaka, the charismatic and respected head of the London Metropolice; and last but not least, Denver, the current Governor's son, but also immensely powerful in his own right. That the candidate list was well know already was in open contrast to the lack of any formal announcements.

Thinking about Denver left Aries feeling troubled. He could feel the tension in his brow. When he had fled to London five years ago, he had forged himself a new identity and life. He had sought to stay out of politics, to keep his head down and lead a normal life – whatever that was, and now this damnable case was already pulling him back into that world. He had slammed the door on his past, and had planned on keeping it that way, but now...

"Damn."

With a dismissive wave, he closed the news feed, pulled on some trousers, boots and a white shirt, to which he added his shoulder holster and pistol, threw on his greatcoat and headed out to the landing pad. *Time to check out the Fox Hunt Club and then find out more about this mysterious trip Charles made to Lower Bricktown.*

As he walked over to his car, Aries' comm beeped. When he answered it Kari's face appeared. She was wearing an overly large cowboy hat and mirrored shades. "Yo Johnny, I have something for you. I ran a trace on your mister CHJ's car, and I found it for you. It is currently sitting in a chop shop in East Vauxhall. I've sent you the address, but you will want to hurry. Looking at the set-up I reckon they are going to strip it in a couple of hours. A hot vehicle like that is too dangerous sitting around. I've sent you the details."

"East Vauxhall. Interesting. That's great work, Kari. Thanks."

"One other thing: take backup. That warehouse is Fist-controlled and there are a bucket load of those fascist meatheads in there.

"Good to know. I had better get moving." Kari signed off and Aries called Lovelace, "Meet me at the location I am sending you, in thirty minutes," - he sent the location - "and bring tactical backup. I received a lead on Charles Hamilton-Jones' car and it is in a Fist chop shop."

"On my way. I'll call in for a tac team now. I was heading that way, anyway." Aries cut the connection, looked at the car freshly repaired from the damage it had taken in the Rock, changed his mind and headed for the lift instead, *Better to take the underground for this one. I do not want to have to get it repaired twice in less than twenty-four hours. That would be plain embarrassing.*

He jumped on the tube at Lower Soho station. The packed carriage was *a sweaty mix of drudges, wearing their corporate jumpsuits and boiler suits, paxers from the Masques and some other gang he did not recognise, and the odd indie like himself. It smelt of too many people in too close proximity. The train rumbled out of the station, its lights flickering, heading South out of Soho, to East Vauxhall via the Rock. Aries stood by the doors, holding tight to a worn strap as the carriage rocked from side to side. He spotted a pickpocket making his way through the crowd, and when he got close John pulled open his greatcoat to reveal the Terminator pistol in his shoulder holster. Without a hint of acknowledgement, the pickpocket changed course and jumped off the train at Lower Rock West. Good move.*

When the train pulled into Lower East Vauxhall, Aries stepped off and made his way through the station. He took his time walking through the station, soaking in the environment, letting the crowd surge around him. The station's walls were covered with fly-posters. Some were for various bands, but most were for gangs or political organisations. All around, huddled in the corners were dirty, dishevelled scavs who had dropped through the murky bottom of the system. Aries noticed that – as a rule – everyone in the crowd pointedly ignored them, fearful that if they made eye contact they would be pounced upon. Others were trying not to think about the thin line that separated them, desperate not to jinx themselves. Finally he reached the barriers and walked out onto the street.

Aries gave one of the scavs ten Sterlings.

The corporate factories and warehouses dominated this part of Vauxhall, covering everything in a thick layer of grease and dirt. The smoke from coolant systems filled the narrow, covered streets. There was a stench of burning metal in the air that blended with the rhythmic machine noises that shook the ground to make it more than a touch hellish.

He made his way to the warehouse that Kari had identified. The route took him down darkened back streets where the only other pedestrians hurried to and from their destinations. Walking around a corner Aries reached his goal.

The warehouse was in the bowels of Ground Zero, East Vauxhall. It was a nondescript building, much like thousands of others. There was a main entranceway, large enough to drive a truck into, as well as a smaller, man-sized door to the right. John stopped on the corner opposite it and looked around. There was an unmarked van parked just a little further down the road. He saw Lovelace standing casually in the shadows besides it.

Aries headed over.

"Glad you could make it. Late night?" Lovelace spoke quietly, but he could hear the arch tone in his voice.

John shook his head, "Its not like you think. Can we talk about that later?"

"Sure." Lovelace nodded toward the warehouse, "Initial sweep revealed no external sentries, but there are cams over both doors, but we can correct that with a short range EM pulse. The doors themselves are reinforced, but nothing a breaching charge couldn't handle. I've got two snipers covering the entrances, code-signs Ravenna and Gateway. We ran passive scans, and we have approximately twenty paxers in there over two floors. Here, put this on."

Lovelace handed Aries an armoured vest and tactical gear. Lovelace held John's greatcoat while he shimmied into it.

"Tac boys are ready when you are. We are on channel pattern Delta." Aries nodded as he put in the earplug/comm units and tactical glasses. Once he had done so, Lovelace spoke "Ravenna – neutralise the cameras."

"Roger. Cameras neutralised," came back the response from the sniper.

"Let's go then." Lovelace banged twice on the side of the van, and the rear doors opened and the black-armoured tactical agents dismounted and split into three teams, one heading for each door and the third heading around to the building's rear to keep it secured. They were armed with compact, silenced autorifles and combat shotguns. Aries and Lovelace split up and each led one of the door teams. Aries felt the adrenaline flood his body in anticipation of the action.

He looked over at Lovelace. Lovelace made a short chopping motion with his hand, and two tac agents moved forward and slapped shaped charges on the locks. Lovelace held up his hand and counted down from three on his fingers.

When he hit zero, the charges detonated, and with well-practised smoothness the tac agents opened the doors and rolled in stun spheres. From inside Aries heard a cry of alarm, then the spheres activated and bounced into the air, releasing their stored-up energy as eye-searingly bright strobes and deafening audio bursts. Aries was glad for the vision- and ear-protection. The teams then stormed the warehouse, each man with the hand on the left shoulder of the man in front. The front man in each team held a full-sized riot shield as mobile cover. As they entered, the team members fanned left and right, each well-practised in room clearance, covering their predetermined fields of fire.

Once through the door Aries performed a quick visual survey. The warehouse was split over two floors, the lower floor being given over to the chop-shop and there were at least three vehicles being stripped. A staircase led up the left side of the warehouse to a balcony, and two offices.

Lovelace's team headed up the stairs, whilst Aries' secured the lower floor. From out of the smoke, a Fist skinhead leaped over a table straight at the tac agent in front of Aries. The agent brought the butt of his shotgun round and smashed the ganger in the face, dropping him to the floor in a bloody heap. From the rear, two gangers opened fire indiscriminately, cutting down two of their own and hitting one of the tac agents square in the chest. He collapsed to the floor. Aries swung his pistol round and fired at the ganger in his field of fire. The heavy 14.5mm autopistol roared, flames shot out of the vents along the sides. The first bullet went wide, but the second struck the ganger in the shoulder and blew a hole clean through, spraying the wall behind the ganger with blood.

A third tac agent stepped past Aries, snapped out his stun baton and smashed it into the chest of the ganger who was about to attack Aries from the rear. Aries nodded his thanks, and checked on the downed agent. The agent gave him the thumbs up sign, and John squeezed his shoulder and moved on.

A crash from above caught his attention as Lovelace landed a spin kick in the centre of a ganger's torso, smashing him through the railing and spinning to land in a crumpled heap. Lovelace smiled at Aries, then shot out his left hand, grabbed the ganger – who was leaping at him – in mid-air and slammed him to the ground. Hard. He then entered the office after the tac agents and disappeared out of view.

Within moments the battle was over. The agents were busily cuffing the gangers and checking their own wounded. The tactical sergeant walked over to Aries and pulled off his helmet. He had short grey hair cut marine-style, and a nasty scar down the right side of his face. His name tag read 'Tynes, J'.

"Warehouse secured, sir. Eighteen hostiles neutralised: four dead, nine subdued and the rest surrendered. Three friendly casualties, none serious. Worst wound was Harman breaking his collarbone."

"Good work, sergeant. Get the ones who can talk rounded up for interrogation. I'm going to check out the cars." Sergeant Tynes nodded, and walked away.

Aries headed over to the cars, Lovelace joined him looking flush but happy. "You really enjoy this don't you, Lovelace?"

"Bloody right I do! Why, don't you?" Aries glanced over at the ganger he had shot. A tactical medic was giving him attention. His shot had pretty much blown the ganger's arm off, but even now he was giving dagger looks at Lovelace. Posters, banners and flags for Fist covered the interior of the warehouse. A fascist gang, their major defining point was a hatred of 'lesser' Human breeds likes Pures, Hulks and Ferals, and of course Echoes, like him, mutating the human bloodlines, or some such bullshit. It didn't matter to them that the breeds were now genetically separate species. It was about hating the 'other'.

"I think of it as a necessary duty. All... this... makes me sad. It is a stupid waste."

"Oh I wouldn't go as far as to say that. This is what I was conditioned for. Every culture has its ignorant zealots. Overlord knows the Pures do." Aries glanced over at Lovelace. In the short time they had known each other it had been unusual for him to talk so openly about Pure culture. "So," said Lovelace, "shall we check out this car?" Aries nodded and they both turned their attention to the car.

It was a 'Stealth-Albion Imperial Scimitar' luxury grav car, fitted with all the option available. The car was worth at least a cool million Sterlings. They opened it up and checked inside. The hand-crafted leather interior seemed clear at first glance, so Aries sent Lovelace to check the boot, while he continued to search. Popping the glove box, he found a custom Stealth-Alvarez Slayer 12mm pistol, loaded with military-grade depleted uranium core rounds. Highly illegal, even for someone like Charles Hamilton-Jones. Beneath the gun he found a scrap of paper with "Malachi, Victory" written on it in shaky handwriting. The flight log had been erased – actually no, it had been set to 'incognito' mode so had never been recorded. Running a systems check, the car was complaining about damage received from a heavy landing.

"John, got something back here." Aries climbed out of the car and walked around to the back. Lovelace was holding a blood test kit. It read positive for human blood. Lovelace's nostrils flared. "I thought I could smell blood in the boot. Your Mr Hamilton-Jones was mixed up in something shady."

"Interesting. Good. I will get this sent back to Central and get forensics to take it apart and see if we missed anything." Turning to the prisoners, he said, "Let us see what our ganger friends have to say for themselves."

Aries and Lovelace walked over. The gangers had been lined up on their knees with their hands behind their heads. Tactical agents stood at ease with their weapons loosely held. Aries heard the gangers muttering insults at him. He turned to face them.

"So who is in charge?"

"Fuck you cop!" Shouted one of the gangers. Aries nodded and tac agent pushed a stun baton into his back with an electric crack, and the ganger collapsed to the floor.

"Right. Lets get a few things clear, shall we?" He spoke in a clear voice and counted the points off on the fingers of his right hand, "First, we are not the police, we are the Agency. Secondly, that means you have no discernible rights. Thirdly, I could not care less about your egos or machismo, and finally if you do not tell me what I want to know I'm going to leave you in the care of Agent Lovelace here." On cue Lovelace gave his biggest, sharpest, smile. "He is a Truthsayer. You know I hear they know all kinds of interesting and painful ways to get information out of idiot *humans*. Do I make myself clear?" The last he shouted into the face of the gangers.

One of the gangers spoke up. "I'm in charge here, Steeler." 'Steeler' was a derogatory term for any servant of the Steel Alliance Accord, such as those who worked for the Agency or Metropolice. With bleached blond hair, cosmetically altered blue eyes and a cheap suit he obviously fancied himself as something special.

"Good choice. So where did you get the car?"

"Jezz and Hawk found it down by the docks."

"How did you crack the security system?"

"We didn't. It was left open and the engine running. Isoke's balls! I knew that freaking car was going to be trouble."

"You got that bloody right," stated Lovelace.

"I need to know the exact location. Was there any sign of the driver?"

The ganger looked over at one of the others with a mohawk. He replied, "Nah. It was just there all on it's own, so we took it."

"Good enough for now. Sergeant, take them away." The tactical agents marched them out of the warehouse. Aries turned to Lovelace. "Why would Hamilton-Jones abandon his car here in East Vauxhall? I know he had recently visited Lower Bricktown in disguise, but then he returns a few days later and abandons his car here. There is definitely something going on and I need to find out what."

Lovelace looked at the time, "Look, I need to go and meet an old mate from the force back in Soho for a quiet drink. You need a lift or are you going to get a ride back with them?"

"A lift would be good, thanks. I left my car at home."

"Let's go, my bike is out front."

*   *   *

Lovelace walked into the Ship of Fools Café in Downtown central Soho, and looked around. The place was full of a mix of people, but he was scanning for one in particular. He spotted Nathan sitting at the back in a booth.

Nathan Sark was a detective in the London Metropolice, and before... the incident... he had worked for Lovelace. He was wearing a dark grey suit and matching tie. He was reading the news from his comm and sipping from a cappuccino. He looked up and Lovelace caught his eye. Nathan smiled. His teeth were bright white.

Lovelace made his way over and slid into the booth. "Hey Detective Constable. Looking good."

"It is Detective *Sergeant* now, Lovelace. When they kicked you out everyone got a promotion." He gave him another big smile to pull the sting from his comment.

"Good for you, Nathan. I always thought you had the chops for a sergeant." Lovelace signalled one of the waiting staff and ordered a black double espresso.

"Yeah, me too. But it was still a ballsed-up way to get it. We were all sad to see you go. Well, almost all of us. The whole thing was political bollocks. Still, I heard you signed on with the Agency, so sounds like you have moved up in the world too." Unable to contain his curiosity, Sark leaned forward, "What's the Agency like, Lovelace? I mean we've all heard the stories and seen the shows, but what it is really like?"

"Like the police only harder. Same politics though. I'm in Investigations, but I'm thinking long-term of becoming a Marshal."

"Bad-ass! I can imagine you as a lawman out on the frontier with nothing but your gun and a huge pair of bollocks," Nathan exclaimed. "So, do you do much spying and espionage stuff?"

"That's the Intel division, but yes, a bit. Though you know I can't talk about it." Lovelace grinned, "We get good gear though. The Agency *has* a budget unlike the force."

"Do you have a partner? Like a new *me*?"

"Yes. His name's Aries. He's a good guy, quiet – keeps to himself, a bit intellectual, offworlder. At least I think he is, from the way he talks. Certainly not a native Londoner."

"Ha! Nothing like me then?"

Lovelace smiled. "How are the rest of the boys and girls?"

"You know, same old, same old. They made Joe Creed the new DI."

"*Creed*? He's ok, I guess. He could be a good Detective Inspector."

"Yeah, he's good, but he doesn't have your brass nuts." Lovelace guffawed, then turned serious.

"It's good to see you Nathan, but I wanted…"

"Wanted to ask a favour. Yeah, I guessed. What do you want to know?"

"I need some more background information on the cases I am currently working on. Can you see what you can find out about Nigel Massey de Sargon, Charles Hamilton-Jones, and Clarice Hamilton-Jones?" Lovelace slid his comm across the table. Sark frowned.

"I dunno, 'Lace. Those all sound a bit posh to me. Might be more than a bit out of our league. Who are they?"

"Massey de Sargon was an Echo who took a dive day before yesterday in an apparent suicide. Charles Hamilton-Jones is a missing Stealth-Albion exec and Clarice is his wife."

"Ok. But what makes you think we'd know any more than you Agency fellows?"

"They are all dirty. My gut tells me they were into some shady stuff, and I need to find out what, but if I do it through the Agency it will get logged by the powers-that-be, and I'm not ready for that yet."

"You are learning, Lovelace! But sure, I'll look into it, be glad to help. Nice to know we have some tricks that are useful to the Agency. I'll make a few enquiries, see what I can find out. Though it might take a little while. The whole sector has been roped-in as extra security for the Governor's Ball in a few days time." Nathan suddenly looked edgy. "Do me a favour though? Don't come by the sector house. We had months of hassle from Internal Affairs, and things have just started to settle down."

Lovelace sighed, and nodded. "Sure." He threw down a couple of notes to pay for the coffees and headed out. He could feel Sark watching him the whole way out.

*   *   *

Aries returned to his flat and picked up his car. He'd run the name/ word 'Malachi' on the way back and come up hundreds of names, but none of them stood out, with or without 'Victory', which he had presumed was the Victory neighbourhood within Soho of the same name. He considered his next move, *Time to visit the Fox Hunt Club, I think.* He changed into a smartly tailored dark brown suit and cravat, and headed out.

The Fox Hunt Club was in uptown Highgate. It sat, strung below a dirigible, permanently anchored between two towers over a thousand metres above the ground, like a floating palace. The 'tower in the sky' symbolism was not lost on Aries, nor the inhabitants of Downtown Highgate, and the Fox Hunt Club was viewed by many as a bastion of snobbishness and elitism. He brought the grav car in to land on one of the many landing pads that jutted out from the club building. The club itself was built in the style of a baroque cathedral, all flying buttresses and huge stained-glass windows. All of course, unnecessary. Aries however also noted the discretely placed missile turrets, and the prickling sensation that told him he approached a Wyld Shield. Designed to prevent the use of Echo powers through them, Wyld Shields were fantastically expensive and only generally found in the Citadels, spaceships and the occasional elite locale such as this. Aries knew he could use his abilities outside, or inside, but unless he could overload the shield, not through it. The elite appreciated their privacy and were not about to let some *hoi poloi* Echo remote spy on them.

Two red-liveried, armed footmen with archaic white pith helmets stood guard by the main entrance. Aries presented his badge. They were unmoved. "One moment, sah. I shall inform the Steward that you wish to visit, unless of course you have a warrant?"

"I will wait."

"Ver' good sah!" Aries couldn't place his accent, it seemed more like the fake Imperial accent from some WeaveNet soap than the product of any actual Imperial world. The footman turned and stepped into the building. The other one regarded Aries with a studied sneer. Aries ignored him.

After a few moments the footman returned and showed Aries in. Once inside the building's true opulence sank in. The floors were gold-inlaid marble, with pearlescent columns holding up the great vaulted ceilings which were themselves covered in rich frescoes. The walls were beautiful wood panelling. He was led into a side office, where he was greeted by a man in formal morning dress who gave a small, forced, head bow.

"Agent Aries, I presume? I am Mr Dorset, manager of this *establishment.*" The emphasis on the last word was unnecessary, given Aries was standing on a marble floor over a kilometre in the sky. Aries had never liked jumped-up little bureaucrats, and from his tone it was evident that the feeling was mutual.

"That is correct. I am indeed Agent Aries, *mister* Dorset." Mr Dorset carried out another of his strange little head bows.

"Normally, I would be required to deny you entry without a warrant. We cannot very well be having our members harassed by the constabulary –"

"The Agency, and you could not stop me."

"As you wish. Apologies, the *Agency*. But in this case, I am pleased to say our purposes are commonly aligned and I am not forced to curtail your enquiries, whatever they may be."

He thought, *You are starting to annoy me now, little man.* But what he said was:

"Mr Dorset, please explain yourself. What do you mean?"

"I mean, Mrs Clarice Hamilton-Jones, one of our most esteemed members has put you forward for membership and, until that review process has been completed, has made you her guest. She asks that you visit her in her suite, once your enquiries are complete."

"She has? Indeed." Mr Dorset stepped forward and offered his white-gloved hand. Aries shook it warily. He then walked over and opened the door for John.

"Welcome to the Fox Hunt Club, sir. I hope you enjoy your visit."

I bet you hated saying that, little man. However, much as I enjoy baiting you, back to business, and the first order of business is to find out who saw Charles last. "Mr Dorset, before I leave you to return to your duties, could you inform me as to when Mr Charles Hamilton-Jones was last here?"

Mr Dorset referred to his comm. "Four nights ago, according to my records."

"And was he here for any special function, or event?"

"Yes. I believe he was here for the monthly dinner event of the London Chapter of the esteemed Honourable Brotherhood."

I've heard that name before. "The Honourable Brotherhood?"

"Yes, they are a very prestigious Imperial society." The words were spoken with cultured disdain as if Aries were an ignorant savage not to have known.

"I see, and are any other Honourable Brothers members of the Fox Hunt Club."

"Yes, certainly, though we don't require our members to tell us."

"Do you at least know who I could talk to who might be able to help?"

Mr Dorset drummed his fingers noisily on his thigh, obviously debating the relative merits, and satisfaction, of stymieing Aries against the cost of potentially annoying the powerful Clarice Hamilton-Jones. Discretion won the day.

"Yes. I believe Mr Cassian Dexter is the local secretary." Mr Dorset again glanced at his comm, "I believe you will find him in the conservatory."

"Thank you."

"Good day, sir."

Aries left the supercilious Mr Dorset and headed for the conservatory.

*   *   *

Aries found Mr Dexter taking tea alone, sat beside a vast panoramic window that gave him an unparallelled view out over the city. Mr Dexter seemed preoccupied, his brow was furrowed and there was a slight nervous sheen of sweat on his forehead at which he dabbed sporadically with a kerchief. His undoubtedly expensive – though dated – suit was struggling to remain crease free.

"Mr Dexter?"

Mr Dexter visibly started. His head snapped around and he stared at Aries, his mouth pursed.

"Yes? Who are you? What do you want?"

Aries pulled his badge, and watched with fascination as all the colour drained from Mr Dexter's face. "Agent Aries. I am here making enquiries into the disappearance of Mr Charles Hamilton-Jones a little over three nights ago, and I believe you might be able to help me."

"Help you? Help you, I don't think so!" Aries noted the bloodshot eyes, twitching hands and heavy five o'clock shadow. Mr Dexter had obviously not slept in quite some time.

"On the contrary, Mr Dexter, I believe you can tell me about Mr Hamilton-Jones' involvement with the Honourable Brotherhood." If it was possible, Mr Dexter paled even further.

"No, no. I can't… talk to you about the Honourable Brotherhood."

"Mr Dexter, I'm afraid I am going to have to insist. We can talk about this here, or back at Central in my office. It is your choice." Mr Dexter's eyes widened.

"You can't arrest… me!"

"Who said anything about arresting? I know you had dinner with Mr Hamilton-Jones and other members of the Honourable Brotherhood four nights ago. I want a list of the other attendees, and I want to know what was discussed. What was Mr Hamilton-Jones' state of mind?"

"I wouldn't know, I… uh… barely knew him." *He's talking about him in the past tense, as if he were already dead.*

"Come now, Mr Dexter. I can hardly believe that you, as the local secretary of the Honourable Brotherhood, did not make it your business to get to know each of your fellow Brothers."

"Well… yes… of course. Look, is this really necessary? I'm frightfully busy."

Aries locked his gaze on him, his voice changing from calm to stern,

"Yes. Yes, it is necessary. Now answer my damn questions. I am losing my patience." Mr Dexter's eyes went wide. Something seemed to give and his postured sagged.

"Oh. Well, he was very energetic, bombastic even. He and those friends of his seemed elated." Mr Dexter bit off the last part as if wishing he had never mentioned it. *Upset that they were his friends and not yours, Mr Dexter?* Thought Aries.

"Indeed. I will need that list of names, and if you could indicate which were his close friends, I would appreciate it. Mr Dexter, do you know what caused this 'elation'?"

"I… the list… right. Right, of course." Mr Dexter scribbled out a list of eight names and handed it to Aries. One name leaped out from the page: Nigel Massey de Sargon. *Of course! The ring! I remember now.*

"I… wouldn't know why they were elated. I'm just the Secretary." The word 'secretary' was laced with resentment. *So many resentful bureaucrats here in the Fox Hunt Club. What a passive-aggressive place it must be.*

He was obviously lying.

"Mr Dexter, I can tell you are holding information back. Simply put, that is a mistake. It would be in your best interests to co-operate willingly."

"I…" He was cut off by another voice.

"I'm afraid Mr Dexter has another appointment that takes precedence, *Agent Aries*." It was John's turn to be surprised. Approaching him from behind, unseen until now, was the London Agency Commander, and Aries' ultimate boss in London, Sir James

Villiers-Cavanaugh, immaculately attired in a pinstripe suit from the finest tailor. His raven-black hair was swept back, emphasising his Echo tattoo. He was every inch the patrician. Aries noted the heavy gold Brotherhood ring he wore as well as the Agency gold pin in his cravat.

"Sir James — Commander, how unexpected!" *What the hells is he doing here?*

"Agent Aries, perhaps you could schedule a time for Mr Dexter to visit you at Central to continue your... conversation?"

"Of course, Commander." Aries spoke through gritted teeth. He turned to Mr Dexter, "I shall be in touch. Until later then, Mr Dexter. Good day, Commander." He bowed to his superior and turned away. Aries struggled to keep the frustration out of his voice. Left with no viable alternative response, he walked away, his thoughts a turbulent sea.

Why is the Commander protecting Dexter?

*   *   *

Aries knocked on the door of Clarice Hamilton-Jones' private suite. A sharply dressed woman opened the door. John guessed she must was Clarice's personal assistant. "Ah, Mr Aries. Ms Hamilton-Jones is expecting you. If you will come in, she will be with you shortly. She is just finishing another meeting."

He followed her into the suite. The woman then slipped out through a cleverly concealed side door. The suite he stood in was decorated in rich reds, with opulent but comfortable furniture and plenty of fresh flowers. Many paintings of idyllic pastoral landscapes, almost shocking in their vibrancy, covered the walls, and the pleasant smell of the summer flowers filled his nostrils. It had a female quality that the mansion in East Hampstead had lacked.

Clarice sat on a chaise longue wearing a simple white silk kimono. Across a small coffee table sat an oriental woman, of the Michiru culture, Aries guessed. Clarice's guest was also simply attired, wearing a pale blue trouser suit with a small Accord star on her lapel. Sat next to her was a steel-haired man in a sharp dark suit and cravat. The three spoke quietly, but after a moment they rose. Clarice and the woman embraced and kissed each other's cheeks. She shook hands with the man, who dipped his head in respect.

As they passed Aries on the way out, he recognised the woman as London Metropolice Commissioner Tanaka. Presumably the man was her chief of staff. She smiled at John as they left, leaving him completely alone with Clarice.

"John, please do come over."

He crossed the room and Clarice leaned in and gave him a kiss on the cheek that lasted a fraction of a second longer than decorum allowed. He could not help but catch a glance of the pale skin of her neck as she returned to her reclined pose and indicated him to sit.

"I hope my intervention at this club helped. I know how fussy they are here. Especially that Dorset. He's a royal arse."

"Yes, thank you, Clarice. Can I ask, was that Commissioner Tanaka?"

"Ami? Yes, she and I are old friends. I must apologise about my rude disappearance last night. Denver and I have history."

"Of course. Not a problem." Aries shifted on his seat, painfully aware that he was alone in her very feminine boudoir. Noticing the unconscious movement, Clarice laughed.

"It's ok John. I won't bite." The glint in her eye gave lie to the statement. "We are very alike, you and I."

"We are?"

"Yes. We both have complicated pasts." As she spoke that word, his eyes snapped up and locked gaze with hers. His pulse raced.

"What do you mean?" Clarice stood, and moved to sit next to him. Despite his caution, he could not help but notice how her kimono clung to her very attractive figure.

"Let me just say I have learned a few things in my time. Discretion is one of them." She reached out and took his hand. "Oh my, you are shaking like a leaf." With her other hand she gently brushed his face and stared into his eyes. He could feel the heat of her hand on his face.

"You have seen a lot of pain, John. I know that. But you are a good man. You don't need to be scared of me." The smell of her perfume was intense and alluring, and he could feel his pulse quickening. *She reminds me of Ariadne in so many ways.* He felt a sudden brief wave of despair sweep through him, which he forced down.

"I am not," he lied, "but what about your husband?"

"Charles? What about him? I know you are doing your best to find him." She looked up at John. "Our marriage is about power. I love him in my own way, but our relationship is complex and often leaves me very much alone." Her eyes held his. "I don't want to be alone, John." He could feel his defences slipping. He looked at her and admitted that he found her irresistible. Sliding toward the edge of the cliff, he decided to jump.

He leaned and kissed her.

When he came up for air, she whispered, "I hoped you'd do that," bit his ear and giggled. A knock disturbed their tryst. Clarice's personal assistant entered.

"I'm sorry to intrude, Clarice, but I am afraid an urgent situation has arisen involving the project."

Clarice whispered, "Sorry." and stood. She continued with a warm smile, "I will see you soon and we will continue this 'meeting' then, I promise." She brushed her index finger on his lips and left.

Aries did not know whether to feel relieved or frustrated. Either way it took a while for his blood to stop racing.

4

Steel Year 2390.09.06 (S-Time)

"Aurelian, my son, it is time for you to marry. I have made arrangements. You will do your duty as a prince of Metropolis and scion of House Favian-DeVir. Make me proud."

Aurelian was confused. It was so sudden. He had looked at his father, the Duke, but his father had been firm and Aurelian could see that he was in one of his intense moods and would brook no questioning from his second son. The statement had whirled around his head for the last two days. *Marry? Me? To whom?* His father, Duke Alexander Memnon Favian-DeVir had been in a powerful, dark mood for many months and Aurelian, like any good son, was worried. He locked himself away, and Aurelian worried that something he had done was the cause, even though Count Morten had attempted to disabuse him of this fallacy many times.

At fifteen, Aurelian was rapidly achieving full-growth. The genetic enhancements he had received, as well as the relentless immersive training in all areas physical, mental and spiritual during his life, had forged him into a powerful man. But his physical maturity was not matched by his emotional. He was still young and this statement by his father had thrown him.

Why does father want me to marry? I am not even the first in line to succeed him, and Darius is already married with children. Besides, father will live forever.

The medical care and gene tailoring his family had received meant that they were essentially immortal, aside from accident or other form of sudden death, such as assassination. The reality was that despite all that, 'immortality' generally only lasted three hundred years before the odds of accidental or intentional death caught up with them, but Aurelian had yet to grasp that subtlety.

But here he was, the young Prince, on his way to meet his arranged soon-to-be-bride and he did not feel prepared. He had learned all about the practicalities, such as sex, of course, how to use it in politics and society, what tricks to be aware of and snares to avoid, but strangely he could not at this moment remember a single instance where he had been taught the art of marriage.

Regardless, he was determined not to let his father down. *I know my duty, and will not fail.* For some reason the calming mantras he had been taught were failing to work, but he pushed on regardless.

He reached the end of the grand corridor that led to the Great Hall, and the Ducal Guard, seeing his approach, snapped to attention. The twin doors silently swung open and with a deep breath, Aurelian stepped through.

There ahead of him wearing a floor-length white dress stood the most beautiful woman he had ever seen. She locked her blue eyes on him and he was lost.

*   *   *

Steel Year 2425.10.02 (S-Time). Day Two, Evening

Lovelace already liked Aries, that was certainly true, but he did not yet quite trust him. He had trusted the wrong person and his career in the Metropolice had been ruined. He was not about to make the same mistake so soon after joining the Agency. Besides he had not had a chance to get to know Aries fully yet, and what was obvious – to Lovelace at least – was that Aries was holding something back. Plus with the 'Clarice' incident at Methadrine last night he did not want to over-complicate things. *I hope Aries can keep his sex drive under control.* Frankly, after seeing how John had looked at her, Lovelace did not think he could. He hoped he was wrong.

He turned his mind back to the case. The truth was, that when digging into the pasts of the high-and-mighty the police records would only tell you so much. He wanted to know who had taken Nigel Massey de Sargon's body and why. To uncover that info he needed to dig deeper and, frankly, the only way to do that was to go and talk to the 'other side', which in this case Lovelace had a hunch were the professionals who had taken the body. They were almost certainly corporate headhunters. Headhunters were mercenaries whose job it was to 'extract' – the euphemism for kidnap – executives from corporations to sell on to other corporations.

Lovelace had requested – and received – a copy of the surveillance vids from the morgue in the Necropolis. It was a long-shot but he wanted to see exactly whom had collected the body. *The Tattooed Man must have smiled on me.* He had been lucky and the effort had paid off. The footage has shown four men, all muscular, all with that ex-military look about them that marked them as mercenaries. One had been an Echo, which while distinctive had not been the real coup, no. What had made his day was that Lovelace had recognised one of them. He was a former pit-fighter.

The violent 'sport' of pit-fighting was a popular underground entertainment in London and because of that it gave Lovelace a clear avenue of investigation to pursue. Because, when it came to pit-fighting, there was only one person to go and see: Jehan sá Fae.

Knowing that, Lovelace had headed to 'Cement', the premier – and illegal – pit-fighting club that moved from place to place within the Rock, always two steps ahead of the police. Cement was a favourite hangout for mercenaries between jobs, somewhere where they could blend in. Many of the pit-fighters were mercs themselves, taking fights for the practice as much as the winnings. Lovelace had needed to lean on a few of his old snitches from his days on the force, but it had not taken long to find out where Cement now was.

He drove his bike deep into the Rock through dark, rain-stained streets, the headlight on his bike the only lighting. Rats, scavs and Overlord-knew what else scuttled out of his way as he roared down the silent roads. Cruising into an officially condemned set of warehouses, he reached a checkpoint manned by mercs. The checkpoint was formed by an armoured personnel carrier parked across the road. A machine gun mounted on top and bright arc-lights kept away the curious.

Lovelace brought his bike to a halt and cautiously raised his hands to show he meant no harm.

"This area is off-limits, mate. Now do us all a favour and piss off!" a voice shouted from the APC.

Lovelace shouted back, "I'm here for the game." A merc with a slung autorifle walked around the vehicle and came up to the bike.

"Who invited you?"

"Jehan sá Fae. Why, what's it to you?" The merc silently evaluated him, his head cocked slightly to one side as he listened to the headset in his helmet. Lovelace noted how the machine gun on the APC stayed trained on him. The moment lasted an age and finally the merc nodded, spoke softly into his helmet mike and waved Lovelace through.

"Have a good one, mate." *Not bloody likely,* thought Lovelace.

Cement was everything the name would suggest: bare cement floors and walls dripping in condensation from sweat, rusted and chipped concrete columns with harsh industrial lighting. Chains hung from rails in the ceiling and pools of oozing oil were scattered around. Loud grinding industrial music echoed off the hard surfaces. The air was heavy with smoke, and the stink of sweat and blood. One of the club bouncers pushed through the crowd, led by a pair of vicious-looking attack dogs.

Lovelace fitted right in.

He worked his way across the club. The patrons were a mix of gangers, city suits, professional criminals, and mercs. There was a large scattering of pretty toygirls and toyboys hanging on to the arms of their risqué beaus.

At the club's centre were two pits gouged out of the floor. Each pit had a sawdust floor, and a chain link fence surrounded it. The audience watched, betted and revelled from stepped seating surrounding the pits. Between the two pits was an elevated area with a welded-steel throne. Sat in the throne was a beast of a man. Over three metres tall he was built like an Avatar of Baal, the heretic Disciple of War. The seated figure was a Hulk, one of the race of giants which was, like Pures, descended – *evolved* – from Humans. The hulk wore a dark suit without a shirt, revealing a chest covered in scars, some self-inflicted, other the trophies of a life spent fighting. Two prize women and one man sat at his feet, naked. A huge sledge-hammer lay across his lap.

Lovelace made his way round the rings toward the giant. He could feel the eyes of many of the crowd on him. In the nearest ring, Lovelace saw a lithe, acrobatic-looking fighter facing off against a cybernetically-enhanced merc. Both were bleeding from a hundred cuts, their blood staining the floor. Lovelace could taste it on his tongue. He felt the *Rage* growl inside him and had to force it down, his fists unconsciously clenching and unclenching.

He turned his face away from them just as the acrobat launched himself at the merc with a high kick. Lovelace heard, rather than saw, the cracking of bone. Despite himself, he salivated, took a deep breath to clear his head and pressed on.

Finally he approached the throne. No guards surrounded it. None were needed. The slaves hissed at him, jealous of anything that might take away the attention of their master. Lovelace ignored them and looked up at the giant. The giant looked at Lovelace, narrowed his eyes and stood, casually swinging the sledge-hammer in his mighty fist.

The crowd abruptly moved away from Lovelace.

The giant walked down the steps and came toward Lovelace. He towered over the conventionally-massive Pure.

"Lovelace." He spat the word out as if it tasted bad. "Samael cut your heart out for showing your face here."

"Samael's busy. You could try, Jehan." Lovelace assumed a loose limbed pose and rose up on the balls of his feet, ready to fight.

Jehan sá Fae, for that was who the giant was, growled. "Don't come into my gaff and square up to me unless you mean it, *Truthsayer*."

"I'm not here to fight you, Jehan."

"Don't have the guts, eh?" Lovelace ignored the jibe. This was a delicate situation. Any wrong move and the odds were long on him walking out of here. "So what *do* you want then, Mr Policeman?"

"I'm not a cop any more, Jehan."

"Yeah, I heard. You are still a badge as far as I'm concerned. Answer the question before I lose my patience, Lokden rot your soul."

"I want your help, Jehan."

Jehan whistled. "You've got brass nuts, Lovelace. You come into my den, after what you did and you have the nerve to ask *me* for help?" Lovelace could tell that despite himself, Jehan was intrigued. "And what do I get if I help you?"

"A favour."

"From you?"

"Yes."

"On your word as a Truthsayer?" Lovelace took a deep breath, *I hope I know what I am doing*, and nodded. "Say it. Say it, Pure." Jehan knew that any oath Lovelace took as a Pure Truthsayer would be binding on his honour, something all Pures took deadly serious.

"You have my word as a Truthsayer." He turned to the crowd watching, "Jehan has my word. I, Tarus Arken Karazhja, Warrior Caste of the Truthsayer Kindred, give it." he turned to Jehan, "Satisfied?"

Jehan sá Fae swung the hammer up and casually rested it on his shoulder.

"Fine. Let's talk. Somewhere quieter." Lovelace nodded and followed the giant away from the rings.

They entered a side room. Jehan sat on a bench and indicated Lovelace to do likewise.

"So, then, Lovelace. What can I do for you?"

"I am mixed up in something that my bones tell me is going to get dark. I need to know what shady stuff three people are into: Nigel Massey de Sargon, Charles Hamilton-Jones and Clarice Hamilton-Jones."

"I know these people."

"You do? Is that going to be a problem?"

"No. All of them have come to my club. That Massey de Sargon asked for my protection … oh a couple of days back."

"He did? Did you give it to him?"

"No." Jehan smiled.

"Why not?"

"The guy was slime. Besides, I'd already told him we were done after the last time."

"The last time?"

"Yeah, he'd asked me to help him dispose of a body."

"Did you?"

Jehan smile grew. It was not a pretty smile. Lovelace took it as a tacit confirmation.

"When was this?"

"Last week. He needed the body of a *person of interest* disposed of."

"Do you know who?"

"Yeah, some suit called Julius Rato." Lovelace did not bother to ask where the body was. If Jehan had made it disappear then it was gone for good.

"What about the other two?"

"They both come here from time to time. Clarice and her lapdog."

"Wait... *Clarice* is the alpha dog? Not Charles?"

"Baal take my soul, yeah. She is the mover and shaker. Chucky-boy wouldn't be anywhere without her and he knew it. At least until recently. I got the impression he was straining at the leash. Wanted to assert himself. Twat. He didn't have the spine to make it. I figured he was going to get himself in serious trouble. Not like Clarice." Jehan stared off into the distance for a moment. "What I would give to have her. She is a shark. A prize catch." He licked his lips.

Lovelace nodded, the continued. "I also need you to find out what happened to Nigel Massey de Sargon's body."

Jehan barked a laugh. It was a cold hard bark of a laugh.

"He's dead? Samael's blade, what a fucking surprise. Good riddance."

"Yeah, and some professional team went in and got his body. I want you to find out who it was. I need to know who ordered it. I recognised one of them as a pit-fighter."

"Yeah who?"

"I don't know what he's called now, but he used to fight under the name of 'Corrosion'."

"Corrosion? Yeah, his real name is Mathers, I think." Jehan shrugged. "He stole de Sargon's body? I'll see what I can dig up."

"Thanks Jehan." Lovelace stood to go.

"About that favour…"

"Yes?"

"I know what I want." Lovelace already knew what it was before Jehan spoke, but he wanted to be sure.

"What?"

"You and me, in the ring. I want to settle this thing between us once and for all."

Lovelace sighed. *I knew this might happen. Well, it was bound to happen eventually. Best get it over and done with.*

"Once this case is complete."

"Once this case is done," agreed Jehan.

Lovelace left Cement.

* * *

Aries gently brought the grav car down to land across the road from Mr Dexter's white Renegade Angel grav car. He glanced down at the map on his vehicle display. His quarry had led him to Downtown near Overlord's Station in the Strip. The weather, still filthy as ever, hammered rain down relentlessly on the street.

His intuition told him that despite his protestations to the contrary, Cassian Dexter was very much involved in whatever had caused Massey de Sargon to kill himself and Charles Hamilton-Jones to go missing. That had made his decision about what to do next straightforward. After leaving Clarice's suite he had checked and found that Dexter was still at the Club. He had decided to follow Mr Dexter and see what he could learn surreptitiously, rather than drag him into Central. After all, he needed to tread lightly if the Commander was involved. He also needed to talk to Lovelace, but wanted to put that off a little longer.

Aries watched Mr Dexter get out of the car whilst attempting and failing to keep the rain off him. Dexter pulled on a hat, coat and muffler and then, with a quick glance around, pulled a pistol from the passenger side seat and dropped it into his briefcase.

Well, well, Mr Dexter. Seems like every gentleman cannot leave the house without firepower now.

Mr Dexter ran across the street, splashing mud all over his fancy suit, and ran into a small café. From where he was he could see Mr Dexter sit down at a table with two other gentlemen.

Aries looked down at the list Mr Dexter had provided of Honourable Brotherhood members who had been at the dinner:

Charles Hamilton-Jones
Nigel Massey de Sargon
Cassian Dexter
Arkell Isadore
Kenton Serrano
Jean Thervessons
Benham Arends
Julius Rato

Eight names. Two missing or dead. Aside from the obvious, only one jumped out at him: Kenton Serrano, the Chief of Staff for Commander James Villiers-Cavanaugh's election campaign. The others Aries did not know, but presumably they were powerful executives if Charles, Nigel and Kenton had deigned to keep company with them. The more he thought about it though, the more he kept coming back to Cassian Dexter.

He was terrified talking to me, and he believed Charles was already dead. Why? What does he know?

He pulled up his comm and ran the pictures of the men Dexter was meeting. They were Benham Arends and by the looks of it, Jean Thervessons, though it was difficult to tell as he was dressed very roughly. Benham Arends put what looked to be a privacy generator on the table and activated it.

Interesting.

They were having a very animated conversation. Several times, one of the gentlemen, Jean, Aries thought, looked like he wanted to leave, but a hand on his arm from Arends kept him seated.

Aries wished he could get in there and listen to the conversation, but the café was too small. They had picked their meeting place well. The question was why? *Why would these wealthy, connected gentlemen, choose to meet in a seedy café Downtown in the Strip of all places.* A quick glance around made it clear that the café was neighbours with strip clubs, bars, gambling joints and, according to the Metropolice reports, a whole bunch of prostitutes and brothels.

It appeared as if Dexter was trying to calm the others down, but whatever he was saying did not seem to be working on Thervessons. The man looked extremely edgy already and appeared to be becoming more and more agitated by the second.

Finally Thervessons abruptly stood up. Cassian Dexter put his palms together and seemed to be praying for him to stay, but it did no good. With a dismissive wave of his hand, Thervessons stormed out of the café.

"Damn." He needed to make a decision fast: was he going to follow Thervessons or stick with Dexter and Arends. *I need to stay with Dexter for now, until I find out more.*

Thervessons stepped out onto the street. Aries got a good look at him. He was wearing a long rain cloak over a woollen coat. He had a thick growth of stubble and dark bags around his eyes. He looked like he had not slept in a week. Thervessons looked side-to-side, pulled the cloak's hood up, and ran off into the rain. *On foot? Interesting.*

Mr Dexter and Mr Arends carried on talking. Suddenly Arends pulled out a handgun and pushed it into Mr Dexter's forehead. Aries was caught in a bind. He was potentially witnessing a criminal act, but if he intervened he would lose any chance to learn more. He looked around, but strangely no one in the café seemed to be reacting to this scene.

Arends' ruddy face was a deep red and the tendons on his neck stood out. Even from here, John could tell that Arends was shouting while Dexter was shaking violently and talking a thousand words a minute. Even from here it was clear he was spraying Dexter with spittle. *Arends is a nutjob.*

The tension lasted just under a minute, before whatever Dexter was saying started to work. Arends face returned to a normal colour and he looked more relaxed. Confident, even. With a decisive move he pulled the gun from Mr Dexter's head and returned it to his holster. *As if nothing unusual had happened. Violence is second nature to this man. I will need to find out more about him and watch him closely, as he is very dangerous.*

Rapping his fingers on the dashboard, Aries made a decision. He pulled out a tracer bug from his surveillance kit and opened the door. Ignoring the torrential rain, he stealthily crossed the road, and moved down the line of cars, careful to keep them between him and his targets. Reaching Mr Dexter's car he attached the bug underneath.

Now if only I knew which one was Arends'...

Taking equal care, he returned to his car, pausing only to throw his soaking greatcoat on the back seat before climbing in. The air conditioning systems hummed to life, quickly sucking the excess moisture out of the air.

Mr Dexter and Mr Arends were still talking. When they stood up to leave, several men stood up with them. The men had a uniform look to them and Aries realised that Benham Arends had brought around ten professional bodyguards with him. He was glad he had hung back from the café. There was no way he could have slipped in unnoticed. Pretty much every patron of the café was one of Arends' men.

He watched them file out, the bodyguards forming a human shield around Arends. An unmarked grav plane appeared from above the buildings and came in to land in the middle of the street. Its landing jets stirred up a storm of dirty water and smoke. Arends waved goodbye to Dexter, then climbed in with most of his bodyguards. The remainder loaded into two other grav cars and the cortège took off and headed South back toward the City.

Dexter waved, then returned to his car and took off. He headed off to the West.

Three men, each seeming disturbed in their own way, each responding to it differently. What are they scared of?

Aries activated his comm and called Lovelace.

"Lovelace, we need to talk."

*   *   *

Lovelace was in a foul mood and showed it by storming around Aries' flat. It was obvious from his expression that Aries regretted having arranged to meet him at his home and telling him everything. Lovelace was storming around the room.

"Isoke's cunt! Our two cases are probably related and you only think to tell me this now? What the bloody hells is wrong with you Aries? You don't keep your partner out of the loop. I could have tailed Thervessons while you went after Dexter. Now, we may have lost him." He reached the end of his circuit, spun and stormed toward Aries.

Aries took a step back and prepared himself for a fight if necessary, but at the last moment Lovelace stopped short and pointed a black-nailed finger at John's face.

"You don't shut your bloody partner out, John!" He ran a hand through his short dreadlocks and let out a hiss. "You should have told me as soon as you found out that Massey de Sargon and Hamilton-Jones were both involved in this damned-toff's-Brotherhood. And then I find out you are about this-bloody-close to sleeping with a witness and possible suspect."

"Calm down, Lovelace."

Lovelace spun on the spot and felt his Rage rise to the surface. The Rage called to him to pull his sword and cut Aries down, to give into the primal urge he felt, but he forced it down. Words from the scripture of the Tattooed Man rang in his head.

A Pure controls his Rage. A Pure who cannot control his Rage is nothing but a sick animal that must be put down without compassion or hesitation.

He closed his eyes and took three deep breaths and finally felt the Rage subside for now.

"Are you ok?" asked Aries quietly.

Letting out a long shuddering sigh, Lovelace replied, "Yes. Yes, I'm ok. I've just had a very hard day. But for pity's sake, Aries, don't cut me out. We are partners, and partners back each other up. Especially when one of them pisses it all up. I thought *you* were supposed to be the senior agent."

"You are right. I am sorry. Look this whole case is starting to get to me."

Lovelace barked a laugh. "Getting to you? No shit. Well it's apparently starting to get to me too. Something stinks and I don't like it, and now you tell me the bloody London Agency Commander — our boss! — might be involved." Lovelace sat down heavily on Aries' couch. "Have you got a drink?"

Aries nodded and walked over to his drinks cabinet and poured them a couple of whiskies. He gave one to Lovelace, then sat down opposite.

"Ok, John. So what have we got?"

"Nigel Massey de Sargon and Charles Hamilton-Jones were both part of the Honourable Brotherhood London Chapter, along with the other men on that list," he handed Lovelace the list, "and possibly Sir James Villiers-Cavanaugh, though if he is Dexter was not saying. They are involved in something underhanded and most likely criminal, something that has got all of them, apart from the Commander as best I can tell, scared."

Lovelace nodded, took a sip of whiskey and spoke.

"My contacts told me that one of these men, Julius Rato, is dead and that Nigel Massey de Sargon needed help disposing of the body. Could be related to the blood stains in Charles' boot. Any word if the tests have come back yet?"

Aries shook his head, "I've not had time to follow them up yet."

"Fine. Massey de Sargon's body was taken from the Necropolis by professionals. My bet is that it was to cover something up, something on the body that they didn't want us to know about. Also he had turned off his own medical unit, for exactly what reason I don't know, but I am guessing it was to prevent anyone from tracking him."

"Yes, I wonder whether it might be the same reason that had Charles go to Lower Bricktown dressed in disguise, or abandon his car in East Vauxhall."

"Do you think this 'Malachi' might be a person, maybe another Honourable Brother?"

"I'm trying to uncover that information, but so far I have hit a dead end. There are just too many Malachis. Without more information I cannot narrow it down. I do know that I want to find out what this 'Book' was that Massey de Sargon mentioned. I feel it might be central to the case."

"Yeah, Aries, but what case? You've still no leads on Charles' whereabouts?"

"No, but I have put the word out with my contacts."

"Me too. So, what's the plan now then, Aries?"

"I want to know everything about Cassian Dexter, Benham Arends and Jean Thervessons."

"What about Kenton Serrano and... what was the other name? Ah, yes, Arkell Isadore?"

"Well Serrano works for the Commander, and we are definitely not ready to tangle with him yet unless we want to kiss our careers goodbye. At least not until we have more of an idea how he is involved. Arkell Isadore I've not encountered yet, so we will need to find out more about him, but the other three were definitely up to something and I want to know what that is. But given what you have learned, we should find out more about this Julius Rato and then after that, you want to track down Thervessons and I'll focus on Dexter? Once we are done with them we can have a talk with Mr Isadore."

"What about Arends?"

"From what I saw the man is primed to go off at the slightest provocation. He is very dangerous and unstable and given that he is walking around with a small personal army, caution suggests we are going to need to plan our approach carefully."

"Agreed. So what do we already know about each of them?"

Aries pulled out his comm and brought up their files, they appeared on the wall next to them, and Lovelace turned to look.

"Let's start with Benham Arends. He is a known arms dealer, unsurprisingly the guy is infamous for having a short temper and displaying outbursts of paranoid psychosis. Frankly that fits with everything I have seen about him so far. What is surprising is that, given his obvious instability issues, he seems to have a clean record.

He was brought in for questioning concerning... let's see... ah yes... the death of his first wife in a train bombing, a shooting over a traffic incident, the disappearance of his aide-de-camp who was presumed murdered. All of those happened in London and none came to trial. In the first a rogue splinter cell of the anti-Echo organisation Firestorm were fingered but they all died when their hideout went up in a fireball. The victim in the shooting disappeared before the trial and evidence was found which led investigators to conclude that he fled offworld. His aide-de-camp was never found, so the charges were never filed."

"All dead, no doubt. Bloody hells! The guy is a nut case!"

"Yes, and that is just London. He was implicated by the Federate Combine in the massacre of the population of a town on the world of Corsair. He is believed to be supplying the arms to at least a dozen terrorist groups, and the Imperial Pathfinders have him on their watchlist, so he is *persona non grata* in both the FedCom and the ICE. He does not appear to care, though, as business is very good. Intel estimate his personal fortune to be about one billion Sterlings."

"Wow. What about... Thervessons?"

"We have almost nothing about him. The gentleman keeps a very low profile, so low that the Agency barely have a file on him. His occupation seems to be landowner, but beyond that the man is a ghost."

"Rato?"

"Rato is a shipping tycoon. Third generation owner of Rato Transport, based out of Gateway. Their second largest hub is here in orbit, at Camelot. They own a fleet of three mega-freighters and at least two dozen smaller cargo ships. The Agency estimates his wealth to be about three billion Sterlings."

"Right. Isadore?"

"Influential lawyer, an Echo himself, he represents rich, well-connected Echoes. He is very good at his job and well rewarded, though frankly financially he is a minnow compared to Rato and Arends. Moving on to Mr Cassian Dexter, real name Marquis Sir Cassian Dexter Tankian — Dexter is his middle name. As far as the Agency can tell he lives above his means and survives on handouts from his friends. The reason they continue to do so is because he is heir to the corporate-noble House of Tankian, which is worth around ten billion. Problem is his father Lord Tankian and son have not spoken in years, but as the only surviving relative in the Tankian dynasty he stands to gain everything. If he can outlive his father. I have not looked at Kenton Serrano's file yet. It will probably raise a whole bunch of red flags in the Commander's office and I am not ready for that yet."

Lovelace nodded then changed the topic.

"So...what are you going to tell the Captain, and more importantly what are you going to do with *Mrs* Hamilton-Jones?"

"I honestly do not know. I want to uncover more... something... about what the hells is going on before we go to the Captain, and as for Clarice..." Aries rubbed his forehead and let out a deep sigh. "Honestly, I do not know. There is something about her. I did not mean to... but there is a connection there."

"You sure? From what I heard she's a serious player. Sure she's not just dragging you around by the balls?" Lovelace looked closely at Aries.

"I... I don't know. Look I will try and keep myself under control — this is not like me — but I have not felt like this in many years."

"It won't end well."

"I know."

Abruptly, Lovelace grinned and slapped Aries on the back hard enough to make him almost spill his drink.

"Well then, nothing like a doomed romance to brighten your day!"

Despite the emotional turmoil, Aries laughed too.

5

Steel Year 2390.10.10 (S-Time)

Aurelian looked up from the floor through slitted eyes. His vision was slightly unfocused, but quickly snapped back into place. *A slight concussion, would render most people slowed.* His genetics were not normal though. He saw the guardsman circling him, casually twirling the baton. Aurelian was unarmed. He quietly tensed all his muscles and when the guardsman circled around again, he launched himself back onto his feet and launched a devastating spin kick. His aim was true and the kick landed squarely in the chest of the guardsman and threw him backward. Seizing the initiative, Aurelian was on top of him in an instant, with the guard in a choke-hold. He spoke.

"Yield." It wasn't a request, and the guardsman, who was rapidly losing consciousness, slapped his hand on the ground three times. Aurelian instantly let go and sprang to his feet and helped the guardsman up. They bowed to one another and Aurelian walked over and picked up a towel. Only now did he allow himself to feel the pain from the repeated strikes the guardsman, *Sergeant Sarrik, I think,* had got in.

Even at fifteen Aurelian was almost fully developed with a strong athletic physique. Having wiped the sweat off his face and arms, he looked up at the viewing gallery and frowned. *Where is father? He hasn't been to one of my training sessions in ages.*

"Your Highness?" Aurelian turned his attention to the figure who spoke. It was Count Morten, the Duke's spy-master and assassin.

"Yes?"

"I need you to come with me. There has been an accident. I'm afraid it is your brother. Something has happened to Darius."

Aurelian felt the bottom fall out of his stomach, as he followed the Count out.

*   *   *

Steel Year 2425.10.03 (S-Time). Day Three, Morning

The blood in Charles Hamilton-Jones' boot had been identified as Julius Rato, also one of the Honourable Brotherhood, which had only further confirmed that they needed to know more about him. So a trip to Rato's residence was in order. The grav car ascended slowly into the dark sky. Aries looked over at Lovelace. Lovelace was still tense after their argument last night, but there was something else. Suddenly it clicked, *Lovelace looks uneasy. He's afraid of flying! Of course! That is why he still uses a ground bike.*

"You are not comfortable in grav vehicles are you, Lovelace?"

Lovelace frowned. "You bloody noticed that, then?"

"Just now. Don't worry, it is perfectly safe."

Lovelace snorted. "Ha! Besides, it's not that."

"What is it then?"

"I grew up in Downtown and Ground Zero, so I didn't get much experience of grav vehicles. They were what the toffs used so they wouldn't have to walk the same streets as the rest of us."

Aries considered his point, "That is true enough." Lovelace turned the tables.

"What about you? You seem very comfortable in grav cars, but not so comfortable in your own skin. Where did you grow up?"

The direct question elicited a small burst of anxiety. Aries pretended to have not heard. "Hmm?"

"You heard me, John. Your accent is fake. You almost have a London accent down pat, but it's not your original accent."

"I... I would rather not talk about that." Aries was shocked. He had underestimated Lovelace. *Stupid mistake to make.*

"I'm your partner, John. Are we going to go through this again?" He heard the edge of anger in Lovelace's voice. Aries sighed and tried to work out how little he could tell him.

"You are right, I am from offworld. Look, Lovelace, it is complicated. I had a different... life... but I left it all behind, and I would prefer to keep it that way."

"I don't get you, Aries," Lovelace sighed, "Ok. You want to keep your past secret, I get *that*. But I got burned by secrets before. I got my balls royally trapped in a vice in the Metropolice. And believe me when I say I don't bloody want that happening again. Secrets get people killed, Aries." A bitter laugh escaped from Aries at the truth of that statement. Lovelace gave him a quizzical look.

"More than you know. Look... Tarus." Lovelace's eyes widened. It was the first time Aries had used his Pure Given Name. "I know. The secrets I have, they have taken more from me than you will ever know. But," he held up a finger, "I can't share that burden with you. Nor can I, nor will I, clear the air. We have not known each other that long, and I do not know you either... yet. I know it is annoying, I know you cannot trust me, but I know that you are not ready for that world of pain, and I am not ready you see you die to keep a secret. Besides, trust takes time, and we barely know each other. We have been partners, what? Three weeks?"

"Four, and thank you!" exclaimed Lovelace.

"What for?" Aries was confused.

"For talking to me like a bloody human being."

"I do not understand."

"Since we started working together I knew something was up with you. You don't need to be a bloody telepath to see you were hiding something, that you were keeping me at arm's length. I couldn't figure you out. Isoke's balls! I even wondered whether you are a traitor!"

"And now?"

"You might be a bloody traitor, for all I know, but I doubt it. However, you and me are alright. Just make me a promise?"

"What?" Aries was guarded.

"If you think I can take it, you can trust me, the stars are bloody in alignment, whatever... promise me you will tell me what happened to you. We're partners, and if I'm going to have your back and possibly meet a violent end, I'd like to know what it was all for." Lovelace grinned. *I underestimated him,* thought Aries, *There is more there than just the warrior, he really is a Truthsayer too.*

"You have my word."

"Good. Now we can get on with our bloody jobs." Lovelace turned to look out the window. The car was still ascending. "How ballsing high are we going in this bloody tin can?"

"This high!" said Aries, grinning, as he pushed forward on the thrust lever and pulled back on the stick. The grav car surged forward and shot up at forty-five degrees into the sky, heading straight for the clouds. The car picked up speed and entered the storm.

Aries flew the grav car through the zero visibility of the storm cloud by instrumentation only. Lightning exploded around the car, shaking it violently as horizontal rain slammed into the windows. Lovelace held tight to his chair and checked his restraints were locked.

"Samael's bloody blade Aries!" Lovelace shouted, "How much further is it?"

"We are getting close!" shouted Aries. Internally he was elated, the simple pleasure of fighting nature with his piloting skills always thrilled him. *Father always said I would have made an excellent aerospace fighter pilot.*

An alert flashed on the heads-up display, and Aries slammed the stick down and then up, diving under a slow-moving grav truck. Lovelace swore colourfully. He swore even louder as Aries flew through and around a set of antennas sticking off the side of a Citadel. John banked the grav car and slid it sideways through the air, letting the wind push him where he wanted to go.

*　　*　　*

Out of the chaos outside, a landing bay appeared, white lit, it was like a portal to another world. Aries pushed the thrust level all the way forward and then car shot into the mouth of the portal. Once inside the calm was instantaneous and, in its own way, just as disorientating. He activated the air brakes, and the g-forces threw both men forwards in their restraints. The car landed with a gentle thump, steam rising from the engines. Aries turned to smile at Lovelace, slapped the release on his restraints while the door fanned open and climbed out.

Lovelace took a little longer, and when out turned to face Aries. "You bloody enjoyed that, didn't you?"

It was true, Aries had a big stupid grin. Lovelace looked around, his eyes pained by the brightness. The landing bay they had landed in was an immaculate white, and the walls, floor and ceiling were lit from within. Behind them lay the opening to the storm, rain clearly sheeting horizontally across the entrance. Lightning flashed in the clouds, the thunder muted despite having been so close. Lovelace pulled on his shades. Aries walked around the car, patted him on the shoulder and said, "This way, big fellow."

They walked across the bay. Lovelace noticed that there were only a couple of other grav vehicles — a car and a plane — in it, and headed for a doorway delimited only by a strip of green luminescence surrounding it.

As they approached, a blue laser scanner ran over them from head to toe. Aries and Lovelace both pulled their badges. The seamless door irised open and they stepped through.

The corridor they walked down was similarly luminescent white. Aries turned to the wall, touched an illuminated green diamond, and spoke, "We are here to investigate Julius Rato's apartment." It was true, thought Lovelace. Despite the difficulty, they had managed to secure a warrant to search Rato's apartment in the Hope Tower. The Uptown Highgate Metropolice detectives had been annoyed that Aries and Lovelace had grabbed their case, but there was not much they could do about it.

Lovelace spoke up, "Uptown is nice. Bit bright though."

Aries, still feeling elated from the flight, grinned. "This is not Uptown, this is the lower part of Zen."

Lovelace's eyebrows raised. Zen was the highest part of the city, it rose above the clouds to the world of sunlight and clean air. Zen was almost Olympian in its stature. Few ever travelled here, and fewer still lived in Zen. Only the valley of Hampstead was more exclusive. Lovelace had only visited Uptown proper once or twice, but never Zen. He took some deep breaths, savouring the air's clarity. There was a slight hint of fresh lemons.

"It is a bit too Federate Combine, for my liking," said Aries with sudden venom in his voice, grin vanished. Lovelace looked at him, *Interesting. Not a fan of the FedCom?*

A disembodied female voice spoke, "This way, Agents," and a beautiful, goddess-like figure in a toga appeared before them, translucent and glowing. She smiled, and indicated them to follow.

"What the fu—! Who are you?"

The goddess turned and spoke to Lovelace, "I am Hope, Agent Lovelace. This is my tower. Please follow me."

She sashayed down the corridor, and despite himself Lovelace found his eyes drawn to the rhythmic movement of her glowing hips. Belatedly he noticed Aries following her, and hurried to catch up. They stepped into a small room, the door closing behind them. Behind him, the wall became transparent, and bright sunlight shined in and Lovelace realised that they were in a lift. He rapidly pulled his shades on.

Once the green spots in his vision had faded, he looked out over the clouds outside. The lightning was roiling within them, and the scene resembled nothing so much as an angry sea roiling against the coast of small islands that were the tips of the Citadels. *It really is another world. Up here you don't even have to see the city below.* He marvelled and was simultaneously repulsed. *So easy to view the city below as existing for nothing beyond your benefit.* It was bright daylight up here, while below it was pitch black.

The lift continued to rise until it was several hundred meters above the clouds. The ride was so smooth that Lovelace did not notice when it came to a halt. Aries tapped him on the arm. "We are here."

Lovelace turned to see that the lift had indeed stopped and the door opened, revealing a sunlit palace beyond. Hope indicated for him to enter. He stepped past her. She smiled at him.

The palace beyond was on three floors. Through the middle of each flowed a waterfall, and it made a soothing background white noise.

Aries turned to Hope. "When was Mr Rato last here?"

"Mr Rato was last in residence, six days ago."

"Did he leave any indication on where he was going to go?"

"No. I believe he had gone to the Fox Hunt Club with Mr Roe, but I have heard nothing for the last six days and am beginning to worry for his safety."

Lovelace paused in his looking around. *The building is worrying about him?* He turned to her.

"We have reason to believe Mr Rato might have been killed. Could you tell me more about this Mr Roe?"

Hope raised her translucent eyebrows and concern filled her holographic face, *She is bloody lifelike. Surprisingly.*

"Oh how terrible! Of course. Mr Brentan Roe is a good friend of Mr Rato and also a member of the Fox Hunt Club. Do let me know if there is anything I can do to help." As she spoke, an image of Rato and Roe appeared in the air next to her.

Lovelace looked at Aries, *Who is this Brentan Roe? That is a new name. Is he an Honourable Brother too, and if so why did Cassian Dexter not mention him to Aries?*

Aries replied, "Thank you Hope. We are going to take a look around. I — we — may have more questions for you later."

"Of course Agent Aries. If you have need of me, all you need do is call my name." She faded out. Lovelace got a wisp of lavender. He shook his head and turned to the palace.

"It's a bit big, John. Shall we split up? I'll take the top floor, you take the bottom and we meet in the middle?"

"Sounds good to me, Tarus." *Again with my Given Name. It was almost as if he needed permission to use it.*

They split up, Lovelace headed upstairs.

The palace, as that was what it really was, *This is no regular apartment*, was immaculate. The walls had an inner glow like the corridors below, but up here it was more muted and subdued. As he approached the master bedroom the two doors silently slid open revealing an impressive vista.

The huge, super king-sized bed sat on a stepped platform, a good half meter above the floor. Behind it was a hundred degree window that provided a stunning vista out over the clouds. Currently the window was dimmed, for which Lovelace was glad. Even with his shades on, much of his experience of Zen so far had been painful.

At least twenty humanoid statues stood by the walls. Each was twisted and appeared to be a plant-human hybrid. Their colours were lurid and the poses gave an impression of the figure stuck in a moment of time. Each statue's head was aligned toward the bed, their faces contorted in grimaces of pain or ecstasy. Lovelace could not tell which. Lovelace was not a fan of art, especially not of this disturbing version. *All those eyes staring at you while you sleep. Rato was a bloody strange man.*

The floor was carpeted, with a huge bathroom suite to one side and walk-in wardrobes to the other. Lovelace walked around the circumference looking for signs of struggle, but there were none to see. Everything was perfect. A vase with several beautiful roses sat on a side table. Idly, Lovelace picked it up, but it was made of some kind of super smooth material and it slipped out of his fingers and smashed on the floor.

The voice of Hope sounded, "Do not worry, Agent Lovelace. The nanobots will take care of that."

Even as he watched the vase disintegrated, the water evaporated and the roses were consumed, until less than sixty seconds later there was no trace the vase and roses had ever been there. Lovelace shivered. *Samael cut me!*

"Are you cold, Agent?" The voice sounded behind him and Lovelace spun on the spot. Hope stood there. Lovelace was momentarily speechless, but finally he did speak.

"Uh… no, thanks. I'm fine. It was the… nanobots. I wasn't expecting them."

"The whole of the Hope Tower is a self-regulating system, Agent. If there is a mess, the nanobots clean it up. If there is damage, they fix it."

"So they would remove any trace of an intruder."

"Yes, I suppose they would. But that is why I record everything."

"In that case, I will cut to the chase — did Mr Rato have any unexpected visitors recently?"

"No, not that I am aware of?" Hope idly straightened her toga.

"You sound hesitant, is something wrong?" Lovelace had to keep in mind that she was just a projection of the Tower's systems. Admittedly, they were highly advanced systems.

"Well, there was a minor disruption in my internal recording systems in Mr Rato's apartment between 03:22 and 03:37 five nights ago."

"That was after Mr Rato had disappeared?"

"Yes, that is correct. It happened during a scheduled maintenance period, however with Mr Rato's disappearance I had decided to forego the maintenance in case he should return. I assumed it was a nanobot swarm carrying out the maintenance as originally planned, as I did not detect any activity in the lifts, or landing pads, and none of the security systems registered any disturbances."

"Yes, but someone could have got in during that fifteen minute window."

"That is highly unlikely, Agent, as my sensor systems are very advanced. My radar detected no approaching or departing vehicles, and my internal sensors use ultrasonic frequencies, infrared, ultraviolet, thermal imaging and pressure monitors. I also have a fully operational Wyld Shield. None of these registered any abnormalities."

"Yes, but the fact remains you had a fifteen minute blind spot."

"I…" The building's avatar seemed unsure of herself. *Itself,* reminded Lovelace. He tried a new tack.

"Hypothetically, if someone wanted to get in during that time, where would they go? Did Mr Rato have a safe?"

"I believe so. Mr Rato has a Quiet Room."

"A quiet room?"

"Yes, it is fully EM shielded and has no internal surveillance."

"Show it to me."

Hope seemed to have an internal debate about it. Finally, she spoke, "I… can't. It would be a breach of trust."

"I have a warrant, and trust me Mr Rato is not coming back."

"How do you know that? Have you found his body? I have been monitoring all hospital channels and that of the Necropolis and there has been no report of his body. Perhaps he has merely been kidnapped?" Lovelace narrowed his eyes, "Look, Hope. You can either show it to us, or I can bring a full Agency forensics team back here and have them pull everything apart. Rato is dead. I know that for certain."

Hope vanished. Lovelace heard Aries call out from below. He left the bedroom and joined his partner on the middle floor.

In a large room lined with mirrors on the floor and ceiling, a whole section of wall had swung open revealing a vault door.

"Was that you?"

"Sort of. I had a word with the Tower."

"Good work."

Aries and Lovelace walked over to the door. Even as they approached, it was clear something was wrong. A neat round hole had been burned through the thick steel. Aries touched the hole, and his eyes and Echo tattoo glowed briefly.

"An Echo did this." It was stated matter of fact, "A Pyrokinetic, like me. Pure plasma stream."

Lovelace reached out and gently pushed the door open, it swung inward silently. Inside, the room was a mess. It was obvious that Rato's Quiet Room had been thoroughly ransacked. His comm units had been completely melted down, and there were several piles of ash — all that remained of documents and several books.

Lovelace turned to Aries, "Echo?" Aries nodded.

"Someone went to great pains to ensure we found nothing. This was a top-of-the-line crew, to get in and out and do all this within a quarter of an hour…" Lovelace agreed. Whoever had organised this had serious clout.

"Yeah, someone is cleaning up loose ends. First Massey de Sargon's body, and now this."

"We need to find out who, and I think there is only one way to find out. I am going to make a call."

Twenty minutes later a new Agent joined them. Another Pure, but as different from Lovelace as could be.

Tall and thin to the point of being emaciated, the Pure was bald and devoid of tattoos other than his Echo one, something that was highly unusual for a Pure. He wore a bodysuit made of braided leather. His Echo tattoo surrounded the left of his two eyeless sockets. His nails were long and pointed. Despite his obvious blindness he walked confidently into the room and over to Aries and Lovelace.

"Lovelace, meet Diarmuid from Ripper." SO-20 Ripper were the elite Echo-only unit within the Agency that dealt with high level Echo crimes. It was they that brought in recently-manifested for the Aegis Foundation. It was also they that administered ultimate sanction on an Echo too far gone to the Wyld Cancer. It was a grim job, but without it thousands, if not millions, of lives would be lost every time an Echo finally went critical. However, their executioner-like profession added to their status as the elite amongst Echoes and made them feared and distrusted with equal measure.

Diarmuid spoke in a curiously lyrical voice, "Hi John, this place is nice, I'm glad I came." Lovelace recognised the accent as Ballaén, which would make him a Ballaétic Pure. A splinter culture that had broken away from the Kapaethjan orthodoxy hundreds of years ago over the nature of the Pure Code, the Ballaén were not exactly popular with most Pures. However, Lovelace had learnt the hard way to put aside his prejudices. They just were not practical for a law enforcer working in London.

Still, when Diarmuid held out his hand he found himself hesitating for an instant before returning the greeting.

"Interesting," said Diarmuid, "the paths were unclear whether you would shake my hand or slight me."

Lovelace looked quizzically at Aries. "Diarmuid is a metapsion," he explained, "an Echo with meta-sensory perception and that gives him limited precognitive abilities."

"Bloody hells," muttered Lovelace. Diarmuid grinned.

"It is ok Lovelace, I get that a lot. Especially from normals. But don't worry I am in the same field as you, Truthsayer. John, show me the room you want me to scan?"

"This way." They led Diarmuid to the Quiet Room.

"How does precognition help us here, Aries?" whispered Lovelace.

"It doesn't," replied Diarmuid, "John asked me to use my psychomancy and chrono-prescience to scan the crime scene."

"Oh, right."

"Now if you will stand clear, Tarus. I am 98% certain that I won't Wyld while I do this, but just to be safe, I recommend standing behind John."

He stepped back behind Aries, and watched the strange Pure Echo at work.

Diarmuid spread his arms wide and his eye sockets and tattoo began to glow white. The glow became brighter until it was the brightest illumination in the room. It was then that Lovelace felt the curious tickling sensation, as if he were standing in a thunderstorm, and strange patches formed in the air that distended, distorted or otherwise altered the light around Diarmuid. Lovelace heard a distant roaring, but the sound appeared to be coming from within his own head. Everything took on a dreamlike quality, edges became sharper, curves warped and straight lines appeared to bend and twist. Diarmuid opened his mouth and more light poured outward from his throat. His finger tips glowed and it seemed to Lovelace that reality was pulled in toward him as everything lost visual focus.

His stomach heaved and he felt the nausea rise. Turning his head as slowly as he could he looked at Aries. Aries stood, perfectly in focus, seemingly more real than the surrounding space. His eyes had a slight shine to them that hinted of a mild glow, but otherwise he was unaffected. Aries looked at Lovelace, saw the disturbance on his face and closed his eyes briefly. A bubble of cold, clean reality, expanded to enclose Lovelace and everything snapped back into place. The nausea quickly retreated.

John mouthed, "Sorry", to Lovelace and returned his attention to Diarmuid, who was now floating a centimetre or two above the ground. Suddenly he touched down and reality returned to normal, aside from a residual glow from Diarmuid. A trickle of black blood ran from Diarmuid's nose. He wiped it away and turned to the other two Agents.

"Your team were professional, there were three of them, plus an Echo. The Echo did his best to hide what they did from me, but he was no match for me. They were meticulous in destroying all evidence linking Julius Rato with the Honourable Brotherhood, specifically to stymie any investigators. They knew the security systems inside out, and I suspect they were working with a Technomancer," — a Technomancer was yet another type of Echo, one who could control machines — "they did their best to disguise their identities, but I picked up a few things. One of the team called the Echo 'Silus'. I also picked up that one of the team was called 'Mathers', but I couldn't tell which one. I am certain that they were professional mercenaries. Oh, and they mentioned someone called Arends." *Mathers! That cannot be a coincidence... this was the work of the same team of mercs that took Nigel Massey de Sargon's body.*

"That is great work, Diarmuid." Lovelace nodded in agreement.

"I'm sorry I couldn't find anything else. They were surprisingly good at covering their tracks. Word of warning, Silus was pretty powerful, I think he might have had more than just Pyrokinesis. I can't put my finger on what, but I am sure that is the case."

"Diarmuid, thank you. You are the best."

"Yes, I am. Good seeing you Aries. I'll show myself out."

Once Diarmuid had left, Lovelace exclaimed, "Isoke's cunt and cock! That was bloody freaky. I need a damned drink." Aries smiled and said, "It is on me. Come on, let us get out of here."

As they walked out, Lovelace commented, "Why don't we get him to scan all our crime scenes?"

"He is picky about where he works, plus we would owe him too many favours. Let's see what we can find on our own first, and then if necessary I'll have another word."

"John, you should know. One of the team of mercs that took

Massey de Sargon's body was called Mathers. It is almost certainly the same team."

Aries nodded. "Good! It is a lead. That is something."

*   *   *

Aries and Lovelace had split up once they had left Rato's apartment. Aries had headed back to his flat to ponder his next steps, while Lovelace went to go see some of his street-level contacts.

They had decided to try and chase down the mercs Arends had used to destroy the evidence at Rato's palace. *Yes, but evidence of what?* Aries was frustrated, they knew that something was going on, but so far they had been vexed at every turn. He hoped that the information that Diarmuid had given them was going to break the case wide open, but it would only do that if they could track down this Silus and Mathers. *Will they crack if we get them? If Lovelace and I get a chance to interrogate them, we at least have a chance of finding out something.*

Aries made a few calls to contacts of his own, putting the word out through trusted contacts that he was looking to find the mercs. He also put a Trace Alert out through the Agency weave. Problem was, he only had names and as yet nothing about the identities behind those names, other than that Mathers was a former pit fighter.

The other new lead was the mention of Brentan Roe by Hope. That name had been missing from Dexter's list. Obviously Dexter had not wanted him knowing about Roe. The question was why? A quick search of the Agency weave had brought up the following:

[Name: Brentan Erasmus Roe; Sex: Male; Age: 82; Race: Human (Truean); Occupation: Banker, Fitzedison Bank; Status: Normal; Medical Cover: Platinum, Nova Response; Current Alerts: No outstanding warrants or alerts.]

He was another rich gentleman banker with aristocratic leanings, just like his Honourable Brotherhood companions, but aside from that there appeared to be nothing special about him. *So why did Dexter leave him out? He might not have been at the Honourable Brotherhood dinner, but leaving him out could only have been purely an intentional act of omission. Perhaps this Brentan Roe is a weak link, someone they fear may reveal whatever the hells it is that they are up to. Obviously Dexter did not want me knowing about him, so that makes him a high value interview target as far as I am concerned.*

After some consideration, he had called Roe and left a message requesting an interview, but so far there had been no reply. *You cannot hide from me for long, Roe. I know where you live and work.*

But that was not enough. He wanted to get some background information on Roe, and he realised that he was dancing around the obvious source. *Clarice...*

He still did not know how he felt about her. It was the first time he had been close to a woman since Ariadne, and he was aware that he was being manipulated by her. Despite that, he knew there was a connection between them. But that knowledge just brought back the pain which he felt well up inside himself. With it came a burst of memories which he forced down. Feelings of guilt and betrayal broke free, despite his certain knowledge that Ariadne would want him to be happy. Clarice had ignited something inside that John had tried his best to bury, and that left him feeling confused and in a state of emotional turmoil.

He wanted to see her again. Needed to, if he was honest with himself, but he also knew he needed some time to think it through. That was without even considering the ramifications of having a relationship with someone like Clarice. Someone who was also a possible suspect in the disappearance of her own husband. Someone who was married.

She was not responsible for Charles' disappearance, came the thought unbidden, quickly followed by, *That is just your lust talking. You cannot possibly eliminate her from suspicion at this stage.*

He sat down on the edge of his bed and forced himself to relax. A few minutes of deep breathing and he felt the emotions subside for now. The decision reached, he picked up his comm and called Clarice.

She appeared on screen and, on seeing him, she smiled. Her eyes twinkled. Then she noticed Aries' frown.

"What is the matter, John? Is something wrong?"

"Can we meet up later? I would like your help with something on the case."

"Of course. Do you have news... about Charles?"

"Not yet, but I am making progress." *Am I making progress? Really?*

"Good. I am glad to hear that. It would be good to see you. Where would you like to meet?"

"Shall I come round to your house later?" He saw her look around the room. Clarice shook her head. A single lock of her dark hair tumbled down over her face and Aries suddenly had the urge to tuck it back. *Concentrate John!*

"Not here. We can meet at a discreet restaurant I know of. We can talk there. I will send you the details."

"That sounds good. Are you alright?"

Clarice nodded quickly. "I'm fine. There are a few things I need to take care of. Since Charles went missing I have been forced to take control over our finances and investments, not to mention the arrangements for the bloody Governor's Ball in three days. It is an extra strain at the moment, but I don't want to bore you with the details. Until later, shall we say 10pm? We could take a late supper?"

Aries glanced at the clock on his comm, it was 3pm. "That sounds good. I will see you then."

"Be careful, John. You have already begun to stir up a hornet's nest." He ended the call. *Good. Maybe this way we will find out what is really going on.*

That gives me seven hours. That should be time enough. Aries got up and headed over to the bathroom. *There is another contact I have that might be able to help me find out about the mercs, but if he is still down in Lower Bricktown I think it might be wise to go low profile.* If he was honest with himself, he still was a bit annoyed at himself for getting his grav car vandalised in the Rock.

He waved his hand over a metal cabinet and a code-lock appeared. Tapping in the code and having his irised scanned, the cabinet unlocked. Inside was a supply of medical patches, stim patches and a collection of various combat drug patches. He reached in and pulled out a small makeup applicator he had acquired from a covert operative in Intel. What he was about to do was highly illegal, though technically was in a grey area for an Agent such as himself.

Moving to the mirror, he applied the special-formula foundation over his Echo tattoo, obscuring it from view. The disguise would only last as long as he did not use his Echo powers. If he did that, the Star of the Overlord tattoo would burn straight through the foundation, just as it would any obscuring material. But until he did, it would hide his identity as an Echo. Useful, as Lower Bricktown was a haven for anti-Echo groups like Firestorm, Fist and even the terrorist group, Blood-299, any of whom would kill him as soon as looking at him.

Checking the foundation was blended in with his dark brown hair at the temples and with his eyebrows he considered himself happy with the effect. *It is always strange seeing myself as a Normal.* It was a shallow deception, as he could still feel the low, burning sensation from the tattoo. *It is a brand, designed to separate us out from everyone else as special and different. And dangerous.*

He had seen how Lovelace had looked at Diarmuid when he had used his meta-sensory abilities. There was an edge of revulsion mixed with jealously and fear. Aries understood the reaction and even accepted it. *Echoes are dangerous. I am dangerous. At any moment I could detonate in a Wyld and kill everyone around me but leave myself unharmed. Every time I use my powers there is a small chance of that. But even when I do keep them under control I die a little every time.* The Wyld Cancer was insidious, building up bit by bit, yet seductive in its call. *Use me,* it called, *You do not have to accept reality as it is. Change it! Shape it! Make it your own!*

Using Echo power was highly addictive, and like everything addictive it was dangerous. Aries prided himself on perversely solving things without using his abilities. *My abilities attract too much attention, and attention is the last thing I want.*

So for him the irony was that he was marked out as an Echo, but functionally was a normal. Unless he was pushed too far. There were many uses for pyrokinetic abilities such as he had. The ability to form, shape and even become pure plasma was useful undoubtedly. Unfortunately most of their usefulness was purely destructive. He could kill and destroy with ease. The beneficial uses were fewer in an age that did not require fire for survival. He sometimes wished he had telepathy, meta-sensory perception, teleportation or one of the other, more socially acceptable powers. But even then he knew that it was not which powers he had, just that he had them.

He reached over and pulled out a temporary tattoo of a spider's web, which he quickly applied to his neck. *A small thin scar applied with practised ease to his right cheek completed the look. Distracts and focuses attention on the scar. If they are asked later to describe me it is the tattoo and the scar they will remember, not my face.*

With a sad smile, Aries returned the illicit foundation to the cabinet and closed it. Getting changed he put on a black docker's roll-neck jumper over the lightweight armoured body suit he wore beneath, black trousers and workman's steel toe-capped boots. He slid a concealed holster onto his belt at the small of his back and put a 9mm Aralyte MIN-101 pistol in it. He pulled a dark grey coat over the top, and as a final touch slid a dagger into the sheath hidden in his right boot. Last, but not least, he fitted three rings onto his right hand. Each looked normal but was weighted down with a mercury core to add a little extra mass for any punches required.

The armour should be enough to stop knife attacks or deflect small calibre bullets leaving nothing but a nasty bruise. He had loaded the pistol with hollow point rounds. Again, highly illegal, but they had the added benefit of stopping unarmoured targets in their tracks without penetrating nearby buildings. Aries wanted to avoid the euphemistically-termed 'collateral damage'. He pulled on a docker's cap, goggles and muffler/breather and checked himself out in his full-length mirror.

I look every centimetre dock scum. Nice.

He pulled out his comm and called Lovelace. When he appeared on screen it took Lovelace a moment to recognise him.

"Bloody blade! Nice disguise, John. I didn't recognise you for a moment. You sure you're not moonlighting as a spook for Intel?" Aries smiled and shook his head.

"Tarus, I want to follow up with some contacts I have in Bricktown. You want to come with me?"

"Sure. I can meet you there. I'm currently in the Rock, so shouldn't take me long, assuming the lug nut I am waiting for turns up."

"Great. See you there in twenty minutes?" Lovelace nodded and he cut the connection, slid the comm into a watertight inside pocket, and headed to the door.

He opened it, revealing a bulky, muscular man in a dark suit with a crew cut and shades standing there. He took off his shades, and Aries knew two things for certain: that this man was a professional killer and that he was in deep trouble. When he spoke it was with a thick London accent.

"John Aries?"

"Uh. Nope mate. You must 'av the wrong flat." *Weak, John. Weak. It is an Uptown apartment. Not a lot of dockers up here.*

The man looked puzzled for a second then shrugged, "Fair enough." He put on his shades again. A second figure Aries had not noticed stepped up behind him and grabbed him in a choke hold. He felt a sudden, familiar coldness on his neck that told him a drugpatch had been applied.

He struggled, but felt the world fall away from him as his vision faded. He quickly began to fade from consciousness. The first man stepped forward and punched Aries incredibly hard. Despite the armour, he felt a rib crack.

The suited man stepped back and absently rubbed his fist. "Damn drudge's wearing armour. He ain't no 'slicing docker." He addressed the figure holding Aries, who remained silent. "The guv' said to nab anyone coming out of his apartment, target's a Steeler, so who knows what he looks like. I ain't bloody taking any chances. Bag him, I'll get him to the guv' and you see if anyone else turns up."

His last thoughts before he blacked out were, *Who sent these thugs?* and *How did they find me so quickly?*

6

Steel Year 2391.08.25 (S-Time)

Aurelian ripped the sword from his scabbard and threw himself over the balcony into the mêlée going on below. A patrol of Ducal Guard had been overwhelmed by a swarm of masked attackers. Aurelian crashed down heavily on one of the assailants, smashing him into the marble floor below as hard as he could. His training kicking in, he rolled off the prone figure and onto his feet.

With a roar he smashed the pommel of his sword into the first assailant's face, spun and thrust the blade through the body of the next. The blade hummed with energy and the stench of burning meat filled the air.

A strike came down at Aurelian, which he parried effortlessly with his blade. With his left hand he pulled his pistol and fired two gauss bolts at close range, blowing head-sized holes in the figure. The masked man was dead before he hit the ground.

Yet above this all violence he could hear them hammering on the door of his son's room. The momentary distraction allowed an attacker to slash him across the arm. Aurelian bellowed like an injured lion and smashed his forehead into the face of the attacker. He felt his opponent's nose shatter and blood sprayed out.

He kicked the reeling figure away and pushed past him, casually firing into his torso. *No man threatens my son and lives. No man.*

Still there were at least another ten assailants trying to get to his son's room. The twin thoughts of *Why are they attacking my son?* and *Where are my guards?* flitted through his mind, but there was no time for thinking, only action.

He ran across the great marble hall, now scarred with battle damage and stained with blood. At the last moment he slid down onto his back under one of the attackers and shoved his blade upwards as he slid past, instantly killing him. His sword became lodged and Aurelian let go and continued the slide, rolling to his feet fluidly. The thought, *Morten would have been pleased with that one,* came to him uncalled for. Without slowing he fired twice with the gauss pistol killing two more.

A return shot glanced his thigh, whilst another punched through his left shoulder. The pain was instantly suppressed by his training and enhancements, leaving him just enough of a remnant to further drive his anger.

He now heard several voices talking quickly. "It's the Prince himself, tell the others, the Heretic's son is here!" and realised that this was no random assassination, but part of a major attack. As if to emphasise this he felt the rumble of a distant explosion. His hearing immediately pinpointed it to the Eastern Gate.

Heretic? My father?

"So Mikael wasn't wrong, the dice really have been thrown. This is it." He knew then that he would almost certainly die, but that no one would kill his new son. He had lost too much and his son would not join his wife with Kali.

"You want me?" Aurelian shouted, "Then here I am!"

With impossible grace he leapt straight over the nearest attacker's head and drove his fingers into the man's throat as he did so, leaving him falling to the floor gurgling on his own blood.

Whilst still in the air, he drew his knife from his belt and threw it into the next attacker's eye. Life as a noble in the Steel Alliance was not for the faint hearted and he had been trained by the best. He remembered the words of his trainer, Count Morten. "You can never miss, never show mercy, never restrain your hand when attacked, or all you care about, all you love will be taken from you."

Morten would have hoped it would never come to this though. He looked around. There were still too many of them and he was wounded and running out of weapons. Steeling himself, he tore open a channel to the Wyld and prepared to release his full power.

*   *   *

Steel Year 2425.10.03 (S-Time). Day Three, Evening

Aries came to with a start. His heart was pounding and a layer of sweat covered his entire body. He opened his eyes, but still could not see. A heavy, musty smell filled his nostrils, and a coarse material tickled his face. He realised that they had put a sack over his head, that either blocked all light or he was in a dark room.

Then he remembered what had happened and forced his heart to calm. Cautiously trying his muscles he could tell he had been bound by his hands and feet, and that he was naked. It felt like they had used manacles or chains on his wrists and ankles. A sharp pain around his neck told him they had put a loop of wire around it, probably also attached to the same metal chair he could feel sapping the heat from his buttocks and back. His breathing was slightly laboured from the punch earlier.

Not good, John. Not good at all. Forces unknown have captured you, and at least one of them is packing some serious strength enhancements.

He invoked a mantra of calm as he had been taught and felt a wave of calm pass over him.

How long have I been out, and where am I? To the first question he had no answer, but for the second he strained to listen. A distant dripping and a certain dankness in the air told him he was either underground or near a water source. Distantly he could hear the sounds of children at play, but it was muffled and confused as if reflected. *What the hells?*

He pondered using his Echo abilities to free himself, but decided that until he knew more he could not risk it. He could just as easily bring the building down on him as get himself free, especially when he was already disorientated. Right now he needed more information. *Besides,* as the tactical part of his mind thought, *whoever these people are they were after me specifically. I need to find out who they are and what they want. Any interrogation is likely to reveal a lot about the interrogator. Whatever these guys have up their sleeves, I have been through much, much worse.*

Invoking a mind-shaping mantra, he dulled his sense of pain in preparation for whatever was going to happen next. It was a risky move, but right now he did not exactly have a full set of cards.

Lovelace, I hope you have realised I have been taken, he thought to himself.

*   *   *

Lovelace was worried. When Aries had not shown up, he had tried to call him, but with no success. His gut told him that something had happened to Aries, and Lovelace feared the worst.

After waiting for a couple of hours in Lower Bricktown, he had decided that he needed to go and check out Aries' apartment as that was the last place he had been seen. On the way he requested a trace on Aries' grav car and his fear only deepened when he learnt that it was still parked at his apartment block.

Now he stood outside the entrance to the tower. He could see the guard on duty inside, seated at his desk. Lovelace looked around, but could spot no obvious surveillance. *Still, just because I don't see them, doesn't mean they are not there.* Lovelace decided on caution, walked back to his bike to pick up a few useful tools and then headed around to the building's rear entrance.

A steel unmarked security door was hidden in a back alley.

Lovelace walked up to it and performed a quick scan with a multi-sensor. The door had a simple alarm on it. Lovelace quickly disabled it, and then moved to open the door. There was no obvious handle on this side, so he pulled out a crowbar, wedged it in solidly and used his considerable strength to lever it over. The tendons across Lovelace's arms, shoulders and back stood out proud. The door warped in its frame and the locks popped out.

Putting the crowbar away again, Lovelace pulled open the door and headed inside.

*　　*　　*

Aries had sat there for what seemed an eternity with only the cold and lack of comfort to keep him company. Distantly he heard the sound of boots walking on concrete approaching. He could hear at least three people, though it was hard to tell as the sound was muffled.

The footsteps stopped and there was the unmistakable sound of a padlock being unlocked and chains being released. The noise of metal grinding on metal was almost deafening.

The footsteps entered the room he was in. He got a strong scent of wet concrete and behind it, sweat. The noise of children playing he had heard earlier was clearer but he was still unable to tell the distance. It was joined by a low mechanical hum.

This is it, he thought, *now the 'fun' begins.*

He heard one of the people walk slowly around to stand at his rear. There was another metallic scraping noise which Aries guessed to be another chair being brought in. It stopped in from of him and somebody sat in it. The third person seemed to be moving a pile of chains to his left.

When he or she had finished, Aries heard nothing besides their quiet breathing.

Nobody spoke.

*　　*　　*

Lovelace moved cautiously up the stairwell to Aries' floor. It had taken a while, but Lovelace did not want to be caught in a lift if things went bad. When he reached the correct floor he opened the door cautiously. The corridor was dark, but that was no obstacle to a Pure like Lovelace. He remained still, spending a few moments watching. In the darkness of one of the doorways he spotted a figure in some kind of stealth suit. The figure was ideally situated to observe both Aries' apartment and the lift.

Lovelace considered what to do next. If he shot the figure with his Headhunter he was likely to kill him, and right now that would not help anyone. Lovelace also realised that his own build, jewellery and alabaster skin, were not exactly subtle.

I'm not going to win this with a battle of who's stealthier. No, I need to neutralise his stealth and keep the bloody surprise.

He looked around for something to even the odds. He saw the fire alarm and then another thought struck him. *Strength versus stealth. More my style.* He knew what he needed.

*   *   *

What are they waiting for? thought Aries. By his best guess it had been at least ten minutes since the three individuals entered the room with him, and in that time they had done absolutely nothing.

Who are they waiting for?

As if on cue, he heard the approaching tap of a single set of footsteps, and something else. *A cane?* The new arrival came to a halt in front of Aries.

The sack was pulled up and Aries found himself squinting in the bright lights. When his vision cleared he saw that he was in a small concrete room with a steel door. Ahead of him stood two figures. The first was a Hulk who had slightly hunched over so as not to hit the ceiling. The second was a face that Aries immediately recognised from yesterday.

Benham Arends.

Arends was attired in a black suit and waistcoat with a white shirt and black cravat. The cravat was fastened by a diamond pin. He wore a long light brown coat and black gloves. In his right hand he held a silver-topped cane. His face was ruddy and his grey hair was short. His expression was not that of a happy man.

"I see you recognise me, *Agent* Aries. I must say you are not the gentleman I was led to believe you were. You look more like a navvy to me. You should know scars do not befit a gentleman."

Aries realised that Arends was talking about his makeup. *They do not know I am an Echo!*

"What do you want Mr Arends?"

"I want to know why you are killing my friends, and why you are trying to kill me."

Aries could not keep the surprise from his face. "What are you talking about?"

Arends scratched his eyebrow and nodded to the figure behind Aries. The wire around his neck tightened.

"Each time you do not give me a satisfactory answer, Aries, my man will tighten the wire. He will continue to do so until it slices through your skin, muscle and throat. You will choke to death on your own blood. It will not be pleasant, nor will it be fast. Should you lose the ability to breathe before I have finished my questions, Mr Mathers there will pierce your chest with a breathing tube. Do you understand, Aries?"

Aries attempted to nod, but was held in place by the wire. Arends, however, noted the gesture.

"Good. Then I shall begin my questioning."

*   *   *

Lovelace stepped out of the stairwell and hurled the fire extinguisher at the stealthed figure as hard and fast as he could. The extinguisher connected solidly with an audible thump and he was gratified to see the stealthed figure collapse bonelessly where he stood.

Not taking any chances, Lovelace crossed the distance at full pelt and grabbed the figure and rapidly bound his arms and legs with cuff tape. He pulled off the stealth mask, revealing an unremarkable human beneath. He checked his pulse.

"Good, you're not dead you toe-rag. You'd be no good to me dead."

Picking him up bodily with his left arm, Lovelace walked over to the entrance to Aries' apartment.

The door was no match for Lovelace, who stepped through its now broken frame. He dropped the unconscious intruder just inside the doorway. It was obvious immediately that Aries' flat had been ransacked.

"Samael's blade! This isn't good, John. Not bloody good at all."

He pulled out his comm, put out a 'Missing Agent' alert and then called Linsbury.

"Boss. We have a big bloody problem. I think Aries has been kidnapped." He turned to the unconscious man. "No, I don't know where he is yet, but I think I know how to find out. I'll call you back in fifteen minutes, but I think you should get a tactical and medical team standing by. My gut tells me that this will get ugly." Lovelace hefted the man over his shoulder and headed for the roof.

Time to get ugly.

*   *   *

"Why are you trying to kill me?"

"I'm not!"

"Don't lie to me, Mr Aries. You killed Julius and you are trying to kill me!"

"No… I did not… am not!" Arends nodded and the noose tightened again. Aries could feel it cutting into his flesh. *What is he talking about?*

"Lying to me accomplishes nothing. I know you were told to kill me. As an arms dealer, I deal in death on a daily basis, Mr Aries, so believe me when I say I know a killer when I see him. You are a killer. You cannot hide that from me."

"Arends," spat Aries, "Get this through your thick *bloody* skull. I. Am. Not. Trying. To. Kill. You. If… if I was, you would already be dead. *You* killed Rato."

"What?" The surprise was evident in Arend's voice.

"You…" Aries was struggling to breathe, let alone talk, "sent those men to his house to cover up the murder." The blood dripped onto his lap in a steady drip. *I cannot take much more of this.* The temptation to use his Echo abilities and kill everyone in the room, and beyond, was becoming harder to resist.

"Incorrect, Mr Aries. I sent a team to ensure that certain information which Julius and I shared did not fall into the hands of my enemies. Enemies such as you." *If you did not kill Rato,* thought Aries, *then it must have been Charles Hamilton-Jones and Nigel Massey de Sargon.*

Arends bent in close to speak to Aries. His face had gone a dark reddish hue and he sprayed spittle into Aries' face as he spoke, biting off every word. "Someone is killing my friends, one by one. First Julius, then Nigel and then Charles disappears. Do think I am a fool? Do you think I cannot see what is going on?"

"What is going on?"

"The Agency, you and your stupid inbred wraith brute, were sent by your Commander to kill me."

"Commander Villiers—" The wire tightened again and Aries started to choke. Arends raised his left hand and the pressure on Aries' neck eased.

"Yes. Commander Villiers-Cavanaugh. It wasn't enough to have our support, he decided to take everything."

"But…I thought he was one… of *you*?"

"He was. But then he got delusions of grandeur. As well you know."
Interesting. So the Honourable Brotherhood are not one big happy family. "So now you will tell me everything he is planning and then, if I am satisfied, I will kill you quickly. If not, not even your bitch of a girlfriend will be able to identify your corpse."

Lovelace hurry up, I cannot hold myself back for much longer.

*   *   *

"Wakey, wakey. Rise and shine, lug nut!" The would-be assassin opened his eyes and screamed. Lovelace held him by his ankles over the edge of the building. Below lay a three hundred metre drop. Lovelace gave him a shake to make sure he was awake. The assassin tried to reach around to grab something, only to realise his arms were still bound.

"Where is Aries?" The assassin, trying to regain some composure, raised his head and glared at Lovelace, but said nothing. Lovelace shrugged and let go. The assassin screamed as he fell, his scream being cut short by the sudden stop as the rope Lovelace had tied to his ankles reached its maximum length.

"Next time, there won't be a rope to save you. Now answer the question. Where is Aries?"

"I don't know what you are talking about, cop!" replied the assassin. Lovelace smiled. It was not a pleasant smile.

"Oh no, I'm not a cop. At least, not any more. Got thrown out for killing too many criminal scumbags like you. No, now I'm an Agent, and we have a whole different set of rules. Turns out I'm not very good at following those either. Tell me where Aries is or I will tear the skin off every centimetre of your body. You see, Aries is my friend, and if anything happens to him I swear blood vengeance on those who killed him, the families of those who killed him, their children, their friends, grandparents and even the bloody man they buy their bloody milk from. I will hunt down each and every one and kill them. You see, I don't follow the Tattooed Man, I worship Samael and we all know what he does to people who piss him off."

The look of confidence faded from the assassin's face.

"So. I will ask again. Where. Is. Aries?" Silence. Lovelace's expression hardened.

"I'm getting a bit hungry, how about you?" A puzzled expression on the assassin's face was contorted with agony as Lovelace bit into his calf. Blood sprayed outward and poured down the assassin's leg. A scream ripped out of the assassin's lungs. Lovelace spat the chunk of meat out. "Your leg tastes bad. How about we try something else?"

"Lokden rot you!" screamed the assassin.

"Tell me where Aries is."

"They will kill me if I tell you!"

"What I will do to you will be worse than death." Lovelace spoke calmly and clearly. The assassin looked up at him, blood poured down his body from his wounded leg and over his face. His eyes went wide, his face drained of all remaining colour, and he appeared to look past Lovelace. At the edge of his hearing Lovelace thought he could hear a voice whisper "*Your… sacrifice… is… accepted.*"

"He's in an old storehouse in Downtown, Perevel, 1280 Ferrius Street, the basement, near the storage yards! Arends owns the whole fucking building!"

"Thank you," said Lovelace. A shadow passed in front of Lovelace's eyes and the assassin fell away from the building screaming. He tumbled over and over before smashing into the street below. Lovelace looked down at his hands. He held a knife and the frayed remains of the rope. Taking a deep breath, he spat out the remaining blood in his mouth and left the roof.

He pulled out his comm and called the Captain. "Benham Arends has Aries. He's holding him in the basement of 1280 Ferrius Street, Downtown in Perevel. Near the storage yards and spaceport. Don't ask me how I found out. Get the tac team and med team to meet me there, and hope we are not too bloody late."

*   *   *

Arends had tired of the questioning and had stepped away from him. Aries realised he had lost a lot of blood, and if he was going to do something he was going to have to do it soon. His head swayed and his eyes stung from cold sweat. Arends was talking quietly to one of his men.

"I don't think I shall learn much more from him. When I'm done with him take care to dispose of his body. I do not want the Agency learning of his fate. Make sure that, as usual, there is nothing left identifiable."

"Yes, sir."

Arends turned to look at Aries while continuing to talk to his man. "No, I think we need to work our way up the tree. I think I should have a word with that ice-hearted bitch, Clarice."

Aries' head snapped up and he looked at Arends. Arends cocked an eyebrow.

"Got your attention, did I? Yes, you heard right. I think it is time I asked a few hard questions of *Mrs* Hamilton-Jones. After all, she is married to a good and dear friend of mine. I am sure she will be delighted to help."

Aries struggled to make the words come out. "Leave… her… alone."

"No, I don't think so, Mr Aries. In fact I think I shall do exactly the opposite."

That is it, thought Aries, *that is it. No more. No more!* He began to open himself to the Wyld. There was a muffled explosion that sounded like it came from upstairs. Then all the lights went out.

Arends spoke into his comm. "What was that?" But before he could get an answer, they all heard a second bigger explosion and then the sound of automatic fire. Arends' face contorted with anger.

"Looks like his little Steeler friends are here. I need to leave." Arends pulled his pistol, turned and pointed it at Aries just as Aries' eyes glowed and the Star of the Overlord burned through the makeup. The reality shifted in the room, drawn in towards Aries. The wire around Aries' neck melted away as did his manacles, the liquid metal running down his body and dripping on the floor leaving his skin untouched. The temperature rapidly climbed and the metal door began creaking as the heat warped it.

"Not this time Arends." Spoke Aries clearly. He raised a hand, but before he could focus his mind, Arends turned and dashed out of the room. His three men followed after him. As he staggered forward, Aries reached inside himself to open a full gate to the Wyld, but as he did so he stumbled. His vision had become confused and he felt the power rapidly slip away. He made it to the doorway and wiped away a few tears of blood from his face. The blood in his eyes burned.

He could clearly hear the sounds of combat from upstairs. Suddenly, bright torches appeared in the corridor and shined in his face. He heard a voice shout, "Agent Lovelace, we've found him. We need a medic over here!" His vision became hazy and his legs gave out underneath him.

Aries collapsed forward just as the first tactical agents reached him. Lovelace swam into view.

"Lovelace…"

"Don't talk Aries. Where's that bloody medic! He's bleeding out here!"

"Arends… He was here. He went that way." Aries reached out.

A medic slid over to Aries and ripped open his kit.

"Is he going to be okay?" asked Lovelace.

"He has lost a lot of blood, taken a very nasty neck wound. Good thing we got here when we did, but we need to medevac him now."

"Do it." Lovelace looked down at Aries. John could see the desire to pursue Arends competing against the need to look after his partner.

"Go," whispered Aries.

Lovelace nodded, and shouted, "Alpha and Bravo squads, you're with me. Delta squad, continue to secure the facility. No one leaves." He stood up and dashed off.

*   *   *

Lovelace hated to leave Aries, but he also did not want the bastard Arends to get away. With a full tactical team at his back he headed off into the corridors the way Aries had indicated. The place was a maze of concrete corridors, pipes and ducting down here. Steam from heating vents filled the air.

Lovelace and his team moved forward as fast as they could while maintaining some caution. His senses were alert to the scene, drinking in everything around him. Suddenly ahead from round a corner someone opened fire. Bullets sparked off the concrete. Chips of shrapnel left trails through the steam.

Lovelace threw himself to the side with a shout of, "Hostile!" and the team took cover. "Flank him!" shouted Lovelace and three Agents moved off down a side corridor. He sighted his Headhunter and fired two booming shots in return, blasting chunks of concrete out of the wall. Lovelace's team opened up, unleashing a volley of fire at the corner behind which the hostile was hiding.

The comm squawked to life. "Lovelace, This is Bravo. We have run into another hostile covering the side tunnel. We are taking fire. Unable to proceed. "

"Hold position, keep him pinned down." The comm squawked in affirmation.

Lovelace turned to the Tactical agent next to him, Sergeant Tynes, and whispered, "Cover me." The weathered Agent nodded and put down suppressing fire on the corner. Lovelace slid his sword out of its scabbard and advanced in a crouched run up to the corner. As he spun around the corner Tynes ceased firing. The merc working for Arends looked up and saw Lovelace emerge out of the mist and raised his gun. Lovelace did not hesitate and swung the sword, decapitating the merc in a fountain of blood with a single swing. The headless body collapsed at his feet.

"Clear. Move up, Tynes, and send two men from Alpha to flank the mercs pinning down Bravo. I am going to push on ahead."

Lovelace stepped over the headless corpse and began jogging quietly up the passageway. *Arends, you are not going to get away.*

The mercs had been set there to delay the agents, that much was obvious, and Lovelace knew that every moment that ticked by gave Arends more time to escape. He picked up speed and barrelled around the next corner, smashing straight into the merc who was standing there ready to ambush him. Lovelace smashed the pommel of his sword into the merc's face and carried on, leaving him for Tynes' tac team to deal with.

He reached a staircase and headed up it. Ahead he heard the noise of engines and Lovelace picked up even more speed as he ran up the stairs, taking them three at a time.

He burst out on to a low roof. A grav plane was taking off. Its thrusters were angled down and the jet wash almost knocked Lovelace off his feet. Arends looked out at him from the window and gave him a small patronising salute. Lovelace pulled his pistol and opened fire, but the heavy calibre bullets bounced off the armoured plane. The grav plane rose into the sky, turned and began heading away.

Lovelace let bellowed a roar of frustration.

But then something unexpected happened. The grav plane veered slightly to the left, then more violently to the right. It clipped the edge of a building and began to spin. The grav plane spun faster and faster and its tail smashed through the walls of an office building and was torn off. One of the passengers was flung out of the plane's rear hatch. The body of the plane picked up momentum and crashed through the buttressed wall of a temple and out through the other side, disappearing from view.

"Samael's blade!" exclaimed Lovelace.

A crack of thunder echoed around the canyon of buildings and a fireball rose high into the sky. A second crack of thunder and Lovelace saw the windows around the crash site explode. He heard distant screaming. Smoke began to rise from several places.

Lovelace began running again. He activated his comm, "Central! Grav plane down! At my position. Scramble emergency teams now!"

7

Steel Year 2425.10.04 (S-Time). Day Four, Morning

The scene was chaotic. Emergency services from the Metropolice, Nova Response and the Agency were all on the scene. Fire crews worked to contain several fires that had broken out in nearby buildings, while civil engineers rushed to try and stabilise the damaged temple before it could collapse. The whole area was wreathed in smoke. Most of the walking wounded had already been taken to the Bastable Hospital for treatment, the dead had been arranged in their black body bags in a clearing. There were over two dozen bags. Bulldozers pushed the wreckage of gutted cars out of the way.

The body of Arends' grav plane itself was surrounded by a circle of spotlights, lasers and hovering drones. Bomb techs, forensic techs and rescue crews picked over the wreckage gently. Already there had been two secondary explosions as overheated boxes of ammunition exploded. No one wanted any more lives to be lost, so everything was being done with extreme caution.

Overhead hovered three grav planes, a Metropolice plane, a rescue plane and one from Enigma Weave News. Their searchlights erratically tracked across the ground like skittish deer.

Around the wreckage the Metropolice had formed a cordon to keep the curious back. Worshippers for the critically damaged Temple of Isoke were turned away. The crash had also damaged and closed Lower Perevel tube station and had thrown local transport in the area into chaos. Roads leading throughout the sector were jammed up solid. Nearby Perevel Spaceport had been forced to delay several shuttle launches for orbit, throwing the flight schedule into chaos. The store yards and container city that housed much of the shipping into and out of London were functioning at reduced efficiency.

Local politicians were foaming at the mouth. They were full of questions: How did a fully armed, but unlicensed, military grav plane come to be operating in South London? What caused the crash? Who was to blame?

The politicians called their contacts in law enforcement and they shook their chains of command. It did not take those calls long to reach Captain Linsbury, and he was now on the scene along with Lovelace.

Lovelace had never been a smoker, but walking through the disaster scene towards the mobile command centre with the Captain he felt a strong urge to light up. Instead he took a sip from the coffee he carried.

"So tell me again what happened, Lovelace."

"I was in command of three tactical squads. We breached the warehouse where Aries was being kept. We overcame the resistance on the upper floor quickly. Heading downstairs, we rescued Aries. I left him with one tac squad and the medical team and gave pursuit to Arends with Alpha and Bravo."

"And?" Captain Linsbury gestured towards the damage all around them.

"We encountered some resistance in the steam tunnels, and fearing Arends was going to get away I took the lead in the pursuit."

"Decapitating at least one hostile on the way."

"Bloody straight!"

"Continue."

"I made it to an open space just in time to see Arends take off in his grav plane. I opened fire, but... there was no way my shots brought it down."

"You carry a... Renegade Headhunter twenty-five millimetre revolver, correct?"

"Yes. Loaded with jacketed Depleted Uranium Rounds." Linsbury's eyebrows arched.

"DUC rounds?"

"I know, they are heavy. But I did not get a good hit, just glancing shots. The plane was undamaged and it flew off, but when it got a few hundred metres away it looked like the pilot lost control and the plane collided with an office tower and led to... this." Lovelace took another sip. His right leg was sore from where he had been grazed by a couple of rounds when storming the warehouse, and his eyes hurt from the overly bright lighting. He watched the Captain carefully.

Linsbury was assessing the scene visually. He wore a tweed suit with a raincoat that was lightly dusted with drizzle. The Captain was rubbing his hands together as if to warm them up, despite wearing black gloves. He abruptly knelt, ignoring the dirt on the road, and picked up a piece of shrapnel from the grav plane. He carefully turned it over in his hand, still saying nothing.

Lovelace nervously rocked his weight from foot to foot. Linsbury pulled out a scanner and passed it over the shrapnel, before placing it carefully into an evidence bag, which he sealed.

The lack of conversation disquieted Lovelace.

"Boss?"

Linsbury turned his head to look at Lovelace while he stood up, brushing dirt off his trouser legs.

"Mmm? Ah yes. I believe you, Senior Agent. The damage to the grav plane is clearly from an internal source. If I had to hazard a preliminary guess I would say that a likely cause was the detonation of a high explosive fragmentation grenade inside the grav plane."

"A grenade?"

"Yes. Though it is certainly too soon to come to a definite conclusion."

"So it was bloody sabotage?"

"Yes. Quite. Very bloody."

Lovelace looked at the crash site again. He took Linsbury's assessment at face value. Lovelace did not like the open questions the assessment revealed. *Why would someone detonate a grenade inside the grav plane? Who would do it?*

Changing subject, Lovelace questioned the Captain. "Captain, any word on Aries?"

Linsbury began walking through the wreckage towards the mobile command centre again. Lovelace kept pace besides him.

"Yes. He is stable. He lost a lot of blood before the medtechs got to him, but the damage is being treated. He should hopefully be up and about later today."

"Good. Good. I am bloody relieved to hear that."

"Yes, small mercies." Linsbury was looking at a woman who was sobbing uncontrollably into the unsure arms of a police officer. "A mercy not everyone will receive," said Linsbury, thoughtfully.

They reached the mobile command centre and entered. Inside it was a buzz of activity. The Senior Agent in Charge, came over to Linsbury.

"G4 Lieutenant Alexander, from SO-10, Sir." SO-10 Shield were the protection division of the Agency and also its internal affairs.

"What is the situation, Agent?"

"Thirty-three confirmed dead, another fifty-six injured of which three are critical and are unlikely to survive. There has been major structural damage to the local Temple of Isoke, Lower Perevel Station has been breached and there is rubble on the track. The fires started by the crash are mostly under control. Local traffic and shipping has been severely disrupted. We are setting up a temporary traffic control centre to take charge of the situation."

"Good, good. Agent Alexander, this is Agent Lovelace, from my Division." Lovelace and Alexander shook hands.

"So what have you learnt about the crash itself?"

"It appears as if the pilot lost control when some sort of device was detonated inside the grav plane."

"So it was sabotage?"

"Yes, it appears so. At this stage we can likely rule out Agent Lovelace having caused the crash."

Lovelace let out a quiet sigh of relief.

"Do we know who carried out the sabotage, or why?"

"Unfortunately not. The bodies onboard were suffered rather serious trauma in explosion and following impact. We brought in a metapsion to scan the wreckage, but it appears as if an Echo onboard managed to shield the craft and passengers from later inquiry. While we cannot at this time confirm this, it is my probably suspicion that the Echo might have been the saboteur."

"Or simply doing his job and shielding his employer against future chrono-scans?"

"Indeed. That is, of course a possibility."

"Still, Agent Alexander, you are correct to focus attention on the Echo until we know more."

"Thank you, sir." Alexander did not appear thankful at all. The Shield agent did not like being questioned by a captain from Investigations. Shield were often a law unto themselves within the Agency, with only Ripper allowed more autonomy.

Linsbury did not appear to notice. "Good. Well do not let us keep you from your work. Agent Lovelace shall be available when you wish to take his official statement." Alexander nodded and returned to his console.

Linsbury stepped out of the command centre and indicated Lovelace to follow. "Walk me to my car, Lovelace."

The Captain spoke quietly. "Be on your guard Lovelace. You have not heard the last of this. Arends was a powerful man with powerful friends. You may have stirred up more trouble than answers."

"Sir, it was Arends who kidnapped Aries. Not the other way around."

Linsbury locked gazes with Lovelace.

"I know that, Agent. But you also know that when politics becomes involved then the truth is the first thing to suffer."

Lovelace let out a bitter laugh.

"True. So what are you saying?"

"What I am saying is that this case is causing annoyance at very senior levels."

"You want us to back off?" Lovelace bristled. Linsbury climbed into his car.

"No, of course not."

"Then what?"

"Brace yourself for a fight, Lovelace. Things will get very unpleasant indeed before they get better." The Captain nodded goodbye, pulled the door shut and indicated to his driver to take off.

Lovelace shielded his face from the dirt and water blown up by the grav car as it took off and thought over what the Captain had said.

Things will get very unpleasant indeed before they get better. Too bloody true.

*   *   *

Aries slowly awoke. Sunlight was shining in on his face. The gentle warmth penetrated his skin. It felt good. He opened his eyes, blinked a few times in the bright light, and looked around.

He was in a private room, the window to his left looked out over the clouds. *This is better than normal for the Agency,* he thought to himself.

His mouth was dry and tasted sterile. The pain in his throat had mostly gone, replaced with a slight tingling sensation. He touched it delicately and found it was not bandaged. He swung his legs out of bed and gingerly put his weight on them and stood up.

He walked over to the window and leaned against it. The view below was spectacular, the cloud cover had broken and in places he could see all the way to ground level. His initial impression was right. He was definitely somewhere in Zen.

A quiet hiss behind him let him know that the door had opened. Turning slowly, Aries looked to see who had come in. Clarice Hamilton-Jones walked in. She was dressed in a tight figure-hugging dark suit, her long dark hair loose around her shoulders. She smiled broadly when she saw him standing.

"John!" She came over and hugged him and gave him a soft kiss on the cheek. Despite having only just awoken, John felt his body stir.

"I am glad to see you up and about. I hope you don't mind, but when I heard what happened I arranged for you to be transferred to my private clinic."

Aries smiled, coughed once before talking and replied, "Thank you. The view is amazing."

Clarice joined him by the window and looked out. She held his right hand in her left. Her touch brought back all the tumult of thoughts and feelings that had raced through him prior to the abduction. He knew where they were going was wrong, and as Arends has shown him, even their tacit involvement so far was putting both of them at serious risk. Yet, despite that he did not want to lose that thread of human contact.

Aries' brow furrowed. "Clarice... I... we..." Clarice stopped him with her right index finger on his lips.

"Not now, John. Just enjoy the sun."

He nodded and turned to face the window. She gently squeezed his right hand and felt calm.

Enjoy the moments, for they are all you have.

*   *   *

Things were up in the air. Arends' abduction of Aries and subsequent death in a grav plane crash had thrown a serious spanner in the works. Lovelace had learned that John had been swept off to some exclusive private clinic to be healed, but that meant he was incommunicado for now.

The events of the last few days had taken their toll on Lovelace. Truth be told, the whole situation with the stealthy assassin outside Aries' flat had affected him deeply. He had used the angle of invoking Samael, the Disciple, god really, of vengeance several times in the past to give an unwilling interrogation subject an extra jolt of fear that would let him unlock the knowledge they had. This time had been different. He could still hear the voice in his head whispering, *"your sacrifice is accepted."*

Then before he had time to think about it the assassin had been falling away from the building to meet a very certain fate on the road below. The problem was, Lovelace did not remember cutting the rope. He had intended to bring the assassin up, cuff him and then go and rescue Aries. But that was not what happened. Worse still, he had not minded.

He had a sinking feeling that for a moment he had become Pledged to Samael. Thought it was a lesser state than being an Avatar of the

Disciple it was still not what Lovelace had planned.

The Overlord, supreme living — though missing — deity of the Steel Alliance and his conclave of lesser gods known as His Disciples, demanded worship from humanity. It was not a question of faith. The gods existed and their power was real and extraordinary. They had saved Humanity from its self destruction. In return they demanded worship, piety and loyalty. A part of this was that they could fill a worshipper with their spirit and make them an Avatar of the Disciple. A living embodiment of the god or goddess. The worshipper became aligned with the Disciple when they became the living embodiment of the concept that the Disciple defined. Albion was progress, usually scientific; Kali, was death and transitional states; Isoke was the vitality and sexuality of creation and conception, and Samael… Samael was the embodiment of bloody vengeance, free from restraint.

Being Pledged was a lesser state, but still one that only the most devout of worshippers ever achieved. It meant the Disciple had taken a *personal interest* in the worshipper. It was a double-edged sword, they could positively intervene in your affairs, but they were also more demanding. Becoming Pledged required the devotee to willingly do so, and unfortunately when Lovelace thought about it, his calls to Samael in aid of his interrogation technique were exactly that.

Bloody hells, Lovelace. You have really done it this time.

That was what Lovelace had been taught. He had been raised to follow the Tattooed Man, Disciple of Judgement. Unflinching, brutally even-handed and devoid of compassion, the Tattooed Man had become the patron Disciple of the Kapaethjan Pures. His way was a clear road where the pure prospered and the corrupt were cut down. It offered moral certainty and purpose. Samael, Disciple of Vengeance was anything but. He lived in the shadows, in the realm between right and wrong.

Now, somewhere along the way, and quite without meaning to, Lovelace had brought Samael into his life. He had not meant to, and although his following was small, worship of Samael was tolerated. He had not been declared heretical like Baal, God of War and Lokden, God of Entropy. But there was a big difference between being tolerated and being accepted. Lovelace realised that he was in spiritual crisis and he needed help.

He reached a decision. He could not talk to Aries about it. He could sense his partner's disdain for all things related to the Disciples, but it was not an attitude Lovelace could understand. It was foolish and dangerous. But for now it was one he would have to accept. But that really only left one source of advice.

I need to go to temple.

Temple was an essential part of life, especially for a Pure. Though genetically related to normal Humans, Pures were a subspecies balanced on a knife edge. They carried within them the seed of their own destruction, an uncontrollable Rage that would render them beast. Temple, for the Pures, was a release. They purged, they bled, they screamed, but all in safety. Lovelace had to admit, he had not been as diligent about temple in recent months as maybe he should have been.

He pulled up on his motorbike outside the small Pure temple he attended in Soho. The entrance was plain. A simple door on a nondescript building, but, with the exception of the massive Temple of Judgement in Tyburn, that was how the Pures preferred it. Their worship of the Tattooed Man and other Disciples was best done in secret. Always a minority, except on Kapaethja, Pures had a culture clouded in secrecy for the rest of society. Too many times in the past they had been the victims of pogroms and other forms of ethnic cleansing, and so they had evolved a discrete culture.

Lovelace walked up to the door. A Kapaethjan Pure stood guard discretely. Though he was masked, Lovelace recognised him, as Warrior Caste of the Guardian Kindred, the Mikaeljans. With two fingers, Lovelace touched the centre point of his forehead, his lips and displayed his open hands, palm upwards, in ritual greeting. The Guardian returned the gesture.

A mind clear of thought, words free of deceit, actions without stain. Am I any of those things any more? wondered Lovelace. The Pure opened the door for him and Lovelace stepped through.

Once inside, the building was entirely different. Beautiful mosaics of geometric patterns covered the walls and vaulted ceilings. The lighting was low, better suited to the sensitive eyes of Pures. Lovelace placed all of his weaponry, aside from his Ascension Sword, into a locker, removed his boots and cleaned his feet and hands in a small fountain. He then used a ceremonial cloth to wipe down his blade, symbolically removing the stain of violence.

The sound of ritual singing in Kapaethjan echoed around the temple. It was the sound of many voices unified in a minor key. Beneath it, almost entirely obscured, was the occasional grunt, scream and clash of metal on metal.

Lovelace continued into the temple. Kapaethjan runes detailing elements of the Pure Code which all Pures, even the Ballaén such as Diarmuid, had to adhere to -- were they not to be considered Fallen -- were written into the patterns on the floor.

Lovelace walked over the red rune symbolising Honour on the floor. It was followed by Loyalty, Truth, Control, Sacrifice, Obedience, Devotion and finally Duty. As he crossed each, Lovelace remembered the lessons of each, as had been intended.

Finally he walked through the open doors of Judgement. The doors were symbolic, unable to close to represent that judgement could not be denied. A Pure's life was built around symbology, around ritual and around the Code. Lovelace entered the Hall of the Disciples.

The Hall was a domed octagon. A niche in each wall contained a statue of one of the Disciples. Albion, Isoke, Kali, The Fool, Thoth, Cai Shen, Samael and, grandest of all, the Tattooed Man. The room's centre held a giant statue of the Overlord, majestic with his braided beard and hair. He wore golden battle armour, simple yet potent. A second statue of the Tattooed Man, only slightly smaller than the Overlord himself, stood at his side holding the Overlord's shield. Each statue, though only slightly bigger than man-sized, was intricate in its detail. Each was painted in strong rich colours and golds and silvers.

A map of the Steel Alliance at its height, some thousand years ago, covered the floor. The strong smell of incense filled the air. The lighting was from burning torches, their flickering flames giving a sense of animation to the Overlord and the Disciples. Around the edge of the Hall were what Lovelace estimated to be at least thirty Pures all knelt in prayer.

Lovelace anointed himself with scented oils from the font by the entrance. His skin tingled where the oil flowed. He looked around, searching for someone in particular. Eventually he spotted her. A tall Pure woman was moving through the kneeling Pures whispering into their ears. She sprinkled blood red petals over each as she moved away.

Lovelace approached her. She looked up at him and held his gaze while he considered her. Her tattoos on her bared arms and throat marked her as formerly Warrior Caste, but now Priest Caste. She was from the Seeker Kindred, entrusted with the gathering of knowledge. A well worn Ascension Sword was slung over her back. It had obviously had as much use as Lovelace's own. She wore body armour which was inscribed with detailed images of the passage of life to death, and a Hand of Kali pendant hung round her neck. The upper part of her face was obscured by a veil, revealing only her mouth and chin. Her naturally grey lips were painted a deep red. He knew her as Tereza Tharn Helja, Priestess of Kali. Taking a deep breath, Lovelace spoke in Kapaethjan,

"May we talk?"

Tereza nodded and indicated him to follow her to a side room.

Once alone, they sat cross legged on low cushions beside a long, low table. As formality required, they each placed their scabbarded swords on the table in front of them, their yellow peace bindings visible. Tereza leaned forward and lit a small brazier. She pulled out a powder from a pouch in her armour and sprinkled it in the flames. A green-tinted smoke billowed up and scented the room with jasmine. Tereza lifted up her veil. She fixed Lovelace with her gaze.

He realised that she was actually fairly young, but her eyes appeared to be dark pools of sorrow. He knew from temple gossip that some terrible tragedy had befallen her and her family, but no one would speak of the details. What Lovelace knew, but which very few others knew, was that she was also security vetted by the Agency. Thus Lovelace could speak to her, knowing that he was not breaking the secrecy of neither the Agency nor the Pure Code.

"Priestess, I am troubled. I have found myself invoking Samael and I believe I may have even been moved by His hand briefly to carry out an act of vengeance."

Tereza nodded, and then spoke. Her voice was soulful and warm. "Tell me what happened, Vesh." Vesh was Lovelace's temple name. All Ascended adult Kapaethjan Pures had four names. Their temple name was the name given to them as a child, then, on Ascension to adulthood, they received their adult, or 'Given' name. Lovelace's given name was Tarus. The name of their Caste and Kindred completed the name. Thus Lovelace's full name was Vesh Tarus Arken Karazhja. Only those most intimate with him such as his lovers, family or priests would call him Vesh.

Lovelace related the events of the last few days. Even the act of repeating the tale lifted his spirits slightly. He finished by saying, "I wish to know what the future holds for me." Once he had finished, there was a long silence while Tereza considered her reply.

"Invoking Samael without proper gravity is extremely dangerous and foolish. You already know this. I believe you have now bound part of yourself to Samael. You have created a holy bond between yourself and the Bearer of the Bloody Knife, and that bond is not easily carried." She frowned, and dipped her fingertips into a small chalice of blood red oil.

"Remove your clothing and stand before me." Lovelace complied, bearing his muscular, tattooed and scarred body.

Tereza stood up and walked around the table to stand in front of him. She reached out and traced the tattoos on Lovelace's face. He closed his eyes as her fingertips followed the markings. Her fingers ran down his face and neck and on to his chest. Tereza stepped in close to him and whispered in his ear.

"Your body has seen incredible violence, your life tattoos tell of a life of struggle. The aspect of your birth was troubled and you could so easily have turned away from the true path. Yet through this all you have sought truth and justice without fail, even when that path would bring nothing but pain, and put you in conflict with your own kind."

Her fingers traced a set of ritual scars on his abdomen which, like those on his face, indicated he had fought many Mortal Duels against other Pures. Her touch was cool, almost cold, yet seductive.

She stepped around him and traced the markings on his back.

"I see more pain in your future and a cross roads. You will have to decide on your loyalties. There will be no easy choices, no clear and bright future. The path you have taken contains darkness so deep that I cannot see through it. You may be required to sacrifice everything for an uncertain future."

Lovelace breathed deeply. The incense filled his lungs and bloodstream. He could feel cool lines from her touch encircling his body.

"I know these are not the answers you seek. But you are not one who retreats from the truth. You orbit another and your role, for now, is to protect him. Within him is the seed of a new future. I cannot protect you from that future, but I can help prepare you. Look at me, Vesh."

Lovelace opened his eyes. Tereza's face was centimetres from his own. Her black eyes were pools of utter darkness. He felt himself being drawn into them. Tereza's voice became dark and heavy,

"I have walked between life and death, Vesh. I have knelt at the right hand of Kali. I have lost all I care for to save that which I loved. I will prepare you for your test. You will not be found wanting."

Lovelace surrendered himself to the darkness.

*   *   *

Lovelace was walking out of the temple and pulling on his shades when his comm rang. His mind felt fresh and clearer than it had in some time. He answered it when he saw it was his old partner Nathan Sark.

"'Ello Nathan, what can I do for you?"

"It is what I can do for *you*, Lovelace. I have something for you. A contact of mine just got in touch. Turns out someone has been trying to use the credit of one Mr Charles Hamilton-Jones."

Lovelace's ears pricked up.

"Go on."

"Yes, I thought that might get your attention."

"Don't bloody mess me about, Sark. Give me the details."

"Your Mr Hamilton-Jones has been spending, or at least trying to, spend his credit down in the Souk." The Souk was a neighbourhood in-between the Rock, Bricktown, Vauxhall and the Smokestack in South London.

"When was this?" Nathan's grin became broader.

"Up until about an hour ago. I also got you something else."

"What?"

"This." Nathan sent over a set of still images from street surveillance cameras. They showed several pictures of an unshaven, scruffy looking man wearing an extremely smart suit jacket that was at least a couple of sizes too big for him. "That toe-rag turned up in the vicinity of the attempted credit uses. My instinct tells me that is your man."

"You are too young to have instincts, Sark. Still… you could be right. Yes, yes. Don't get bloody cocky. One good call and you think you're a detective."

Sark's grin grew so wide it threatened to make the top of his head fall off. Lovelace knew what he needed to do.

"Seriously though, Nathan. Good work and thanks for the tip off. I need to call my partner and go and take care of this."

He cut the connection and called Aries. He was relieved when the call was answered.

"John, I have a possible lead on Charles. Are you good to go?" Aries replied in the positive, "Good. Meet me on Victory Bridge. We are going into the Souk." Lovelace walked across the road and climbed onto his bike. He attached his sword and scabbard to the bike. *It will be good to make some forward progress on this damn case. I don't like constantly being on the bloody back foot.*

He roared the bike to life and shot off down the street weaving through the traffic.

*   *   *

Aries was excited. He had left the company of Clarice in a hurry, without mentioning why. He did not want to get her hopes up, and frankly a big part of him did not want to remind her about her husband. It was childish, he knew, but right now he could not help himself.

The grav taxi dropped him off on the Soho/Victory side of the bridge and he ran over to where Lovelace was waiting. He paused briefly as he approached. Lovelace looked somehow bigger. Not physically, just in sheer presence. Aries could not think of any other way to describe it other than it was if he was more real than the environment around him.

Lovelace climbed off the bike as they approached and they grabbed each other's right forearms in greeting.

"Tarus. Good to see you. I have not had a chance to thank you for saving my life." Aries switched to Kapaethjan, "You do your Kindred proud."

Lovelace's eyebrows lifted.

"You're welcome, John. I didn't know you spoke Kapaethjan?"

"Just a little, I learned as a child. Shall we go find this mysterious credit thief?" Lovelace nodded and indicated to Aries to climb on the bike behind him, which John did.

They roared across the bridge, skirting the Rock's edge, heading South into the Souk.

The Souk was so named as it had become populated with a large number of immigrants from the human Arish, Uranni, Zan and Couresaad cultures. They lent the whole area an exotic quality, and, even though over the last century or so the ethnic makeup had grown more like the rest of London, the Souk still retained its culture.

The streets were narrow, with the only large roads being elevated, running several stories above their heads. Staircases, hidden courtyards, alleys and tunnels dominated. Bridges crossed from one block to another, and many of the intervening alleys had tarpaulin roofs. As its name would suggest, the Souk was one giant market. The traders sold everything from fresh meat brought in from the Wytchwoods beyond the Wall, to exotic fabrics brought from across the Steel Alliance. You could find almost anything in the Souk, and if you were so inclined, behind closed doors you could acquire the less-than-legal. Both the London Metropolice and the Agency had dedicated teams investigating and shutting down the people traffickers as fast as they could, but new ones always appeared. Slavery was illegal in the Accord, but that did not stop the trade. Immigrants from the more repressive worlds of the Imperial Commonwealth or

Federate Combine sought new lives in London and other worlds in the Accord, but many were snared by callous so-called 'snakeheads' who would force them into lives of indentured prostitution, slavery or sometimes even worse.

Despite that seedy underbelly — or perhaps because of it — the Souk was a vibrant place.

Lovelace parked up and they headed into the maze's heart. Under cover of the tarpaulins existed a fabulous bazaar. Aries breathed in the strong scent of spices from a thousand worlds. Traders attempted to sell him fruit and vegetables, many of which he had never seen before. They competed for his attention with cloth salesmen offering glittering, shimmering and even glowing fabrics.

Aries waved them away and they pushed onward, heading down staircases packed with bustling people. Lovelace occasionally checked the map on his comm. Finally he indicated that they were near the last reported site of the credit thief.

Both Agents slowed in their approach and put a few paces between each other. They entered a busy square with a café on one side and the entrance to a covered market on the other. Lovelace walked over to the café and took a seat. As a Pure he was the most distinctive, so he settled for a spot sat on the square, making no attempt to hide. He ordered a spiced coffee.

Aries moved round the outside of the square and hung back in the shadow of a carved arch by the market. Both had switched their comms to sub-vocal communication mode.

"Do you see anything, Lovelace?"

"Nah. He should be round here, the reports Sark gave me showed him moving in this direction. This is bloody good coffee, John. You should get some. It is strong, what do you think they put in it?"

"Cinnamon, cardamom and other spices you will not have heard of. You see him yet?"

"Still no. Offworld spices?"

"Definitely. Can you concentrate on the task at hand?"

"I can do two things at once, John. What spices?"

"There is a cinnamon variant from Byzantium that contains a mild hallucinogenic. It is slightly poisonous. They are probably using that."

Aries saw Lovelace spit out his mouthful of coffee. He grinned.

"Just pulling your leg."

Lovelace frowned, then cleaned up the coffee. The patron at the next table was staring at him.

"Coffee was too hot. I burnt my tongue." Lovelace stuck out his black tongue to make the point and the patron hurriedly turned his attention back to his own table. Lovelace looked up.

"John, target moving your way. He is coming out of the market, you can't miss him. He apparently thinks jackets come in a one-size-fits-bloody-all."

Aries glanced around the corner. Sure enough, there was the man from the surveillance images Lovelace had showed him working his way through the market. His sleeves were rolled up. As he passed a fruit stall, the man slipped an orange into his pocket.

"Looks like he is a high-end criminal," said Aries, sarcastically. "Run his face, find out who he is."

Lovelace glanced down at his comm. "Looks like he is river scum called… Varn. Chas Varn. Minor record, theft, robbery, small time cons. Nothing heavy. Not exactly a premier league scumbag."

Varn stopped and pointed at something in one of the market stalls. As he did so he snaked his other hand out and lifted what looked like a pendant from the stall. Varn shook his head and moved on toward the exit. Aries waited until the man had just passed him, before stepping out.

"Chas Varn. We would like a word."

Varn's head spun around, his eyes wide. Their gazes met and Aries knew then that he was going to run. With surprising speed, Varn turned and sprinted off across the square.

"Varn is running," shouted Aries unnecessarily.

"I can bloody see that!" replied Lovelace.

Varn leapt over a table and dashed down an alleyway. Aries stormed after him, Lovelace headed off down a parallel alley to try and flank him. Aries had to hand it to Varn, the little thief was damn fast.

Varn dived down a side alley and when Aries followed him, Varn was already running up a fire escape.

"Do not make me shoot you, Varn!" shouted Aries. Varn briefly looked down at him, his eyes wide. He replied, "Piss off, copper!" and continued climbing.

"Lovelace, he is making for the roof. See if you can get ahead of him."

"On it!"

John started up the fire escape. Two floors above him, Varn stopped, backed up against the wall then charged towards the edge of the fire escape and vaulted the guard rail. He flew across the gap and smashed through a window on a neighbouring building.

This little man is not going to make this easy!

Aries reached the same level and also leapt the gap, rolling as he hit the floor. An Arish family, watching WeaveNet, stared at him as he rolled to his feet.

"Agency! Which way did he go?"

Four hands all pointed down the hallway. Aries nodded and set off once more. He ran out into a stairwell. Varn was three floors below, rapidly descending.

"He is heading for street level at my location, Lovelace!"

"Isoke's balls! First you go up, then down. On my bloody way!"

Aries leapt over the railing and dropped two floors. He rolled with the impact as he had been taught and came up running. Varn, now only a single landing below swore and redoubled his speed.

They reached the ground floor passage with Aries hard on Varn's tail. Just as Varn reached the street exit, Lovelace stuck his leg out across the entrance, tripping Varn and sending him flying. Varn crashed to the ground heavily and pulled himself over to find Lovelace's Headhunter revolver in his face, and his boot on his chest. Varn raised his hands in surrender.

"Don't bloody move!" said Lovelace. Aries reached the end of the corridor and slowed to a halt. He was breathing heavily, and his neck itched like crazy.

Lovelace glanced over at him, "Careful there, John."

In between heavy breaths, Aries panted, "Why. Do. They. Always. Run?"

Lovelace considered the question. "Because there are predators and prey, and prey always run. It is what they do. Varn here. He's prey, aren't you, you little toe-rag?"

Chas Varn looked uncomprehending. Lovelace reached down, grabbed him by the collar, and with one arm pulled him up, lifting him clear off the ground.

"Yes. Definitely prey."

Varn suddenly rediscovered his ability to speak.

"What you want, coppers? I ain't done nothing wrong. You can't hold me like this. It's illegalised harassment."

"*'Illegalised'* harassment, eh?" said Lovelace contemplatively. "Varn, you can't just go making up new words."

Aries spoke up, and flashed his badge. "Varn. We are Agency, not police, and you can start by telling us where you got that suit jacket and the credit you have been splashing around."

The colour drained from Varn's face.

"Ah, Samael's pointed cock!" Aries' eyebrows lifted at the expletive.

"Answer the question." Lovelace gave Varn a little shake for encouragement. In his grip, Chas Varn looked like a child.

"I found it, alright? I ain't hurt nobody, mate."

"You found it? Where?"

"Here. In the Souk."

Aries glanced at Lovelace, who arched a black eyebrow, then turned his attention back to Varn.

"Give me the jacket, and everything that was in the pockets, and I mean everything. Then take us to where you found it."

"It is mine!" pleaded Varn.

"The jacket is evidence in a missing persons inquiry, Varn. That means if you hold on to it you are part of whatever happened to the owner. Like murder. You know what they do to scavs like you who murder gentlemen? Your only chance to save your scrawny neck is to help us. It is your choice." Aries held up a pair of cuffs to emphasise his point. He could see Varn's mind working furiously, trying to find an angle.

"Will there be a reward?"

"Possibly."

"Good enough for me. Put me down, please?" He looked up at Lovelace who lowered him to the ground while very obviously keeping one hand on the butt of his pistol. Varn took the hint and shrugged out of the jacket like a snake shrugging off its skin. He handed the jacket to Lovelace, and then shoved his hands in his pockets and fumbled around.

"Stop playing with yourself, toe-rag."

"I ain't! I'm going to give you what I found. Well, what I have left…"

Lovelace growled and Varn shrank back.

"No no! There was a roll of cash and I spent some. That was it, I promise!" Varn pulled his hands out of his pockets. He was grasping several items. Aries pulled on some clean forensic gloves and took the contents gently from him. It was a wallet, a roll of hundred Sterling notes, a set of keys, a mini-comm and a serrated knife in a sheath. Aries put them all into an evidence bag to sort through later, but both he and Lovelace shared a glance about the knife. That was definitely not the kind of thing a gentleman carried, but then to a lesser extent neither was a roll of cash. The elite never used cash at all. If they spent money themselves it was just credit via their comms, such as the mini-comm.

"Is that it?"

"Yes! I swear it, may Samael strike me down if I lie."

John could not help noticing the uncomfortable look on Lovelace's face when Varn said that, but he did not comment. *Something to mention later, if I get a chance.*

"Good. Then take us to where you found the jacket."

Varn looked worried.

"Look, guv. Do I have to? I'll tell you where it was, but I don't want to go."

"Yes, you do Varn. Now get moving before I decide to file a Termination Order on you." He opened his greatcoat, revealing his shoulder holster and Varn's eyes went wide. *Of course, he has no idea I can't just get a Termination Order without evidence.* Termination Orders were issued when the target, a known and proven serious criminal, such as a terrorist, was unlikely to ever be brought to trial, or if such a trial would be too damaging. In those cases a Termination Order would be issued, and any Agent would be required to terminate the subject on sight. *Drastic measures,* thought Aries.

Varn's head nodded rapidly, and he headed off slowly down the alleyways. Lovelace and Aries followed closely behind him.

They walked for about a quarter of an hour and in that time the weather worsened. The light drizzle from earlier became heavy rain. Aries pulled up the collar of his greatcoat, Lovelace pulled up a hood on his jacket. Varn, now clad in just a soaking t-shirt and trousers plodded on resignedly. He brought them to a small square where rubbish was piled high around the edges and the ground was a mess of mud and filth. The whole place reeked.

Varn stopped in the middle of the square and pointed at one pile of rubbish. It was a big pile of empty boxes, bins and bags. Aries indicated to Lovelace to stay with Varn and cautiously approached the pile. The rain was sheeting down now, and he could feel it dripping down inside his great coat and matting his hair.

Despite the rain, there was a strong odour of rotting meat hanging like a miasma around the rubbish. With a sinking feeling, Aries began to very carefully peel back layers of the waste.

It did not take long before he revealed a hand jutting out from the pile. Aries turned to Lovelace and said, "looks like we have a body." In response Lovelace clamped his hand down on Varn's shoulder.

Searching for the face, Aries followed the arm up the body. He felt himself conflicted, *Is this going to be Charles? Am I going to have to tell Clarice I found his body in a back alley in the Souk, tossed out like so much mouldy fruit?* and then to his shame he also thought *Would that be so bad?* Mentally chiding himself for even having that thought, he dug at the rubbish with renewed vigour, while water poured off him.

Suddenly the last piece came free, revealing the face of a man. A face contorted in agony. With relief, John realised it was not Charles Hamilton-Jones.

He pulled back the rest of the rubbish to reveal the body of a man, whose body shape suggested he was probably in his thirties, though so prematurely aged as to seem many times older. Heavy lines of worry and weariness were etched into his face. Aries touched his own face, largely free of such marks. *And yet this man was young enough to be my son.* The thought brought a sudden stab of pain and Aries stumbled.

"John, are you ok?" came the voice of Lovelace. Aries picked himself up and replied.

"I am ok. Just lost my footing."

The man had obviously been dead a few days. His rancid shirt had been pulled open and his chest was a congealed mass of blood. Flies swarmed out from the body, and maggots were busily at work in the wounds. The stench was unbearable, and Aries staggered back and struggled to control his nausea.

His eyes bright with anger, he turned and walked over to Varn, "Tell me what happened."

"I was in the area, when I heard a fight and a scream, so I snuck over. I saw some old geezer standing over that scav's body." He indicated at the corpse. "He was putting the jacket on him. He was scary mate, the man, he had the scav's blood all over his face and hands. I shouted, and he took one look at me. At first I thought he was going to attack me too, then his face... he was terrified, and he ran off down there." Varn indicated the northern exit. "Once he had gone, I took the jacket and then got the hells out of here."

Aries bent in close to Varn, so he could clearly see the Echo tattoo. "Do not lie to me, Varn."

Varn's eyes were wide and his voice was pleading, "I swear I ain't bloody lying to you, that bloody 'gentleman' you are searching for...

he killed that scav. I swear it on my mother's life!" Aries searched his face, but could find no sign of duplicity. The story was just too strange for a little gutter rat like Varn to make up. Aries nodded.

"When was this?"

"Erm…" Varn counted it out on his fingers, "five nights ago." *The night Charles disappeared.* Aries could see Lovelace made the same connection.

He pulled out his comm and called for a forensics team. He looked back at the corpse.

Charles Hamilton-Jones. In the Overlord's name, what did you do, and where did you go?

He looked to the North. He had been heading towards the Rock, and perhaps, beyond that, the Victory Bridge that crossed the Thames Canyon.

8

Steel Year 2425.10.04 (S-Time). Day Four, Afternoon

Back in the SO-50 offices in Central, Aries and Lovelace considered the personal effects they had recovered from Chas Varn that were laid out before them on the table. The pinstripe jacket; a wallet; a roll of hundred Sterling notes; a set of keys; a mini-comm, and of course the sheathed serrated knife.

Lovelace summarised what they knew. "The jacket was made by Xi Volker, tailor to the rich and famous, for Charles Hamilton-Jones. The wallet has his identification. There is a little under ten thousand Sterlings in the roll. The difference is probably what Varn was able to spend. The keys have Charles' prints all over them, and are for a mechanical door lock, but for what door we don't know. The mini-comm is his, and the knife came back positive for human blood, at least one person's but possibly more."

Aries picked up the keys and the money roll and weighed them thoughtfully in his hand.

"A gentleman like Charles Hamilton-Jones has no legitimate need for either cash or mechanical keys. Doors are either opened for him by others, or respond to his bio-signature. Charles was up to something that he did not want any official record of, that much is clear. But cash is not used in polite society. No, he was up to something in Downtown or Ground Zero, and given the site of his grav car we recovered and now his jacket, my bet would be somewhere in South London."

"That doesn't exactly narrow it down, John."

"No, but it is a start. We can work our contacts to further narrow it down. These," Aries indicated the evidence, "tell a story. They tell of a powerful rich man who wanted something that was beyond his every day world. He needed to be able to operate surreptitiously, and he did not feel he could trust it to his usual agents. He had to do it personally and that meant he had to get his own hands dirty." Aries paused for a moment before continuing, "Actually, given what his butler, Six, told me I think the door that these keys unlock is somewhere in Lower Bricktown. After all, it is a likely explanation for why he travelled there dressed as a drudge."

Lovelace nodded. "Sounds plausible, at least until we dig up more. That doesn't tell us why he went mental and murdered a bloody scav in the Souk, left his jacket and then ran away. Assuming you believe Varn, which I do."

"You are right, it does not. It does tell us that something very terrible happened. There is no evidence so far to suggest he was a homicidal psychopath intent on murder, and even if he was, a brawl with a scav in some back alley in the Souk seems unlikely."

"If you say so. Though, I have seen some horrific shit in my time on the beat. If I learned one thing it was that people are capable of anything."

Aries nodded.

"You are of course right. We cannot make that conclusion about his personality yet, though it does give us a line of enquiry. We… I… need to find out more about Charles."

"John?"

"Yes?"

"About your abduction by Arends. I wanted to talk to you about that, but since then things have been bloody crazy and we've not had a chance to talk. What happened? Why didn't you fry the bastard with your Echo powers?"

Aries sat down, and rubbed his neck.

"I… I promised myself I would not use my powers unless there were no other options."

"The lug nut had a wire around your throat and was trying to pull your head off. That not reason enough?"

"No. Besides, I wanted to find out what he knew."

"And?"

"He thinks *we* were sent to kill him, Rato, Massey and Hamilton-Jones."

"What? That's mental. Who did he think bloody sent us?"

Aries looked around the room.

"Not here, Tarus. Ask me later."

Lovelace looked at him askance, but let it slide. He changed the subject, "Before all… that… we were going to find out more about Brentan Roe."

"Balls! I forgot all about him. I left messages for him before Arends' men got me. Yes, you are right, Lovelace. We need to find out more about him and why Mr Dexter left him off the list. Ok, how about I find out more about Charles and you hunt down Brentan Roe?"

"Actually I'd like to take a crack at Jean Thervessons. From what you said he is hiding out at street level and that is more my domain, and I reckon Roe can keep another day. One thing, John. Don't keep me in the dark about what you find?"

Aries nodded solemnly.

*   *   *

Lovelace walked cautiously down the staircase and into the small square between several tenement buildings deep in the Strip. The quality of 'life' here was poor, the urban smog, heat haze and high humidity levels created a toxic fog that kept visibility down to less than fifty meters and life expectancies similarly short. Lovelace wore a white, faceless mask with a small breather built in. As he also wore a hooded black cloak, the contrast was extreme.

He had released the fastener on his holster as trouble had a habit of appearing at the least expected moment round here, and he rested his hand on the butt of his Renegade Headhunter. He peered at the tenement street numbers. *512 and 514. Thervessons' hideout should be the next building.*

It did not take him long to reach the entrance way to the block. A metal gate hung open, the corridor beyond was cast into darkness. Lovelace pulled out his Headhunter, held it loosely and entered.

If my contact was right, Thervessons should be on the third floor.

He advanced cautiously toward the stairwell at the end of the corridor – his nerves on edge as if expecting imminent attack. It was only as he began to climb the stairs that he realised something.

This place is completely silent. Isoke's balls! Where is everyone?

The only sounds he could hear were his own footsteps and breathing. No screaming, no crying, no WeaveNet boxes turned up too high. Nothing. Just a curious stillness in the air. There was a charged feel to the environment. Lovelace could feel the static electricity raising the hairs on his arms and as he moved through the foggy corridor his passage left faint luminescent trails. *I hope this isn't an Echo thing.*

Despite himself, he muttered a quiet litany to himself. "Tattooed Man, Lord of Pures, make me your instrument of Judgement. Defend me from the corrupt, remove my hesitation and let me have the will to do what must be done." Since his visit to temple, he had felt the need to be more focused in his faith.

He cautiously stepped around the staircase's last bend onto the third floor.

Second on the right.

As he approached the apartment, he noticed the corridor's walls corridor were covered in symbols, sigils and runes and in front of the apartment door was a thick line of what appeared to be salt. The Star of the Overlord was painted on the door in what Lovelace guessed to be blood. His training as a Truthsayer was shouting at him that these signs were all markings of ritual magic.

Lovelace pulled back the hammer on his heavy revolver. His gut told him this was not going to end well. He listened carefully but could still hear nothing from inside the apartment. Carefully he stood to one side of the door and reached for the handle.

He turned the handle and the door swung silently inward. *Unlocked? What the hell?* No light emerged from the hallway inside. The darkness was impenetrable to him, even with his natural low-light adjusted eyes (a trait all Pures had). He brought up a dim torch and shone it into the corridor.

Hundreds of what appeared to be rats were nailed to the walls, their blood congealed in each other's fur, ruptured internal organs hanging down. The floor of the corridor was sticky with brownish blood.

"Samael's bla—"

Lovelace did not get the chance to finish swearing as a cloaked figure barrelled out of the darkness at an incredible speed and slammed into him at full force. He felt a sharp pain in his side and, despite his superior size, he was pushed over.

The cloaked figure landed on top of him and raised a vicious curved knife dripping black blood. In the dim light Lovelace saw his assailant's face, it was Jean Thervessons, but his face was twisted with animal fury. Thervessons screamed into Lovelace's face, "Die! Die! Die! You fucking thing!" Spittle sprayed over Lovelace.

Thervessons raised the knife to strike and Lovelace lashed out and smashed the butt of his pistol into Thervessons' face. He felt teeth and nose break as Thervessons was hurled backward in a spray of blood by the force. Moving quickly, Lovelace rolled to his feet, the pain at his side telling him that Thervessons had got in at least one hit. He brought his gun around and saw Thervessons run along the corridor and leap through the closed window, smashing straight through the glass.

Lovelace, without thinking, ran after him and leaped through the gaping window frame. He rolled as he hit the ground three floors below with nothing but a grunt and looked around.

Thervessons was already running down a side alley.

"THERVESSONS! STOP! AGENCY!" shouted Lovelace as he gave pursuit. Despite himself, he was impressed, Thervessons was seriously fast, and Lovelace, despite his augmented build struggled to keep up. He roared and chased after him.

As he chased him up the sloped alley, Thervessons pulled bins and other rubbish down behind him, but Lovelace jumped over the obstacles. He pursued him down the alleyway and onto a nearby street. Thervessons was already running down the far side of the street. Lovelace raised his pistol and took aim, but before he could fire he staggered, suddenly dizzy. He pulled open his cloak and looked down. Thick black blood was running down his hip and thigh. Like all Pures, his blood did not clot easily, they suffered from haemophilia.

There was nothing he could do at that moment, only trust that his medical implants would do their best to staunch the wound. He lowered the gun and set off after Thervessons once more. His quarry was now running up a metal staircase to an elevated set of streets, some four stories above. Struggling to breathe in the mask, Lovelace ripped it off and, muttering a series of expletives, gave chase.

Reaching the top of the staircase, he found the elevated street largely empty. Thervessons stood in the centre in a pool of street light, rapidly turning around, his knife held in front of him. His face was twisted into a rictus of fear. His voice was unclear as he spluttered through his broken teeth, spraying blood, spittle and teeth fragments as he spoke.

"You can't have me! I won't let you! I am invulnerable! I am protected! You must obey me!"

At first Lovelace thought Thervessons was shouting at him, but then realised that the shouts were directed more generally, as if Thervessons were blind, or at least disorientated.

Grimacing from the pain, Lovelace advanced cautiously. His left leg was dragging.

Abruptly, Thervessons' head snapped around and he stared directly at Lovelace. His gaze was intense and his face went strangely expressionless. When he spoke it was in a quiet voice.

"Please don't let them take me!" he pleaded.

"Who? Who wants to take you?" asked Lovelace quizzically as he approached. *Five metres. Stay there. Four metres. Just stay there.*

An engine roared deafeningly behind Thervessons. He spun around to face the noise. Out of the darkness a speeding black truck appeared. Its lights flicked on and the glare drove needles into Lovelace's eyes. He cried in pain and held up a hand up to try and block out the light.

In the centre of the road, Thervessons sank to his knees, making no attempt to get out of the way. His hands were raised in supplication, and it appeared to Lovelace that he was crying. Thervessons' lips moved, but Lovelace could not hear him over the approaching truck's roar.

The truck smashed into Jean Thervessons, snapping him under the wheels where his body ruptured, being pulled apart and spraying blood over the street. The truck's brakes screamed and the truck came juddering to a halt, smoke billowing from the tortured brakes.

It happened so suddenly that Lovelace stood there for a moment, unable to move. Finally as the driver climbed out of the cab Lovelace staggered over. The truck driver's expression was panicked.

"Overlord save me! I didn't see him! I swear I didn't see him! He came out of nowhere! You have to believe me!" He turned his terrified gaze on Lovelace. Lovelace pulled his badge and cuffs and arrested the driver. "Stay where you are. Agency." Reaching inside his cloak he pulled out his comm and hit the alert button, calling for emergency response backup. He cuffed the driver to the truck and, feeling his legs failing him, slowly sat down on the kerb.

Thervessons' blood flowed thick and dark across the street and into a nearby storm drain. Holding a hand to his side, Lovelace let out a long sigh.

"Jean Thervessons, what the bloody hells did you do?" He toppled slowly over to one side, the voice of the truck driver pleading his innocence droning in his ears.

*   *   *

Aries brought his grav car in to land in the space indicated by the agent waving lit batons standing in the light rain below.

The scene below him was best described as organised chaos, with several ambulances parked up around the truck. He spotted at least one forensics truck, and several white-suited forensics agents painstakingly examining the road, the truck and the surrounding area. The flashing lights of the police vehicles fought for dominance with the blindingly bright floodlights set up by the Agency. Through it all drifted the ever-present miasma of the Strip.

Once safely down, Aries shut down the car and climbed out. A white-suited forensics Agent stood there with an umbrella. *Small mercies,* thought Aries.

"Agent Aries? I'm Agent White, from AMRED. Captain Linsbury sent me." AMRED was the medical, research and forensics division of the Agency.

"Good to meet you, White. What is the situation?"

"One fatality, a Jean Thervessons. Agent Lovelace sustained a stomach wound, and is currently over there," Agent White pointed at one of the ambulances, "refusing to go to hospital until you got here. The truck driver," White pointed at a police truck, "has been arrested and is awaiting transport to Central. He appears to be in shock. My team are currently examining the truck involved in the fatality before transporting it back to Central. I have a second team standing by at Mr Thervessons' residence. We've sealed off the entire block, but I thought you would want to see it first. From first glances, Thervessons' flat is rather unique."

"Thank you Agent White. It seems like you have all the bases covered. I would like to have a word with Agent Lovelace, and then we can head over to Thervessons' residence. Give me a moment with Agent Lovelace, and then we can go?"

Agent White nodded, handed Aries the umbrella and returned to his forensics team. Aries approached Lovelace. Lovelace sat in the door of the ambulance. He was bare-chested, with several medpatches covering parts of his heavily tattooed and scarred torso. The medpatches were already stained black from his blood. A paramedic was tending to several smaller wounds on Lovelace's arms. Lovelace's eyes were narrowed to slits as he gave Aries a weak smile.

"Hey John."

"Hey Tarus. What happened?"

"Thervessons did not want to come quietly."

Aries looked back at the long bloody streaks on the pavement under the truck.

"So I can see. Are you alright?"

"Yeah, got scratched by Thervessons' knife. Nothing serious." He picked up a long curved silver knife in a sealed evidence bag that sat next to him. Aries handled it carefully. "Careful with that, the blade has a serrated monofilament edge, an anti-coagulant coating and a neurotoxin applicator." Lovelace absently scratched at the antidote patch on his neck. The medtech swatted his hand away.

"Leave it, Agent Lovelace, unless you want some form of permanent paralysis." Chastened, Lovelace dropped his hand back to his lap.

It was a nasty weapon, designed to cause devastating wounds that would make the target bleed out while in maximum agony. *Lovelace was lucky, true, but he is one tough bastard to have kept going. That was an assassin's weapon.* Aries looked at him with a new level of respect and politely ignored the blood packs that Lovelace was hooked up to. *That wound would have been fatal to almost anyone else. It would have been fatal to me.*

"Tell me what happened. From the beginning."

"I went to Thervessons' flat. An old snitch of mine helped me track it down. Before I could go in, Thervessons came barrelling out like a crazed demon on stims and attacked me. In the scuffle he winged me, I broke his nose, and he dived out a cocking window. I followed him here, and he freaked out in the middle of the road, before getting flattened by the truck. You should have seen him. He was completely out of it. Tried to pray to the truck as it approached, if you can believe that."

"Is that it?"

"Yeah, aside from how creepy Thervessons' flat is, and that was just the entrance. I asked forensics to hold back because you have to see it first. From what I could see it's a bloody rat abattoir. He was into some dangerous shit."

Aries nodded. "Let's go and have a look then, if you are up to it?"

"Just try and bloody stop me." Lovelace grinned weakly.

*   *   *

Aries, Lovelace and White stood outside the door to Thervessons' flat. *Lovelace was right, this place is creepy.*

The walls, ceiling and floor of the corridor were covered with painted runes, sigils and magical characters. In the forensic lights' harsh glare they lost much of their power, but even then they disturbed Aries in a way he could not quite put his finger on. They implied a strong belief in the supernatural, something Aries was reluctant to do. In a world where ordinary humans could be gifted with abilities to reshape reality he did not see the need for anything to be classified as supernatural. To do so merely cloaked the activities in false mystery. *Better to shine the light of inquiry on such things, regardless of what the Disciples tell us. They have their own reasons for the artificial separation between Echo and Divine.*

There was a disturbed line of salt outside the door itself, and the signs of Thervessons' and Lovelace's struggle were clear to see. A black, dried pool of Lovelace's blood was smeared across the worn floor.

White pushed open the door and indicated Aries to look inside. A cloying abyssal stench of the abattoir flowed out. Aries took a moment to settle his stomach.

Before going in, Aries turned to White. "Get your agents to knock on the neighbours, see what they saw or heard?" White nodded and gave the order over the comm.

The walls were covered with hundreds of rats, each nailed to the concrete while still alive. Their blood had run thick over each other's fur, creating a matted, reeking mass. The blood had reached the floor and flowed down grooves which had been chiselled into the concrete. The grooves formed whirls, spirals and labyrinthine patterns. The corridor beyond was pitch black.

White spoke, "This is as far as we've been, so be on your guard."

Aries nodded, and pulled his pistol and torch and stepped over the threshold. Lovelace followed, with White taking the rear.

Taking care not to step on the grooves, Aries advanced cautiously down the corridor. The sense of weight in here was almost overwhelming. Aries could feel it bringing on an edge of claustrophobia, but he willed it away. The corridor had a door on either side and a dark room at the end. Aries indicated for Lovelace to check the door on the left, White the right. He pushed on.

A pair of long, straight scratches on the floor caught his attention. He crouched down to examine them. They were not deep, but were about shoulder width apart. "Lovelace, looks like Thervessons dragged someone here." Now he looked in more detail there appeared to be more than one set of scratches. "Actually, make that more than one set." Aries had a sinking feeling.

Lovelace nodded, and opened the door in the left wall. "Bedroom," he grumbled, "or what's left of one. This bloke lived like a bloody animal."

"Just rubble in here, Agent Aries," said White, on examination of his room, "it looks like the ceiling collapsed in."

A thought occurred to Aries, "White, could you find out who owns this block?"

"On it," came the quiet reply. Aries advanced on. He noted another set of drag marks.

"Got another person dragged in by the looks of it." He looked ahead. The light from his torch lit the miasma in the air, though it was still unable to illuminate the room at the end. Flies buzzed around his head. Aries swatted at them absently. He was aware of the stench of rotting meat.

"Thervessons owns this block, and all the surrounding ones." Aries nodded. It was as he feared.

The darkness ahead was thick and organic, appearing to be more of a wall than a simple absence of light. Aries steeled himself and pushed through. A light from above him drew his eye up.

He entered a hall, hollowed out of much of the apartment block. It was hacked out from at least another four stories of the block. The corridors and rooms in the flats hung open to the air. A single shaft of light fell from above, illuminating a circle in the centre. Aries' gaze slowly lowered to the ground.

In the circle, piled carelessly atop each other was a mass of corpses. They hung upside down, right way up, entwined amongst other bodies, all without apparent rhyme or reason. The bodies of men, women and children discarded like so much detritus. Many were torn open, their viscera spread over the bodies surrounding and it was clear that they had been thrown down from above.

The stench was appalling this close. Maggots writhed over the bodies and flies swarmed in the air above. Surrounding the circle was a stinking gutter full of congealed and caked blood, and viscera. Aries could hear the sound of the hardened forensics agent, White, vomiting behind him and the sound of Lovelace emitting a low, animal growl.

Aries closed his eyes and forced his mind to focus. When he slowly opened them again, he looked around the room. With one small exception, every square metre of the walls and floors was covered with the same occult sigils, runes and signs. Some in blood, others in various paints.

The exception was a two metre circle of salt within which lay a filthy stained mattress, a chamberpot full to overflowing, and the wrappings of various food packs and drinks. Aries looked and understood that the patterns in the room, all the signs, every bloody thing, emanated from this this small area.

It was Lovelace that spoke first.

"I recognise this. It is a circle of protection. Everything else here feeds into that circle. Every. Single. Thing. This is an abomination."

White, who had recovered, spoke, "Even the bodies... even the bodies feed into it?"

"Yes. This is heresy. Proscribed by Divine Edict. He should have died slowly and bloody painfully for what he bloody did. We have to get the priests of Kali in here as soon as bloody possible. This unholy place needs to be destroyed. Destroyed utterly."

Aries arched an eyebrow and thought to himself, *Lovelace is too enthralled by the power of the Cults of the Disciples. There must be a better explanation then simply declaring this all 'heresy'. But if that is true, then why do I recognise this?* He looked around the room. Everything felt familiar yet also utterly alien. *I feel the power here. Lovelace is right. All that death, it was to feed... something.* He looked at his hands. They were shaking uncontrollably. Aries did not know why. Try as he might, the memories associated with this scene were locked to him.

Suddenly he heard something. It was a faint sound of crying.

"Aries, did you hear me? I said—" Aries held up his hand for silence.

"Shut up!"

The sound was faint. It was coming from the pile of bodies. Aries leapt into motion and ran over to the bodies and began pulling them off.

"What the bloody hells are you doing?"

"There is someone alive in here!"

In moments he was joined by Lovelace and White. They pulled off body after body searching for the source of the sound. They ignored the terrible stench, the gore and worse, possessed by the need to find the source.

Finally Aries pulled aside the body of a woman to reveal a small child, a girl. She had been protected by the way the woman had fallen, creating a small pocket of space in the horror. Aries reached down to her. Her eyes were wide.

"It is ok. We will not hurt you. My name is John and I am here to help you. Come with me, take my hand." With painful slowness the girl reached out and took Aries hand. He gently lifted her out and held her in his arms. Lovelace and White assisted Aries in climbing down from the pile. Aries could hear White calling for medical teams on his comm.

He walked her carefully out into the hallway outside the apartment. Medtechs swarmed him and gently took the girl off his hands. She stared at them in terror. "It is alright, they are here to help you. I promise."

Seemingly accepting his promise, she passed out. The medtechs carefully carried her out. Aries brushed off the medtechs examining him and shouted after them, "Make sure she gets the best care and round the clock security. If anything happens to her there will be hells to pay." He turned to the medtechs around him, his eyes alight with anger. "Leave me alone. I'm fine. Go and help her!" They hurried off.

He turned and saw Lovelace walk out of the apartment. Both of them looked like they had emerged from the grave themselves. Lovelace's gaze was glazed, his breathing shallow. When he spoke his voice was low and gravelly.

"You know he killed all those people — all those people — to try and save himself?"

"I know," replied Aries, "but what from?"

"I don't know. But it didn't work. One thing I do know is that those damnable so-called 'Honourable Brothers' must be bloody stopped. Those bastards did something. Something terrible and now they are paying the price for it and are doing anything in their power to try and save themselves. But we... I... will kill them if I have to. Or something even worse will happen. I don't care what we have to do."

Aries simply nodded. He agreed with Lovelace, but he also knew something else. He needed to know what they had done and even more he needed to know why all this felt so familiar.

9

Steel Year 2391.09.11 (S-Time)

Aurelian stood in front of the funeral pyre and watched as the black smoke billowed into the blue sky. The stains of dried tears lined his face. He was alone on the top of the tower in the palace, having ordered away all the Guard and his family. His whole body shook, but there were no more tears, just a terrible hole inside.

It was an accident. That is what he had been told. It had been a terrible accident. *It was an accident.* They kept telling him that, as if it would make it better. There was no explanation for why the shuttle had failed its re-entry approach and slammed into the upper atmosphere and exploded as it did. *I should have been on the shuttle. Not Ariadne.* He has been in the hospital sitting with his infant son. They had been required to attend the investiture of a new Governor, and normally he would have gone in Ariadne's stead, but a unexpected bout of ill health had forced him to stay.

It should have been me. Every victim of tragic loss thought this, but Aurelian knew that in his case it was true. It really should have been him.

Ariadne's blue eyes and bright smile had brought such joy into his life. He still could remember the smell of her dark hair, it was a scent of strange worlds and beautiful unknown vistas. She had been in his life less than two years, before being cruelly taken from him. This same year he lost his older brother Darius when his aerospace fighter had collided with another during a routine patrol.

It was whispered by courtiers that *such things did not happen.* There must be a curse on the family.

Aurelian barked out a short angry laugh. A curse? Metropolis was one of the most advanced planets in the Steel Alliance. A glittering city world, home of tens of billions, the hub of an interstellar trade network unimaginable in size. The Dukes of the House of Favian-DeVir were second only to the Emperor on forbidden Elysium in power. Their fief contained some of the most industrious and prosperous worlds ever known.

Yet despite this, people would talk of 'curses'.

Perhaps we are cursed. It would be one answer for why we have suffered so much ill fortune of late.

The loss of Darius and now of his daughter-in-law had affected his father badly. The Duke had retreated even further into his intense gloom. He was barely seen by his family or his people now, preferring to delegate much of the administration to others. Others who were not as competent. Others who sought political advantage. Others who plotted. When he looked at Aurelian, he seemed to stare straight through him. *I remind him too much of Darius.*

Despite his unhappiness, Aurelian did not believe the talk of curses. Something else was afoot. The instincts that had been sharpened by the training he received told him something was building. A change was coming. He could feel it. But what that change was, he did not yet know. There was growing tension everywhere. His father may not see what is happening, but Aurelian was determined not to be so blind. He had his baby son to care for and given the recent attack. In that, he prayed he would not fail.

The White Masks, the secret police of House Favian-DeVir had rounded up the colleagues and confidants of the attackers. They had questioned families and co-workers, but they did not break, there was just the mutterings of heresy and curses. Despite his order to go gently – which his father had subsequently countermanded – the actions of the secret police had merely stoked the fires of resentment. *Why had they attacked me? Why had they sought my son?*

Change is coming. Emptied of all emotion, Aurelian turned and left the tower.

*   *   *

Steel Year 2425.10.05 (S-Time). Day Five, Morning

It had taken a long shower before Aries had started to feel clean and for the shaking to stop. The results of Thervessons' hubris had shaken him badly.

He wrapped a towel around himself and walked into his bedroom and picked up his comm. Aries looked down at the list and notes of Honourable Brotherhood members that Mr Dexter had given him, along with an additional two names he had added:

Charles Hamilton-Jones - Missing, presumed dead?

Nigel Massey de Sargon - Dead (Suicide)

Cassian Dexter - Secretary of the Honourable Brotherhood

Arkell Isadore

Kenton Serrano - James Villiers-Cavanaugh's Chief of Staff

Jean Thervessons - Dead (Road traffic accident)

Benham Arends - Dead (Grav plane sabotage)

Julius Rato - Dead (Killed by Charles and possibly Nigel Massey de Sargon?)

Brentan Roe - ?

James Villiers-Cavanaugh - ?

What was clear was that of the ten names on the list, five were missing or dead, all within the last week. Whatever was happening to the Honourable Brothers was happening fast, and if he and Lovelace wanted to find out what was really going on, they were quickly running out of potential interviewees. *The problem is that I cannot just walk up to the London Agency Commander or his Chief of Staff and interrogate them. At least not yet.* That meant they were limited to Cassian Dexter, Arkell Isadore and the mysterious, and thus far absent, Brentan Roe. The problem was that, so far, when they had approached a target directly things had gone down hill quickly. Dexter had been shielded by the Commander. Arends had become psychotic and paranoid, and Thervessons... well, Aries did not want to think any more about Thervessons.

Aries realised that he needed more inside information on each of them if they were going to catch them off guard. He needed to meet with Clarice. After that he might go and have a quiet talk with Denver. After all, if he was a potential rival to the Commander in the upcoming election, he might be more forthcoming on Villiers-Cavanaugh's dirty secrets.

The blood on Charles' knife had come back from forensics as well. Trace amounts of flesh identified that it had been used to kill the scav, Julius Rato and one third person, as yet unidentified. *Charles, what have you done? What kind of homicidal psychopath are you?*

Lovelace had suggested that he put Cassian Dexter under surveillance as that had previously revealed both Benham Arends and Jean Thervessons to them and Aries had quickly agreed. They had both needed some time apart to decompress after the horrors of Thervessons' abattoir. *No news on the little girl, yet. Last I heard she was in a state of complete catatonic shock. I hope she recovers, though what kind of life she has to look forward to...* He had done what he could. He hoped it would be enough, but the life facing her as an orphan was not going to be easy.

John had called Clarice and she had agreed to meet him in a couple of hours at 'Liebers & Kesserich', an exclusive Uptown grand café in the shadow of the Stealth Tower in the City, the central-most district of London. He needed somewhere neutral and just-public-enough so that he could concentrate on the subject at hand. He did not trust himself alone with Clarice as she seemed capable of piercing his bubble of calm at will. It had not been since the death of Ariadne that he had felt anything serious for another woman, and that was part of the problem. This case was unravelling the new life he had carefully constructed faster than he could ever have imagined.

He mentally recited one of the calming mantras he had been taught, stood and prepared himself for the day.

Given he was heading uptown, Aries pulled on an armoured body suit over which he wore a white shirt with a wide-cut black cravat, a dark red silk waistcoat, black trousers with a navy blue stripe running down the outside of the legs to his square-toed boots, and a black frock coat. He wore a concealed shoulder holster with an Aralyte MIN-101 autopistol. He donned his customary greatcoat, a pair of black leather gloves and a derby hat.

When he considered himself in the mirror he flashed back to his earlier disguise as a docker and he smiled at how utterly different he looked. Aries headed for the door and quickly checked the new, improved external security system installed yesterday. The hallway outside was clear, and a security guard stood guard at the lift. The building management company had been scandalised over the whole abduction affair and had substantially beefed up their security.

Aries took a deep breath and headed out to meet with Clarice.

*   *   *

'Liebers & Kesserich' occupied the entire floor of an elegant corporate tower in the City, literally in the shadow of the mighty Stealth Citadel. Unlike the rest of London, the City had no Downtown or Ground Zero. The Stealth Tower filled those areas with its massive base, geothermal systems and vast vaults. The street levels started in Uptown, and so L&K, as it was known, occupied the 'ground' floor. A ground floor over three hundred metres above ground level.

The white ceiling was domed, held up by black onyx pillars expensively shipped in from offworld. A white and black geometric pattern decorated the floor. Fine details decorated with gold leaf covered every surface. All the tables had white marble tops, the chairs were clean black leather, and the room was lit by icy glowing lights on black chandeliers. The interior walls were black wood panels inlaid with gold. Sound suppressors kept the noise muted and soft, despite the hard edges. A set of large gold and white clocks told the time on Earth, Mars, Venus, and one in the centre displayed the decimal Steel Alliance Standard Time marked out with the 25 hour Standard days used by interstellar travellers.

The staff were immaculately attired and well schooled in their service. They moved efficiently and unobtrusively through the seated guests, always at your hand when you wished to order, yet out of hearing range when private matters were discussed.

The whole place oozed classy elegance. It was also a hotbed of corporate espionage. Aries knew this and had suggested it for exactly that reason. Clarice and he would not seem out-of-place. In fact it was unofficially deemed neutral territory, and to date in the two hundred and fifty-seven years L&K had occupied this site not a single criminal act had ever been recorded.

That did not mean that there had not *been* one, just that, for whatever reason, no one had *reported* it.

Aries walked in from the rain through the gold-and-glass revolving doors and handed his greatcoat and hat to the waiting concierge.

"John Aries. I am expecting a guest."

"Of course, Mr Aries. We prepared a table for you in our booth section as requested. Your guest has not yet arrived. If you will kindly follow me?"

Aries followed the concierge across the room. A quick glance showed Aries at least seven faces he recognised, though none from his current case. He slid smoothly into the booth facing the door so he could see when Clarice arrived, and ordered tea for them. This meeting was going to be on his terms.

He did not have to wait long. Clarice came through the revolving door. She was wearing an elegant pale white long coat and hat. Underneath she wore a white shirt, suede waistcoat and, in the latest fashion, a brushed twill convertible riding skirt. A misnomer really, especially now as she wore it fastened as loose trousers. Black pointed boots completed the look. Her long black hair was loosely bound up. He dress was simple and it enhanced her beauty. She was led over to the booth.

As she approached, Aries tore his eyes from her, and looked around to see who was noting her approach. At least three of the other tables had noticed her. As she passed one table, the gentleman sat there, who, by his attire, Aries guessed to be from the human Kanchurian culture, stood and gave her a deep bow. Clarice returned his bow with one noticeably shallower, spoke a few quiet words with him and moved on. The Kanchurian man's eyes never left until she reached his table. The other two people who were watching her were an academic-looking woman and a stern looking man with steel grey hair and a severe black suit. Aries recognised him as the man who had been with Commissioner Tanaka at the meeting with Clarice at the Fox Hunt

Club. He did not look happy, though by the deep etched lines in his face, Aries guessed he did not exactly smile much.

Switching his attention back to Clarice, John stood and they embraced. As they sat, Clarice leaned forward and whispered, "This is rather cloak-and-dagger, John. Is everything alright?" She looked deeply into his eyes. "It isn't alright, is it John? Has something terrible happened?"

Aries let out a long sigh, then activated a white noise secrecy generator. He had not realised he had held his breath.

"I have information about Charles, and I am afraid it is not good."

"What have you found? Tell me, John. Have you found... him?"

"Not yet, but I think we are getting close. I... I do not really know how to say this discretely, so I am going to just have to say it. I believe Charles was on the run. Something he did, or was involved in with the Honourable Brotherhood caused him to be in deadly fear for his life. During his flight – for an unknown reason – he..." Aries paused, *How do you tell her 'Your husband murdered a scav, and I have no idea why'.*

"What is it, John? Did Charles do something wrong?" Clarice reached out and took his hand. Aries noticed her hand was soft and warm. "Tell me what he did. You can tell me anything."

"Charles... Charles... We believe Charles to possibly have been involved two murders. The first, we know for sure, he committed during his flight and we have credible evidence of the second. I am sorry Clarice, I wish I did not have to tell you this. The Honourable Brotherhood are a bad lot."

Clarice sat back, withdrew her hand from John's. He felt the absence of her warmth. She appeared to consider this information. Then, she nodded.

"I believe you. I knew those so-called Honourable Brothers were anything but. A rich clique of elite... men. Charles was neither a strong man, nor a leader. Despite his position and background, he always felt the sting of a lack of greater success. He wanted what he could not have." The way she said that last sentence, Aries realised there was a trace of sadness and regret there.

When Clarice looked up, he could see her eyes glinted with moisture. He leaned across the table and took her hand in his.

"Are you alright, Clarice?"

"Yes." She sniffed and gave him a small smile. "Sorry. Old memories. The past really." The way she smiled lit Aries up. "Thank you for telling me the truth, John." She pulled out a handkerchief and dabbed away the moisture. A waiter arrived with their tea and cakes.

Once the waiter had gone, Clarice looked at Aries, her eyes steely calm. "John, promise me you will find out whatever they were up to and stop them?"

"I promise." Clarice nodded, satisfied. "Telling me about Charles was not the only reason for meeting me, was it?"

"No." She studied his face.

"You want my help?"

"You are very perceptive, Clarice. I want to find out everything you know about the Honourable Brothers on this list." He handed her his list. Her eyes immediately went to the bottom of the list.

"James Villiers-Cavanaugh? The London Agency Commander, and your ultimate boss?" Aries nodded. "John, if you tangle with him you will be playing a very dangerous game. Villiers-Cavanaugh is a very, very dangerous man. A dangerous man who does not react well to not getting what he wants." The look on her face told Aries that she spoke from personal experience.

"I believe him to be involved." Clarice chewed on her bottom lip in an uncharacteristic act.

"Look, everything I just asked you to do, about stopping them. Forget it. Just step away from the case. Let it go."

"I cannot, Clarice."

"Why?"

"It is my duty. But it is more than that. This damned case is tied up with my own past. Besides, after what I saw yesterday… they have to be stopped. These are people who will stop at nothing to get what they want. No matter who gets killed. No matter the consequences."

Clarice gripped his hand hard. "They will kill you, John. If you cross them any further, they will kill you."

"They will try. They will not be the first. But even if they do, I have to do this. I will not go down easily."

"You are sure?"

Aries nodded. Clarice took a deep breath.

"In that case, tomorrow evening is the Governor's Ball. It is the last big event before Governor Sagacious steps down. Everyone of importance will be there. That includes all your so-called Honourable Brothers. Come with me, as my guest. Until then, I will get you everything I can find out about those bastards."

"Guest? But will that not cause a scandal? After all your husband is still missing."

Clarice looked him straight in the eyes and gave him a wicked smile. "Screw the scandal. Let the Overlord care what they say. This is war, and you need my help."

10

Steel Year 2425.10.05 (S-Time). Day Five, Afternoon

Aries flew over to Imperial. The sector bordered Soho to the East, but that was where the commonalities ended. Imperial was all grand frontages on houses and towers. Ground Zero and Downtown in Imperial were among the most orderly in London, populated by a mix of the servants, valets, and butlers for the grand houses' residents in Uptown (Imperial had no Zen) and the storekeepers that served those same houses. It had a uniformity of grandness that Aries found bland. Every house shared an elegant similarity, the same portico entrances, the same graceful windows and cultured lines of perspective. The streets in Imperial were clean and well maintained by a mix of automated drones and cleaning crews who worked with a forced level of 'chipper-ness' that was cloying.

Imperial was a sector where everything was *just so*. It was stifling.

By choice John would not be here, but Clarice had insisted. If he was to attend the Governor's Ball with her, he had to look the part and without even looking at his wardrobe Clarice announced with certainty that nothing he owned was suitable. If he was to even get in, let alone mix with the powerful, then he needed a change of image.

He knew that was true, but still found himself stubbornly wanting to refuse. The truth was, this Ball was bringing him too damned close to his past life. The problem was he had to go. It was the best opportunity so far to penetrate the wall of elitism and murder that surrounded the case. It was an opportunity for him to seize the initiative. After all, the surviving members of the Honourable Brotherhood would not expect to see him there.

Still, a sense of unease gnawed at him from the inside.

John forced it out of his mind and brought his attention back to the present. He checked his location and saw he was almost at his destination. He brought the grav car in to land on the illuminated pad with a slight bump and jumped out. He walked into the offices of Xi Volker.

Xi Volker was London's premier designer, her clothing ranges setting the trend on a hundred worlds, able to compete with the finest fashion houses on Elysia, Victoria, Metropolis and Vortek. She attended the annual Steel Alliance Fashion Month on Insanity, an event that was legendary for inducing sensory-overload.

Aries was surprised to note her offices in London were very

understated and simple. Once you entered the building itself, the uniform grandeur of Imperial was replaced by a very minimalist modern chic. Clean lines, bare walls, indirect lighting. Nothing detracted from the clothing. Her eye for interior design was accomplished and understated.

From a side door a beautiful, tall, pale-skinned blond woman walked in. Her attire gave Aries pause. She wore an ethereal clinging white dress that split at the front to bare her breasts. There was a delicate snake-like pattern embroidered into the dress in gold thread, and she wore a gold and jade snake talisman that hung between those same bare breasts. Gold and jade bracelets and anklets completed the look. She was barefoot and stood there completely calm, as if unaware that her bosom was on display. There was no hint of sexuality to the pose.

Aries found himself staring. *If that is next season's look, things are going to get very interesting in London.* His mind immediately started pondering Clarice in that dress.

The blond smiled, "Mr Aries? If you would like to follow me, Xi will see you now."

Aries nodded and followed her sashaying form down the hallway. On the way he passed two other women, a blond and a brunette, who were both similarly attired. The one man he passed was essentially bare-chested, so at least there was some kind of parity.

His guide led him into a room where all the walls were mirrored. Awaiting him was a stunning oriental black woman. She wore a high collared black dress that, aside from being figure hugging, revealed nothing. There was a pattern of spirals seemingly engraved into the fabric and each spiral was slightly luminescent. The dress reached the floor and obscured even her feet. The look was completed by black long gloves. Her hair was shaved, designed to reveal the delicate snake tattoo that started on her head and wound its way around her head and neck, disappearing into her dress. Two stunning green-almond eyes stared out from her delicate features, a beautiful dark chocolate colour.

Despite — no because of — her demure dress and the contrast with the revealing dresses of her associates, Xi Volker was stunning. Stunning, classy and full of mystery. Aries realised that everything he had seen so far in this building was designed to focus all attention in on her.

Aries felt a little warm. She was powerful.

Xi Volker smiled at him, her smile flawless.

"Hello Mr Aries. Clarice told me you would be visiting." She stepped forward and began to examine him with an experienced eye. Her right hand trailed over the muscles on his torso. She stepped back and nodded.

"Yes, I think we can do something with you. Take off your clothes and we will begin."

"I'm sorry?"

"You heard me, Mr Aries. Take off all your clothes and we will begin. You do not construct art on poor foundations, and believe me you have nothing I have not seen before."

The comment about poor foundations stung a little. He had thought himself well attired. He was acutely aware that three of Xi's female assistants and two of the male were standing in the room. They were all looking at him. Evaluating him. He was not afraid of nudity, nor was he ashamed of his body, but he was more than a little uncomfortable at being sized up like a piece of meat.

"Come now, Mr Aries. Clarice did not tell me you were shy. If it would make you more comfortable, Darrienne here could *relieve* your tension? She is an Acolyte of Isoke and is very good at that." The stunning blond who had greeted him at the door approached. Aries coughed and raised a hand for her to stop.

"Um. No. That will not be necessary." He began to undress, handing each piece of clothing to one of the assistants who appeared then disappeared rapidly, Aries' clothes vanishing off out of sight. He hoped they were not just throwing them away.

Once naked, the assistants moved in and began taking very detailed and personal measurements. They had him strike a variety of poses, and all the while Xi Volker looked on, carefully evaluating everything.

She circled him. "Tell me Mr Aries, your accent. Where is it from?"

"What? Oh. Here and there."

She smiled. "Indeed." She then shook her head, "Your posture is wrong. Vendahl, I can quite clearly see his lower back is misaligned."

Aries felt a strong pair of hands grasp his torso, and a male voice quietly whispered, "Relax," in his ear, followed by a sharp twist and an audible crack that echoed around the room.

"It should be corrected for now, Mistress Xi, though Mr Aries you should avoid slouching over to the right, there is a slight right-ward lean in your spine which you should watch out for."

Aries looked up, puzzled. Xi raised an eyebrow, "As I said, one does not build art on poor foundations, and your posture was poor." She examined him more closely.

"You are a trained sword fighter and martial artist in addition to your use of a… gun." She spoke the word 'gun' with distaste. "Nonetheless, your physique is in excellent condition for a man of your age."

Aries snapped his gaze round to lock eyes with her. His body tensed up.

"No need to worry, Mr Aries, your secrets remain secrets. Though if you do wish to keep your past to yourself, you should work more on your poise. The way you hold yourself reveals much about your past. For example, you have had cosmetic surgery on your features, though the quality of your original features did not require it. That tells me you wished to alter your appearance beyond mere cosmetic change." John's eyes narrowed.

"It is very, very good, but you cannot hide such a thing from me. Also, your accent: though you attempt a London one, I hear a trace of accents from Insanity and… either Metropolis or Hammer. Standard is not your first language, you use Jensian inflection on your hard consonants and you are uncomfortable with contractions in Standard. You might wish to correct that."

Aries began to wonder if this was really a dressing session at all or merely a disguised interrogation. Xi looked at him and laughed.

"My dear Mr Aries, it is my job to know these things. I am a tailor, and a true tailor considers every aspect of their client's life to create clothing that enhances that life. It is not telepathy, it is merely a pursuit of perfection in my career. That is the reason that all the powerful come to me. You wish to ask me a question, yes?"

"You made the suits for both Charles Hamilton-Jones and… uh…" – he felt a hand measure a rather delicate part of his anatomy – "and… uh… Nigel Massey de Sargon?"

Xi smiled and nodded. "Of course, you know this to be true. I also design all the clothing Clarice Hamilton-Jones wears, or does not. I design the appearance of many of the rich and powerful, and above all the discerning."

"Right. Do you know Brentan Roe?"

"Yes. Mr Roe is one of my clients, though I fear something may have happened to him."

"Oh?"

"Yes, he has missed his last two scheduled appointments. In fact, a pair of rather muscular gentlemen came to visit me. This would have been four days ago. They told me that Mr Roe would no longer be requiring my services."

"Could you describe them?"

"Of course I can. I can tell you all about them. Both were mercenaries, 201cm tall and 206cm tall, both were fitted by amateurs and were carrying concealed sidearms. They were ex-Astro Marine Corps, I believe one had originally trained as a pilot, though they were now working as mercenaries. One had extensive reconstruction of his left leg and torso, the other had received several upgrades to his central nervous system. Their accents were blurred from living in several locations, though most recently they'd been operating in the Imperial Commonwealth. One had recently received a shoulder injury, and of course the other was an Echo. They certainly did not work for Mr Roe. This, plus the missed appointments, led me to fear the worst."

I wonder if that was Silus and Mathers from Arends' crew. Certainly sounds like them. That means Roe is probably dead. I will need to find out for certain though.

"Thank you, Xi."

"You are welcome Mr Aries. I think we are almost done for now." They dressed him in a simple white robe, which he was pleased to note was not bare-chested. "If you follow Darrienne while I get to work, I will have a new line of clothes made for you shortly." As John turned to leave, Xi added, "I can see what Clarice sees in you."

He followed Darrienne to the waiting room.

*   *   *

Lovelace returned to his flat. A day of following Cassian Dexter had revealed absolutely nothing, and he was fed up. Surveillance had confirmed that the little bastard had stayed in his apartment in Uptown all day and after a full twelve hours of it, he had handed over to a junior agent from SO-50.

So here he was, back home. Unlike Aries' flat in Uptown, Lovelace still lived in Downtown Soho. He lived in a modest apartment block in the Compton neighbourhood within Soho. He parked his bike on the street and jogged up the steps to the entrance. Unlocking it, he made his way down the corridor. The first door he passed was that of Mrs Connelly, the building manager. Lovelace knocked on her door. A muffled voice from within spoke as the locks were undone, "Oh Mr Lovelace, it is you."

The door swung open revealing a kindly, motherly figure. Lovelace handed her a carton of milk from his bag of shopping. "Thank you Mr Lovelace, that was very kind of you to pick me up some milk. How did you know?"

"You always run out when your grandkids are visiting, and they visit every Thoth's day."

Mrs Connelly smiled. "Well that was most observant of you. Thank you. That reminds me. Earlier today another Pure lady came past and asked after you. I told her you weren't in. Her name was... let me see... I think it was Therese?"

"Tereza?"

"Ah yes, that was it. Anyway I said I would tell you she had been by."

"Thank you, Mrs Connelly."

Lovelace let her return to her grandchildren and continued down the hall. *I wonder what brought Tereza down here?* He was not surprised that she knew where he lived, that was easily discoverable from the temple records. *Hmm... something to think about. After I've had a beer.*

Having reached his flat, Lovelace fished out the keys. Unlike Uptown residents such as Aries, or that Rato-guy, his door still needed keys. He looked down at the keys and a thought came to mind. *It is very strange that Charles had a set of keys. I can't think of any reason a man like him would have a set of keys to some flat or building somewhere that doesn't have a dubious motive. Power, sex, money, or compulsion. It usually comes down to one of those things. Perhaps he was shagging someone on the side? Doubtful. Power? He has lots of that, but that has never stopped men like him wanting more, so that is a possibility. Money? Maybe, but I doubt it. He had all the money he needed, though he was carrying that roll of bills. I wonder if he had some deep, dark fetish? Something he had to hide away. Something that would destroy everything he had if it was revealed? The knife was not for bloody cooking, that is for sure. Was he some kind of thrill killer? It was certainly a possibility. Extreme power and a love for your fellow man do not often go together. I know he attended Cement. Perhaps that was not enough for him.*

Lovelace weighed the keys thoughtfully, then unlocked his door and stepped into his apartment. He flicked on the light. His flat was small but it had been his home for the last ten years and he was loathe to move, even though the Agency paid him a lot more than the Metropolice ever did. His living room had a WeaveNet box in the corner, a faded sofa, two armchairs and a coffee table. Mounted on the wall between two windows there were six swords arranged, from a short parrying wakizashi blade to a long curved naginata.

The paint was peeling in a few places and it was a little rundown but it was home. It was his sanctuary and Lovelace instantly felt himself relax. Three doors led to his bedroom, the guest room and the bathroom, and an arch led through to the kitchen.

He put down his shopping and walked over and lit the two candles and stick of incense on his small shrine to the Tattooed Man and Overlord. Once completed he grabbed the bag and walked through to the small kitchen and put the it down on the surface. He quickly packed away the fish and meats in the fridge. Like all Pures, Lovelace's diet was primarily carnivorous. He could eat vegetables, but got almost everything he needed from meat, usually served in a sushi style. Still, Lovelace had always had a penchant for noodles and he put away a couple of cartons of those too, along with the milk and beer he bought for himself. That chore complete he pulled one of the beers from the fridge and returned to the living room.

In one corner of the room stood a fighting dummy wearing his practice armour and Lovelace slung his sword and gun belt over it and pulled off his coat and boots. Feeling the tension in his neck, he used the heel of his palm to push his chin around to ninety degrees until his neck made a satisfying loud crack as the vertebrae were released. He then vaulted over the sofa to land on it. An action he immediately regretted as he felt a stabbing pain in his side.

The wound he had received from Thervessons was still healing. It had been deep, and only his own dogged insistence that he could cope had stopped him being rushed to hospital. The truth was, Thervessons had almost killed him, and he knew it.

He gingerly put his feet up on the coffee table. A meow greeted him from the floor and a small tabby cat leapt up onto his lap.

"Hey Flames, how have you been?" Lovelace scratched the cat under its chin, and it responded by purring and curling up on his lap. Lovelace leaned back and sipped from his beer while considering the last two days.

The whole Thervessons thing had been nasty. *What the bloody hell had you been up to? What would drive a man to kill over sixty residents in his slum apartment blocks and then live like some kind of bloody animal in a tiny space? He ate, slept, pissed and shat all within a space the size of a prison cell. Why? The man was rich.* Lovelace had looked into his financials. Thervessons had owned over a hundred apartment blocks at all levels of the city. The income was enough to keep him extremely well off and able to live in the best bits of Uptown, yet he had chosen to live like a caged animal in the worst part of Downtown in the Strip. It did not make sense.

The mention of Tereza's visit by Mrs Connelly had reminded him of something. He wanted to see if he could find out what all that magical stuff — all the runes, sigils and other shit — had been for. There must have been a purpose. A twisted purpose of a sick bastard, to be sure, but a purpose nonetheless. *I wonder if Thervessons' was the darkness that Tereza had spoken about?* He hoped it was, but knew that it was probably not that.

He made a decision. While Aries went off to the Governor's Ball, he would get on with some actual investigative work and go and talk to Tereza and the other priests and Truthsayers he knew about the purpose of Thervessons' sorcery. If he knew exactly what he had been trying to do, it might give him an insight into what was going on. Cassian Dexter could wait.

The combination of a decision made and an insistent nudging of his hand and low purr from Flames told him the cat was hungry, and the rumbling in his own stomach told him he was also hungry. Lovelace finished the beer, picked up the cat and headed into the kitchen.

"Come on Flames, let's get our dinner."

*   *   *

Lovelace led Tereza into Thervessons' apartment block. Agency warning tape sealed the place off. In a place like the Strip that usually meant nothing as scavs were quick to move in, but this time the building was still empty. Lovelace was not surprised, it had a bad atmosphere.

He had gone to the temple to see Tereza and to see if she and the other priests could shed any light on the specifics of what Thervessons had been up to. Tereza had quickly told him that in order to help she needed to see this place of darkness. The power to the neighbourhood was off and both held torches, their beams catching the floating specks of dust and mold in the air.

"Is this the place, Tarus?" asked Tereza when they reached Thervessons' flat. Lovelace nodded. Outside the temple, Tereza used his Given Name. Tereza kneeled and began casting an eye over the occult markings in the hallway.

"Your human was attempting to keep something out. He was using corrupted sorcery to do it."

Lovelace thought back to his religious training that was part of his upbringing as a Truthsayer. Sorcery, what was sorcery in a world of Echoes?

The Wyld was the source Echoes tapped. Echo powers were the

physical manifestation of the abilities of some people to reshape reality around them through force of will and the channelling and focusing of the Wyld's raw power. They were visceral, vital and immediate.

The Disciples, such as Albion or the Tattooed Man, worked through a combination of Echoes and their own subtle transformations of reality, less immediate than those of an Echo, but powerful nonetheless.

He had learned in the history books that the Disciples originally came from, or *through*, the Wyld, that it was the appearance of Echoes and the subsequent tearing of the fabric of reality that allowed them to exist in an in-between state and manifest in the forms of their Avatars. Each Disciple represented a strand of energy in the Wyld, each strand becoming a defined concept such as death, judgement, or progress in our reality. The Overlord was order.

Beyond the pantheon of the Overlord and His Disciples, which were lesser deities, were the fallen Disciples: Baal the God of War and Lokden the God of Entropy, and worship of them had been forbidden for over two thousand years. People did worship them, however, their cults surviving underground into the present, living in secrecy, for heresy was a serious crime.

But the Disciples were not the only strands of energy within the Wyld. It was not like any place in our reality, it was subject to strange currents, riptides, whirlpools and, occasionally, storms. It was an unimaginable space that intersected with our reality but was not of our reality. Beyond Baal and Lokden were the demons known in Kapaethjan as 'Rezhadi'. The word brought fear. The word-concept had no direct equivalent in Standard, but translated loosely as '*soul worms*'.

Rezhadi emanated from the Wyld, same as the Disciples, same as Echo powers, but they were like blood stains spreading through the fabric of everything the Disciples and Echoes represented. They twisted and coiled and gnawed at reality. They were elemental forces of putrefaction, madness and corruption that tear and burrow and spread.

To define their needs in human terms was to misunderstand them, they were not sentient in any way that a human could comprehend, more forces of natures than distinct beings. Humans of any kind could never truly understand their motivations, their hunger.

But that did not mean people did not try.

The insane worshipped Rezhadi in the dark corners of the Steel Alliance, but aside from those damned, there were those who sought to trade, to bargain with Rezhadi for power that they could not otherwise legitimately gain. That was a true heresy, for it could endanger whole worlds. They would spread like a rot through good flesh, corrupting, shifting and altering not only the people around them but the very fabric of reality itself, weakening it and pulling it closer to the Wyld, closer to their ravening ever hungry maws. They were elemental, insatiable and almost unstoppable.

This was sorcery, the desire to extract power through terrible pacts made with the inhuman. That was why it was heresy.

Is this a form of Rezhadi? Is that what this is all about?

That Thervessons had been trafficking in such… filth… shocked even the hardened Lovelace. They proceeded into the apartment. Tereza examined everything. When they entered the central space which had held the bodies, now removed, she gave a low whistle. She slowly rotated, taking in the markings on the walls and ceilings, taking it all in.

"This… man… he sought protection. Everything here focuses in on that." She pointed at the circle where Thervessons had ate, shat and slept. "He used twisted versions of holy protections on the outside to mislead, to deflect and to protect. But within here, within this… place… he went one step further. He used those people, their energy, to hide himself. This was all about obfuscation. He was very scared of something, something he would go to any lengths to hide from. This was not about power, it was about burying himself in the earth and pulling the soil over the top."

Lovelace nodded. "What could he have been so scared of? What had he done?"

"I do not know, but whatever it was, it was powerful. Incredibly powerful. One thing you should know, Lovelace."

"Yes?"

"It did not work."

"What?"

"All this sacrifice, all this murder, this waste and misdirection. It failed. I believe that was why he came after you." Lovelace's side twinged at the memory. "He had failed. Whatever he was hiding from found him. He perhaps hoped that by killing you, he might buy himself more time. But once that had failed, he was left with nowhere to run. His fate had been sealed."

He thought back to the truck that had seemingly appeared out of nowhere, and of Thervessons' pleading to be saved. It certainly had not worked.

"This place, this place needs to be destroyed if the taint is to be lifted." Lovelace looked around. He certainly agreed with Tereza, there was nothing good about this place.

"I agree. Can you arrange it?" Tereza nodded. "Good, then let's get out of this bloody abattoir."

11

Steel Year 2425.10.06 (S-Time). Day Six, Evening

Aries looked out the window of the grav limo that he shared with Clarice for the short journey from her mansion to the Governor's Palace in East Hampstead.

Six, her butler and their driver this evening, brought the grav limo down to land among the hundred or so other grav cars parked on the well-tended lawns outside the Palace. Massive arc-lights illuminated the grand palace as well as the skies above. The lights picked out the swarm of Metropolice and news grav planes buzzing around like angry bees. The banners of the Accord and London flapped wildly in the wind and down drafts caused by all the air traffic.

There was a charge in the air. Aries could feel it and it gave him goosebumps.

This was to be the Governor Sagacious' last major event before his retirement and it was shaping up to be a truly major event. Sagacious had ruled London with a firm and thoughtful hand for the last twenty-eight years since the end of the terrible period of internecine conflict now known as the Civil War. Sagacious was not exactly a popular administrator, but he was respected and trusted, and there were many anxieties about his stepping down as Governor of London. His rule had been so stable that people had almost forgotten there had been a time when he had not been there. The announcement of the election had shocked them out of their complacency.

All that added up to stellar attendance with guests from London and far beyond. For the millions who could not attend, segments of the Ball would be broadcast live over the WeaveNets to viewers throughout the Governor's domain. The Ball promised to have all the glamour and glitz of the finest awards ceremonies.

It was already giving John a massive headache. For someone who worked as hard as he did to avoid attention, this was the antithesis of all that. He started as he felt Clarice brush against him. He turned to look at her and she said, "You will be fine, John. Remember this is business, not play. Keep your mind focused on gathering as much information as you can."

Clarice was wearing a formal ball gown. The dress was matte black and sleeveless, starting with a high, almost chaste, neckline that revealed her neck and shoulders and a body-hugging black top, over which was a laced bodice of a reflective black quality cinched in tight but which opened up to hang down to her mid-thigh. From beneath it the dress flowed out into a many layered flouncing skirt with stiffening under-dress and an irregular hem. The layers were a mix of black lace, the same shiny material and matte back fabric. Her arms were bare but for black silk ribbons wrapped around her arms running from elbow to finish at her ring fingers. To complement our outfit she had her black hair tied up high and she wore a simple black choker.

The whole look was distinctly modern with a hint of melancholy. He was impressed. The look spoke to her classiness but also of her status as the wife of a missing husband, possibly in mourning.

He considered how he was dressed. Xi Volker had provided him with a tailored black tuxedo. The single breasted black jacket was worn open with a silk Nehru collar. He wore a mandarin collar white shirt underneath made of the most elegant material he had encountered. Around his neck he wore a full length orange and white striped cravat. Pleated trousers to match, fastened with a black belt and elegantly simple silver buckle, and handmade leather formal half-boots were a nice touch. He wore a small Accord pin in the cravat. Everything about it was clean and simple and yet elegant.

He had to admit that together they made an elegant couple. One that would certainly set tongues wagging in society. At this point in the investigation, stirring things up would be a good thing.

Six, the butler, climbed out of the car and walked around to Aries' side. John nimbly jumped out and turned to offer a hand to Clarice who took it and managed the feat of climbing out of the car smoothly and with dignity. John took her arm, and they walked across the lawn to the palace. He was pleased that tonight it was not raining, indeed, the sky above was clear and he could see both moons. The silvery Luna and the bronze, second moon of Troy. All around them other couples, individuals and groups were making their way to the palace.

The Governor's Palace itself was as much a temple as a palace. It stood slightly raised on eight steps above the surrounding lawns, a glowing vision of white marble. The architecture was mathematical graeco-roman, with great Doric columns eight metres tall holding up the capital, which supported the entablature holding up the architrave and triangular pediment. Between the pediment and the architrave were glorious gold and marble friezes retelling the stories of the founding and ancient heroic past of the Steel Alliance. The centre of the pediment held a golden eight-pointed star of the Overlord.

The main entrance was formed by a double row of eight columns, and Aries recalled from some set of facts learned long ago that for reasons of correspondence, this front approach was exactly sixty-four metres wide. Between each pair of columns hung one of the flags of each of the worlds and territories in the Governor's realm. Earth, Luna, Venus, Titan, Ravenna and Gateway were most prominent, but they were not the only ones. Every element about the palace was mathematically and artistically designed to offer worship and respect to the Overlord. From the top of the pediment flew the flags of London, the Steel Alliance Accord, and at a lower level, the Federate Combine, Imperial Commonwealth of Elysia and Dominion of Kapaethja, signifying the binding of all the states into the Steel Alliance Accord.

The palace had been badly damaged in the Civil War, but Governor Sagacious had spent vast sums of money painstakingly restoring it to its full glory, and many of the population of London felt with pride that this represented the Governor's own desire to rebuild London to a level equal with its own ancient past as the seat of imperial and divine rule.

John and Clarice made their way up the steps and through the colonnade. Marines from the Astro Marine Corps, in ornate, white ceremonial dress uniform, stood in two ranks forming a corridor through which the guests flowed into the Palace.

They entered the main foyer, again decorated in the graeco-roman style. A gold statue of the Overlord dominated the room, in full armour his hammer raised and pointed out through the entrance. His eyes blazed, set deep within his fierce bearded face. One leg was bent, standing on the dead bodies of those who challenged his rule. A ring of incense burners encircled the statue, surrounding it in a pungent fog. The statue towered over the guests, and each guest ritually drew the eight-pointed star in the air before continuing.

The archway from the foyer opened up into the ballroom that filled the front part of the palace. At the rear of the ballroom was a pair of grand staircases that curved around to rise to a landing and balcony, some three stories above the ground. At the entrance to the ballroom stood an announcer who called out the identities of each arrival as they entered the room. He announce the couple ahead of John and Clarice.

"Lord Shatrughna Kilbraith-Ravana, Seventh Earl of Corballo Minor, Marquis of Victoria and Lady Kathleen Kilbraith-Ravana, his wife and Seventh Lady of Corballo Minor, and Chief Mercantile Officer of the Rami Agricorp."

Aries looked at the announced Earl and Lady. They looked pretty ordinary to him, but before he could disappear off into reverie, they were introduced.

"Lady Clarice Hamilton-Jones, Eighteenth Viscountess of the Charter Corporation Stealth-Albion, and her companion, John Aries, Agency."

John was perversely pleased with the brevity of his title. In a world of Governors, Commanders, Dukes, Ambassadors and Lords, being a simple Agent turned heads. He could see several of the other guests thinking, *How did he get here? What is his relationship with Clarice Hamilton-Jones? Is he powerful? Should I talk to him or ignore him?* Aries knew he upset the social order, though perhaps less so than, say, if Lovelace had attended in his stead. He was at least an Echo which made him a person of minor note.

Clarice took his arm and they proceeded into the ballroom. They were handed glasses of champagne from the Governor's own vineyards, somewhere in the twisted and dangerous Wytchwoods near London.

Aries surveyed the room, looking for familiar faces.

Clarice nodded at one small huddle of people. He spotted Commissioner Tanaka at the centre of the group, holding court and chatting with her admirers and confidants. She wore a blood-red ball gown that, like Clarice's, opened out into a layered flouncing skirt. Clarice walked over and Aries accompanied her.

"Ami! How good to see you!" With the skirts preventing any ability to get close to each other with decorum, they merely shook hands. Ami Tanaka smiled warmly at Clarice.

"Clarice, darling. How good to see you! This smart gentleman at your arm must be Mr Aries. A pleasure to meet you again, Mr Aries."

He smiled. "It is good to see you again too, Commissioner Tanaka."

"Oh please! Call me Ami?" Clarice had turned to greet some of the other people around Commissioner Tanaka.

"Only if you call me, John."

"Very well, John." Her smile grew wider and she leaned in towards him. "Tell me, John, how goes the hunt for Charles?"

"We are making progress tracking back his movements up to his disappearance, though so far he remains... elusive."

"I see." She took hold of his forearm in a grip that was surprisingly firm. When she spoke it was in a low quiet voice that belied the broad smile and easy-going posture she took. "You are making yourself some powerful enemies, John. I heard about your recent abduction. To put it poetically, you are swimming in a lake of sharks wearing nothing but a chum wetsuit. If I were you, I would be careful." She released her grip, smiled and said, "Next time you see him, send my regards to Lovelace." Then she turned to greet another approaching man.

Everyone is warning me off. He was amused by her metaphor. For a Commissioner she sounded an awful lot like Lovelace. *It must be a cop thing.*

He took a sip of his champagne, pacing himself, while he looked around again. Hanging back near the wall he spotted Cassian Dexter looking surprisingly shifty in his tuxedo. He did not give the impression of someone who wanted to be there, which was ironic given how in demand the invitations for the Ball had been.

Looking over at Clarice, he saw she was engaged in conversation with a pair of corporate-looking gentlemen. He caught her eye and raised an eyebrow and she gave an almost imperceptible shake of her head. *They are not people I need to meet.* He nodded in return and set off across the ballroom towards Mr Dexter.

When he was halfway there, Xi Volker and her assistant Darrienne intercepted him. In contrast to her earlier bare-bosomed appearance, Darrienne was wearing a formal, traditional gentleman's black tuxedo. Xi Volker held her arm and wore a gothic black dress, all lace and silver straps. They surprised him when it was Darrienne who spoke.

"Mr Aries, you look very handsome tonight." Xi merely smiled.

"Thank you. Both of you." He stepped back to give them a quick twirl. Darrienne leaned in and whispered in his ear, "You are a good-looking man, Mr Aries, perhaps later we could have a… um… dance?" The comment surprised John, but before he had time to reply, Xi and Darrienne were off once more. *I wonder what the story is there?*

Aries downed the last of his glass of champagne, placed it on the tray of a passing waiter, and continued towards Mr Dexter. The look on Cassian Dexter's face when he saw Aries approach was anything but pleased. He desperately searched around for some distraction he could use to escape the incoming Agent.

"Mr Dexter, how good to see you."

"Ah. Yes. Um… Agent… Aries was it?" *As if you do not remember who I am.* Internally, Aries smiled. He decided to go for shock tactics.

"That is correct, Mr Dexter. After our conversation the other day, I have been meaning to follow up with you, but unfortunately the recent grisly deaths of Mr Arends and Mr Thervessons rather distracted me. It is a shame they died, but that seems to be happening to a lot of your Honourable Brothers at the moment, does it not?"

Mr Dexter went pale, as all the blood drained from his face. "I… uh… don't really know what you mean? I…"

"Oh that is right, you were probably too busy wondering what happened to Mr Julius Rato? He is dead too. In fact, counting Nigel Massey de Sargon, four of your close friends all dead within a week. Things are not looking too promising for Charles Hamilton-Jones either. It is amazing really. That list you gave me is growing shorter by the day. There are what? Three names left on it. Including yours, Mr Dexter."

He could see Dexter swallowing. *Right about now, his mouth has gone dry and his heart is trying to batter its way out of his chest. Good.* Aries continued, "Yes, indeed. That list is getting shorter by the day."

"What… what do you…want?"

"Me? Oh nothing of import, Mr Dexter," Aries' tone hardened, "aside from you to tell me what the hells is going on. What I know is that you are in extremely serious, and probably terminal, trouble. Whatever it was that you and your 'Honourable' brothers did is the cause of the nasty deaths of your friends. Your one chance to save yourself is to come in and talk to me. You know you cannot hide behind the Commander forever, and if you want to make this right, you will turn yourself in. Maybe then I can protect you. Think about it Dexter, but not for too long because time is running out."

With that pronouncement, Aries turned away from Mr Dexter and returned to Clarice's side. A quick glance over his shoulder showed Cassian Dexter downing a glass of champagne and quickly hurrying away.

Good! I hope that puts the cat amongst the pigeons. This cloak and dagger charade has gone on long enough and I want to see what I can shake out of him.

The Ball itself began. A gong rang out around the hall, silencing the crowd and drawing everyone's attention to the balcony. The silence was so acute Aries fancied he could hear the breathing of those around him.

A pair of mighty curved horns, each standing over three metres tall, sounded. The doors to the balcony opened and three figures emerged onto the balcony. The lead figure was Governor Sagacious. He wore the formal military uniform of a General in the Astro Marine Corps, a position awarded to him by the AMC in recognition of his commitment to the Accord's stability. His white uniform was immaculate, the gold braids looped from his shoulder in perfect positioning. His left breast displayed the medals and colours earned in his duty. He did not wear the formal peaked cap of an officer, instead revealing his grey hair. He had a grey goatee and moustache and his Echo tattoo stood out, clearly visible, surrounding his bright blue eyes. He was every centimetre the embodiment of the patrician, something he had cultivated over the years of his rule. Despite his power, his background before the Civil War was unremarkable. When Michael Warren (his real name) had completed his Echo training he had served as an officer in the AMC before retiring to take on a role as a corporate operations and logistics executive. Nothing about him marked him out as exceptional, and yet here he was, and with his own rags to riches story.

His eyes were serious and intense, and John was reminded of his own father's.

Besides him stood his wife, Lady Elyssia, a former athlete and model, many years his junior. She wore a refined and elegant pale blue dress, and, like her husband, she was also an Echo. The third person on the balcony required no introduction. Everyone in the room immediately recognised Denver, who – for him – was dressed extremely conservatively in a dark red suit, though with no shirt underneath.

The crowd burst into applause. Governor Sagacious let the applause continue for a few moments before raising his hands for silence. The crowd obeyed.

"My Holy Avatars, Lords, Ladies and Gentlemen, Citizens and Kindred, I bid you welcome to my annual celebration of the Signing of the Accord that brought the dark days of the Civil War to a close."

The crowd burst into applause again, though this time Sagacious quickly quieted them.

"Before we begin the festivities, as is traditional, I would begin with a prayer. Please join with me in offering your obeisance and fidelity with Her Divine Apotheosis, Highpriestess-Keeper of the Temple of the Overlord, Nebhotep Neteri, to the Overlord and His Disciples with whom humanity in all its forms bound the eternal Alliance of Steel almost two and a half thousand years ago."

The pair of grand doors beneath the balcony opened and the Highpriestess-Keeper entered, escorted by the Temple of the Overlord's white-and-gold robed priests and priestesses. Each carried a hammer in one hand and flaming bowl of incense in the other. A thick pungent smoke was given off by the incense burners. The Highpriestess-Keeper was clad in beautiful golden armour. In her hands she held a double-headed hammer, an ancient relic from the founding days of the Steel Alliance. Her visage was stern.

She began to chant in the ancient religious language and her cortège joined in.

Aries evaluated her. Nebhotep Neteri was known to be a religious fundamentalist that held to the absolute word of the Overlord. She had been brought in three years earlier from offworld over the heads of the local priests and priestesses to lead the Terran Temple of the Overlord by the High Council on the world of Teushpa following a land scandal that had engulfed the previous Highpriest.

Her imposition had been a major blow to the self-esteem of the local temple and her hard-nosed, no-nonsense approach had not exactly improved the situation. Aries knew that she was referred to as the 'barbarian queen', or less eloquently, 'that bitch' in private by the priesthood.

Still, while she had the backing of the High Council, her position was unassailable and she had managed to forge a working relationship with the Governor.

Aries filtered out the prayer himself, he had heard it a thousand times before and right now he was more interested in seeing who else had arrived. Although almost without exception everyone had their heads bowed in prayer there were a few who were doing other things. In the crowd he quickly spotted Commander James Villiers-Cavanaugh and his Chief of Staff Kenton Serrano. They were quietly talking to a tall woman in a luminescent white suit. Her pure white hair, violent eyes and suit marked her out as a Jensian from the Federate Combine, but beyond that he did not recognise her. He made a mental note to get a better look later.

Likewise, Commissioner Tanaka was easy enough to spot. She had her head bowed in prayer. Her staff and companions were likewise similarly pious, or at least acting it. Cassian Dexter had either disappeared, or Aries was simply unable to make him out in the crowd. He recognised the lawyer, Arkell Isadore of the Honourable Brotherhood, from his picture in the case file. Isadore, a well-built, dark-skinned Echo in a dark suit stood at the room's rear with several companions. He was sipping champagne and chatting jovially. Clearly the stress that was eating at Dexter was not affecting Isadore, or at least he was better at hiding it. *Much better at hiding it, I think.*

Aries made another mental note to try and talk to him before the evening was over. Returning to scanning the crowd, John was surprised to spot the familiar figure of Captain Linsbury. Linsbury caught his eye and raised his glass in toast. Aries nodded in return, surprised to see the Captain here. *I had no idea Linsbury was so well connected. Interesting. I should talk to him in a bit, these last few days I have barely briefed him.*

Unable to spot anyone else he recognised he turned his attention back to his companion. Clarice looked stunning, and he had to admit it. His feelings for her were very confusing, but the attraction was extremely strong. The kiss they had shared the other day was vivid and fresh in his mind, like spilt blood. He breathed in her scent, it was intoxicating. She reminded him in so many ways of Ariadne, but had her own distinct charms. But he was not convinced she was uninvolved in the disappearance of her husband and deaths of the Honourable Brothers. After all, she certainly held no love for any of them, and in Arends' case at least the dislike had been more than mutual. *I must see if I can discover what Mr Dexter or Mr Isadore think about Clarice. That might help me get more of a grip on the relative power plays. After all, Arends was extremely paranoid and may not have been representative.*

Plus there was also her friendship, or alliance, with Commissioner Tanaka, as well as her previous, as yet undefined, history with Denver. She was well connected, powerful and shrewd. An accomplished political player. What she saw in him he was not sure, and that was the problem. At the back of his mind was the inescapable knowledge that she was manipulating him to achieve her own goals. Yet despite that, she had done nothing but help him so far. If that was manipulation then it did not rankle.

It left him feeling like he was standing on very unstable ground. Either way he was going to have to do something about it. Problem was, as yet he was not sure what he would do.

The twin giant horns sounded again, indicating the end of the religious ceremony by the priesthood of the Overlord. They retreated back the way they came. Before conversations could resume at the same level the Governor spoke once more. Waiters quickly passed through the crowd refilling everyone's champagne glasses or providing those without with replacements.

"My dear guests, welcome once again. I hope you enjoy yourselves, but before we begin the dancing I wish to raise a toast: To London, the Accord and the Steel Alliance. May they never fall into darkness!"

The crowd met the toast and drank, then from amongst them rose a voice, "And to Governor Sagacious in gratitude for twenty-eight years of wise rule!" The response this time was enthusiastic with massed shouts of "Hear! Hear!"

Out of the corner of his eye, Aries watched the Commander politely sip from his glass. *So it is true, he really is going to stand as Governor.* Formal announcement or no, Villiers-Cavanaugh was definitely looking to further his career.

So, possible candidates in the election so far were the Commander,

Commissioner Tanaka and Denver, though those were just the candidates from London. Sagacious' realm extended throughout the solar system (with the exclusion of Mars) and beyond. The Viceroy Governors from Venus, Ravenna and Gateway were certainly likely candidates and were almost certainly here, though Aries had no idea what they looked like. *But I should. If Villiers-Cavanaugh is looking to this election, so should I.* He mentally chided himself, *May be I have been looking at this case all wrong. Maybe this is not about the Honourable Brotherhood at all, but about the Commander. A group of rich, powerful scheming men and an upcoming critical election. That is an unlikely coincidence. I need to look into that angle more.*

"Agent Aries, what a pleasant and unexpected surprise to see you here, tonight." The voice of the Commander shook him out of his reverie and he spun to face his boss.

Sir James Villiers-Cavanaugh hawkishly stood there looking anything but pleased, but then he never did. Alongside him was the reptilian-looking Kenton Serrano, his Chief of Staff. Average build, average height, average Caucasian skin tone, brown eyes, brown hair. Aside from the unblinking look to his eyes, there was absolutely nothing distinct about Kenton Serrano.

"Commander. Mr Serrano." Aries nodded at each in turn. Neither side offered their hands. "Indeed, I was invited along as a last minute replacement for your dear friend, Charles, by Mrs Hamilton-Jones."

"I see. Yes. How *is* the case progressing? I have been more than a little perturbed by the lack of updates on the case. I had expected better from you Aries. Everything in your file had led me to believe you to be a diligent agent. Was I wrong?"

"No, sir. It is just that things have taken some unexpected twists."

"Really, do tell? As I am discovering, you are indeed a man full of surprises." The last was said with a definite edge. Serrano smiled. It was not a pleasant smile.

"Yes indeed. Unfortunately I was delayed by my abduction and torture by Mr Benham Arends, and his subsequent unexpected death. That would have been only a trifling inconvenience, but I am afraid that Mr Jean Thervessons attempted to kill my partner, and Thervessons too died. I am making good progress and hope to have uncovered the whereabouts of the Viscount soon." He found himself growing angry and before he could stop himself, he added, "Before any more of your friends do something stupid and then die."

The Commander's face coloured red and Serrano's smile vanished abruptly. Villiers-Cavanaugh raised his index finger to retort, when another voice cut in. It was Clarice.

"James! How wonderful to see you! I cannot thank you enough for assigning Agent Aries to the investigation into poor missing Charles. He has been doing a superb job. You should give that man a commendation. You really are a good friend, James."

She held out here hand and, with painful slowness, Sir James Villiers-Cavanaugh bit back his anger and leaned forward to take her hand and kiss it.

"It really was nothing, Clarice. We all miss Charles and pray for his swift return. As for Agent Aries, indeed he has turned out to be quite the dogged investigator with many hidden depths. I shall be keeping a very a close eye on him from now on. To make sure he is properly rewarded, of course." His look at Aries was all smiles and friendliness, but his jovial expression did not make it all the way to his eyes. They were very cold.

"Oh, see that you do. Agent Aries has been of great comfort during this most trying time. I might also go so far as to say he has become a close friend. Friends are very important, are they not, James?"

Villiers-Cavanaugh's eyebrows lifted in surprise. "Why… yes. Yes they are, Clarice."

Clarice smiled. Her smile was cold and hard like a diamond. "It really is good to see you, James. You have done so well for yourself, who knows how far you might rise? But if you will excuse John and I, I believe the dances are about to begin."

The Commander nodded stiffly and Clarice walked away with Aries. She leaned in and whispered in his ear, "What did you say to him? He looked fit to burst."

"I just reminded him that his friends were hindering my investigation and are dying. The correlation was obvious."

"Careful, John. James is not a man to be trifled with. You do not rise as far as he has done without being dipped in blood. Like all of us, he was not always the eminent person he was today."

"What was I going to do? He told me to investigate your husband's disappearance, and when it appears as if I might actually succeed he is not exactly pleased."

"John, he picked you because of your record. Nothing showy, nothing too good or bad. You were, from your file at least, a perfect bureaucratic agent. But we both know there is a lot more to you than that." *What do you know about me, Clarice?* "And now, so does James. He is a powerful man, and would make a powerful enemy. He is going to examine everything about you now."

Aries felt a sharp coldness in his stomach as the truth of that comment sank in. *Perhaps I was too rash.* He looked back at the Commander, *Or not. Damn.*

Clarice took his hand in hers and gave it a squeeze. "Don't worry, John. You have made some powerful friends too. Perhaps more than friends." She stopped walking and turned to face him. He could feel the heat in her hand as she locked him with her gaze. "But you have reached a decision point. Will you finish what you have started, even if it means facing losing everything you have worked so hard to build. Or will you flee into hiding once more? Are you ready to stop running, John?"

His eyes grew wide. *She knows who I was!* He opened his mouth to speak, but Clarice raised her right index finger and placed it on his lips.

"Do not answer now. I want you to really think about it. Make your choice soon, John. Time is running out."

The time for talking ended, as the band took up their instruments and the music began. Clarice stepped into his arms for the first dance.

John's mind was a-whirl as they danced. That his past that he had worked so hard to bury could have been uncovered by Clarice, and possibly Villiers-Cavanaugh was a terrifying concept. It meant that Clarice, at least, held him in her power. Terrible forces of destruction and retribution were held in check merely by her inaction. But with the smallest move she could rain death down on him, and if she really did know his true identity, then she knew that too.

But she had in no way threatened him. Exactly the opposite. Their relationship was becoming closer by the day, though it was clear that their relationship was unequal. It had been played on her terms, at times of her choosing.

"John, you are an amazing dancer." He thought back to the thousands of hours spent practising all the formalities of the court, something a typical agent would have no experience of. He mentally kicked himself for allowing that part of him to show through, but it was too late, the damage was done and he could not suddenly become unskilled. He was not *that* good.

He felt her body press against him as he twirled her around to the music. He breathed her in deeply, *Gods! She is intoxicating!* His body responded strongly to her presence. It was mutual, there was no doubt of that. He could hear her breathing, it was fast. Faster than the simple exertion of the dancing should have caused. He could see a flush on her cheeks.

She looked at him and her eyes sparkled, transformed into the eyes of a girl.

They danced and spun and twirled beneath the beautifully painted domed ceiling of the ballroom, alone in a crowd of thousands. Politics and espionage put aside in the moment. For a moment all knowledge of the danger he… they… were in was gone. They were just two people, a man and a woman, dancing, their bodies wrapped in tempo and step.

They had danced for what seemed forever when, finally, there was a break.

Clarice pulled him up the staircase. They had found a quiet corner of the palace. She was laughing in a carefree way. They were both flushed with the exertion of the dancing. They reached a bend, and Clarice pulled him to her and they kissed. First gently, and then with growing passion as their bodies pressed together.

Aries reached down and under her dress and ran his hand up her thigh, savouring the softness and warmth of it. Clarice responded by pressing herself more firmly into him.

She whispered into his ear, "Make love to me, John. Forget about everything else and make love to me, John. I need you."

Aries, unable to hold back any more, mouthed the word, 'yes.' He gripped her thigh firmly and ran his other hand through her hair, messing up her immaculate styling. Clarice smiled and bit his earlobe, then stepped away and pulled him by the hand up the stairs as they sought some privacy.

The memory of Clarice saying, *"Remember this is business, not play,"* flitted through his mind. *Is this business or play?*

*   *   *

Lovelace stood by the manhole cover that led to the sewers below. A rancid stench rose as a visible mist from the black hole. Standing with him was Detective Sergeant Nathan Sark and a municipal engineer in a bright orange jumpsuit and hard hat. On top of the sewer hole was a tripod winch with a cable disappearing into the darkness below.

Sark turned to the city worker. "You say you found him down there?"

"Aye. Central registered a pressure build-up just next to the Imperial/Soho mainline. One of the side feeds was backing up something terrible, so they sent me down to check it out. Usually it is just all the congealed fats and oils from people's cookers mixed with compacted faeces."

Nathan held up his hand, "Yeah, um that's too much information.

Thanks."

"You asked." The worker looked surly.

Lovelace cut in, "And you found a body instead?"

"That's right. All jammed up in the grating. Must have floated down the upper primary from Imperial. Damn thing should have gone down the main feed, but looks like it got caught up in a vortex caused from a pressure wash and got sucked down to the lower and fired down a secondary pipe."

Lovelace did not pretend to have followed that in detail, but he did not need to. "Wait, does that mean you know where it came from?"

"'Course. I know all the flows round here. Worked these lines for near-on twelve years."

"Good. Then once they get the body out of there you can tell me where it came from. How did you know to call it in?"

"'Cos of this." The worker pulled out a plastic mortuary tab. It was engraved with 'Massey de Sargon, Nigel.' "It's not unusual to find stiffs in the sewers. I checked it on the comm, and saw that your man here," he nodded towards Nathan, "Had put out an alert on the body and I called it in."

"Good job. If only more people were as diligent as you." The worker visibly swelled with pride at the compliment.

From below came the muffled sound of swearing from two uniformed police officers in chest high waders carrying the body. "Pull up the bloody winch!"

The city worker pressed a button on the winch and it began to wind the cable in. It only took a few moments for the black body bag to rise to the street level. Lovelace, who was now wearing gloves, pulled the body in and laid it down. The stench rising off the bag was unbelievable and even Lovelace, long hardened to the unpleasantries of the city had a hard time not retching.

He unzipped the bag, and sure enough it contained the filthy corpse of Nigel Massey de Sargon. The last few days since his abduction from the morgue had not been kind. The wounds he had suffered in the fall were torn open with definite signs of the body having been harassed by vermin. Lovelace nodded. "Yes, that's the bastard."

Nathan crouched down next to him, holding his nostrils closed with one hand. "That's your missing city gent?"

"One of them."

"An Echo?"

"Yes. Not that being one helped him."

Lovelace noticed something else. Massey de Sargon's body showed signs of having been autopsied. Which would have been unremarkable, except that the doctor at the Necropolis had told him they had not been able to perform an autopsy. *That meant that someone else autopsied him. Why?*

"This cadaver's been autopsied, but not by us. Why?"

"Maybe someone else wanted to find out how he died and did not trust us to do it properly, or maybe they thought we would cover something up."

"Of course! Arends was a paranoid bastard. When he kidnapped Aries –" Lovelace ignored the look of confusion on Sark's face, "he ranted on and on about how he thought *we* were trying to kill him."

"Were you?"

"Don't be silly. I'd have done a better job. So... thinking it through, Arends learns that Massey de Sargon is dead, thinks the Agency had him snuffed and decides to swoop the body out from under us before we could cover it up so that he could get his own trusted doctor to perform the autopsy."

It made sense. *You stupid fool, Arends, I wonder how you reacted when you were told that he died from the fall?* Still, at least that nagging loose thread could be tied off.

Sark posed the next logical question. "So if he got abducted from the Necropolis, what is he doing in the sewer?"

"You fancy a trip to Imperial to find out?"

"Sure."

Lovelace turned to the city worker. Behind him the saw two bedraggled policemen emerge from the sewer. "You think you could show us where you think the body went in to the sewers on a map?"

"I reckon so. What's in it for me?"

Lovelace smiled. "A warm feeling in your heart, and maybe I put in a good word to your supervisor."

"Good enough. Got a comm?"

Lovelace nodded and handed him his comm after removing his gloves. The worker brought up the maps, scrolled through them muttering to himself, 'Nah that's the tertiary pipe. Sealed up since last year. If he went in there he'd have gone straight down to Riverside.' With a firm point, he indicated a spot on the map.

"He must have gone in from this block, only way he could have got into that side pipe."

Lovelace took the comm and looked. It was a nondescript block in

Imperial. However one thing immediately jumped out at him: there was a current fire alert on one of the houses. He showed the comm to Nathan.

"Let's go."

They took Nathan's car. Lovelace did some further checking on the burning house. The owner of the house was none other than the recently-deceased Benham Arends, psychotic arms dealer and kidnapper of Aries. *I was right!* "Put your lights on, Nathan, and stop driving like your granny and get us there before the fun is over."

Sark turned on his police lights and powered off down the streets, heading West towards Imperial.

The drive did not take long. The gates between Imperial and Soho were opened for them just before they arrived, and shortly afterwards they were parked in the regal-looking square. One of the grand houses was surrounded by fire engines, ambulances and police. Fires licked out of the windows and thick, heavy black smoke poured out of the shattered windows. An emergency rescue grav plane hovered overhead, its searchlights scanning the building, looking for trapped people.

Lovelace climbed out of the car and Nathan accompanied him as they walked towards the building. Lovelace flashed his Agency badge at the police. "Who's in charge of the scene?"

The police officer pointed at a woman in formal police uniform. Lovelace approached her.

"You in charge here?"

"That is correct. I am Chief Inspector Willoughby. Who are you?"

"Agent Lovelace, Agency Investigations. Tell me what you know." Nathan stayed silent and simply watched, enjoying the chance to see the Agency at work.

"The fire appears to have been started about thirty minutes ago."

"Started? You suspect arson?"

"Oh yes, the airborne unit," — she pointed at the grav plane overhead — "detected alarmingly high quantities of an accelerant."

"What accelerant"?

"Incendiary white phosphorus."

Lovelace nodded. When Sark looked blank he turned to him and said, "White phosphorus is a military grade incendiary, used in incendiary grenades and bombs. It's bloody nasty stuff, will burn the skin right off you in seconds. Burns happily under water too." Lovelace turned back towards the Chief Inspector.

"You should know that the house belonged to one Benham Arends, a known and now deceased arms dealer. There may be a whole cache of ammunition and explosives in the building. Have you cleared the surrounding buildings?"

"Of course. I cleared the entire block."

"Good." A muffled crump sounded from inside the building and a section of the roof collapsed in releasing a fireball into the sky. "You saw the grav plane crash in Perevel?" The Chief Inspector nodded. "It is the same lug nut."

She pulled out her comm and spoke into it, "All units, be aware there may be unexploded munitions in building. Proceed with extreme caution."

"Wait, you have men in there now?"

"Yes, of course. I sent in a fire team to look for survivors."

"Get them out!"

"They know what they are doing."

"I don't bloody care. Get them out of there now! The place is probably rigged with traps. You need a bomb squad!" The Chief Inspector narrowed her eyes and reached for the comm again. Before she could speak there was a mighty explosion and fire exploded out of every window and door, spraying shattered glass and masonry on the emergency services vehicles and personnel. Lovelace pushed the Chief Inspector to the ground and ducked. A big piece of stone smashed into her car. When the initial explosion had passed, a second groaning noise filled the air and Arends' house collapsed in on itself like a deck of cards, collapsing with a great spray of dust and smoke that covered everyone.

Lovelace stood up. "Isoke's cock and balls!" he shouted. Grabbing the Chief Inspector's comm he shouted into it, "Check for survivors in the rubble but do it bloody carefully, there may be more unexploded bombs!" He threw the comm down and walked back to Sark's car. Nathan hurried to catch up. Behind them the visibly shaken police officer stood up and dusted herself off.

"What do you think happened?"

"My guess is that one of Arends' men decided to clean up the bloody mess his cock-sucking, paranoid psychopath of a boss had left behind. They got what Arends needed from the corpse, and not wanting to be tied to it the minion threw the body into a sewer, grabbed what he could and torched the bloody place."

"So your Arends bloke had your missing corpse?"

"Yes. Bloody looks like it. Question is why? What was it about the body that he did not want us to see? I am going to get a new autopsy done, but this time no one is going to bloody walk the body out of there. I will see to it myself if I have to nail it down my bloody self." He glanced back at the rubble as he climbed into the car. "Arends, I hope you are bloody being flayed and violated senseless in whatever of the bloody hells you find yourself in!"

12

Steel Year 2425.10.06 (S-Time). Day Six, Evening

They had found a storage cupboard and Aries had taken her there, up against the wall. There had been nothing graceful about it, their passion had overwhelmed them. Their lovemaking had been frenzied to begin with and his body tingled from where Clarice had run her fingers down the scars on his back. When they had come the release almost made him black out.

Afterwards they had fallen to the floor, his jacket acting as a poor substitute for a blanket, and now John held her to him, gently. Despite his confusion about Clarice, despite the knowledge that Lovelace would be really angry, and that he had possibly just thrown his entire Agency career out of the window, he felt calm. At peace.

He revelled in the sense of contentment, well aware that it was only transitory. He could feel the heat of her skin against his chest. Her hair had broken free of its restraints and her bodice was untied and lying on the floor. Clarice stirred and rose up revealing her breasts. She kissed him. He returned the kiss and felt his passion stir again. He had not been with a woman for longer than he could remember. No one since Ariadne. He had had offers, sure, but he had not felt that spark with anyone. He had thought that he would never feel that again. That is, until Clarice. There was something about her that called to him on a deep, primal level. The contrast between the powerful, restrained, and even, he admitted to himself, manipulative woman, and the unbound girl full of passion he caught glimpses of in her eyes, stirred him.

He knew their relationship was wrong, that is was based on an imperfect balance of power and that it might even cost him his life, but for the first time in a long time — longer than he cared to admit — he felt *something* for another person. But it was more than that, more than just a sex thing. He needed that connection.

He also knew that he was failing miserably to push forward his investigation at the Ball. So far, aside from a brief encounter with the Commander, he had only really talked to Dexter and then only to pressure him in the hope that he would crack. Mentally ticking off the other Honourable Brothers present he decided that he should at least talk to the Echo lawyer, Arkell Isadore, and maybe after that, see if he could get Kenton Serrano alone. At least that way he could salvage something of the evening.

Clarice reached up with her hand and gently touched his Echo tattoo. John started.

"Did it hurt?" she asked. She started pulling her hand back and he grabbed it softly and guided it back to his face. He remembered the ceremony that had given him the permanent mark of his *otherness*.

"Yes. More than anything you could imagine. It felt like my whole body was on fire. It is impossible to describe, but the closest I can get is that it felt like they tore my soul open and ripped out part of me from deep inside" Clarice continued to gently trace the eight-pointed star with her fingertips.

"What is it like? Using your Echo powers, I mean?"

"It is the most amazing rush you could imagine. There is nothing else like it. Drugs, sex, nothing compares. But then the burn of the cancer follows the rush. You can feel the Wyld Cancer eating you up inside, corrupting and twisting you. You use your powers, you can change the world, but you also die. But the rush… and the power to reshape reality… it is addictive. Many people who fail during training do so because they cannot fight the addiction. They crave that feeling and it eats them up."

"Have you ever become addicted to it?

Aries closed his eyes. "I came close… it is so seductive, and easy. The truth is that if you begin to rely on it, people die."

"But to have all that power and then not use it can't be easy?"

Aries smiled a pained smile. He nodded. "Nothing is easy, but what about you?"

"I'm hardly normal, John. My family spared no expense gene-tailoring me. Everything about me was designed for my role, since before I was born. My looks, my health, my intellect. Everything."

"I know that feeling. My… father… wanted only the best for me. It was not enough that, like my parents, my latent Echo talents were detected young. I also received every enhancement they could give me. I run faster, leap higher, see and hear better, punch harder and heal faster than any normal human. But that is not what I mean. Our world is dominated by Echoes, like me. Look at the Governor: he is one, and so is every single potential candidate. Do you ever feel there is a glass ceiling?"

It was Clarice's turn to look pained. *All that power, and yet she is still as much under the thumb as any of us.*

"Sometimes. But as I said, I have a role. A role I was *made for.*" And then he saw it. In many ways Clarice was made to be a perfect society wife, clever, urbane but… submissive. Somewhere along the way something had broken that part of her. He wondered what it could have been. He stroked her face.

"Clarice, you are more than that. You are more than what they made you. You are a complex and strong woman, Clarice, and from what I can see, far stronger than you husband." Clarice looked at him, an unreadable look in her eyes.

Poor Charles, he probably never knew what he had.

"If I find Charles, what will you do?"

She looked unsure of herself. It was not something he had seen before. "Honestly, I… don't know. I can't go on the way things were. I can't go back. Too much has changed." He wondered if he was part of that change. He knew he should not say anything, but the words slipped out before he could stop them.

"What about us?"

"I… I don't know. Can't we just not think about that for now and enjoy the moment?" John nodded and they kissed again, her body moving against his.

A shout outside startled them both. "Someone call the Metropolice! I found a body! There's been a murder!" John's eyes went wide. Without the need to say anything, they quickly stood and pulled their clothes on. He helped Clarice redo the ties on her bodice. It took a few moments, but they quickly stepped out into the hallway. John turned to Clarice. "Go find the Governor, I need to find out what has happened."

He grabbed a wide-eyed servant who was running past and flashed his badge. "Agency. Take me to the body. Now!" The servant nodded rapidly and led Aries down the hallway. They hurried towards the rear of the palace, towards the Governor's private temple. Two marines stood guard at the door. Both looked on edge. Aries flashed his badge, "Lieutenant John Aries, Agency Investigations, let me in," and, combined with his air of authority they complied and opened the doors. "Get on the comms and get the palace locked down! Nobody leaves and I mean nobody!"

He felt the tingling of a Wyld shield as he entered, which gave him pause. One Wyld shield around a major building was unusual in general, though expected for any secure premises, but to have a second, internal shield was highly unusual, and prohibitively expensive.

Lying there in a rapidly spreading pool of blood on the immaculate marble floor of the small private temple for the Governor and his family, was the body of Her Divine Apotheosis, Highpriestess-Keeper of the Temple of the Overlord, Nebhotep Neteri.

At least he believed it was the body of the Highpriestess-Keeper, for her head was missing. He kneeled down and examined the body. From an initial visual inspection she had been shot twice in the chest, both roughly in the central torso region, perhaps aiming for her heart, though the aim was not exact. Lying next to the corpse was a bloodied antique axe. Her head had been crudely hacked off – and as evidenced from the chips in the marble – it looked like it had taken more than a single blow.

This was not the work of a professional, though the fact they had taken the head (most likely to prevent any kind of medical aid) was a sign that this was no spur of the moment attack. It took a level of focus beyond an instant rage-driven strike to decapitate your victim and then leave with their head. *Either that or a form of advanced psychosis. But in that case if the attacker had poor impulse control he would not have stopped with just the head. Nothing else on the body appears to have been touched.*

Aries looked around for blood drops from the severed head, but could see none. That implied that the head had been placed in a bag, another mark against a crime of passion.

He considered the location: a private temple, where, presumably, Nebhotep Neteri had been praying in solitude, offering unrestricted access to anyone who could get into the guarded room. The Wyld shield provided protection from the use of metapsions to see through time and space to identify the attacker. It was a good place for an attack. Quiet and obscured.

He considered the victim. The priestess was no untrained civilian. Her order required her to be able to defend herself, and certainly no one rose to her rank without having survived at least one plot or even assassination attempt. Thus for such an amateur attack to succeed implied she most likely knew her attacker or considered them no threat which, ironically, gave them enough of a window to strike.

He stood and looked around the room. How had the attacker fled? There appeared to only be a single door to the room, but the marines had been standing guard there. *No, in a palace this old, that has been the seat of Imperial power, survived civil wars and insurrections and seen revolution and violence, there will be a network of hidden passages and chambers.*

With a sinking feeling he realised that his earlier promise to himself to question the Honourable Brothers at the Ball had been thoroughly blown out of the water. He mentally kicked himself for not sufficiently dogged earlier.

His consideration of the crime was abruptly interrupted when the main doors slammed open and a crowd of priests and the Governor's entourage stormed in. Aries pulled his badge and imposed himself between them and the body. He was a rock standing proud against an angry sea.

"Governor. This is a crime scene, stand back. The Highpriestess-Keeper has been murdered!" shouted Aries.

The crowd came to a halt. The Governor himself stepped forward.

"Who the hells are you?" he demanded.

"G4 Agent John Aries, SO-50 London Agency Investigations, m'lord. I was attending your Ball when I heard the alert."

The Governor nodded. Next to him another figure pushed forward, a robed priest who threw back his hood revealing a wan, bald man with pale blue eyes.

"By the Overlord's Grace!" He pushed forward and Aries raised a hand and stepped in front of him.

"Who are you to dare stand before me, blocking access to the body of her holiness?"

"I am the embodiment of the Agency here in the palace, and you might be?"

"I am Priest-Keeper Malachi, deputy of the Highpriestess-Keeper." *Malachi!* thought Aries with shock. Governor Sagacious put his hand on Malachi's shoulder. *Malachi! That name!* Aries flashed back to the note he had found in Charles Hamilton-Jones' car: 'Malachi, Victory'. *Was it this Malachi? How had I not found him?*

The Governor spoke, "Priest-Keeper Malachi, I agree with this Agent and I must insist you stand down. If we are to get to the truth of this terrible crime, we must preserve the evidence." Malachi looked like he was going to object, but then backed down.

"Of course, m'lord." Aries noted that Commander Villiers-Cavanaugh, Commissioner Tanaka, Denver, Clarice and even Captain Linsbury were in the crowd. All eyes were on him. It did not exactly make him feel comforted. His mind was still reeling with the possibility that the Priest-Keeper, deputy to the deceased Highpriestess-Keeper, might be the mysterious Malachi, that he might have had a direct hand in, or have critical information about the disappearance of Charles.

It was the Governor who spoke again and snapped his mind back to the present.

"So, Agent Aries," started the Governor, "as you seem to have taken control of this crime scene, what would you have us do?"

"I've ordered that the palace be sealed, if you could ensure that order is carried out? I believe the perpetrator may still be in the building. If you will approve I would request that an Agency forensics team be brought in immediately. I would also like to liaise with your security staff to review all the vid footage from tonight, to see if we can spot the killer in the crowds. After that I will need to begin carrying out interviews with all the staff and guests. That… uh… includes yourself and everyone else present here."

The Governor smiled. "Of course. But perhaps you may require some assistance? After all there are over a thousand guests and approximately the same number of staff."

"Yes. Yes. Captain Linsbury, could you assist me?" Linsbury nodded and stepped forward. *This situation is likely to spin out of control.* "Captain, with the permission of yourself and the Commander…" he glanced at Villiers-Cavanaugh, "I would like to bring in the entire SO-50 Investigations team to assist?"

Linsbury looked over at the Commander, who nodded. "Agreed." *Next I need to stop any kind of whitewash.*

"Good. Commissioner, in order to ensure we get to the bottom of this as quickly as possible, could I request you bring in detectives to work with our agents on the interviews?"

Commissioner Tanaka nodded and smiled. "Of course." Villiers-Cavanaugh's face went cold.

"Then I would like everyone out of this room until forensics have cleared it."

Governor Sagacious clapped his hands together. "You heard the Agent. Everyone out!" As the crowd started to leave, the Governor turned to Aries and quietly said, "Expertly done, Agent." Aloud, he said, "I suggest you start your interviews with myself and the other people in this room."

"Of course, m'lord."

It is going to be a long night.

*   *   *

Lovelace, like the rest of SO-50 Investigations, got the call to the Governor's Palace. He had just finished the call and was walking out of his flat when his comm rang again, though this time the identity of the caller was hidden and his comm told him it was coming in on an encrypted channel. He answered it. It was audio only.

"Truthsayer?"

"Yes?"

"It's Jehan. I have some information for you which I am sending through." After he had made the agreement with the merc, Lovelace had half expected — no hoped — that Jehan would not find anything.

"What have you got?"

"I dug up a few things that I knew you'd fucking love to know about those Chakka-loving toffs you are investigating."

"Go on." He knew the file was downloading, but he wanted to get Jehan to summarise it.

"I ain't your assistant, Truthsayer."

"Just tell me what you bloody found, Jehan."

"Fine. First up, Charles Hamilton-Jones has a little love nest in Lower Bricktown that he pays cash for and keeps a rotting secret from pretty much everyone, but especially his bitch of a wife."

"So how did you hear about it?"

"I have my sources, which I ain't about to share with you."

"Then just bloody get on with it."

"Him and Nigel were there a few days before Charles disappeared and Nigel took his swan dive."

"Interesting."

"There's more."

"Yes?" Lovelace could hear Jehan take a deep breath,

"I got you all of their medical files. They have all been enhanced about as much as you would imagine, nothing unusual. Nigel Massey de Sargon got several enhancements to his tackle. Corpse puppet! As if that would make a bloody difference? Your rich strumpet, Clarice Hamilton-Jones though, formerly Clarice de Varabonde, Samael's blade! She was interesting. She is from the fallen old minor pre-Civil War imperial house of Varabonde that lost all of its lands on Tiberia during the Civil War. They had the misfortune to be nobles in what became the Federate Combine. She fled with her family, but they lost almost everything. Guess they were not content with being poor, ordinary drudges like us. Clarice was their best bet to get back up to the level they were before the Civil War took it all away.

"She has enhanced central and peripheral nervous system, enhanced hearing and sight. All the usual shit. But here is where it gets interesting: she has pheromone emitters, vocal control including the ability to use subsonic and ultrasonics and, I shit-you-not, a poison gland and hollow incisors. The whore can bite you to death. Still, with a body like hers, it might be worth it and you'd love every bleeding minute of it. You see, the pheromone emitters allow her to mess with other people's heads something chronic.

"I got to say, she is kitted out like Albion's whore, a professional assassin. If she didn't kill you with her bite she could probably just break your neck. You don't want to know how I got hold of that information, but it weren't easy. She had the additional enhancements made in... ah yes... 2407, so... eighteen years ago. Just before she got involved with the Hamilton-Joneses"

Lovelace was silent as he considered the implications of what Jehan was telling him. "Wait. Hamilton-Joneses, as in bloody plural?"

Jehan continued, "Oh yes. I saved the best until last."

"Oh?"

"Yeah, it turns out that Charles Hamilton-Jones was not the first Hamilton-Jones Clarice banged."

"What?"

"Charles had an older brother, Simon Hamilton-Jones. About fifteen years ago he and Clarice were screw buddies and then all-of-a-sudden he disappeared completely off the grid and she moved on to banging Charles, who as far as I can tell controlled the money. I've scoured my contacts, but no one knows what happened to Simon. He fell off the face of the rotting Steel Alliance. You want my opinion? Poor sod's probably in a shallow grave somewhere."

"What else do you know about the older brother, Simon?"

"He was the soft, quiet and artistic type – apparently their mother, the ruling matriarch, felt he would never amount to anything and pretty much cut him off. He trained as a priest of Thoth, but for some reason dropped out. After that he became a painter and got some local attention, but frankly it's not to my taste. Too disturbing." The image of Jehan, perhaps the single hardest man Lovelace had ever met, as an art critic was strange. "When the matriarch died in 2410 there was a legal fight between Simon and Charles, which Charles eventually won. I figure Clarice decided to change-up, around the same time he disappeared."

"Thank you, Jehan."

"No thanks required, Truthsayer. Just remember our bargain."

"I do. I will be there."

"I know."

Jehan disconnected the call. Lovelace's mind was a-whirl with the deluge of new information. *Charles has a secret flat in Lower Bricktown, and a missing, probably dead brother called Simon. But the thing that shook him the most was that everything Jehan was saying seemed to confirm his worst fears about Clarice. She is extremely dangerous and is manipulating Aries. When she is done with him, she will most likely kill him, just like she did Charles and Simon.* A cold certainty descended on Lovelace. He had to stop her. *If John could think straight he would agree with me, but she has him under her spell.*

Isoke's cunt! I am going to have to stop her, and to do so I may have to fight my own partner. She is at the centre of all of this.

He checked the file Jehan had sent over. As promised it contained the details on the Lower Bricktown flat, all of their medical records as well, as the short file on Simon Hamilton-Jones. Lovelace slid his sword into the bike scabbard, and climbed on. A sense of cold certainty settled on him as he drove North out of Soho to a pick-up for the flight into East Hampstead.

I'm going to have to stop Clarice Hamilton-Jones to save my partner and solve this case. The only questions remaining were when and how?

*　　　*　　　*

It had been a long night, one of the longest in Aries' memory. The questioning of the guests and staff of the Governor's Ball was no small undertaking. There were thirty or so agents from SO-50 Investigations joined by another forty-ish from the London Metropolice.

When it had started John had quickly realised that leading the investigation was going to be a big job. Not to mention the possible awkwardness of having his boss, Captain Linsbury, answering to him for this stage of the investigation.

Interviewing the Governor himself had been a challenging experience. The Governor was so mild-mannered, so softly spoken that it was easy to forget how effortlessly he wielded power. The subtle administrator had a steel core. Aries had kept the interview short, because frankly, he did not think the Governor had committed the murder. He did not stand to gain, and in fact the death of the Highpriestess-Keeper hurt him. Besides, he had been out front in the Ball entertaining giving a live interview to Enigma WeaveNet News when the murder had taken place.

After four hours of juggling interviews, law enforcement personnel and trying to keep the high and mighty attendees of the Ball calm, Aries' nerves were beginning to fray. He had stepped out of his tenth… no eleventh interview for a coffee before he realised how tired he was.

He had requested two of the other SO-50 Agents carry out the interviews of Clarice, the Commander and the Commissioner. Each had strong alibis for their whereabouts during the murder. Clarice's alibi was going to be tricky if they decided to look into it further, but that was a worry for later.

Now he was sat in the staff canteen in the Palace hunched over a rapidly cooling cup of coffee.

"May I join you, Aries?"

He looked up, guiltily aware that he had been avoiding his next interview with whomever it was. Standing next to him was Captain Linsbury, also holding a cup of coffee. Aries smiled and indicated the seat next to him. Linsbury sat.

"Not an easy case to take on, this murder, is it?"

Aries shook his head. "No, not really."

"Then maybe next time you will exercise a little caution and won't rush to the front of the queue and take control?"

"Maybe."

"Can I make a suggestion?"

"Yes. Of course."

"Let me help. Hand the organising of the interviews over to me. You can still be the primary investigator on the case, if it is your career you are worried about. Though, in your case, your Agency career has never exactly been exactly stellar."

John frowned. "That would be... damn it, yes thanks. Your help would very much be appreciated." He paused, "Wait... I'm tired... what did you mean about my career?"

"You have not always been my favourite subordinate, but you have a personality type that indicates you should be. In your evaluations you score extremely high on command abilities, decisiveness, controlled aggression and self-motivation. Yet that has never been how you have acted during your time working for me. Your personality type is that of a leader, yet you hide from it. Natural, or shaped by your environment, I don't know. But command is in your blood."

Aries gave Linsbury a troubled look, the Captain continued.

"Actually that is not quite correct. It isn't command. It is a death wish."

"What?"

"I have seen that look on many Agents before you, Aries. You are far from the first. It is blindingly obvious to me that up until now your career in the Agency has been that of someone trying to keep a low profile, to hide from their past and from their own potential. It was almost like you were in suspended animation. Frankly, I'd been thinking of trying to get you transferred out. Your heart just wasn't in it. How you made the rank of G4, I'll never know. When I partnered Lovelace with you it was in the hope that he would shake you up. He is a hardened street cop and you needed that influence. I can also see that this Hamilton-Jones case has woken you. It is in your eyes, your posture and in the set of your face. You're hungry for it."

Linsbury was right, they had never really had a working relationship that 'clicked'. But this was the first time he had heard that he had been so close to being fired.

"I don't know what your background was before joining the Agency. Oh, I tried to find out, but you did a damn good job of burying it, but that doesn't matter. Something happened to you, something that broke you — or at least you thought it did. Up until this Hamilton-Jones case. Your problem now is that you have to make a decision: are you going to try to bury your head in the sand again and return to your sleepwalking state, or are you going to embrace the potential of this darkness in you — this death wish, and risk everything and throw yourself into solving the case — damning the consequences — and probably kill yourself along the way like you almost did when that arms dealer kidnapped you?"

"Those are my choices? Frankly, Captain, I do not like the sound of either one, much."

"No, those are not your only choices. There is a third option. You can take whatever was done to you that made you hate yourself so much and you can turn it into a positive. You can, as they say, seize the day. Of course maybe everything will blow up, but your previous Agency existence was just a slow form of death anyway. Maybe your past — or this investigation — kills you, maybe it doesn't. But you need to turn around and face whatever you're running from, if you are to move forward. You need to try to turn it into something positive. That will mean some difficult choices. But the important choices always are difficult, especially in a world as crazy as ours."

"Why are you telling me all this?"

"Partly because, despite my better nature, I like you John. I think you have the potential for a powerful good or a powerful evil. Partly because I am your boss and I want you to stop wasting your abilities. But mostly because I would hate to see you fail. And you will fail, John, if you do not pull yourself together."

"What about this new murder case? This murder of the Highpriestess-Keeper?"

"Tell me what you think, and leave nothing out."

"I think it is connected to the Hamilton-Jones disappearance and the suicide of Massey de Sargon." Aries lowered his voice to a whisper, "The whole of the Honourable Brotherhood, of which they were both members, are involved in something dark and nasty, something to do with the upcoming election of the new Governor. What exactly, I don't know. But I do know they are all dirty, up to their necks in whatever it is and it has been killing them off. One-by-one. My intuition screams it." He paused. "Even the Commander."

To his surprise Linsbury nodded. "Then do your job. Do as you were trained: follow the money, or in this case the power. Wherever it leads. I'll do what I can to help. But if it does lead to the Commander, you have to take the investigation all the way. Whatever the cost. Otherwise the same rich, pampered bastards will keep getting away with flouting the rule of law, and that just pisses me off."

Aries' head sagged and a sigh escaped him. Linsbury patted him on the back and stood. He was smiling.

"Don't worry old boy, that can of worms is for tomorrow. Right now we have a whole palace full of murder suspects to be interviewed."

John finished his cold coffee in one gulp and stood.

*   *   *

Aries was in the palace's security control room along with a commtech and a couple of junior agents from Investigations, looking at the vids taken during the evening. They had reviewed the footage immediately prior to, and following, the murder, but no one had entered the private temple until the servant who discovered the body, and even he was in the room for less than thirty seconds. There were over fifteen hundred cameras in the palace. They had then run an analysis of the vid footage from across the entire palace to try to identify a suspect moving towards the temple. The commtech had the program track every individual guest and staff member through their appearance on the cameras and the in-building sensor grid and use that information to plot their movements on to the palace's schematics.

The schematic and overlay were projected into the air in front of Aries. The palace was vast. Far vaster than Aries had initially guessed. It was a veritable warren, and that was just the sections he was being allowed to see, as he had no illusions that some areas were classified, even from him. Initially the picture was overwhelming and confusing, to say the least, as thousands of dots moved in seemingly random patterns through the palace. It was a storm of fast-moving dots. Aries had a thought. "Can you remove any of the suspects who remained in the ballroom or its adjoining areas the entire time?"

The commtech nodded and quickly almost half of the dots vanished. Aries looked at the schematic again. The kitchen area was almost diametrically opposed to the temple, so that was another good target for elimination. Again the commtech complied and roughly a third of the remaining dots vanished.

He looked in the bottom corner of the projection and saw that the total number of targets was hovering around three hundred or so.

"Alright, can you filter out targets who remained stationary the whole time and who can be positively identified by their ID tags as guards?"

Another hundred or so targets vanished. The remaining third of the palace showed dots in time-lapse rapidly moving in or out of the hundreds of rooms and corridors.

"Damn, that is still a lot of targets."

The commtech peered at his display on which was scrolling technical information about the scans. "I've found a problem. A mistake in the system."

"Yes?"

"One of the catering staff... his ID appears to have been instanced twice. Even weirder, the system did not automatically pick it up."

"Twice? Display his information and then show me the vids of both instances."

A second split-screen projection appeared in the air next to the first, with vid footage of two targets. A third projection displayed the staff member's personnel file.

"Scott Winfield, aged twenty-five, a member of the catering staff." Aries looked at his picture and then at the split-screen projection.

The target on the right, clearly Winfield, appeared to be a servant and was serving champagne to guests in the ballroom. The second target — on the left — also appeared to be a servant and was pushing a trolley through the corridors. But everything about the second vid footage raised Aries' hackles. The servant was never facing the cameras and in each of the segments of vid footage in which he appeared he was facing the other way. He was also shorter and darker haired. Aries felt his heart beat faster. This was a definite lead.

"Get me everything on this second person. That is our man. I want to see his face. Also find out from the footage who else saw him, and get that information to their interviewers. Someone will be able to provide a description. Also I want Scott Winfield brought in and questioned. I want to find out how he managed to get his ID cloned to the most high security event in London."

Who fits the profile of an inexperienced killer, but one who somehow knows how to avoid being identified on camera? You are not going to get away, whoever you are, and I bet someone else is pulling your strings.

"Agent Aries, I think we may have something."

"Show me." The commtech brought up a video shot. It was only a partial image, but is was enough for Aries to recognise the face. "Cassian Dexter! What in the name of the Overlord!" *That spineless fool assassinated the Highpriestess? But why? How?*

Aries' comm rang, he looked down but did not recognise the ID. He answered the comm.

"Agent Aries?"

"Yes, who is it?"

"This is Cassian Dexter." His voice was querulous. *Mr Dexter? Now that is a surprise.* "We need to talk."

"Yes we do. I am in the middle of a murder investigation." *I need to tease the information out of him, cannot let him know I've identified him as the killer yet.*

"I know. But we still need to meet, right now. You said you would help me."

"I know I did, but your timing is… unexpected. Why now?"

"Because it is only a matter of time before you discover that the person you are searching for is me. I did a terrible thing. I killed Highpriestess-Keeper Neteri and I need your help. There isn't much time.".

"Where and when?"

"Meet me on the Victory Bridge in thirty minutes. Come alone or you won't see me."

13

Steel Year 2425.10.07 (S-Time). Day Seven, Early morning

Aries found himself standing on the Victory Bridge that crossed the Thames canyon from Soho to the Rock. All around him the buildings towered high above. Leaning against the wall, he looked over the edge. Some hundred meters or so below him flowed the Thames river. Once a mighty thoroughfare for traffic and trade, it now existed in the gaps between hundreds of towers that formed a man-made canyon. As London had regrown from its almost complete destruction some two and a half thousand years ago, much of that growth had been upwards. The Thames canyon was the most literal representation of how far the ground level had risen.

Still, despite the Victory Bridge's location at the centre of the city, offering one of the handful of vehicle and pedestrian crossing points that spanned the canyon it was almost completely deserted at this time of night. Aries looked around. He could not see another soul in sight, though already visibility was dropping rapidly as a thick fog billowed up from the river below. Each lamppost provided a pool of light, and the buildings towering above provided a vista of twinkling lights, their windows turned to stars.

The scene gave the illusion of being eternal and unchanging, and for a moment, Aries could imagine the people who had stood almost exactly where he now stood over the twenty-four centuries before his birth. It was a spooky thought, and added to the general sense of melancholy he had felt since getting the call from Dexter. It had forced everything else from his mind.

His mind was whirling with theories and counter-theories as to why Dexter would have killed the Highpriestess-Keeper. It concerned him, but what concerned him even more was wondering why Dexter had contacted him. After their brief encounter earlier in the evening at the Ball he had hoped to crack him open later, but this… this was unexpected. *What does he want from me?*

Aries had come alone, near enough. Lovelace was parked in a nondescript car on the Soho side of the bridge, observing the location. Aside from his partner though, Aries had told nobody, not Linsbury, not Clarice and certainly not Commander Villiers-Cavanaugh.

Thinking of Lovelace brought a new concern to the fore. Lovelace had been surprisingly quiet when he had arrived at the palace, John would go so far as to say brooding. Something was weighing heavily on his mind, and the Pure was doing a poor job of disguising that. Aries was worried that whatever it was it might interfere with his ability to do the job, and at this moment he needed him focused. Things were coming to a head, John could feel it in every bone in his body.

"Tarus, do you hear me?"

"I hear you, John."

"Any sign of Dexter?"

"No, not so far. I'll let you know if I see him and I'll monitor your comms. Lovelace out."

Not exactly communicative this evening — no, morning now. In the short time they had been partners, John had not seen Lovelace be this taciturn. Taking a deep breath, Aries forced the thoughts from his mind and concentrated on the situation at hand.

He started as a delivery van rumbled by heading from the Rock to Soho on some early morning errand. The fog was getting thick now. Aries had not seen the van until it was almost on top of him.

You picked a good meeting spot, Dexter. Very hard to be spied on, almost no distractions. Would be the perfect place for a secret rendezvous. Or an assassination.

Feeling the cold lump in his stomach return, John scanned the bridge. *If you have come here to kill me Dexter, I will not go down without a fight.*

Out of the fog from the Rock end of the bridge emerged a figure. Wrapped in a heavy coat and wearing a hat pulled low to obscure his face the figure approached Aries. John felt his adrenaline kick in and his muscles begin to warm up in preparation for possible fight or flight. His palms itched. *Is this it? Is this where they decided to eliminate me?* His senses were keyed up for an attack, but the figure made no hostile moves as he slowly approached, and in fact at the last second turned to face the wall to look out over the canyon.

"You came. Good." Dexter sounded both surprised and relieved.

"What the hells is going on Dex—"

"No names." Aries nodded.

"Fine. My question still stands. What the bloody blade of Samael do you want?" He saw Dexter physically cringe at the his choice of language. *Yes, I suppose invoking the name of the Disciple of Vengeance might upset him.*

"You need my help, and I need yours."

"What can you offer me?"

"Don't you want to know what is going on? Don't you want to know why all these people — all my friends are dying? Why I had to kill the Highpriestess-Keeper? Don't you want to know what all the death is for?"

"You know I do. What do you want in exchange?"

"I want your protection, and I want a new life. I want to get away from all of this."

"You want the Agency's protection?"

Dexter laughed. It was a sour laugh.

"The Agency? No. Don't make me laugh. With them my death will be certain. No. I want your protection, Aurelian."

John felt his blood go cold. He disconnected his comm. He did not want Lovelace to hear any more.

"What did you call me?"

"Aurelian. I know who you are. It took some doing, but I pieced it together. I listen. People ignore me. I am just 'that silly Mr Dexter'. But I listen. I watch. They underestimate me. No matter what you think of me. I'm nobody's lackey."

"What does… that name… have to do with anything? Who else knows?"

"Not many people, just myself and two others. I know you can protect me. You can help me start a new life, to escape all this. If anyone can, you can. After all you did it for yourself. You know how to disappear, to vanish and to escape your fate. You can do that for me. That is what I want, and in return I will tell you everything."

Aries was torn. He wanted to know what Dexter could tell him, but that would risk putting him at odds with the entire Agency. There was also that name. If he knew, then others did too and that meant that he had been found. Sooner or later *they* would find him. He thought back to what Linsbury had said earlier. *I can run, I can die, or I can try and turn this into something greater.*

Without knowing when the change had happened, Aries realised he was done running. He nodded with firm decision.

"Deal. But if you cross me, I will kill you myself. I am going to take you somewhere safe now with my partner, Lovelace. Do not speak the name Aurelian again if you want my help."

*   *   *

Following the encounter on Victory Bridge, Aries had taken Cassian Dexter and Lovelace to the Rock. Having navigated the corridors of gangers, scavs, filth and urban decay they now stood in an airlock fashioned into the entranceway of an apartment in the bowels of Ground Zero. Despite having been to the Rock on many occasions Lovelace had not been to this place before. The smog had been so thick that they had all had to don breathers and now they stood in the cramped airlock while the air was purged and cycled.

Lovelace was edgy for many reasons, but right now two things concerned him. Firstly, why Aries had shut off his comm when Dexter had called him "Aurelian". Secondly, that he was standing next to the self-confessed killer of the Highpriestess-Keeper in the depths of the city and not having him locked up in an interrogation cell. *What the bloody hells is going on?* The whole thing had acquired a mental patina of a conspiracy, and he could feel himself being pulled deeper in.

Of course the irony was that while his partner was miring him in a conspiracy, Lovelace was in turn conspiring to stop his partner's girlfriend. With that realisation Lovelace forced himself to relax. *I need to learn what I can, if I am to act at the right moment.* With something this delicate he had to do it right. Aries was clearly bewitched by that woman, and Lovelace was his only chance of being rescued. *I only hope it hasn't affected his performance at his job. Isoke's balls! Who the bloody hells is 'Aurelian'. Is that who Aries really is? And if so, who is he? That's a bloody noble's name.* He looked at his partner anew with close interest. *Is that it? Is he — was he — a noble? If so, why the new identity. What did he run from? And is Clarice holding that over him as a weapon?*

His thoughts were brought to an abrupt halt as the airlock completed its cleansing and the inner door swung open revealing a vision of a warm space full of soft flowing fabrics, low lights and a thick smell of incense and spices. In contrast to the soft, inviting scene in front of him there sat the largest dog Lovelace had ever seen. *The thing's a monster, a bloody Hound of Baal!* Almost the size of a large pony, the dog sat and examined them, both relaxed and alert. Standing next to the beast, and dwarfed by its size, was a small woman — Lovelace guessed she was from the Couresaad culture by her tanned skin tone, slender build and deep blue eyes.

"Johnny! You brought me guests!" *She's talking to Aries!*

"Hi Kari, yes. I need a place to talk to Mr Cassian Dexter here." Aries indicated Dexter then nodded towards Lovelace, "And this is Lovelace, my partner." The woman, for despite her youthful appearance was not a girl, approached them and shook Dexter's hand and then stood in front of Lovelace and gazed up at him. She was at least half a metre shorter than him, and probably less than half his weight, yet her gaze was penetrating and Lovelace almost found himself stepping back. Eventually she reached out her hand and Lovelace took it gently, afraid he might crush it, and shook.

"Lovelace, eh? That's not a Pure name. What is your real name?"

"Tarus Arken Karazhja."

"Warrior caste Truthsayer, eh? Good to meet you Tarus." She indicated towards the dog, "This is Zeke. They can come in Zeke." Turning, she skipped off into the room, and gingerly, Aries, Dexter and Lovelace followed.

They made themselves comfortable on low cushions. Kari brought over a tray of spiced coffee and cakes.

"Kari, I need you to hide Mr Dexter here for a few days, is that ok?" Dexter seemed on edge, and started on hearing his name mentioned.

"Sure. What's he done?" Dexter's eyes went wide.

"You will hear in a minute. Relax, Dexter, Kari can help you. Trust me." Dexter's head bobbed twice in quick succession in agreement. "Good. Right, now you can tell me everything."

"Right… I… what do you want to know?"

"I want to know why you killed the Highpriestess."

"I had to! He told me I had to if I was to survive."

"Who?"

"Malachi. After the the Hunt began killing everyone I turned to him for help. But he was lying, it was all damned lies!"

"The Hunt? Ok Dexter, start from the beginning. I want to know what Charles Hamilton-Jones and the Honourable Brotherhood were up to."

"Charles? It was all his bloody idea! Ok… ok… where to begin? I don't know everything, but I will tell you what I do know. It started as a heated discussion at one of the dinners I organised. Well, it was more of an argument. About the future of the Steel Alliance. That in itself was normal, they always discussed politics and power and the stupid little games they played, but this time was different."

"What was different?"

"Kenton — Kenton Serrano — was there and he was in a rage. James Villiers-Cavanaugh, his boss — your boss — had just learned from his sources that Governor Sagacious was going to step down, but that he wanted to put Commissioner Tanaka in his place. Villiers-Cavanaugh had been driven into a psychotic rage by the news. As far as I could tell he had always assumed he would be a shoo-in for the Governorship. He had been betrayed, and despite a meeting which Kenton described as 'traumatic' the best he could convince the Governor to do was to enact a formal election using the old, pre-Civil War rules. You see, no one had revised the laws since the election as frankly there had been more important things to deal with, like reconstruction, and Sagacious has been Governor in the whole period ever since ruling via the act of martial law, which had never been rescinded."

"How does this link to Charles Hamilton-Jones."

"Well Charles, who was long on pomp and circumstance, but short on actually ever doing anything — he was considered the puppet of his wife — exploded with rage. He went on and on about how that 'stupid bitch' Commissioner Tanaka could not be allowed to become Governor. She was everything the Honourable Brotherhood hated. Powerful, self-made, popular and a keen political player. But as far as he was concerned her worst failing was that she was best friends with his wife, Clarice. I seem to recall him shouting something about how 'this was too far, he could not let her have it.' That kind of thing."

"When was this?"

"About four months ago."

"Carry on."

"Anyway, he and Nigel swore they would not let that happen. The others agreed with him — especially Kenton and Benham Arends. Others at the table, Julius, Brentan and myself, were fairly quiet. The problem was, what were they going to do? Charles admitted it himself, that his wife controlled the purse strings, and if they directly attacked Tanaka it would quickly be traced back to them, as friends of Sir James Villiers-Cavanaugh. Kenton, who was Sir James' Chief of Staff for his election campaign, urged caution. He was all in favour of stopping Tanaka, but they needed to find a subtle way to do it. It was then that Jean – Jean Thervessons – said that it was a shame that she — Tanaka — could not be struck down by divine vengeance. Charles went very quiet and pale at that. He quickly excused himself and after that the conversation went on to other subjects."

"And?"

"Well at our next dinner a month later, Charles announced that he had an idea. He knew of a way we could strike down Tanaka and everyone who worked with her and keep our hands completely clean. He swore everyone to secrecy. He said he knew how to call in the divine vengeance of Samael on her. He said he knew how to learn of a ritual that would invoke something called the 'Wyld Hunt' to destroy her and anything that stood between it and her. Well, we all laughed.

It was ridiculous. Except for Jean. Jean said calmly that it could be done, if the correct ritual could be found, that such a ritual had been used in the past. He had been experimenting with the occult. Jean explained that he had read up on the Wyld Hunt before, that it was known to be an aspect of Samael, Disciple of Vengeance, and that the Wyld Hunt was summoned in times of need and that the summoner became an avatar of the Wyld Hunt through the ritual and then would be able to direct it to destroy targets of the avatar's choice. Problem was that the copies of the rituals needed were all believed to have been lost."

"I see, carry on."

"Well, Charles said that he knew where to get hold of the ritual. He would not say where it was from, just that he was certain of its source, but that he would need certain extremely rare materials that could not be acquired by conventional means. This was when Malachi's name first came up. You see, Kenton Serrano had recently met with Malachi on behalf of Sir James. If the old rules were to be followed in the election then there would be four colleges that would vote to determine the new Governor. The first was the eligible electorate of the worlds of the Governor's dominion: Earth, Venus, Ravenna etc. Second was the corporate vote, third was the vote from the Council of Terra made up of the planetary Governors, and last was the vote from the Temple of the Overlord. Malachi was going to be key for that. The Highpriestess-Keeper was a close ally of Sagacious, but was undecided on the election — at least she was then — and Sir James needed her vote, and the best way to do that was via her deputy, Priest-Keeper Malachi. He was an Honourable Brother too, like the rest of us, but from Corballo."

Lovelace's mind was a-whirl with the politics and conspiracies. He realised he had, up until this point, had no idea how the new Governor was to be elected. That all of this could be tied to an election campaign stunned him with its arrogance and insanity.

"Kenton said we could approach him, if we did it right. Charles, Nigel, Jean and that psychopathic bastard Benham were all for it. Julius and Brentan were against it. Arkell and I stayed quiet and they took that as tacit agreement. Benham and Julius had a huge row about it. They were old friends but I had never seen them disagree about anything, until this. Julius said that they risked heresy, Benham called him a coward."

"So what happened?"

"Charles and his cronies went to go and get this ritual and then work on Malachi. Convince him to help them stop Tanaka. I thought it was never going to happen, but then at the last dinner, that was eleven days ago, Charles was full of energy and excitement. He said they had what they needed to do it, and he had acquired a place for them to carry out the ritual in secret. Julius was scornful, he said he did not believe them, that there was no power in the occult at all and I remember Charles got really angry. It was Nigel who suggested that perhaps some kind of test was in order. After all this was new territory for them all. He invited Julius to join them for a test of their abilities. Apparently Jean had uncovered a related, but lesser, ritual that would act as a 'trial run' for them, as it were. What cinched the deal for Julius was that Charles said that Sir James would be there, as would Malachi. You see, Julius had been recently investigated by the Agency and was looking at a potential full fraud investigation. The chance to meet Sir James in person was too good not to miss. Julius was always networking. Benham couldn't make it along, and frankly I was not even asked. Arkell, Kenton and Brentan had other matters to attend to, not sure what, but they were not going to go."

"And?"

"We all got the call the next day, it worked! The target had died in circumstances that could not be linked back to us."

"Who was the target?"

"I don't know for sure. They never told me. But now, now I think the target was actually Julius, poor bastard. Now they were going to do the final ritual, but they needed all of us. Apparently it required a certain number of people to invoke the Wyld Hunt. The potential power — it was exciting! So Kenton, Brentan, Benham, Arkell and myself were picked up by Charles, Nigel and Jean and taken to a secret location and when we got there it was all set up. Sir James and Malachi were not there, and neither was Julius. They told us that Julius had said he had not wanted to take part, and they had respected his decision. I only later found out, from you, that he was dead."

"Where was this?"

"Like I said it was a secret location, I had to wear a blindfold to prevent any Echo metapsion being able to use me in the future to identify it. We drove around in circles and random patterns for hours, but while I was there I heard the bells of some temple ringing. They made us deactivate our medical bio-status units," *Just like Nigel Massey de Sargon,* "and we had to leave all our comms before we went with them. It was all to stop us being tracked or, like I said, some Echo metapsion finding out where we went in the future."

"So what happened? Something went wrong. What was it?"

"I don't know. We carried out the ritual as we were told to. Charles had some ancient tome where he had acquired the ritual from. How he got hold of it, I still don't know. The ritual, it worked. At least it appeared to. This terrible darkness formed in the centre of the circle and a voice sounded in my head. The voice was like nothing I have ever encountered. It was the voice of all my fears. It said, 'Your sacrifice is accepted. Give me Charles.'"

Lovelace unconsciously shivered. Aries, however, appeared more sceptical — As he was every time religion and the supernatural were discussed. *He doesn't believe. Still at least he is keeping that to himself and letting Dexter talk.*

"Then something happened. The darkness grew rapidly, it filled the space then broke through. It lashed around, but when it hit Charles, it was like it hit a solid wall and it recoiled. Charles went crazy and tore some necklace he was wearing off, it was bright red with heat. He ran, we all ran. But before I got away I saw it surround Brentan. We... we all heard his screams. It peeled him and tore him apart. It was the most horrible thing I have ever seen. I turned and ran. When I reached the outside I realised I was right, it was definitely Whitetemple somewhere but I don't know that area well. I did not stop running until I found a cab. The next thing I heard was that Nigel was dead, Charles was missing and I panicked. I tried to tell you that first time we met. That was why I gave you the list, Aries. I was trying to tell you, but Sir James stopped me. He told me to say nothing to you about the whole affair. He said he would protect me, and I believed him then."

"So what happened?"

"The voices. Ever since the ritual I have heard the terrible voice of that thing in my head. It never stops. I can feel it closing on me. It wants Charles. I thought I had gone mad, it seemed like a terrible nightmare, but then when Benham and Jean died I realised it was real and Sir James could not protect me. I panicked. I could feeling it getting closer all the time, so I went to see Malachi. He told me that if I was to save myself I had to kill the avatar of the Wyld Hunt, that somehow the ritual had been perverted and we had become the targets of it. Until the avatar was stopped the Wyld hunt would continue to destroy us one by one until we were all dead. The trouble was, that I had no idea who the avatar was. But he gave me a necklace. I recognised it — it was like the one Charles had been wearing at the ritual. Malachi told me that it would help me see through the illusions and see the true form of the avatar, that I would be able to see the darkness surrounding them. When I saw that person I would have to kill them to stop it. Malachi told me that it was required. That I had to do it if I was to seek forgiveness from the Overlord. I was wearing it at the Ball when I saw the Highpriestess-Keeper. It was her! At least I believed it was. I had to act, and so I killed her. But then I realised it was all a lie."

"How?"

"The voice of the Hunt. It did not stop. Malachi just used me to kill the Highpriestess-Keeper. He used me, Charles used me, they all bloody used me. That is when I decided to find you. You are the only person who has told me the truth from the beginning, and the only person who can help. But even if you can't help, and the Hunt does get me I refuse to go quietly. That is why I am telling you all of this."

Dexter looked physically exhausted by his confession. He was pale and wan. Aries sat back and ran his hands through his hair. Lovelace let out a low whistle.

14

Steel Year 2425.10.07 (S-Time). Day Seven, Morning.

Their interview with Cassian Dexter had given them a huge amount to think about, so much information it almost overwhelmed Aries. They had left Dexter working with Kari to try to work out exactly where the ritual had taken place in Whitetemple. He also realised he had not made a decision about whether to honour the deal he had made with Dexter or not, so until he had, he was going to keep him holed up with Kari. At the very least he did not want the Commander getting hold of him. Still, Aries was not exactly comfortable letting Dexter use the network he had built up in his escape from Metropolis. It was, after all, still his escape route should everything fall apart here in London.

Regardless, Aries realised that they had to push forward with solving the case now, more than ever. Lovelace had received a lead on Charles Hamilton-Jones' secret flat in Lower Bricktown, so after double checking that Dexter was safely stashed away at Kari's, they left to follow that tip. Given that he also now knew who killed the Highpriestess-Keeper he decided to leave the murder investigation at the palace to others for a bit. He sent Linsbury a message letting him know he was out and about chasing down leads. In the back of his mind he knew he would need to come up with some kind of resolution to the murder, but not quite yet.

On the drive to Lower Bricktown Lovelace, who was driving, had been strangely quiet and Aries was concerned. *We learned so much from Dexter, it really is a lot to take in.* He attempted to make conversation.

"How did you find out about the flat?"

"You don't bloody want to know."

"Did you find out anything else?"

"No." Aries picked up on the stress in his voice. *There is something he is not telling me. He is probably just trying to work something out in his head before presenting it to me.* Aries let the subject drop and instead checked the ammunition in his carbine.

Upper Bricktown, to the North, and Lower Bricktown, its Southern neighbour, were the neighbourhoods where all the refugees and immigrants from other places in the Steel Alliance came to when they could not afford to go anywhere else. It was a tightly-packed melting pot of cultures, races, languages and, frequently, violence.

The Metropolice in the sector were renowned for essentially being riot police with their main role to keep whatever happened in the Bricktowns in the Bricktowns.

The irony was, that within Bricktown, Upper Bricktown was considered the gentrified area — where many immigrants moved when they had 'made it'. This brought tensions between the 'haves' and 'have nots' which was insane given that in the greater scheme of things there were no 'haves' here at all.

Lower Bricktown was primarily made up of tightly packed brick tenements, known as 'rookeries', usually around fifteen stories high with up to ten people sharing a single room. Conditions were cramped and unhygienic and the area suffered from frequent bouts of dysentery and cholera, both of which were easily treatable if you were part of the system. Most people here were not. They sneaked in on cargo shuttles, the transnaught or through the city gates strapped to trucks and vans.

The road they drove down was punched through a series of blocks – literally punched – as the road builders had decided a long time ago that what London really needed was an express-way to the Wall through Lower Bricktown. That meant that it was primarily a tunnel, with brief glimpses of the streets below as it exited one building before plunging into the next. Lower Bricktown barely had a level that classed as Downtown, with most of it firmly in Ground Zero. This, and the easy access to the tunnel from the buildings, many of which had doors that opened directly on to it, meant that the tunnel was used by heavily-armoured convoys and that was about it. The streets were strewn with empty packaging material, fuel drums on fire, and other detritus of humanity. If the convoys did not roar down here every other day, Aries suspected that the road would become just one more long tenement.

They had decided to make the drive in an armoured car, more of a big-wheeled armoured personnel carrier, than a typical road vehicle. Around them they felt the eyes watching them all the way until their turn off.

The off-ramp brought them down into the maze of small streets within Lower Bricktown. Aries glanced up and saw the huge Citadel of the Sun towering abandoned and forbidding over them. Despite its name, the Citadel was a dark, soul-crushing spire that loomed oppressively overhead. It reflected the mood well. Everything about Lower Bricktown was grim. There were none of the Souk's colourful markets to the North, just buildings simmering with resentment and primed to explode at any point. The whole area was a powder keg.

Aries was wearing tactical armour under his greatcoat, as was Lovelace. In the back of the car they had a squad of similarly armoured agents commanded by Sergeant Tynes. The armour gave them all a bulky appearance, but it could not be helped. It was not how Aries liked to operate, but frankly he did not want to take any chances.

Lovelace brought the car to a stop outside their destination.

Aries looked up at it. The whole building was unremarkable. Nothing marked it out as different from its neighbours at first glance, but as he considered it a few unique features did emerge. There were security cameras cunningly placed, the doors were all reinforced and all the windows on the lower floors appeared to have been bricked in. The brick work itself was curiously absent of gang graffiti.

When Lovelace turned off the engine the silence was oppressive. Aries turned to Lovelace and the team, "Alright, gentlemen, let us keep this clear and clean. Lower Bricktown may be a free-fire zone, but do not open fire unless you are attacked first and for Overlord's sake check your targets. We do not want to start a riot. No one who lives here needs that kind of trouble, so let us not give it to them. Understood?"

Lovelace nodded and the team voiced their agreement. *All of them are tense, Isoke, I'm tense too. This place, it is not good. Not good at all.*

"Let's do this."

They opened the doors and climbed out. Everyone's eyes were peeled and scanning the buildings around them. Despite thousands of people living within a stone's throw, the streets were completely deserted. Just the mournful sounds of a police siren in the distance and the cawing of a murder of crows kept them company. Aries indicated Lovelace to take point and the team moved out in a lightly-dispersed pattern.

This does not look like the love nest Lovelace described it as. It was pretty much as far from a love nest as it was possible to be. *It looks more like an abandoned meat packing factory.*

They reached the front door to the building. A heavy mechanical lock sealed it and Lovelace pulled out the key they had recovered from Chas Varn and tried it. The door unlocked and swung open. The team cautiously entered, with the last member closing and locking the door behind them.

The building inside appeared to be derelict. They moved through room after room filled with nothing but the detritus of former residents, but it was clear that no one had lived in most of the building for quite some time. Rats scurried out of their way and they had to clear thick spider webs from their path. Their torches picked up the motes of dust in the air. They circled around before heading up to the next floor. After almost an hour of carefully searching the building they reached the top floor. At the top of the stairs was an armoured door, with a code lock.

"Breach it."

Sergeant Tynes moved up and pulled a multi-launcher loaded with breaching rounds. He aimed at the door's hinged edge and fired three times, from top to bottom, blowing big holes in the door. A second tactical agent moved up with a small ram and smashed the door down, while a third provided cover with a riot shield.

With the door down they moved in quickly. It took only moments to secure the apartment.

"Sir," said Tynes, "you and Agent Lovelace will want to see this room."

Aries and Lovelace moved through the flat to the room Tynes was in. The room had been cleared as a ritual space, with a large circle inscribed with chalk on the floor. Aries had flashbacks to Thervessons' flat. *It seems Mr Dexter was telling us the truth.* Aries was not sure whether he was relieved or not, though. Part of him – a big part – had hoped that everything Dexter had told them had been a lie. The circle was surrounded by hundreds of painstakingly drawn sigils. A table had been placed in the centre as a crude altar of sorts. Leather straps dangled from the four corners. The table itself was stained with dark brown blood stains. As they approached, a swarm of flies took off and buzzed around the room.

Aries could not shake the nagging sensation of familiarity that this place gave him, just as Thervessons' had.

Lovelace turned to Aries, "You reckon this is where Hamilton-Jones and Massey de Sargon killed Julius Rato, like Dexter said?"

"It seems likely, though we should get this altar to forensics to carry out a DNA test to confirm."

What caught Aries' eye though, was that to the side of the circle was a book case. It was packed with physical, hardback books and sagged under their weight. The books had titles in numerous languages. He spotted titles in Extasia, Zani, Couresaad, and several other languages, as well as scripts that he did not recognise on the oldest books. They all appeared to cover various occult and mathematical subjects. There was a comm, which when he turned it on displayed a complex mathematical-occult tome written in Jensian. However what focused his attention was that there was a gap. A gap for a large tome. The dust around it showed that it had been there, but when he looked around the room he could not spot it.

"Sergeant?"

"Sir?"

"I want your men to check every corner of this flat. We are looking for a book about 'yay' big."

"Yes, sir. You heard the Agent, find it." The agents dispersed and began a thorough search of the flat.

Lovelace turned to Aries, "You don't expect to find it do you?"

"Not here. My intuition tells me it was taken somewhere else — most likely the location in Whitetemple that they took Dexter to."

"Do you think it is 'The Book' that Massey de Sargon jabbered on about before his death?"

"I think that is a distinct possibility. Lovelace, you have more experience with these things than me, what do you think they were doing here? Was Dexter telling us the truth?"

"He was. It is a summoning circle."

"Really? You can be that specific?"

"Yes. I did some digging around after our encounter with Thervessons. Where his circle was designed to keep something out, this is designed to pull something in."

"The Wyld Hunt?"

"I don't bloody know! But look at the lines, the markings, they all flow inward towards the circle. The sacrifice of poor old Julius Rato, that was the focus of what went on here."

"It is difficult to tell, but from what Dexter told us this place was last used a couple of days before Charles disappeared. So… nine days ago. Does that seem correct to you?"

Lovelace walked over to the altar, bent forward and sniffed the congealed and hardened blood.

"Yes."

"Why did they not carry out the main ritual here? Why somewhere in Whitetemple?"

"Your Charles Hamilton-Jones seemed pretty paranoid, probably worried they would work out what happened to Rato here. Also maybe he wanted somewhere more disposable, after all it looks like he's been bloody using this place for a while."

"True. But of course, that still does not answer the question of why they killed Rato at all. He was one of them, and with their resources, if they needed someone to murder it would not have been that hard for them to grab someone off the streets. Sure he was not keen on the plan, but it is a big step from having a heated discussion to deciding to kill him. There must have been some specific reason for killing Rato."

"I don't know. They all seem pretty bloody psychopathic to me. They'd probably kill people for less. But, thinking about it, it might be because they *did* know the poor bastard."

"What do you mean?"

"A sacrifice is meaningless unless it is a genuine sacrifice. Killing some random bloke would not have been a real sacrifice, just a thrill kill, and wouldn't have bloody counted as such. Whereas killing Rato, that was a real sacrifice. People were going to come looking for him, after all he lived in Isoke-loving Zen with a sentient AI. He would be missed and it placed them in real bloody jeopardy. For the first time in their lives. Maybe they needed that for the ritual to work."

Aries nodded. "Of course there might be more to it than that. Julius Rato wanted out and they felt he was not committed enough. If he reported them, all this would bring serious charges of heresy at the least, if caught, and probably much worse."

"True. Isoke's balls! And to think I almost felt sorry for Massey de Sargon. The lug nut got what he deserved."

"Let's collect up everything – especially these books, image this room and get the hells out of here."

"Agreed."

Sergeant Tynes returned to the room. "Sir, we found this comm." He handed it to Aries who turned it on. It was an easily-available, low-end comm of the type owned by millions of drudges and corporate wage slaves. Checking the owner details, he found it it was registered to Charles Ulialias Nuan.

"Charles Ulialias Nuan. A second identity for Charles? That last name, where have I heard it before?"

The name was agonisingly familiar, but he just could not place it. But a quick check on his own comm revealed the name, "Simon Ulialias Nuan." Aries looked at the name, and the name clicked in his mind. "Simon Ulialias Nuan was the painter of the piece in Nigel Massey de Sargon's office. Now why would Charles create himself a second identity with the same last name as a famously reclusive painter? What else is on this damnable thing?"

Lovelace was silent, his brows furrowed as Aries searched the comm. "This comm seems set up to monitor and control payments to

Hampstead Asylum. Why would Charles be making payments to the Asylum under a false name?"

Lovelace head snapped up as realisation struck. "Simon Ulialias Nuan. Simon Hamilton-Jones. Bloody Samael's blade!"

"What are you talking about?"

"Charles had… has an older brother called Simon. He disappeared fourteen years ago. I thought he was dead, but what if Charles had him committed to the Asylum?"

"When did you find this out?"

"Earlier."

"And you did not thing to bloody tell me?"

"You were busy at the Governor's palace screwing Charles Hamilton-Jones' wife."

"What?"

"You heard me. Her scent is all over you. You didn't make much of a bloody secret of it."

Aries looked over at Tynes who was quietly watching them both.

"We will talk about that later. But why did you not tell me about Simon?"

"I thought he was bloody dead. Didn't seem to bloody matter at the time."

"Overlord save me, Lovelace! It matters! What else did you find out about him?"

"After his and Charles' mum died they got into a legal battle and then one day Simon disappeared. Guy was troubled, trained to be a priest of Thoth, then took up art. Everyone assumed he had gone somewhere quiet and committed suicide, or else left London for climes unknown. Oh and he was your girlfriend's squeeze before Charles."

"She's not my girlfriend."

"That's not what it looks like. Your cock is ballsing up this entire investigation."

"We will talk about this later."

"Yeah, right, whatever." Lovelace was visibly fuming. Aries was similarly angry, but now was not the time to thrash this out.

"I need to go and see this Simon Ulialias Nuan. If he is in Hampstead Asylum that might explain his reclusiveness."

*   *   *

Aries and Lovelace walked out of Charles Hamilton-Jones' secret flat. Their tactical team had almost finished loading the car up with evidence.

Out of nowhere, there was a roar of engines overhead and two grav planes rose up from behind the surrounding buildings. Their searchlights switched on, blinding Aries and Lovelace. Loud speakers blared.

"AGENT ARIES. AGENT LOVELACE. STAY WHERE YOU ARE. THIS IS THE AGENCY."

Aries looked over at Lovelace then over at Sergeant Tynes. John indicated to Tynes to finish loading the car with the evidence.

One of the two grav planes landed in a cloud of stinking water, the rear ramp slammed down and two black-suited men and at least ten heavily armed Agency Marshals rapidly exited and made their way over to Aries and Lovelace.

"Sir?" asked Tynes. The sergeant looked unsure.

"Sergeant. Get your men in the car and get the evidence out of here. I want you to keep it safe until I see you next. Do not hand it over to anyone except Lovelace or myself. Now go!"

Tynes nodded, climbed into the car with his men and drove off back into town. The approaching Marshals spread out in a loose horseshoe around Aries and Lovelace, their guns held ready, if not actually pointed at them.

The two black-suited agents approached. One was bald and the other had a crew-cut. They both had a severe look to them. Before they even showed their badges both Aries and Lovelace knew they were from Shield, the security and internal affairs division of the Agency. It was the crew-cut Shield Agent who spoke first.

"Agents Aries and Lovelace. You are to come with us. The Commander wants to see you." *No names, typical Shield.*

Aries nodded. "Of course. Nice of him to send us an escort."

"I will need you to hand over your weapons." After their fight in the secret flat, Lovelace was tensed like he would welcome a fight.

"Why, are we under arrest?"

"Not at this time." *But you would like us to be, wouldn't you?*

"In which case, no. I think we will hang on to them."

Lovelace added, "Unless you would like to try and take them from us?" Lovelace's hand was on the butt of his holster. Aries smiled. He found himself itching for a fight, to personalise the nebulous enemy they had been fighting. *I reckon our chances are good. There are twelve of them, but I'm an Echo and Lovelace is very dangerous.*

The Shield Agent's eyes narrowed, but he made no move to enact his refused command. It was his companion, the bald headed agent, who spoke next. "That won't be necessary. Who was in the car that just left?"

"A tactical team that came with us to this location. I sent them back to base. Why? Is that a problem, Agent…? Oh I'm sorry I did not catch your name. Or Rank."

The bald Shield Agent did not reply, but Aries saw his jaw clench. *Shield Agents are such a bunch of jumped up little fascists.* The first Shield Agent indicated with a sweep of his hand that they should enter the grav plane. As they walked towards it, Aries could not help but notice that the Marshals followed both his and Lovelace's movements closely.

It is almost as if they did not expect us to come quietly.

As they climbed into the grav plane, Aries turned to Lovelace and quietly said, "Well, this should be interesting."

"Aye. Looks like someone wants to give our balls a roasting."

Aries nodded and then settled back into the seat. He turned to the Shield Agent who sat next to him. "Be a good man and wake me when we get there?" and closed his eyes before the Agent had time to respond. He heard Lovelace snort with laughter.

*   *   *

Aries and Lovelace had been escorted to the top of Central in no uncertain terms. At every stage of their journey through the London headquarters of the Agency they had been surrounded by Marshals flanked by their two Shield escorts.

John had been surprised that since the initial confrontation they had made no move to try and disarm either himself of Lovelace. Aside from that fact everything else could easily have been mistaken for a formal arrest of the two of them. Now they rode the final lift up to Commander Villiers-Cavanaugh's office in silence. Lovelace looked around and gave the tactical agents a broad smile, taking care to bare the maximum amount of teeth. Lovelace stretched, his own armour creaking, and rolled his head, producing a series of loud cracks from his neck which sounded excessively loud in the packed lift.

Lovelace is just letting me know in his own way that he has my back and is not worried. Good. This could get nasty.

Finally, after a seeming eternity, the lift came to a halt and the doors opened, bathing the lift in light. They had emerged into the

Commander's offices in Zen and the sun shone brightly outside the glass walls of the pyramid that sat on top of the tower of Central.

Aries and Lovelace were escorted out of the lift by the two Shield agents, but the Marshals remained in the lift. *The Commander probably does not want them tramping their filthy boots into his office.* He looked down at his own mud-encrusted boots and smiled. Lifting his gaze up again, he looked around and considered the location they found themselves in. The rapid shift from the depths of a free-fire zone in Downtown/Ground Zero of Lower Bricktown to the splendour of the London Agency Commander's office in Zen could not have been more striking. They may have well been uplifted to the Overlord's own empty palace on the second moon of Troy.

They were led towards a pair of large golden doors engraved with a scene of the Overlord liberating London. To the door's right was a golden statue of Albion, sword upraised, and to the left the Tattooed Man holding a shield. The doors swung open and they entered.

Inside, sat behind a vast black desk, sat Sir James Villiers-Cavanaugh. Behind him, framing him, rose a pair of pillars. From the top of each hung a long banner with the colours of the Agency. Between the two columns hanging from the glass was a large eight-pointed golden star of the Overlord. Glancing around, Aries saw that the walls were covered with artwork, medals and various relics. A holographic representation of the Steel Alliance worlds were projected in one corner, with the Accord's worlds, the realm of the Agency's jurisdiction, a narrow strip along the middle between the mighty Federate Combine and Imperial Commonwealth of Elysia.

This place is more throne room than office. It appears as if our good Commander thinks very highly of himself.

They came to a halt in front of the massive desk. There were no chairs, so they were forced to remain standing. With the slightest of movements of his right hand, Villiers-Cavanaugh dismissed the two Shield Agents and they retreated silently the way they had come. *No unnecessary witnesses? Worried what we might say in front of your cronies?* Sir James studiously ignored them for quite some time. Instead, his focus appeared to be on a heavy book on his desk. Aries tried to make out the title, *'The Writings of the Akonites'*. The act was a sham, and everyone in the room knew it. Aries could see the veins at Villiers-Cavanaugh's temples pulsing.

I — we — know all about your dirty sordid schemes.

This charade went on for a good couple of minutes and would have perhaps gone on longer if Lovelace had not noisily cleared his throat.

Sir James looked up and fixed his hawkish gaze on them. *Is it just me, or is his Echo tattoo glowing?* Aries closed his eyes and focused his perception on the energies of the Wyld. There was a definite pattern of ripples emanating from the Commander. *What have you been using your abilities for, Villiers-Cavanaugh? In fact, I wonder what your abilities are?*

"Agent Aries, Agent Lovelace, good of you to join me on such short notice."

Aries smiled. "Not at all Commander, thank you for sending us an escort."

"Indeed. As I mentioned last time we met, Agent Aries, I have been very disappointed in your lack of communication concerning the Charles Hamilton-Jones disappearance case, and now it seems also on the murder of Highpriestess-Keeper Nebhotep Neteri. Very disappointed indeed, and so I felt it appropriate for us to discuss the cases now and your career in the Agency. Without interruptions." *Not a fan of Clarice, are you, Sir James?*

"As you wish. Sir." Sir James smiled. It was not a nice smile.

"Agent Aries, I do not appreciate your constant hounding of my friends, and your insinuations against them."

"I can imagine."

"No, I don't think you can, Aries. You see, you have caused a lot of problems for me, and London. I believe the fatalities of Jean Thervessons, Benham Arends and now Arkell Isadore are directly attributable to your investigation and could have been avoided if you had proceeded in a more professional way."

Arkell Isadore is dead? How? I heard nothing of this. That leaves only Kenton Serrano alive from the ritual. No wonder the Commander is so enraged.

Lovelace placed his hand in front of his mouth as if to cough and muttered, "Bollocks!" Aries smiled. Sir James' reaction was anything but amused. His face went very pale, his jaw muscles clenched and the pulsing veins on his temple went into overdrive. He abruptly stood up.

"What did you say, Agent Lovelace?"

"Nothing. Sir. Just a cough."

Villiers-Cavanaugh's eyes narrowed and he rested his fists on the desk top and leaned forward.

"Agent Lovelace. The Agency gave you a second chance because we felt you had potential. Were we wrong to help you? Because if you like I CAN SEND YOU BACK TO THE PIT WE FOUND YOU

IN?!" The last part was delivered as a shout. "You see this star on my face? It means I can destroy you with a thought. I can crush you like a fucking bug! Do not challenge me, Agent. I do not tolerate insubordination. Ever."

Aries heard a low growl start in Lovelace's chest. He reached out his right arm and put it on Lovelace's shoulder. The Pure's head snapped round and John saw how barely in control his partner was.

Aries asked, "What do you want, Commander?"

Sir James turned his attention to Aries.

"Agent Aries, I suggest you reign in your partner before he does something he will not live long enough to regret. As for you, I am giving you formal warning to stay away from the Honourable Brotherhood. Your harassment of them has gone far enough and has cost the lives of several people already. I am ordering you off the Charles Hamilton-Jones case. Linsbury can assign some other agents to solving it. As for the murder of the Highpriestess-Keeper, I would throw you off that too, but the Governor, for his own reasons, feels you are the correct agent to be heading the case. I expect to be informed about every movement you make, every lead you find, every theory you come up with. Everything. Do you understand me?"

"You are taking me off the Hamilton-Jones case? You can not do that!"

"Yes I can. You are off the case, or are you disobeying a direct order, Agent?"

Oh you are just hoping I say yes, aren't you?

"I understand. Commander."

"Good. Do not think you can disobey me, Aries. Now you two can get out of my office, Kali take your souls!" With that, Sir James sat, the two agents dismissed.

15

Steel Year 2425.10.07 (S-Time). Day Seven, Evening.

Lovelace rode his bike like a furious angel, screaming through the dense traffic, heedless of the risk of injury or even death. The wind and rain slammed into both him and his bike, forcing its way into cracks in his leather jacket. Lovelace did not care. He was burning bright with anger.

It is the same bloody thing all over again! Lovelace thought to himself. *The same bloody politics and plots and Baal-be-damned bullshit. The Commander is neck-deep in it, that much is obvious. Heresy, politics and murder, a potent bloody mix. I swore to Aries I'd stop it, whatever the cost and now I know the cost. I cannot do it alone, I need Aries as well, but while he's caught up by that she-devil Clarice, he will never be able to see the situation objectively.*

After they had left the Commander's office, Aries had immediately headed off to East Hampstead to see Clarice. He was obviously bewitched by her, any objective person could see it. As if that was not enough, he had struck some sort of secret bargain with Cassian Dexter. The guy was a murderer, and while his confession was useful, Lovelace did not know how much of it to trust. *And at what price was the confession? What did you promise him, John?*

Easing back on the throttle, Lovelace parked on a bridge over a road somewhere in the Strip and climbed off. He walked to the edge and pulled off his helmet which he held loosely in his left hand. He looked out over the streets below. The rain had cleared much of the Strip's semi-permanent fog, revealing the faded, stained façades of the buildings in all of their decrepit glory. Lovelace felt a twinge in his side, a vestige of the sharp pain he had felt when Thervessons had stabbed him. The wound had already healed, but the psychological scar was still there.

His mind was a storm of emotions – anger, betrayal and fear. He could feel his Rage growling inside him. It almost erupted in the Commander's office. For a Pure, giving into that bestial uncontrollable Rage was a deadly sin. It marked the passage of a Pure becoming one of the 'Fallen'. The Fallen were outcast Pures. He had always been told that they were no better than animals, driven insane by the Rage. When they were found they were put down like the sick animals they were. Lovelace had even administered that final rite to several Fallen himself.

It was never easy, staring into their eyes, searching for a glimpse of recognition. All he ever saw was fear and the Rage. It consumed them, and they had to be stopped. At the time he had never thought too much about it — truth be told, he had not allowed himself to think too much about it — but now… now… he *was* thinking about it. What was the line between Pure and Fallen? Between man and beast? Had he really understood them, or had he just seen what he wanted to see?

He needed to vent some of his excess anger before it overwhelmed him.

"I need a bloody drink!"

With a strenuous mental effort, he forced his attention outward, away from the dark whirlpool in his mind and looked around. He quickly saw what he was looking for, a bar. He locked up his bike and walked into the bar.

It was a rundown place, the clientèle — aside from himself — entirely normal human. He walked over to the bar itself and sat down on a stool. The bar man approached. He did not look happy to see Lovelace.

"We don't get many Pures in here."

"That's nice for you. Give me a beer." Lovelace dropped a ten Sterling note on the bar-top, the barman snatched it away and replaced it with a beer. Lovelace downed it in one and signalled for a second. The second followed the same way, and Lovelace was on his third when he heard a voice behind him.

"You are in my spot." The figure behind the Pure could not see Lovelace's expression change, but the barman could and he backed away. Lovelace was smiling. It was not a happy smile.

"Get another seat."

"Did you not hear me, wraith? Lokden rot you! I said, that is my spot."

"I heard you. Are you really that stupid?"

"What the fuck did you call me?"

Lovelace slowly rotated around on the chair and stood. Standing in front of him was a well-muscled human meat-head in a faded Astro Marine Corps t-shirt. The veins on his forehead and neck were pulsing. *Just like the Commander.* They were eye-to-eye.

"I called you an idiot. Why?" All around them many of bar customers were hastily making an exit. The meat-head did not seem to notice, or care. He swung a punch that connected solidly with Lovelace's head, snapping his face around. The punch was strong enough to floor most normals, but not Lovelace.

Lovelace merely turned his head back towards the human, drained his beer and then spat out a mouthful of black blood and beer onto the human's shoes. Lovelace smiled.

"You punch like a child." Blindingly fast, he reached out with both hands, grabbed the man's t-shirt and smashed his forehead into the meat-head's face. There was a sickening crack of bone as the human's nose broke. The meat-head staggered back and looked up with rage. Blood was pouring from his broken nose and a cut on his eyebrow.

"You broke my bloody nose!"

"No one will notice, you're still ugly."

The meat-head swung another punch which Lovelace blocked, which the human followed with a spin kick.

He's trained. I guess the t-shirt wasn't just for show. Good!

Lovelace moved in and they traded rapid punches, kicks and head-butts, smashing their way through most of the furniture in the bar. The fight went on for several long minutes, until finally Lovelace grabbed the meat-head, lifted him over his shoulders and threw him through the front window and into the street. The meat-head smashed into a parked car and crumpled onto the pavement.

Lovelace climbed out after him. The meat-head was down for the count. Lovelace checked for a pulse, which he found. As far as he could tell the human would live, though with some nasty bruising. Lovelace heard several people approaching, he looked up and saw that the meat-head had friends. Lovelace smiled, and with one hand he pulled back his jacket and revealed his Headhunter revolver and Agency badge. His other hand held the grip of his sword strapped to his back.

"Trust me, gents. This is one fight you don't want. Take your friend here home and get him patched up. He fights well."

They decided that he was right and dragged their friend off. Once they were gone, Lovelace sat down on the pavement himself and leaned back against the parked car. The fight had helped clear his mind, but as much as he wished it had not, he knew that if was going to break the hold over Aries that Clarice had, he was going to have to stop her somehow.

The question was how? Despite his misgivings, the only way this was going to work was to at least try and convince Aries. He had to try and get through the fog that Clarice had put in his mind. If that failed he would need to incapacitate Aries somehow and have to act alone. There was no other way for it: he needed to meet with Aries.

*   *   *

Aries had no intention of dropping the Hamilton-Jones case, no matter what Commander Villiers-Cavanaugh threatened. *I am getting too close to the truth and that is the last thing he wants. He picked me because he thought I was a bad agent, someone who would be unable to solve the case, someone he could push around. He was right. In the past I was, but no more. I am going to crack this case wide open and stop whatever schemes he has in motion.* After what Sir James had said to them both in their dressing down he had looked into the death of Arkell Isadore. He news had shocked him. There were not many Honourable Brothers left. *How did he die?*

From the report he learned that the Echo lawyer was found smashed to death in the elevator in his apartment which, despite all the safety features, had dropped the one hundred and eighty floors in virtual free-fall with Isadore in it. Aries was certain that the Hunt had struck again.

That left only Kenton Serrano and Cassian Dexter still alive. Dexter's confession had led to Charles' secret apartment in Lower Bricktown which had, in turn, led to Aries learning of Simon Hamilton-Jones (and his pseudonym of 'Simon Ulialias Nuan'). Now that it was possible, Aries needed to meet Simon, but he wanted to see him alone. So Aries had told Lovelace that he was going to see Clarice. He did not like deceiving his partner, but after their argument at Charles' secret flat he felt he had to. Lovelace had intentionally, and wilfully, kept information about Simon's very existence secret from Aries. John needed to know why.

Hampstead Asylum was in East Hampstead, just like the Governor's palace and the Hamilton-Jones estate, yet it could not be more different. It was a maximum security prison capable of holding the most deranged Echoes hidden behind the façade of civility. Heavily fortified and Wyld shielded, the place was impregnable. But that was not its key feature. No, that was that very few people even knew it existed. The powers that be ensured that the Asylum did not feature in news reports or guides to London. That made it the perfect place for Charles to have secreted his brother. *Once he had him there it could not have been too difficult for a man of Charles' means to erase all evidence of his existence. Others in his social circle would have assumed some family scandal and closed ranks as they always do. Poor Simon.*

Aries' return to East Hampstead was no more reassuring than the last time, and this time he was bound for the heart of darkness. Torrential rain poured down, drastically reducing visibility. He landed his car on the dimly illuminated landing pad and reluctantly climbed out. Aries looked at his comm to check the time. It was ten o'clock at night. He looked up at the Asylum. *'Welcoming' is not a word I would use. No, 'brooding' is more appropriate.*

Taking a deep breath he walked up the path to the front door. The words 'Hampstead Asylum — In The Overlord's Name' were engraved in gold into the stonework above the door. Aries reached out and grabbed the archaic knocker and banged it down three times. Each bang echoed with unsettling volume. In the distance a flock of startled birds took to the skies. He felt the hairs on the back of his neck stand up and knew with absolute certainty that he was being watched, though the source was unclear. He waited a full minute, yet there was no answer.

He banged the knocker again and waited. Finally the doors swung silently inward. Blinding light spilled out from inside. Aries stepped into the light and into a vaulted reception room. The floor was a checker board pattern of black and white marble squares and the walls were a sterile white.

As silently as the doors had opened, they sealed behind Aries once more. Aries composed himself and walked confidently across to a nurse who sat behind the reception desk. She wore a starched white uniform that was immaculate in every detail, the very archetype of the prim nurse. She looked up and smiled. Aries noticed that the smile never made it to her eyes. They were still pools devoid of emotion.

"Yes? How can I help you, sir." The tone of her voice was clinical and utterly businesslike.

"I am here to see Simon Ulialias Nuan."

"I'm sorry, sir, but visiting hours finished four hours ago. I am afraid you will have to come back tomorrow." Now it was Aries' turn to smile. He casually placed his Agency badge on the table.

"No. I think I must insist that I will see him now." The smile on the nurse's face remained totally static.

"I am afraid that Mr Ulialias Nuan is asleep now, sir."

"Then wake him."

"We don't like to disturb our patient's rest, sir." *She is giving me the run around, that much is evident.*

"That is sweet, but I am afraid I must insist."

"I'm afraid those are the rules, sir."

"Make an exception."

"If we were to make an exception, sir, then they would not be rules would they?" Aries paused and took a deep breath.

"I am here to see Simon Ulialias Nuan and I will see him now, or will I have to call in an Agency tactical team to pull this building apart stone-by-stone until we find him?"

"I'm sorry, sir, but—" The approach of a stick-thin scarecrow of a man in a white doctor's coat interrupted her. On his beak-like nose he affected the wearing of glasses. He smiled at Aries with a smile identical to the nurse's.

"I'm sorry to have kept you, Agent Aries. I would have come down straight away, but I am afraid I was unavoidably detained. Please allow me to introduce myself, I am Doctor Smythe." His expressions belied his conciliatory tone. He did not appear sorry.

He held out his hand. Reluctantly Aries shook it once. He had the feeling that he had staged the entire conversation between the nurse and him in order to assess the agent in some way.

"I believe you are here to see Mr Ulialias Nuan? Well then, allow me to take you to him?" Aries retrieved his badge from the desk and followed Dr Smythe to a cunningly-concealed armoured bulkhead. Reaching it, the good doctor pulled out an identity card and held it to a reader. He then placed his hand flat on the scanner. On a small comm screen the words, 'DNA scan complete. Identity confirmed,' appeared and the bulkhead slid silently open. He gestured for Aries to go first.

Reluctantly he complied.

As they walked down the darkened corridor, lit only sporadically by overhead light panels, Aries noticed two things. *I am no longer able to sense the flow of the Wyld. We have passed through a Wyld Shield. I had expected that because many of their patients are psychotic Echoes that are too useful or possibly salvageable to destroy.* The second thing he noticed was the general aura of torment and suffering that the very walls of the institution exuded. Hampstead Asylum was a place devoted to containment. Neither observation filled Aries with confidence, but it was too late to retreat now. The bulkhead had shut itself behind them.

I am beginning to wish that I had stopped to tell Linsbury where I was going, but there was too great a risk he would be forced to tell the Commander.

Doctor Smythe led Aries to a lift, they entered and the compartment began to rapidly descend into the bowels of the building. The lift stopped sharply and Aries felt his knees buckle slightly.

The doors opened and they stepped out into another identical corridor. Aries followed Smythe through a disorientating labyrinth of corridors as the doctor led him to Simon Ulialias Nuan. Along the way they began to pass cell doors, each fitted with a small square window of armoured glass. Faces pressed themselves to the glass. Many started to moan or wail as they saw Doctor Smythe. From some of the cells Aries could hear insane chanting and scratching. From others he heard rhythmic thumps as if someone were repeatedly smashing their heads against the walls. Aries hurried on to catch up with Doctor Smythe. The doctor turned his head and smiled at him. Aries was not reassured. Then, without warning, the doctor stopped outside a cell. He turned to face Aries.

"Mr Ulialias Nuan is in here. I warn you to keep out of his reach. Please try not to get him too excited. Just call an orderly," he said, pointing at the bulky men in white who had just appeared out of the darkness, "When you are finished." Smythe unlocked the door and motioned Aries to enter. *I have come this far and I am not about to back out now*, and so he entered the cell.

It was difficult to make out anything at first, but then in the gloom Aries saw a figure bound to a chair. Simon Ulialias Nuan wore a restraining jacket and his hair was wild and unkempt. Aries circled slowly around him looking at the walls of the cell which were covered in strange runic symbols that Aries did not recognise. In one corner was an easel, a half-painted canvas on it, piles of paint tubes scattered around it. It was the only splash of colour in the room. The painting was a riot of colours. It drew Aries' eye in.

Simon was the first to speak. "You've come about my brother, haven't you?"

Aries nodded. "Do you know what happened to him?"

"Yes." Simon smiled and Aries saw the madness in his eyes. *I will have to be careful.*

Simon continued, "Charlie is so desperate for power. He has spent his entire life searching and searching for power. Greedy. Greedy. Greedy. Honourable Brothers, just as bad. They had to have it all. He put me in here, you know. His own flesh and blood. In here. Because I am older. Because I had her. Jealous. Jealous. He always wanted more. Now he finally got what he wanted." Simon began to laugh, but was quickly overcome with a fit of coughing instead.

"Her?"

"Yes. Clarice. She and I were going to marry. Did you know that? No one knows that. Charlie knew it. He wanted her. So he made me disappear like smoke. Erased my existence. Gave me this name. Do you know what it means? It means '*hidden one*' in an ancient language. Ha!" A look of immeasurable sadness filled his face. "She visits me, you know? We talk."

"What do you talk about?"

"Everything. About Charlie, about her, about my art and about that damned book."

"Book?" Simon looked straight into Aries' eyes. His gaze became dark and intense and Aries was forced to break the contact first.

"Oh yes. Book. The book Charlie wanted to have. Had to have. After mother died I became... obsessed. I tried to understand the patterns of the universe. I went to places I should not have gone. Broke me. Broke my mind. But I wanted to control the universe. I did not understand the price, no one ever understands the price. It cost me everything. My life, my love, my mind. Everything, and left me with nothing. Nothing but my art. He takes the pictures and I never see them again. Why does he take my pictures?" The strain of talking so much was obviously tiring Simon quickly.

"But Charlie came to see me... oh, not long ago. Or was it? Time is strange here, so hard to track the days. Do you know, I never see the Sun any more? I miss the Sun. He asked me to teach him the words. The rites. He was searching for the power to summon the Wyld Hunt." Simon looked closely at Aries. "You know of the Hunt?"

"Yes. Where is your brother now?"

"I don't know. But if he became the prey of the Wyld Hunt then it will stop at nothing until it finds him and destroys him. It will destroy anything that comes between it and its prey. Many people will die. So many people. Why does he hide so?" Again Simon was wracked by a coughing fit.

Aries had to know more. "Do you think it has found him? Is he dead?" Abruptly Simon looked very small. His voice was similarly quiet.

"I do not think so. The rite is the key. He knew rites of protection I had not taught him as well as how to summon the Hunt. I showed him the way... the words he wanted. But not the words he would need. As I was told to. He knows how to survive. Charlie always knew how to survive."

Charles is alive?!

"Wait. You said you were told to give him the words. Told to? By whom? What did you tell him about the ritual to summon the Wyld Hunt?"

"It was upside down... It was too powerful. I had to stop him you see? I had no choice. He should not have it. The rite is the key! The key! THE KEY! THE KEY!" Simon began to shout and violently thrash about in his chair. "THE KEY! THE KEY!" Spittle flew from his mouth as he was overcome by a coughing fit. An orderly rushed in, the other one walked up to Aries.

"You have to go now. Please follow me." Aries looked at Simon, but he was caught in some kind of seizure. As he turned to leave the small cell, Simon suddenly quietened down. He whispered quietly to Aries as the sedatives took effect.

"It is different. It was changed. Beware the Hunt!" The orderly shuffled Aries out of the room.

Shortly afterwards he stepped out into the cool rain in the night air. The rain was still falling heavily and Aries revelled in it, feeling it splash on his upturned face. Questions tumbled around inside his head now. *What rite and what trade? And how was is it changed? Given her visits, was it Clarice who changed it?*

*　　*　　*

As soon as he left Hampstead Asylum, Aries knew he had to go and see Clarice. Somehow she had a hand in all this, Simon had said as much. The revelations that Charles had an older brother and that he had made him disappear were shocking, but so was the realisation that Clarice knew of it and went to see Simon. But what was most shocking was that Charles might still be alive. Aries had made the assumption during this entire case that Charles Hamilton-Jones was dead, but to have that challenged potentially changed everything.

What does it all mean? And if he is alive, where is he now? Was this Wyld Hunt hunting down all his friends to get to him? If so, how did Charles become the prey rather than directing the Hunt? Was there even a Hunt? Should he believe the ravings of a mad man in the asylum and the confession of Dexter?

Clarice, what did you do?

He flew the car over to her estate. The rain had not eased up at all since leaving the Asylum and visibility was extremely poor. There were very few lights on at the mansion. He brought the car in to land, but his agitation made the landing a hard one. He had not slept for almost two days now and it was beginning to take a physical toll. He climbed out and rushed down the path, his greatcoat pulled over his head to shield him against the rain.

He reached the door and banged on it. No answer. He banged again, but again there was no answer. He turned his back to the door and slid down to lean against it. His eyes were so heavy and his limbs felt like they were made of lead.

He had been thrown off the case by the Commander, he no longer knew if he could trust his partner or Clarice, and try as he might this case kept digging up his past. A past that was better left gone and forgotten.

Without realising it, his eyes slowly closed.

*   *   *

Steel Year 2392.01.22 (S-Time)

Aurelian knew his whole world was falling apart. Throughout his father's domain the revolution was spreading like a contagion. There was talk of open civil war erupting. His entire world was crumbling before his eyes.

First, he had lost his brother, then his wife and now his son. After he had fought so heroically to save him from the assassins, he had lost Zhevan to illness. He had been consumed by the Wyld Cancer, he had manifested too young as an Echo and the uncontrolled energies consumed his young body like wood on fire. There was nothing anyone could do. Aurelian was forced to sit and watch him slip away before his eyes.

No one had seen his father for weeks. Since he had issued the decree of martial law, he had vanished into his private chambers, refusing to allow anyone in. Even his own son. Aurelian tried his best to manage things in his father's absence, but no one could have managed this.

His world was dying and a new one was in the process of being bloodily born. But, truth be told, Aurelian no longer cared. After the death of Ariadne and Zhevan, Aurelian had lost the will to live and he was sleepwalking through the motions.

Count Morten found him standing on the balcony overlooking Hammer Square. In the distance fires raged, the crack and thump of weapons fire was muted, the tracers and energy fire like so many fireworks.

"Prince Aurelian. I have been looking everywhere for you."

"How goes it, Morten?"

"Badly. The revolution is gaining momentum everywhere. I honestly think the entire Steel Alliance is going to be torn apart by civil war."

Aurelian nodded.

"Your Highness, you are needed."

"Needed? Me? What for?"

"I need you to begin organising an evacuation."

"What?"

"Metropolis wall fall soon. We need to begin planning for the future."

"What future? There is no future, Morten. Everything is falling apart. What does it matter? Let it all fall apart." Aurelian heard the Count take a deep breath.

"Your Highness, Aurelian. I know you have been terribly hurt by the death of your wife and son, but you have a duty to your people. To your followers."

"Duty? What does duty matter now?"

"Duty matters. It is all we have. You are needed and you can either choose to stay up here like a coward, like your father, or you can choose to do your damned duty."

"A coward! You dare to call me a coward?" Aurelian spun to face Morten, his eyes blazing. "After everything I have done? You call me a coward? You call my father a coward? I should kill you where you stand for that."

Morten smiled. "Then kill me. If you can. I am prepared to die doing my duty. The question is, are you?"

Aurelian looked at Morten, momentarily speechless. No one had every talked to him that way before. Eventually he found his voice. *Morten is right. I have been avoiding my duty.*

"What do you want me to do?"

"I need you to go and see your father. He cannot hide any longer, his edicts be damned. I need you to confront him. But if that does not snap him out of it, then I need you to give me authorisation to begin evacuating our people before the fighting closes our escape routes. I need you to act like a Duke."

Aurelian took a deep breath and slowly exhaled.

"I understand. Begin making the preparations for evacuation." Morten saluted and turned to leave.

"Morten?"

"Yes, your Highness?"

"Thank you."

"Don't thank me yet Aurelian. We will be lucky if any of us survive." The Count left.

Aurelian took one last look out over the burning city and turned to do his duty and confront his father. It was long past time.

*   *   *

Aries awoke suddenly, shivering and soaking — from the rain or cold sweat he could not tell. His memories had been so clear in the dream, as if the decades in-between then and now had never happened. Thinking of his time as Aurelian was always troubling, but until recently he had managed to keep all those memories buried deep. He had forced himself to think of Aurelian as dead, for in a very real sense he was. Everything from that part of his life was dead and gone, and to be nostalgic about it was to invite disaster.

The Federate Combine that had grown out of the revolution and subsequent Civil War still deemed him an enemy of the state because of his lineage. If their feared elite secret police, the SSG, were to discover his whereabouts again they would not hesitate to kill him and everyone he cared about. There was still the paranoia that he might return and try to stir up royalist sentiments in the population and incite them to rebel. The Federate Combine thrived on paranoia. He was the "Enemy".

Aries had no desire to do any such thing. The world he had grown up with had been utterly destroyed and was never coming back, and nor did he wish to try and recapture some of it by fleeing to the Imperial Commonwealth of Elysia. He did not wish to be anyone's figurehead for counter-revolution. As far as he was concerned, Aurelian Darius Favian-DeVir was dead. John Aries, on the other hand, was alive and wished for nothing other than to be left alone in obscurity.

At least that was until recently, now he was not so sure. At least not so sure that he wished for a quiet life. His past was gone, but he still had his future. This case had reawakened his ambition and his drive, and despite himself, he was glad.

Then he realised something else, something shocking. The whispering he had heard in his nightmare… he could still hear it! The words were unclear as if they were a conversation he could almost hear. He tried to mentally dismiss it by thinking *I must be more strung out than I thought*, but the truth was he was unnerved.

Struggling to his feet, he checked the clock on his comm. He had been asleep for nearly two hours and in that time no one had disturbed him. *Where is she?* His shoulders and back ached and he felt like shit. He needed to go and get cleaned up. He still needed to talk to Clarice, but right now he could barely see straight. There was a missed call from Lovelace and the simple message, "Call me — we need to meet in person urgently."

Maybe Lovelace has discovered a clue? I will follow up with him after I've been home. I can meet Clarice later.

The rain had died down, which was a small mercy as he crossed back over to his grav car. He took off and headed back towards Soho.

16

Steel Year 2425.10.08 (S-Time). Day Eight, Early Morning.
Lovelace waited for Aries. His heart was racing and he could feel the adrenaline pumping through his system.

He sat on a quiet bench in the London Arboretum. Thick foliage surrounded him on either side, with many trees soaring into the air towards the glass-domed ceiling. The sound of bird song and small animals crawling through the undergrowth competed with the gentle gurgling of the nearby stream.

The London Arboretum in Greenwitch, was an almost unique space in London, a splash of nature in the city that was accessible to ordinary people, unlike the secluded sanctuary of East Hampstead. Unlike Hampstead it did not have its own weather management systems, instead it under a great dome. At the apex of the dome hung an artificial sun that provided the light that the city beyond could not. The sun was providing a warm twilight. The air was heavy and humid with a moist, leafy smell that Lovelace found refreshing. Although open to the public, it was always fairly quiet and offered a discreet venue for clandestine meetings. Mostly lovers, but in Lovelace's case, informants too. This had always been a favourite spot of his to meet informants when he had worked in Soho. It was far enough across the city from the sector that their chances of being spotted by familiar faces was almost non-existent.

He also liked it because it had a calming effect on him, and given its neighbouring proximity to Central it provided an easy, small slice of escapism for him. Right now he needed that calming effect. This conversation with Aries was going to be tough. If Aries refused to listen to reason, Lovelace did not know what he was going to do, but somehow he had to stop Clarice.

If he came to it, he might have to... *kill* her, but that would be a last resort. An extreme option.

Where is he? I spoke to him almost an hour ago. It was not like Lovelace to fret, but this was new territory for him.

Finally just as he was about to reach for his comm to call him, Aries appeared, walking down the path. Lovelace stood. Aries looked exhausted and distracted. There was a certain level of standoffishness between them. *Things between us have not been easy for the last few days. Wait... is he muttering to himself?*

"What do you want, Lovelace?"

"Thanks for coming."

Aries nodded.

"We need to talk."

"About?"

"Clarice."

"You have not liked her since the moment you first met. What about her?"

Lovelace took a deep breath. *Here we go.*

"This is bloody difficult to say, but she is using you. I think she is at the centre of all of this." Aries' eyes narrowed slightly, but he remained calm.

"Go on."

"I found out some things about her that I think you need to know. I think this whole time she has been manipulating us… manipulating you, to control the case. She is the power in their marriage. She… is more than you think she is… I found out that she has had extensive modification." Aries turned and walked to the edge of the path, looking out over the small stream. Lovelace followed him over.

"You talk about that like we have not all got enhancements of some sort or another."

"Not like this. She's built like a bloody professional assassin. Also you should know people around her have a habit of vanishing in mysterious circumstances. Look, she's not telling you everything about her husband's disappearance."

"What are you saying, Lovelace? And careful how you say it." Aries sounded angry, his voice had deepened.

"I think she had a hand it in."

"You do? You have evidence to back this up?"

"No not yet, but I will get it. The woman is evil and must be stopped."

"What the bloody hells are you talking about? 'She must be stopped'? You do not know her like I do, Tarus."

"I know, and that is the problem. You are too bloody close to her. Everything about her allows her to manipulate men like you. Isoke's balls! She even has pheromone emitters to bend you to her will!"

Aries squared off to Lovelace. *Is he going to fight me? Have I pushed him to far?*

"Baal's teeth! You don't know what you are saying Lovelace! It is not that *bloody* simple! There is so much more going on than you know." *He really is angry, I have never heard him swear like this before.*

"So you say, but you aren't thinking straight. She's got you by the balls, John. If you do find out she is behind all of this are you willing to stop her, before it is too late?"

"Lovelace you are putting me in a tough situation." Aries abruptly turned and moved away from the stream and walked towards the bench. Lovelace followed suit. Lovelace looked up towards the dome, his heart heavy. He kept his voice even.

"I know. But I need to know where you stand."

"Where I stand? Where I stand? Don't you understand Lovelace? I think I love her."

"Shit." *This is going to be more difficult than I hoped.*

He looked over at Aries. His attention was drawn to movement on his back. His eyes widened as he spotted an infra-red dot tracking up Aries towards his head, invisible to the naked human eye, but not to a Pure like Lovelace.

"Look out!" He shouted and leapt forward, pushing Aries out of the way. He felt a blinding pain as if he had been struck by a train. Distantly afterwards he heard a sharp retort, but he was already falling towards the ground. His head struck the ground with a dull force, but everything seemed so distant. He could hear someone's voice shouting, but the words were indistinct. There was a warm wet feeling on his face and he wondered if it was raining, but it was too dark to see. The blackness overwhelmed him.

*   *   *

Aries did not even hear the sniper shot, not until long after it hit, at any rate. One minute he was arguing with Lovelace, then suddenly Lovelace was throwing him to the ground. By the time he had spun around, Lovelace was already lying on the floor in a rapidly spreading pool of thick black blood. There was so much blood it was difficult to tell where it was even coming from.

He wildly scanned around, trying to find the sniper, but he could see nothing. Fearing a second shot he kept low and crawled over to Lovelace on his hands and knees. His partner had been shot in the neck. Aries pulled off his greatcoat and shirt and tried to staunch the wound with the shirt. Lovelace was losing blood so fast, he did not know if it was going to do any good.

He activated his comm. "Agent down at my location! I need immediate medevac!" The reply from Central was a dim blur to him.

The blood was everywhere, it had already soaked through the shirt. *I need to do something.* He could feel his heart racing as panic set in.

"Panic benefits only the enemy." He could hear the voice of Count Morten in his head.

"You are right. Calm. Must be calm. Breath slowly." He was talking aloud to the voice of a dead man in his head. *I really am losing it. What can I do?*

An idea struck him. It was dangerous, and might kill Lovelace, but it might save his life too. He had to do it.

Closing his eyes he summoned the Wyld's power. He focused the raw energy, feeling reality subtly change around him as the tips of his fingers became white hot. Gently, every so gently, he peeled away the shirt and applied the heat to the blood, forcing it to congeal around the wound. The smell of burning meat filled his nostrils, making him want to vomit, but he persevered. The shot had gone straight through without detonating. Lovelace had been lucky. Sniper rounds usually detonated once they were inside the target for maximum damage. Forcing his mind back to the here-and-now, Aries worked his intricate binding at the smallest level. The effort was exhausting. It was relatively easy for an Echo to summon large amounts of unconstrained energy, but this... this required a level of control he had not known he was capable of.

Slowly the wounds closed. When they were crusted over with thick black blood, Aries let the Wyld energy go. The exertion had almost made him pass out. But he could not quit yet. Staying low, he grabbed Lovelace under the shoulders and began to drag him down the path towards the entrance. In the distance he could hear the approaching sirens and engine roar of a grav plane. He saw other visitors to the Arboretum around him, the horror written large on their faces. Looking around he spotted a large, well-built man.

From the whispered part heard in his own head, three words emerged clearly: *Let him go!* The shock was so much Aries almost dropped Lovelace. *Am I going insane?* He forced the thought aside and concentrated on the present.

"You! Help me get this man outside to the ambulance!" When he hesitated, he shouted, "NOW! THAT IS AN ORDER!" The man jumped into action and grabbed Lovelace's legs. The two of them gently carried the heavy Pure outside. Aries had never appreciated quite how big his partner was until this moment, when he was almost literally dead weight.

The ambulance crew met them outside and lifted Lovelace onto a stretcher.

"He was shot by a sniper round through the neck. I sealed the wound as best as I could."

The paramedic looked at the wound then turned on Aries.

"You cauterised it? What were you thinking? Were you trying to kill him?" When Aries took a breath while considering his answer, the paramedic carried on, "Forget it. I don't want to know." The paramedic spoke into his comm, "Get him on plasma immediately, 5cc of Tiranine, 10cc Green Bond and I want his vitals monitored continuously. Tell the Bastable we are bringing in a Priority One case now. He will need immediate surgery then full immersion in a bioregen tank."

As they wheeled him towards the plane, Lovelace began to convulse.

"He's going into arrest! Get me the paddles, now!"

A second paramedic ran over with a small box. The first tore open Lovelace's shirt and slapped the two small pads he was handed onto Lovelace's chest.

"Now!"

The second paramedic pressed a button on the small box and Lovelace's entire body went tense. The first paramedic looked at his hand-held sensor.

"OK! I've got a pulse! Let's get him out of here!"

They wheeled him into the plane. Aries watched as they loaded Lovelace on, then tried to climb on himself. The first paramedic raised his hand and stopped him.

"No room for passengers. Leave him to us."

The grav plan took off, blinding Aries with the combination of steam, dirt and wind. It rose quickly into the air and turned north, heading to the Bastable Hospital.

Aries looked down at his own hands. They were stained black with the blood of his partner. *Who sent the sniper? Commander Villiers-Cavanaugh? One of the remaining Honourable Brothers? Who?!*

*   *   *

Aries did not even remember how he got home. He had stumbled into the bathroom and passed out under the shower. He awoke sometime later and managed to crawl into bed. He collapsed and fell into a deep sleep.

The sound of a gunshot! Cool air rushed into his lungs as Aries sat bolt upright in his bed. Cold sweat drenched his body. He looked down and saw that his legs were bound in the sheets, trapping them. *A nightmare!* Aries forced himself to relax. Slowly, he released his breath, willing his hands to stop shaking. Aries felt a soft arm snake around his waist.

"Lie down." Clarice? He let himself be pulled back into the bed. Aries felt movement beside him and felt her warm mouth kissing its way down his body. The release when it happened was intense.

"Was it good for you too?" asked a strange, cold voice. His eyes snapped open and then Aries saw her face hovered centimetres from his own. But it was not her face. Thick black blood dripped down her neck from a bloody wound. Her skin was alabaster white and her eyes were pools of darkness. Blood covered her body and soaked the sheets. It was as if she were half herself and half a Pure, like Lovelace. Around them he could hear whispering, as if of many voices. He tried to look, but he could not take his eyes from her. She saw the expression on his face and laughed. It was not a kind laugh. Her laugh grew louder and louder until Aries tried to cover his ears against the deafening noise, but he could not. Aries felt a series of sharp cold pains all down the sides of his chest and stomach. He tried to struggle, tried to escape but he could not. He was trapped. The pain became unbearably tense, overwhelming him and causing him to black out.

He awoke with a start, naked on the cold floor. His whole body ached and he felt drained of all energy. The images from last night flooded through Aries' mind once more, causing him to curl up into a protective ball. Breathing slowly, Aries relaxed and pulled himself back onto the bed. There was no sign that anyone other than himself had been in the bed last night.

It was just a nightmare. Then he remembered the real events of last night. *Lovelace!* He scrambled to his feet and pulled on clothes as quickly as he could and stumbled towards the door. As usual he had left his WeaveNet screen on with the sound muted, showing a news channel. On the way past, he saw the face of Commander Sir James Villiers-Cavanaugh on the screen. The sound was off, but he was talking on a news programme. He was all smiles and false friendliness.

"Turn the sound up!" he shouted. The screen had cut back to a news reporter.

"...heard the formal announcement that London Agency Commander Sir James Villiers-Cavanaugh will be standing as a candidate for the upcoming election of a new Governor to replace Lord Sagacious, who announced his intention to retire recently. We contacted the office of Commissioner Tanaka, currently the perceived front-runner in this upcoming election, for a statement on her possible candidacy but none of her spokespeople were available for comment."

"The Commander standing for Governor! What a bloody surprise!" Aries' voice was thick with sarcasm. He shook his head and headed out the front door.

*　　*　　*

He arrived at the Bastable Hospital still feeling groggy and half-asleep. He picked up a cup of coffee from the little store in the lobby and headed over to the reception. As London's biggest hospital, the Bastable dealt with thousands of patients every day. Hundreds of patients, and their families and friends moved through the well-worn reception hall.

The receptionist looked up. She was dressed very similarly to the cold-hearted nurse he had met at Hampstead Asylum, but unlike her, her face was pretty and warm, if more than a little weary.

"I am here to see Agent Lovelace. He was brought in last last night."

"And you are?"

"Agent Aries, his partner." Aries showed her his badge.

"One minute, let me check for you. Ah yes, your partner is in intensive care in the secure unit. I'll get you escorted in." She pressed a button and two security guards appeared, both had the look of being ex-military. "Please escort Agent Aries to Secure Wing One. Agent Aries, I will need to request that you do not take any food or err... drinks in with you."

"Oh this? Of course." Aries downed his coffee, slightly scalding his mouth, and handed her the empty cup.

The two guards led him to the secure wing reserved for Agency and Metropolice personnel. They left him sitting in a small waiting room. It was not long before a doctor appeared.

"Agent Aries? I am Doctor Pritchard. You are here about Agent Lovelace, yes?"

"Yes. How is he?"

"I'm afraid he's in a critical condition. The bullet passed straight through his neck and nicked his spine. It also caused his left lung to collapse and with the extensive blood loss. There may have been permanent brain damage."

"Overlord save him."

"He's in surgery now. We have our best people working on him, but he only has a fifty-fifty chance of making it. But he's a tough one. Frankly he should have been dead already, but he is a fighter and hung on. If anyone will recover, it will be him."

Aries sank back into the chair and a deep sigh escaped him.

"Is there anything I can do?"

"Aside from pray to Isoke, no, not really. We will let you know the moment we have any news, but for now all you can do is wait. I am sorry the news isn't better."

"That is ok, Doctor. Thank you for being straight with me."

"Of course." Doctor Pritchard got up and returned to his duties. "*You are going to die.*" The voice spoke with cold certainty.

"Excuse me? What did you say?"

"I said, 'of course'." The Doctor looked confused.

"I… I thought you said something else. Never mind." *What is going on with me? Whispered voices, imagined threats, what the hells is happening?*

Aries pondered what to do next. He was undoubtedly shaken. There was nothing he could do for Lovelace right now, that much was obvious. He still did not know how to resolve their argument about Clarice, and it was eating him up that if Lovelace died, their last encounter would have been so angry. The Commander had ordered him off the Charles Hamilton-Jones case, but had allowed him to keep pursuing the murder of the Highpriestess-Keeper.

He knew what he needed to do. He needed to go and have a talk to Lord-Keeper Malachi. After all, he was connected to both the murder and to Charles' disappearance, as well as the upcoming election. The man was at the centre of everything, especially if what Dexter had said was true. Aries' expression became one of grim determination.

"It is time Malachi and I had a serious talk."

He left the Hospital to go to the Temple of the Overlord.

* * *

The Temple of the Overlord in Tyburn Square was the single largest temple in London. It dwarfed the nearby Necropolis and Temple to the Tattooed Man, though not the black monolith that was the Tower of Judgement. In all his time living in London, Aries had never been into the Temple of the Overlord. For him it was too monumental, too impersonal, too ancient. When he did go to a temple it was usually the local temple of Isoke or Kali. Yet now, here he was standing outside the heart of the cult of the Overlord and his Disciples, where the Overlord himself had consecrated the ground centuries back. It was an intimidating building weighed down with age and secrets. It was here that the original Alliance of Steel was forged between the Overlord and the surviving humans.

A cold wind whistled through Tyburn Square, somehow penetrating Aries' greatcoat and chilling him to the bone. The square was largely empty, with a few handfuls of civil administrative, law enforcement, legal or religious personnel quickly hurrying to and from meetings in the various buildings. The people were dwarfed by the scale of the square. In the centre stood the ancient gibbets, for here had been performed all the public executions to great acclaim and fanfare until they had been banned in London after the Civil War. The scaffolds stood rusting and creaking in the wind. No one had the authority to remove them, so they stood there slowly corroding.

Aries forced his attention back to the here and now. His mind had been wandering, and he knew it was due to a desire to avoid thinking about his present situation too hard. The thoughts about Clarice and Lovelace were intermingled and too fresh. He could not think clearly. He knew that he should have gone to see her first, but after everything that had happened with Lovelace he could not face it yet. What would he say? What could he say? If he were honest with himself going to confront Malachi seemed like the easier option. Or at least it had until he found himself standing before the mighty Temple of the Overlord. Now things did not seem so clear.

You need to do this. Malachi could know more about the disappearance of Charles, the murder of the Highpriestess and the schemes of Villiers-Cavanaugh than almost anyone. Men like him hide behind the power of the Disciples and the so-called supernatural to justify their existence. Well I, for one, will not defer to anyone. It is time for to answer for your actions. Problem was, this was a big step. Once he had confronted the new acting-Highpriest there would be no going back. The dice would have been rolled. There would be consequences to his actions. Once he crossed this threshold there was no going back. He would have to see this thing through to the end.

He hesitated, then in his mind's eye he saw Lovelace go down from the sniper's bullet. He remembered being pushed out of the way. He, and not Lovelace, had been the sniper's target and Lovelace had been willing to give his life to prevent that. He felt determination harden in his heart. *Who am I kidding? The dice have already been rolled. You know what you have to do.*

He checked the rounds in his pistol.

One way or another, Malachi, I am not leaving without you telling me what I need to know.

Aries stepped over the threshold and passed through the great gates to the Temple of the Overlord.

*   *   *

His Agency badge had got him past all the guards and checkpoints in the Temple, and he stood before the entrance to the Chambers of Brass, the apartments of the Highpriest-Keeper or Highpriestess-Keeper. So named because it was in the supposed style of Troy, the second moon and home of the Overlord before his disappearance. The moon had a brass colouration and hung fat and heavy over the Earth. Aries remembered a rumour he had heard that, once upon a time, there had only been a single moon. The night sky must have looked strange back then.

Aries reached out and banged the great brass knocker. The Chambers of Brass were a sub-complex within the Temple of the Overlord, a small palace for the head of the Cult of the Overlord in London, formerly Nebhotep Neteri and now Malachi di Combibos di Mercator. A junior acolyte answered the summons and led Aries through. The place reeked of antiquity. The air had a curious stillness and mustiness that set Aries' nose on edge. Candles – *so archaic!* – lit the passages and cast flickering shadows on the tapestries, paintings and decorations. It created voids absent of light, hidden nooks that lent themselves to scheming and rumour. It was as if the candles and incense that had burned here for thousands of years were impregnated on the walls themselves, lending everything a sense of crushing weight.

They arrived at the entrance to the office of the Highpriest and the acolyte withdrew. Two temple guards in ceremonial brass armour stood vigil outside. Aries sized them up, their armour, though appearing ornate was functional and the ceremonial halberds they carried contained carbines in the hafts, lending them use as both a close combat and ranged weapon. Aries was wound up tight, his anger bubbling away just below the surface.

If it comes to a fight, these two will be troublesome. I wish I had Lovelace to back me up.

He nodded at them, knocked, took a deep breath and entered.

The office he entered surprised him. There was none of the finery of the Chambers outside, the walls were plain white, a large tapestry of the Battle of London hung to the left. The opposite wall was dominated by an impressive set of bookshelves and scroll holders.

Facing him was a small desk sat in front of two huge windows leading onto a balcony that provided an impressive view over Tyburn Square.

That view is so similar to the one I remember of Hammer Square, back on Metropolis.

In fact the only elaborate area of the room was the personal shrine to the Overlord, at the centre of which was a single armoured glove from the Overlord's own armour. Given its size the Overlord must have stood at least four metres tall. Candles and a prayer mat surrounded it.

Malachi stood facing the windows looking out over the square beyond. He was silhouetted, but Aries could tell his hands were clasped behind his back. He wore the simple robes of a priest of the Overlord, not the ceremonial attire he had worn at the Governor's Palace.

Without turning, or acknowledging Aries' arrival in any other way, Malachi spoke aloud.

"To think that the Overlord *Himself* stood where I now stand some two thousand four hundred and twenty five years ago is humbling."

"What do you think he would say if he was standing there now?"

Malachi turned his head and gave Aries a sideways glance.

"*He* would lament the state of the mighty Steel Alliance *He* forged. Fractured and fragmented into petty warring states, thousands of settled worlds now lost to anarchy beyond our borders. Heresy and deception rife. The remaining Disciples arguing amongst themselves, whole worlds lost to apostasy. Corporations abandoning their divine mandates in search of ever greater ways to exploit the masses. The future lost. *He* would be angry. Angry that the compact *He* made with humanity has been broken." Each use of the male pronoun was emphasised. It was an unusual way of speaking.

"Angry?"

"Oh yes. *He* has been betrayed, and when *He* returns I fear the bloodshed will be beyond reckoning."

"He will return?"

"Of course. *He* left as a test of our faith, of our character, and we have all failed *Him*. The Temple of the Overlord has failed *Him*."

"Is that why you did it?"

Malachi turned from the window to face Aries. The Star of the Overlord Echo tattoo on his face became visible. *I missed that the first time we met, how did I miss that he was an Echo? I wonder what his powers are?*

"Why I did what, Agent Aries?"

"Why you arranged for the murder of Highpriestess-Keeper Nebhotep Neteri?"

Malachi smiled, and walked calmly over to his desk. He indicated Aries should sit and he himself took a seat and began signing the scrolls on his desk.

"Kill the Highpriestess-Keeper? Why would I do such a thing?"

"You tell me. Perhaps you thought she was failing the Temple, or maybe it was just that she blocked your own ambitions."

Malachi's smile grew.

"Really now, Agent Aries. Do you really think I would murder my own superior over something as trivial as my own career? Is that why you have come here to confront me and… possibly arrest me?" Malachi did not look worried.

"Perhaps not, but I have evidence linking you to the murder."

"Evidence you say? Then you should present that evidence to your superiors, should you not? If you already have the so-called proof you say you do, what need have you to talk to me? I am sure Mr Dexter would be delighted to help."

Aries ignored the comment about Dexter.

"I want to know why. I want to know why you aided Charles Hamilton-Jones with his plotting, and now why you are supporting Commander Sir James Villiers-Cavanaugh in his bid to become the next Governor. If not for personal ambition, then why?"

Malachi put down his pen, steepled his fingers and leaned back in his chair. His smile faded, though humour was still visible in his eyes.

"You do ask a lot of questions, don't you, Agent Aries?"

"It is my job."

"No, I think it is more than your job. This is not about the Agency, this is all about you, isn't it?"

"What do you mean?"

"Everything is changing around you and you need answers. Answers to questions much older than this case. This case goes beyond any mere investigation for you. Do you deny it?"

"I am asking the questions here, Malachi. Stop evading."

Malachi's smile returned.

"Charles Hamilton-Jones, like many of his friends, abhorred the sorry state of the Steel Alliance. Unlike many others he had the will to create change. I, however, had no direct involvement in his plans. He merely asked me some questions. Questions I provided answers to. What he did with that information was his own doing, not mine, Agent."

"And Villiers-Cavanaugh?"

"You are politically savvy, Aries. I can see it in your eyes as much as you seek to deny it. Sir James is destined for greatness, but he is his own man, I would not deign to speak for him. If you have questions for him, I suggest you ask him yourself."

"Yet you say you did not do these things for the sake of your career."

"What things? I am but a vessel, Agent. My role is to carry out the Overlord's will until such time as *He* returns. What Charles or James do is their concern, not mine"

He is lying, I need to try to bait him out of his smug cleverness.

"And the Wyld Hunt? What do you know of the Wyld Hunt."

Malachi looked down. A momentary frown crossed his face.

"The Wyld Hunt is a force of divine vengeance. To call it for material matters is an act of hubris. It sees through the self-deceptions to the truth behind. Should you wish to know more about the Hunt, I suggest you examine yourself, Agent Aries."

"Why?"

"For you have the mark of the Hunt upon you. This is not the first time you have encountered the Hunt in your life."

The voices in his head coalesced on one word: *Remember!*

In the back of Aries' mind a door opened and a flood of memories came pouring out, overwhelming him.

17

Steel Year 2392.01.22 (S-Time)

The doors to the apartments of Duke Memnon Favian-DeVir burst open. Aurelian stepped over the unconscious forms of his father's guards. They had refused to allow him entry, but he was not to be stopped. Aurelian glowed with rage as he advanced into this inner sanctum.

He was shocked at the state of it. Dust covered much of the furniture. Chairs, tables and sofas had been pushed to the edges of the rooms and piled haphazardly. The storm shutters had been sealed over the great windows, leaving the only light in the room the torch that Aurelian himself carried. The state of disuse had sapped much of the energy from his advance, but now he redoubled his efforts. Something was very wrong here and he was determined to find out what.

Room after room was similarly disarrayed, but as he advanced things became worse. The floors and walls were covered in arcane markings. Circles within circles, spirals within spirals, complex shapes reminiscent of runes and other, almost primitive markings scratched, painted or marked with chalk covered every available surface. Scattered liberally around were torn sheets from books. Aurelian picked one up, but he could not make head nor tail of it. The script was not even one he recognised and he was fluent in over nine languages.

"In the Overlord's name, what is going on here?"

He stepped over silver trays with plates of food left to moulder. *Whatever has happened here is not good. Father, what have you done?* Eventually as he advanced through the many rooms, he spotted light coming from ahead. He also heard strange chanting, the voice raw and cracked, the words unfamiliar to Aurelian. It was a form of Jensian, the language spoken on this world, but not a form Aurelian recognised. The words seemed almost archaic, the phraseology was verbose, especially compared to the geometric simplicity of the modern tongue.

Steeling himself for the worst, Aurelian advanced.

"Father? Duke Memnon? Your Grace?"

He entered a room that had once been his father's study. Now it was chaotic and disordered. The bookshelves smashed on the ground, books scattered far and wide, many with their pages torn out. The pictures had been ripped from the walls, the desk was overturned, his chair smashed to pieces against it. The room was a scene of rage and frustration. In one far corner was a bed, more of a nest really, made from sheets and cushions dragged over. *This is the den of some animal, not a Duke of the Steel Alliance!*

The centre space had been cleared. Markings similar to those he had passed were scrawled on the floor or painted, and by the looks of it, the paint was blood. Flies swarmed around the room and there was a terrible acrid stench from the candles that guttered around the circle.

In the centre of the circle was a man. His hair was matted, his clothing filthy, he whispered and shouted to himself in the archaic dialect while continuing to paint shapes on the floor. In one hand he held an open heavy book.

"Father?"

At the sound of Aurelian's voice the man spun around. Aurelian staggered back. It was his father but he barely recognised him. His eyes were bloodshot, a thick beard had covered his normally clean shaven face, his hair was matted into thick dreadlocks. His expression was full of terrible rage, then fear then confusion. It was several seconds before he seemed to recognise his own son.

"Au... Aurelian?"

"What in the name of the Overlord are you doing, father?"

At the invocation of the Overlord's name Memnon rocked back, as if he had been physically struck. His expression changed, became feral and he bared his teeth.

"Do not use his damned name here! He is a liar! A thrice-damned liar! He betrayed me! Us! He is the deceiver! Abandoned us!"

"That is heresy father! What the hells is going on here? Your people need you and yet here you are living like some kind of sick animal while your world burns around you!"

Duke Memnon's face — his father's face — went slack then contorted in anguish. Tears poured down his filthy face leaving streaks in the grime.

"They took him from me... they took all of them. They are going to take you too. Don't you understand?"

Aurelian crouched to his father's level.

"What are you talking about? Who?"

"Those damned revolutionaries. They all have to die. They took Darius and I will kill all of them!" Aurelian had not heard his father mention his dead brother's name since the funeral. The anger in his voice was thick and heavy.

"What?"

"They have to be stopped, and I am almost ready! The Hunt will have them!" The lights in the room seemed to shrink, becoming weaker as the shadows lengthened. Their breath began to frost in the air.

"The hunt? What is the hunt?" Aurelian was really worried now. "What have you done, father?!"

"My final act of vengeance. You have to go now, son. The Hunt comes and I will not have it mark you! Goodbye, son!"

Memnon's eyes blazed as he called on his own Echo abilities. His Echo power was that of teleportation and he was far more powerful than Aurelian. Aurelian felt the Wyld surround him. He fought it, but it was no good, his father was just too powerful. He could not stop his father from teleporting him away. The power so overwhelmed him that he felt himself blacking out. He tried staying conscious, but it was no good. He blacked out as he faded away.

*   *   *

Steel Year 2425.10.08 (S-Time). Day Eight, Late Afternoon.

Aries' snapped back to the room with Malachi. The priest had walked around his desk and was standing next to him staring intently at his face. It was unnerving, to say the least. His mind was reeling over the memories unlocked. *My father called the Wyld Hunt! No wonder Thervessons' and Charles' flats felt so familiar! I had seen it before! Overlord save me, my father was a heretic! Why could I not remember it until now?* All the intellectual barriers and arguments denying the orthodoxy of the divine had been pushed to breaking point. Was he wrong? His father had certainly thought so.

"What?" Aries stood up rapidly.

Malachi's smile returned.

"I was just saying I hope your partner survives. What a terrible thing to have happened. You appeared to zone out for a few moments. I was concerned for your well-being."

"My well-being is just fine, thank you."

"Of course. Well, if there is nothing further? I wouldn't want to keep you from Mrs Hamilton-Jones. I am sure you are dying to get back to her."

Aries felt the anger well up inside him. He took a deep breath and forced himself to remain calm. *I am not going to rise to your baiting,*

Malachi.

"I'm not done with you yet, Malachi. You arranged the murder of the Highpriestess-Keeper and I am going to see you put to trial."

"You are going to arrest me?"

"Damn straight."

Malachi's smile vanished as quickly as it had arrived.

"Careful there, Agent. What makes you think you can arrest me?"

Aries pulled out his Agency badge.

"This. Highpriest-Keeper Malachi, I am arresting you under the powers invested me by the Steel Alliance Accord. If you have the right to Legal Counsel, you have the right to remain silent. If you attempt to escape you will be stopped by any means necessary. Do you understand?" He pulled his handcuffs out.

Malachi laughed.

"You have no idea what you are getting into, do you, Agent? Be careful or you will end up like your partner, Lovelace. Wouldn't it be a shame is something like that happened to you, or… perhaps to Mrs Hamilton-Jones? Yes… Clarice."

The implicit threat pushed Aries over the edge. Before he knew what he was doing his anger took hold and he smashed his fist into Malachi's face. He grabbed the priest and threw him into the bookcase, scattering books everywhere.

Malachi turned, his smile still in place despite the blood pouring down his face from his nose and a cut on his forehead. He spat out a mouthful of blood and began laughing. The laughing brought Aries up short as he advanced towards the priest. He could hear banging on the door behind him.

"Why are you laughing, priest? Do you think this is funny?"

The door behind him crashed open. Aries pulled his pistol and pointed it in the faces of the two guards who entered. They in turn pointed their staff weapons at him. They had him out-gunned.

"I am laughing because you are through. You attacked the Highpriest-Keeper in his own office. You defile the Temple of the Overlord. You are done Aries. Look at yourself."

Aries looked down. His fist was covered in Malachi's blood. His anger was dashed by cold reality.

"You are still under arrest for conspiracy to murder your former superior."

Malachi laughed.

"You have no evidence, just the word of the killer against me. You have NOTHING, and now you are nothing." Aries knew he was right, he knew the truth was he only had Dexter's word against Malachi's. If he took Malachi in now he would be out in hours. The Commander would see to that. Hells, the rules would see to that. *Then it is time to stop following the rules.* Aries now knew what he needed to. Malachi had perhaps unwillingly let him break the last mental barriers to his memories of his father. It was time to banish the Wyld Hunt and put an end to this tragedy.

"You are wrong Malachi. It is not me who is nothing, it is you. I may not be able to take you in yet, but you won't escape justice. I promise you that. You may have escaped for now, but I will not rest until you and the rest of you and your scumbag friends fry for your crimes." Now it was Aries' turn to smile. "You see, I am just getting started. Enjoy what is left of your life, priest."

With that Aries turned and pushed past the two guards and left. His face was a mask of grim determination.

Malachi had stopped laughing.

*   *   *

Aries was barely out of the Temple of the Overlord when he got the call from Linsbury. It was a secure, encrypted call.

"I don't know what you did Aries, but you stirred up a hornet's nest. I just got a call from the Commander's office. He is screaming mad over something you said to the Highpriest-Keeper. He wants your badge and gun. He wants you suspended. I've never seen him so mad."

Aries smiled.

"Good. I needed to shake things up, and it is long past time I stopped following that bastard's rules. I plan on playing this through to the end, but Captain, I don't want to drag you down with me. If you want me to come in I will."

"No, I don't want you to turn yourself in. Screw Villiers-Cavanaugh. I told you to take this all the way, whatever the cost. No one should be above the law, though now you know the cost. You will need to lose the badge and comm, Shield will activate the trackers in both shortly. You need to go underground now, John. I will help you as much as I can, but you need to see this through. If not for your sake, then for Lovelace's."

"I will… Captain. What about you? If they find out you warned me they will have your badge."

"Don't worry about me, John. I didn't make Captain without knowing a few tricks and knowing where the bodies are buried, so to speak. I will be fine."

"Thank you... Paul."

Linsbury smiled.

"No thanks necessary. I suggest you grab whatever you need from your flat now. I will also keep an eye on Lovelace. Close this case, John."

"I will."

"One other thing you should know. Kenton Serrano is dead." *That just leaves Cassian Dexter and possibly Charles.*

"Dead? How?"

"I don't know exactly. Sir James hasn't let anyone from Investigations near it. Shield are handling the investigation directly, which is bad news. It means they think it was an inside hit."

"That is not good. Not good at all."

Linsbury nodded. Aries cut the call and pulled out his Agency badge. The eight-pointed gold star was full of memories and meaning, but it was also full of advanced friend/foe identification, emergency trackers and much more. It no longer empowered him and if he hung onto it, it would sink him. He rubbed his thumb over the gold as if polishing it, then turned and dropped it into a nearby rubbish bin. His comm followed suit along with his Agency grav car key. He felt a mixture of sadness but also release. His anger had hardened into a focused beam of light. He would not be stopped. This case was not just about his future, it was about his past and he wanted answers.

He was free to finish this his way now, and he knew where to start.

Simon Hamilton-Jones was his key to defeating the Wyld Hunt. After all it had been him that had told Charles how to summon the Hunt in the first place. But to get Simon's help, he would need to get him out of Hampstead Asylum, and he could not do it alone. He needed the help of Clarice. *If Lovelace was right and she is behind all this, this will tell me one way or another, but I can't get Simon out without her.* He pulled the collar of his greatcoat up and disappeared into the night.

*   *   *

He had made a quick trip via his flat to pick up some essentials, including a stack of fake IDs he kept for emergencies, and had made himself scarce before the agents from Shield arrived. He had a single bag of personal items and equipment.

Not a lot to show for a life.

He had jumped in a cab nearby and had the driver take him to Imperial, where he changed onto the tube heading North. A couple of quick changes of the tube, a clothing change in a café, and short a bus ride later he was reasonably confident he had shaken a tail, if he had had one. He had arrived at the central London transit hub that was Overlord Station. He found a quiet spot deep in the echoing arched vaults away from the tens of thousands of people passing through the huge station. He needed to make a call, and with its hundreds of known exits (as well as more than a few lesser known ones — some of which he had learned of during earlier cases) he was confident he would be able to evade any pursuit should they be able to trace his call.

His senses were alert. He felt the final few pieces that had separated him from his past self fall away. He was on the run, and unlike most people, it was something he was very good at. He visually scanned the people nearest. No one was paying him any attention, and nor should they. He was dressed as a typical businessman, in a slightly dishevelled pinstripe suit. *Xi Volker would skin me alive if she saw me wearing something like this!* The thought amused him and brought a brief smile to his face.

He pulled out a disposable comm he had picked up for just such an occasion and called Kari.

"Shakti," while making a call from outside, he used one of her pseudonyms, "I need you to get me an untraceable connection to Clarice."

"Ok. Give me a sec." She cut the connection. Moments later the comm beeped and Aries answered. Clarice's face appeared on the screen, and despite his inner turmoil, he found himself smiling. *It is good to see her face.*

"John! Where have you been? I've been trying to get hold of you but you vanished off the face of the Earth. I heard what happened to Lovelace! It was terrible. No one at the Agency would talk to me. What is going on?"

"Sir James kicked me off Charles' case and then suspended me."

"What? He can't get away with that!"

"It does not matter. I think I know how to solve the case, but I need your help."

"Of course. Anything."

"I need you to help me get Simon out of Hampstead Asylum, and with Charles gone only you can help me."

Her eyes searched his face. *Will she lie to me? Will she pretend not to know who Simon is?* Finally, she simply nodded and said, "Very well." Her expression was solemn.

He was relieved that she had not attempted to deny knowledge of Simon, or fabricated any other kind of excuse. So much had happened since he last saw her at the Ball.

"I need you to pick me up here," he sent her map locations, "as I cannot get into Hampstead on my own."

Again, she nodded, and said, "You must have questions."

"I do, but they are for later. Right now I need your help. I need you, Clarice." The last slipped out without conscious thought. A gentle smile appeared on her face.

"I'll be there. Be careful, John."

"Good. I... I will see you there." He could see she detected the hesitation in his voice. He ended the call and purged the comm. As he walked away, and with the smooth action of a professional thief, he slipped it into the pocket of a passer-by. *If Shield do trace the call back that will make life a little more complicated for them.*

He vanished into the crowd, his destination a rendezvous with Clarice.

*   *   *

Clarice's grav car was waiting for Aries in the back alley. The lights were off and only the gentle hum of the grav repulsors could be heard. Mr Six, her butler stood by the car under a simple black umbrella. Unlike his white suit last time, this time he was dressed entirely in black. Six ignored the heavy rain that poured down from the laden skies above.

"Mrs Hamilton-Jones sent me." Six's voice was neutral. Aries searched his pale face and white eyes for some sign of deceit, but he could find none.

"Where is Clarice?"

"As she was about to leave several black-suited gentlemen from the Agency arrived. They wanted to ask her some questions concerning yourself, I believe. Following her instructions and our own security protocols I left via one of our other exits, brought my car and came to the rendezvous, whilst my mistress kept them busy. She will meet us at the Asylum. I trust that is acceptable?"

If this is all a cunning trap, I am damned. But frankly Shield have no need of subterfuge. If they knew where I was they would already have had me surrounded and arrested.

"Indeed it is acceptable, Mr Six."

The butler opened the rear door for Aries noting, as he did so, "It is just Six, sir. No 'mister' is necessary," before returning to the driver's seat and gently taking off. The journey was not long, though he did circle round Hampstead and enter from the West, rather than the South as Aries normally did. They flew low over the trees and Six kept all running lights off. Startled birds erupted into the air behind them, but aside from that, their journey was without incident.

Six brought the car in to land outside Hampstead Asylum. Aries climbed out. He put up his own umbrella, the rain was falling heavily enough to be almost deafening. The window on the driver's side smoothly rolled down and the enigmatic butler spoke.

"The mistress asked me to wait. She will meet you by the entrance, sir."

Aries nodded and quickly made his way through the storm to the portico outside the Asylum. Clarice stepped out of the shadows. She was wearing a long ankle-length coat and in the light Aries could not tell if it was dark blue or black. She had it cinched tight against the rain and cold. Her expression was pensive and her eyes scanned his face.

"I came as quickly as I could. I had to make sure those Agents could not follow me. They said you were under investigation for corruption and wanted to know when I last saw you. I told them the truth, that I had not seen you since the Governor's Ball. I think they wanted to bring me in for questioning, but Jrgen, my lawyer made it clear that was not going to happen. Jumped up little shits, they didn't know who they were tangling with."

Aries smiled and Clarice's face softened briefly. There was a tension between them, but it was not oppressive.

"You look... good. I was going to say 'bigger', but that sounds silly. But you do look like a weight has been taken off your shoulders."

"You could say that. Some things from the past fell into place."

"Your past?" Her eyes widened. "I need to tell you something... I know who you... who you were. I've always known."

Aries wanted to stop and talk to her about everything, but now was not the time. The agents from Shield could track them down at any moment, so they needed to act.

"Later. We can talk then. Right now I need your help to get Simon out of here."

Clarice nodded and gestured for him to go first. Aries turned and rapped the archaic knocker. This time the door opened almost immediately, bathing them both in cold white light. They stepped in.

Dr Smythe was already there to meet them. He immediately addressed Clarice, all but ignoring Aries.

"Mrs Hamilton-Jones, what an unexpected pleasure. We had no notice of your intention to visit Mr Ulialias Nuan. Is everything ok?"

Clarice gave a tight smile.

"I am here to take Simon home with me. He has been away from his family far too long."

"Ah… well you see he was placed here in our care by your husband, so I would need his assent to release Mr Ulialias Nuan into your custody."

"My husband will not be coming back so I am afraid you will have to deal with me. Besides which, he illegally had his own brother, Simon Hamilton-Jones, committed here against his will under that ludicrous pseudonym. I intend to rectify this crime. Now, Dr Smythe, you and the administration of this facility can comply with my request, or I can take this to the Governor, the press and my army of overpaid lawyers. This man besides me is also a member of the Agency, as you know. I know how much you and your clients value your discretion, after all we move in the same circles. How do you think they would react in such a situation?"

Dr Smythe frowned. It was a strange expression, as if only his forehead muscles moved. The rest of his face remained placid and still. It gave him the aspect of a mannequin.

"Mrs Hamilton-Jones… Clarice… there is no need for such actions. We are of course aware of the disappearance of your husband, I simply meant that I would need to consult with the administration to formally release Simon into your care. He is an ill man, and we would not wish to see his health further risked."

"Really, Dr Smythe? I can assure you he will be perfectly safe under my care. Quite safe indeed."

"Of course. Well, if you will just accompany me, we can get the release paperwork completed." Dr Smythe turned abruptly on his heel and set off across the atrium. Clarice and John followed closely behind. He led them into the offices of the administration which were so utterly mundane and standard that it was almost shocking compared to the rest of the Asylum's Gothic splendour. Dr Smythe's office was behind smoked glass doors. They entered and he gestured to them to sit. He pulled out a comm and began going through the release forms with Clarice.

Aries looked around. The offices were largely empty at this time of night. Most of the lights were off in the rest of the office which made the glass walls of Dr Smythe's office appear almost mirror-like. After a few minutes of Clarice completing various forms, some reflected movement on the glass caught his eye. He could see the screen of Smythe's desk comm. It was showing the video feed from the front entrance to the Asylum. There were two men standing there, both wore identical suits. Aries recognised them. It was baldy and crew-cut from Shield. There was only one reason they would be here.

Aries stood and walked around the desk, pulling his gun as he did so. He shoved it into the good doctor's face.

"John! What are you doing?"

"Smythe told the Agency we are here. Why did you do it, Smythe?" He cocked the trigger on his pistol to emphasise his point.

This time all the muscles in his face moved as the doctor took on the expression of abject fear.

"I… I had to. We received an alert requiring us to inform the Agency if you were spotted. We were to keep you busy until they arrived to take you into custody. They said you were wanted for murder!"

"Murder? Whose murder?"

"I don't know!"

"Fine." Aries reached down and grabbed Smythe by the collar and pulled him roughly to his feet. "Then I think we need to hurry this along. I want you to have the agents stalled while we all go and get Simon and then you are going to help us get out of here without being seen. If you hesitate, deviate, or set us up I will put a bullet in your brain. Do you understand, doctor?"

Smythe nodded hurriedly. A drip of sweat ran down the side of his face from his temple.

Clarice stood as well. Smythe's eyes searched her face for some help. He was out of luck. "I am disappointed in you, Smythe. Very disappointed. Do as he says, or, should he not kill you, I will destroy you. Remember, I do not need a weapon to kill you. Now, enough of this play, stall them and take us to Simon!"

The doctor activated his comm and called the front desk. "Esmeralda, I need you to stall the two agents who are at our front door. Hold them off until I give you the word, and under no circumstances let them into the facility. We have a Code Red alert, so I am ordering the building into lock down."

The cold voice at the other end replied, "Of course Dr Smythe." The Doctor cut the call.

"A Code Red alert?" asked Aries suspiciously.

"It is the alert for an escaped patient. It allows us authority to lock down the building and deny anyone entrance. After all, the majority of our patients are Echoes and we cannot take any chances."

Aries nodded and then touched his own Echo star with his left forefinger.

"You had better be telling the truth. Do not forget that I am an Echo too, and I could incinerate you from the inside out in an instant. Now let's get moving."

"Of course... of course."

Smythe led them out of his office and down the hallway to a service lift. Once they were inside, Dr Smythe had to provide a genetic, voice, and iris scan as well as type in a twelve digit code and swipe his personal key. *That is some pretty tough security.*

A computer voice said, "Identification confirmed, Dr Smythe. You are cleared to enter. Lift shaft unlocked. Defence systems deactivated."

The sense of descent was subtle, and it only took a few moments for them to reach their destination.

"Secure Ward Blue." The doors opened and they walked out. The reached a security checkpoint and Dr Smythe produced his id again. He also presented the release papers for Simon. The guard grunted.

"Nuan's getting out? There's a surprise."

Smythe gave him a cold smile and they proceeded. Aries felt the tingle of a Wyld Shield as he passed through the checkpoint. They continued on to Simon's cell. This time the journey was significantly shorter and less circuitous.

The doctor unlocked the cell. Aries indicated for him to go first. *No way I am leaving him outside the cell.*

In the darkness of the cell they saw Simon. He was already dressed in a dated suit and was sitting cross-legged on the bed. Aries looked askance at Doctor Smythe. "He's been like that all day."

At the sound of his voice, Simon started and his eyes opened. "Clarice! You came!"

Clarice moved forward and crouched down in front of him. She gently took his hand.

"Simon, we have come to get you out."

"I made a new painting. I made it for you." He handed her a picture. She took it and then passed it onto Aries.

"Simon, it is time to leave. Are you ready?"

Simon looked at her, looked around the room. John could tell he was nervous. Despite his false imprisonment, this cell had been his home for years. Aside from his visits from Charles, Clarice and Aries, he had had no outside contact in a very long time. *I had not even considered that he might not want to leave.*

Simon swallowed and nodded rapidly. "Yes. I am ready."

"Good," said Clarice.

They returned to the lift where they had entered. The guard stepped forward. Aries tightened his grip on the pistol in his pocket.

"Dr Smythe, there is a call for you from the front desk." The guard handed Smythe a comm.

"Yes?"

"Doctor Smythe, I am afraid the Agents are insisting. They have called in additional support, something called 'HTA'? There is a grav plane landing outside now. I thought you should know."

Smythe cut the call and turned to Aries.

"HTA?"

"It is an elite Agency tactical unit. HTA is an abbreviation of High Threat Assault. They are heavily-armed Agency tactical teams. Or at least usually they are. It is often used as a cover for bringing in personnel seconded from the Astro Marine Corps SALVO special forces. Either way, they mean business, and they are skilled at breaching high security installations. We need to get out of here now. Is there another way out?"

"No, the front door is the only way out."

Aries smashed his knee into Smythe's guts, causing the doctor to bend double. The guard went for his gun, but before he could pull it, Aries back handed him with the butt of his own pistol. The guard crumpled to the ground. Aries turned to Clarice and tossed her a pair of his cuffs.

"Cuff him." Clarice did as she was told, while Aries returned his attention to the doctor. "Smythe, I am not going to ask you again. Is there another way out of the Asylum?"

The doctor nodded and gasped. "Yes… yes there is another way out. One of the emergency escape passages. The patients don't know about them, only the top level staff do. For our use in a Code Black situation."

Aries could not help himself. "Code Black?"

"Yes, in the event of a full-scale riot or other such prisoner escape scenario, we would activate a Code Black response. The Asylum, and everyone within it — including most of the staff — would be killed."

"That is pretty cold, but I suppose that it might be necessary. Anyway, get us to one of these escape tunnels."

Smythe nodded and then, clutching at his side, led them away.

*   *   *

They emerged from a secret entrance concealed in a copse of trees in Hampstead near the border to Highgate. They left Dr Smythe tied-up in the tunnel. Neither John nor Clarice had any illusions that he would betray them at the first opportunity. Once out of sight they made their way towards Highgate. This close up Aries could see that the sides of the buildings facing Hampstead were in effect massive screens providing the illusion of forest stretching away into the distance. Clarice led the way. Rain swirled around them and they were all drenched and miserable except for Simon. He stared into the sky regardless of the rain in his face, his expression almost euphoric.

How long has it been since he last felt rain on his face? wondered Aries, but he had no time for whimsy. They had to get away before the Assault Team were on them.

"Clarice, do you know a way we can get out of Hampstead on foot?"

She nodded. Her hair was falling in wet clumps over her face and her dress was clinging tightly to her. Aries wanted to hold her close, but he knew that he could not. Not until this thing was done and the things between them had been resolved. She pulled her closed hand out of her purse and slowly opened it revealing a silver brooch. It appeared plain, but she held it gently, implying that there was more to it that it first seemed.

"Yes. This key is given to all residents. It unlocks the access points to and from Hampstead, should we ever need to come and go on foot, or discretely." She pressed her thumb on the grip of the key and a small dull green holographic arrow appeared in the air. "Come on, the nearest exit should be this way." She led them in the direction the arrow pointed.

Minutes later they reached the edge of Hampstead and Clarice held the brooch up. A section of the wall swung open and they headed in. A short lift ride up to street level in Highgate and they were once more in the city. Aries hailed a cab and the three of them climbed in. Aries got the taxi driver to take them south to Soho.

He reached into his backpack and pulled out another disposable comm. He again got Kari to set up a secure link and he called Captain Linsbury.

"What is going on, Paul? The Commander sent an HTA Team after all of us."

"He did more than that, John."

"What do you mean?"

"About an hour ago Governor Sagacious collapsed and was rushed into hospital. He is in a critical condition."

"That is not good, but how is that related?"

"As soon as it happened Sir James was free to act. The Governor was the only thing that held the Commander back from bringing the hammer down on you. It is bad, John. Very bad."

"What did he do?"

"He issued a Termination Order on you, along with several charges of terrorism, heresy, corruption and — you are not going to believe this — the murder of his Chief of Staff and Honourable Brother, Kenton Serrano. Highpriest-Keeper Malachi co-authorised the order. Rumour from Intel is there are three Kill Teams from SALVO tasked with eliminating you. They are reporting directly to the Commander, part of some deniable black ops personal unit he has."

SALVO were the elite special forces unit of the Astro Marine Corps. The 1st Rapid Reaction Force of the AMC were based on Luna and were often seconded to the Agency for tactical operations. SALVO Marines were specialists and excelled at many things, but in this case it was their training in black operations and assassination that was most pressing. They would relentlessly hunt him down. *Three teams? That is fifteen heavily armed black ops marines.*

"I had nothing to do with Serrano's death. Damn, of course that means that was not an Agency High Threat Team at all. They were the Kill Team. How they tracked me down to… well it does not matter where we were. Isoke's balls! A Termination Order on me? Sir James has gone insane! He cannot get away with that, surely?"

"Additionally, he is trying to get a state of emergency edict issued, but the Deputy Governor has holed up with Commissioner Tanaka and Sagacious' son, Denver, and without the Deputy's counter-signature no edict can be issued. The Termination Order is thin, but I think he hopes by the time everything calms down you will be dead and he will be Governor."

"Wow… I am speechless."

"It is a bold and desperate move, certainly. Regardless, whatever you are doing, you are seriously enraging the Commander, and right now that makes you his number one threat."

"Will the Kill Team go after Lovelace, or Clarice?"

"It is possible they might go after Clarice, but Lovelace is probably considered a non-threat at the moment, at least for now. John, whatever you are going to do, the clock is ticking. If she is with you she is a target. On her own, not so much, as Villiers-Cavanaugh knows that the shit will really hit the fan with her allies — like the Commissioner — if she is killed."

"Thanks for the heads up, Paul."

"Sorry to be the bearer of bad tidings, John."

Aries smiled and cut the connection. He turned to Clarice. Simon was staring out of the taxi window his eyes taking in the city around them.

"You heard that?"

Clarice nodded. "A Termination Order. Villiers-Cavanaugh has overstepped the mark now, he will not be allowed to get away with this."

"We need to split up. If we are together the risk to you is too high, and you are probably the only person I know who can do something about this Termination Order. Also I want to ask a favour."

"What?"

"I want you to get Lovelace to safety. I do not buy what Linsbury said. I know these Kill Teams. I have tangled with their kind before and if they think they can use Lovelace, or you, to get to me they will not hesitate."

Clarice nodded. She reached out and gently ran her hand down Aries' face.

"There is so much we need to talk about. So much you need to know. But not now."

John smiled.

"I know."

"What about Simon?"

"I need his help." John turned to Simon. "Simon. I need your help, to stop the Wyld Hunt and to make sense of everything that is happening. Can you help me?"

Simon turned his attention back to the interior of the car. His eyes searched John's face, looking for... something. Finally he quietly spoke.

"Yes. I can help you. I know how you can banish the Wyld Hunt."

"Good. Thank you, Simon." Aries rapped on the divider between the passenger and driver cabins. "Driver, pull over here."

They paid the cabbie and as he drove off Aries threw the used comm into a bin. He turned to Clarice.

"This is it. At least for now. I will not see you again until this is done. First the Hunt, then the Commander."

Clarice nodded then leaned in and kissed Aries. The kiss was soft and gentle. He pulled her to him and they embraced. He could feel her heart beating against his chest. After what felt an eternity she broke the embrace.

"Stay alive, John." He smiled and Clarice turned and walked away, rapidly disappearing into the crowd. A passing police patrol car reminded Aries that he was a fugitive and he turned and led Simon south. Towards the Rock.

18

Steel Year 2425.10.09 (S-Time). Day Nine, Early Morning

Back in Kari's flat in the Rock, Aries sat with Simon, Cassian Dexter and Kari around a table.

"Dexter, did you manage to find where in Whitetemple the ritual took place?"

Cassian smiled. "Yes, with the help of Kari and some traffic drones we were able to identify the building. It was here." He stabbed at the map displayed on the table.

"Good. Now, Simon, you said the banishment ritual had to be performed at the same place?"

"Yes. You must close the gate the Hunt came through and it is easiest there. That is where it crossed from the Wyld to our world. I have almost finished writing the ritual of banishment for you."

Aries noted how Kari looked at Simon. She was starstruck. When they had first arrived at her apartment after leaving Clarice, Kari had whispered in his ear, "Is that *the* Simon Ulialias Nuan?" Aries had confirmed that he was, though his real name was Simon Hamilton-Jones. Kari had seemed in awe. "His paintings are amazing. He is the most gifted artist I've ever seen. I can't believe he is really here!"

In amongst all this murder, intrigue and violence there is still space for surprise apparently!

It gave him a wry smile and some slight small hope that maybe things would turn out alright in the end. He shook his head and returned to the subject at hand.

"Good. Will it take you much longer?"

"Maybe a few hours?"

"That will give me time to put in place the arrangements for our deal, Dexter." Dexter seemed genuinely surprised and pleased that Aries was going to honour the deal. He had given it some thought, and despite the rather huge detail that Cassian Dexter had killed the Highpriestess-Keeper whilst under the malign influence of Malachi, he had decided to honour the deal. Partly from his own personal code, partly because he knew it would fester like a sore wound with Malachi and Villiers-Cavanaugh, and partly because he liked the man. In some ways he reminded him of himself. In his flight from Metropolis, in the period between when he was Aurelian and when he assumed the 'John Aries' identity he had been forced to do some very dark things that he was not proud of. He had been given a second chance and everyone deserved that.

Except for Villiers-Cavanaugh and Malachi. They had used up their chances for redemption long ago as far as he was concerned.

"Thank you."

"Thank me when it is done."

"Aries, have you thought about using the Wyld Hunt to strike at Villiers-Cavanaugh and Malachi?"

"I have, but I dismissed it. Fooling with powers of the Wyld such as the Hunt is dangerous and unpredictable. No, when justice comes to find the Commander and the priest, it will be delivered by me. In person."

Dexter nodded, apparently satisfied. Aries had not had the heart to tell Dexter that he was the last surviving Honourable Brother from the ritual.

"In that case while you all finish the preparations, I have some errands to run. Kari have you picked up any chatter on the Kill Teams?"

"Not much, I'm afraid. They are keeping a low profile, but they are definitely out there. A Marine dropship landed in Central late last night. It was an unscheduled flight, and I am pretty certain it was them. They are definitely in London. You should probably stay here for now."

"I cannot. If I let them control the situation, I am dead. I can take care of myself. Just make sure everything is ready when I get back." Simon, Dexter and Kari all nodded.

Aries pulled on the leather jacket Kari had provided him with and checked himself in the mirror. His hair was no longer his usual styled dark brown, but was instead short and bleached blond, and his Echo tattoo was again covered by makeup. It was not a perfect disguise, but it should help. It would not fool the Kill Team, but the last thing he wanted was to get picked up by some beat cop. He checked the ammunition in his pistol, slid it into the concealed shoulder holster, pulled on a breather mask and headed out.

*   *   *

The old memories of being on the run rushed back to Aries as he moved through the city. He travelled from meeting to meeting, from one location to another always alert for pursuit, always employing the tricks and tactics of counter surveillance he knew. He was very good at it. Unfortunately he knew that eventually they were going to find him. After all, he had only to make a single mistake for them to find him. In the scheme of things their mistakes almost did not matter, though SALVO Kill Teams were very, very good at what they did. They had almost found them at the Asylum. One tiny advantage he had, was that, as an Echo, it was very difficult if not impossible for them to use a metapsion to track him.

So he could keep running for now, but sooner or later they were going to find him. They were faceless, implacable and unstoppable. In many ways they were like the Hunt itself. At some point in the last day he had realised that the whispers he had heard in his nightmare were audible to him all the time when awake. If what Dexter had said was true, then he was closing in on the Hunt. Or it was closing in on him. *Either way, this will soon be over.*

As he dashed into another alley in the back streets of Soho he realised that he had to change the game around. He had mentally danced around the issue, but the truth was he needed to become the hunter. He needed to turn the tables on the Kill Team if he was to survive long enough to banish the Wyld Hunt and bring the Commander and Highpriest to justice. He needed to send a clear message. But that meant crossing a line he had fought so hard to avoid crossing. He had always tried to avoid unnecessary killing, but Kill Teams were implacable. They were also professionals who were well aware of the risks. *These are men and women honed into killing machines. They are not innocents, which helps a little. Still does not make what is necessary also right. But I must be resolute.*

The final arrangements had been made with his contacts. Dexter, Kari, Simon and, if she wanted, Clarice would all be able to escape London. Everything was ready. He had even ensured that if he died they would get away.

He needed a neutral place where he could face the Kill Teams on his terms, and Charles' secret flat in Lower Bricktown was perfect. He knew that Charles had acquired the entire building and the neighbouring ones were derelict. It was a good site. It was unlikely that any civilians would be caught in the crossfire, and frankly the building deserved to be torn down.

Nodding with grim determination, Aries made his way to South London.

*   *   *

Once he was in Charles' block, Aries made a calculated 'mistake'. He called the Bastable Hospital and enquired after Lovelace. He gave a false name and details, of course, but he knew that the Kill Team would be monitoring any attempt to contact his partner.

Overlord save me, I hope Clarice got him out of there in time.

He did not have to wait long. Their response was shockingly fast. In less than a minute he spied a pair of grav planes silently descend nearby. The pilots were good. If he had not known exactly where the only good landing points were nearby for approaching the building undetected, he would have never known they were there.

Sixty seconds. Impressive. The Kill Teams must have been holding station above the city, waiting for a sighting to move in. It is what I would have done.

Aries watched from one of Charles' cameras placed on a nearby rooftop. The two five-man teams spread out quickly, moving towards the building he was in with easy efficiency, neither appearing over-confident or over-cautious. A swarm of small flying drones launched from each of the planes. Their role was to provide aerial reconnaissance and control. Moments later his external camera feed went dead as they neutralised it with a targeted electromagnetic pulse.

Aries smiled a grim smile to himself. He sat in the dark, in one of Charles' chairs he had dragged to the centre of the ritual space. A comm tied into Charles' security systems sat on his lap. Already his eyes were glowing as he began to gently tease open a tear in reality. He did it subtly, trying to ensure that if they had any Echoes on their team they would not detect the build-up of power. It was not an easy thing to do for any Echo, but Aries had manifested young and the training he had received, as a prince of the House of Favian-DeVir, had taught him a level of finesse above most Echoes.

I just hope it works. They know I am an Echo, so I will have to move quickly before they can seek to neutralise or eliminate me.

The security systems on his comm started failing, one after another. They were simultaneously entering through the ground floor and the top floor. They were going to strike from every direction at once to prevent him having an opportunity to escape. Aries suppressed a small flash of nerves and continued summoning the Wyld. The outer circle of security systems were all dead now. They were very close.

He closed his eyes and activated the circle of stun spheres he had placed in the room. The whole room was sharply lit as if by lightning. Surrounding him and entering through every door, through every window were the Kill Team. Head to toe in faceless poly-mimetic powered armour that provided maximum camouflage, their stealth systems were momentarily overwhelmed by the multiple stun sphere blasts as they attempted to mimic their surroundings and lighting.

I have but a second.

Without wasting an instant, Aries unleashed all the powers of the Wyld he had summoned. He tore a massive hole in reality and let the uncontrolled energies of the Wyld rush through him. The pain was overwhelming, but through sheer force of will he twisted and shaped the vast surge of energy in his body, focusing it and applying the template of control as his teachers had taught him. But where they had taught restraint, where they had taught him fine control, he now sought only fury.

Opening his eyes that were blazing with energy, he gazed around the room. The Kill Team had him cornered and they were not here to take him alive. The Star of the Overlord on his face burned bright, a searing pain to remind him of his training. He had sought to avoid this. He hated indiscriminately taking life, but the Commander and his cronies had pushed and pushed and pushed until he would be pushed no further. His carefully tempered self-control melted in the face of his anger, and now these people, this Kill Team from his own organisation had hunted him like an animal.

Seeing his summoning of the Wyld, the attackers realised the danger they were in and moved quickly to kill him. Even if they had been ordered to take him alive — which they had not — capturing him was no longer an option. But they could not move fast enough. Aries released the chains on the energy. Raw plasma exploded out from his mouth, his eyes, his nose, his fingers, every pore on his body. It radiated out as he became for a moment a new star. A star so bright that it blinded anyone who saw it. The plasma rolled, roiled and boiled across the room incinerating everything it touched. Man, metal, clothing, skin, organs, bones, blood, all boiled. Armour was no protection, nor were the vertical columns of the apartment. The plasma burned so fiercely that it took the very oxygen out of the air behind it.

In less than a second, ten highly-trained marines, were reduced to ashes. The windows of Charles' apartment violently imploded as the air outside forced itself into the vacuum, extinguishing the remaining fires. The shattered glass filled the air like a storm.

And then it was over. Silence replaced noise and fury and Aries was alone.

He collapsed to the floor, the light fading from his eyes. A fine sweat of blood covered his naked body, soaking the floor. The blast had been so fierce it had vaporised his clothing. All around him the building shook as it began to collapse in on itself. He pulled himself to his feet, groggily. He could feel the tenderness from where he had been touched by the vacuum, and capillaries had been ruptured. Aries also felt the gnawing sensation from deep within his bones as the Wyld Cancer took ever greater hold. Each step was torture. But there was no time for self-pity. Destroying the Kill Team had given him a reprieve, but it would be a brief one. All too soon, another team would be sent to complete what the others had not. He had to get out of here. Now!

Aries staggered out of the building as the entire edifice came collapsing down behind him. He crossed the street and pulled his duffel bag out from beneath a pile of rubbish. He pulled on a change of clothes and headed North, back towards Kari's apartment. It was time to banish the Wyld Hunt.

*   *   *

Lovelace slowly regained consciousness. Every single part of his body felt like it was on fire, all of it except his throat, face and upper chest. From those three locations he felt nothing. It was not a pleasant feeling. His eyes felt heavy. He tried to remember where he was, or how he got here.

The Arboretum... I met up with Aries. We were talking and then... what? The memories would not come. He could see himself talking to Aries and then it was now. There was no transition. It was as if he had been literally 'turned off'. *Turned off? The only way I would have been turned off was if I lost consciousness or... Samael's blade! Or if I died. What the bloody hells happened to me and where am I now?*

With renewed urgency Lovelace forced his eyelids open. Every millimetre was exhausting. His vision was blurry, the light that hit his optic nerve was overwhelming. It was like staring into the sun. He resisted the urge to close his eyes, even though he felt like he was about to black out from the strain.

Work, Lovelace! Work!

A woman's voice spoke quietly. "Lovelace, you are awake! Can you hear me? Lovelace?"

"I hear you." His voice sounded weak and hollow, every word made his vocal cords crack. His voice sounded different, like he spoke from another body. "What the hells is wrong with my voice?!"

"Shh... you have been very ill, you are healing. Give it time."

His eyes had gradually desensitised and he could see blurry shapes. He was in a room with a large window, behind which were... clouds? The sky? There was a woman standing near him. Leaning over him. He tried to focus. Tried to concentrate. Slowly the figure came into view.

It was Clarice.

Lovelace's entire body started and he tried to move away. *What is she doing here? Is she here to kill me?* He wanted to escape, but he could not. His body betrayed him and he was left lying there, breathing as if he had run a marathon. Distantly he heard quiet alert noises.

"What... what are you doing here?"

"John sent me. Try to relax, Lovelace. You are safe."

"I'm not safe. Not with you! I know all about you! Are you here to kill me?"

Clarice gave a small smile. "I suppose I deserve that. No, I am not here to kill you, Lovelace. I am here because John asked me to be. He asked me to protect you."

"Protect me? From what?"

"From... you are not well Lovelace... try to relax."

With grinding effort Lovelace forced himself up on his elbows. Every muscle in his body was taut and sweat beads began appearing on his face.

"No! Tell me. Protect me from what?"

Clarice sighed.

"From the Agency Kill Teams sent after Aries by Commander James Villiers-Cavanaugh."

"Kill Teams? What are you talking about?"

"Aries has been suspended from the Agency and branded a terrorist."

"Did you do this?"

"No! Of course I did not."

"Then what the bloody hells is going on?"

"It is a long story. You... you were shot by a sniper that was trying to kill John. You saved his life."

"A sniper? I don't remember any... Samael's blade!" The tangled memories came flooding back. The infra-red spot. The massive impact. The sudden cold.

"Yes, the sniper almost killed you. John had to try and cauterise the wound. It was a desperate gamble but you were bleeding out. He kept you alive just long enough for the paramedics to arrive. Then you went into arrest. Actually you went into arrest several times and underwent extensive emergency surgery. The shot pretty much killed you. The surgeons did the best that they could, but you were terminally wounded and even if you survived there was a high risk you would be a paraplegic."

Lovelace looked down his body, the sheets had fallen away from his hand. He clenched his hand and mercifully it complied.

"But... I can move."

"Yes. When John asked me to protect you from the Kill Teams I had you moved from the Bastable to my own private clinic. London's best surgeons and biogeneticists have been working on you for the last twelve hours. Your body was pumped full of surgical nanites and they have grafted on an entirely new throat, grown from your own cells. It will take some time for you to fully heal, but you *will* heal."

"I... why?"

"John asked me to protect you. So I did."

"That is not enough. There must be more."

"John knew the Kill Teams would try and get to him via you and I. He made me promise to help you, and I could hardly be doing that if you were going to die of your injuries, could I?"

"But won't they find us here?"

"They already have." Clarice pointed across the room.

"What!" Lovelace looked in the direction she was pointing, while trying not to move his head.

Five faceless armoured Marines stood there. They were so still and their poly-mimetic armour mimicked the background so well that they were almost invisible. They were like statues.

"Are they...?"

"Yes. They are all dead."

"Why? How?"

"The Hunt... the Wyld Hunt killed them."

"The Hunt? Why? How?"

"How? I do not know. As to the 'why', you know why, or at least you suspect you do."

"Because of you?"

Clarice nodded sadly.

"I... don't understand."

Clarice took a deep breath. "This is all my fault."

"Tell me."

"After Charles had made Simon disappear into Hampstead

Asylum, he came to me in my grief. I thought — everyone thought — that Simon had committed suicide or fled Earth. He had disappeared so utterly. I had no idea that he was less than a kilometre from where I lived. I only found out a couple of years ago. But by then, Charles and I were married. He was good to me, at first I thought he was my saviour. But over the years I realised he was my burden. Charles always over-reached himself. In business, in love, in power. It became a full-time occupation for me to save him from himself. That relationship morphed over time until he became my puppet. Everything he did was because of me. He was not a bright man, but even he realised what was going on over time. We began to resent each other, something that blossomed into a full-fledged hatred from me when I discovered what he had done to poor Simon. I had taken to visiting Simon in secret. Charles thought he was so clever with the pseudonym of Simon Ulialias Nuan, he never suspected I knew the truth."

She paused to breathe, before continuing. Lovelace said nothing, he listened.

"When Simon told me that Charles wanted to know the ritual for summoning the Wyld Hunt, and what the Wyld Hunt was, I decided to find out more. What I discovered was that this was all part of some stupid rich man's power scheme. Charles wanted to be king maker for Commander Villiers-Cavanaugh in the upcoming election. Stupid little Echo prick thought he'd be the power behind the throne along with all his Echo cronies. He wanted to use the Wyld Hunt to destroy Villiers-Cavanaugh's opponents untraceably, and then hold that same power over him. But to do that he needed Simon's help. You see Simon had always been fascinated by the occult, by the blending of Wyld from Echoes and the powers of the Overlord and His Disciples. He'd tried to become a priest of Thoth, but Charles had put paid to that."

"When I learned all this, I agonised over what to do. With Simon's help, Charles might well be able to pull off what he intended, though more likely he would destroy everything around him, including me. You see, I knew Charles wanted rid of me. I had no doubt that I would be the first target of the Wyld Hunt. But even with that threat, I did not know what to do. It was only when talking to Simon that I realised that I could subvert the ritual. You see when the Wyld Hunt is summoned the summoner becomes infused with a part of the Hunt, they become in effect a minor Avatar of the Hunt. It is through this divine link that they are able to mark targets for the Hunt. At least, that is what I learned from Simon. I have since realised that it is far more complicated."

Lovelace's eyes widened.

"You summoned the Hunt first!"

Clarice again nodded.

"Yes. The ritual that Simon prepared for Charles was subtly different. It summoned the Hunt, yes, but it did not allow the summoner to become an Avatar of the Hunt. When those… men… summoned it, they called the Hunt, but without control. I had already done so, and in my bargain with the Hunt I promised to release it, if it destroyed Charles."

"But things didn't go as planned?" Lovelace could see that Clarice was under stress. Each word she spoke was like a physical blow.

"No. Somehow Charles managed to evade the Hunt at the summoning and flee. It was the Hunt that made me get John assigned to the case — it made me manipulate him, but I do not know why. Since then the Hunt has been tracking down and killing Charles' companions in an attempt to get closer to him. It has been beyond my control. The Hunt is an unstoppable force of vengeance and it was summoned and fed by my hatred of my husband, but it is now beyond my control."

"But you are the Avatar of the Hunt?"

"Yes, part of me is bound to it. But that pact is not about giving me control, it works both ways. Part of me has become the eyes and ears of the Hunt. That is why I left John. Not because he sent me away, but because I did not wish to betray him to the Hunt. Now the Hunt is angry at me, and is going to punish me."

"Why did you do all of this? Why?"

"It knows I care for John, and it will try and destroy him, and then it will turn on me. That it has not done so thus far is a mystery to me. All I know is that I cannot help him defeat the Hunt. But I can help him by saving you. So that is what I have done. I love John, and if I cannot help him, then I had to see that you could. I know what I did was wrong, but I won't run away from it. Whatever my fate. It is in the hands of the Hunt, John and now you."

"Where is John — Aries now?"

"I do not know. He has gone to stop the Hunt. But after he stops the Hunt he will still have the Termination Order on him. I know he will confront Sir James. I also know that however good he is, he will lose. He will need your help."

"My help? I can barely move. Let alone help him."

"Your movement will return. My doctors have seen to that. He will need you. He will need his partner."

Lovelace let out a long sigh. Everything he had suspected was true — but subtly different. He had no idea what he was going to do about Clarice, at least for now. But she was right, Aries would need him.

"What do I need to do?"

Clarice told him.

*   *   *

Aries staggered into Kari's apartment. Kari ran over to him with Dexter and Simon a few steps behind.

"Samael's blade! You look terrible! What happened?"

John gave a weak smile. The tendons on his neck stood out proud. He was obviously in a lot of pain.

"The Kill Team found me."

"What?! Are you ok?"

"I am fine. But that particular team will not be coming after me again." All of them knew what that meant and they let the subject drop. Instead Kari helped Aries sit down. "Thanks. Cassian are you absolutely sure you and Kari been able to identify the ritual location in Whitetemple? We are only going to get one chance at this."

"Oh yes, most definitely. With Kari's extraordinary help we were able to locate the building quickly. I have the address here." He passed a slip of paper over to Aries.

"Good. Simon, do you have what I need to close this damned gate and banish the Hunt?"

Simon looked more serious. "I do, but you should know this will be very dangerous. We are dealing with intense powers here. The Hunt is an aspect of Samael, Disciple of Vengeance and that is no small thing. I am worried you might not survive."

"I have to banish it, to stop the killing and to make sure that someone like Malachi does not get control of it. The Hunt is too dangerous. Besides… I can hear it calling me."

Cassian Dexter went pale. Simon's brows furrowed.

"Oh! You hear the whispering? That is not good. You have been marked by the Hunt somehow. It is going to come after you."

"That is what I figured. So you see, I do not really have a choice. Either I defeat the Hunt or it destroys me."

"I understand. The ritual is very… dangerous, but it is least risky at the site of the original summoning. Anywhere else would require terrible sacrifice, but we can use the original sacrifice to seal the gate at that spot. Here…" Simon pulled out a stack of hastily organised sheets covered in spider-like scrawls. "This is what you need. I apologise about the writing… I am out of practice… at everything actually. Look, John — may I call you John?"

"You can call me anything you like, Simon."

"Good. Good. John, I think I should come with you."

"It is too dangerous Simon. Things could go bad very quickly and I… might not be able to protect you. Besides, this is not your fight."

"I feel partially responsible."

"Don't. Charles used you, I am using you, hells even Clarice used you. You had your life — your freedom — taken away from you. I know what that is like." Simon cocked an eyebrow in confusion. Dexter gave Aries a thoughtful look. Aries finished, "I do not want you to give any more of your life away, Simon. I am going alone, and that is the end of it."

Simon looked like he wanted to say more, but stayed quiet.

"Kari. When I am gone I want you to get Dexter and Simon to Clarice's mansion. I have arranged that our contacts will collect Dexter from there and get him off world." He looked at Dexter. "As promised, all the arrangements are in place. These are for you." He handed him an unmarked package. "That is your new identity. It will stand up to all but the most intense scrutiny, so do not get scrutinised."

Dexter smiled. "Thank you, John. You are a man of your word."

"My word is pretty much all I have left."

"No, not all you have. You still have your life. You should leave with me."

"I cannot, and I will not. I am tired of running away. London is my home now, and I am making my stand here. Besides, if I do not stop this madness here then soon enough there will not be anywhere to escape to. I have seen this before, remember."

Dexter nodded and smiled. "Good luck, John. For an Agent — an ex-Agent — you are a decent human being."

Aries snorted with laughter, then his demeanour hardened.

"Time to stop the Hunt." He grabbed the ritual and the address and headed out. Before he reached the door Kari grabbed him in an embrace.

"Stay alive, Johnny."

"I will see what I can do."

He left.

19

Steel Year 2425.10.09 (S-Time). Day Nine, Late Night.

Whitetemple at this time of night was not a nice place to be. *Actually, Whitetemple at any time is not a nice place to be.* Looming large over the whole district to the North was the Wall that sealed off the ruins of North-East London, now known only as the 'Shadows'. The whole area had been fundamentally *altered* by a major Echo rebellion over two thousand years ago. The Wall was originally built to keep scavengers out, but now it acted to keep the Shadows out of the rest of London. The whole area was littered with dark tales of horror.

Whitetemple sat in its literal shadow, and more than a bit of that darkness spilled over into the district. It was an area of mists, tight alleyways, looming overhanging buildings and pools of blue light from flickering street lights. It was commonly believed that the area got its name from the profusion of temples within it. Every Disciple had multiple small temples to which worshippers flocked, fearful that monsters, killers and slave traders haunted the darkness. They were right to be worried. Aries knew that the name was a bastardisation of the area's ancient name, one that pre-dated even the Chaos that led to the birth of the Steel Alliance, a name that hung heavy even then.

Now he worked his way from shadow to shadow, from alleyway to doorway, always on the lookout for pursuit. As an instated Agent he had walked proud and free, daring those who would attack him, alert to the vermin of the city. Now he was vermin, banished from the light.

The voices in his head were louder now, the words still just out of reach, but he could feel their calling. Even without the address provided by Dexter he fancied he would have been able to find the ritual site by the increasing pressure of the ethereal whispers.

His whole body ached, he was tired — more tired than he could ever remember having been before. His nerves felt aflame from his recent Echo use. His head throbbed from the constantly tormenting voices and his skin crawled. Every step was difficult, but he pulled his greatcoat tighter and staggered on with a sense of dour fatalism. Luckily the streets seemed mostly deserted and even those residents he did pass seemed as keen to avoid contact as he was.

Finally he reached his destination. He looked up. The building was a nondescript five-storied terrace house made of dark grey bricks. The windows were boarded up and the white paint on the front door had almost entirely flaked off, revealing a pitted and corroded steel door behind. He tried the door, it was locked.

Glancing from side to side and seeing he was alone, he pulled out the crowbar he had secreted in his greatcoat and jammed it into the door between it and its frame. He pulled with all his might and with a loud cracking noise the door came free. He dropped the crowbar, caught his breath — he was panting heavily — and swung the door inwards. There was no lighting beyond, so he pulled out his torch. There was a smell of decay — of mold and rot — but also a strangely animal smell of stale sweat and a hint of blood. Aries took a deep breath to steady his nerves and then pushed in.

Once through the door, he felt the hairs on his neck rise. The building was rife with a static charge. *Dexter had said that the ritual had taken place on the first floor.* He walked down the corridor and climbed the stairs. It was clear from the disturbances in the dust that many people had been up and down these stairs recently. He knew he was at the right place.

The first floor was knocked into one structurally-unsafe room. There, much as in Charles' now-destroyed private flat, was the ritual space. In the centre of the ritual spiral was a ruptured and rotting corpse. Dark, congealed arterial blood was sprayed liberally around the room. The stench of decay was overpowering. *Brentan Roe, I presume.*

It was obvious they had left in a blind panic. Around the room were discarded cases, coats and other personal effects. Circling carefully around the ritual spiral, Aries saw the blackened and charred remains of an amulet. *That must have been what Charles was wearing. What Malachi gave him to protect him.*

He could imagine Charles Hamilton-Jones, Nigel Massey de Sargon, Jean Thervessons, Kenton Serrano, Brentan Roe, Benham Arends, Arkell Isadore and Cassian Dexter standing around the circle. They would have been brimming with a mix of anticipation, excitement, fear and, of course, arrogance. They thought they were on the cusp of unbridled power, but instead all they were on was the cusp of destruction. Now only Cassian Dexter still remained alive… for now.

Who else is the Wyld Hunt going to kill? This has to stop. This is where it all started, and this is where it is all going to end.

Shining the torch on the scraps of paper that formed the ritual he read through it all one more time. It was not as if the ritual was complicated, but he could not afford to make a mistake. Finally, as sure as he could be that he had memorised it, he folded the notes up and put them back into his pocket. He took several long slow breaths to control his heart. His hands were shaking slightly. He lit the eight candles around the spiral, pulled out the ritual knife they had recovered from the petty thief Chas Varn and made a small cut on the palm of his left hand. He walked around the edge of the spiral dripping blood as he did so.

In the old tongue, so unfamiliar to him, he began the chant that Simon had prepared.

"Wyld Hunt, your work is done. The Hunt is over, it is time for you to return to the Wyld. It is time for you to leave. The time of vengeance is past." He repeated the words over and over. Simon's notes had been very clear. *The words matter, but not so much as your intent. You must empower each word through force of will, you must use your Echo nature to amplify the words, you must force the words through the barrier of our reality and into the Wyld where the Hunt resides. Your words must sew together the tear in reality, bind that which has been unbound, and heal the wound in our time and space.* He felt the words building in power inside him. The feeling was similar to the sense of summoning powers for his Echo ability, yet subtly different. The power felt strangely... colder... more ancient, as if the energy itself were laden with memories and history. His eyes and tattoo began to glow, as did the circle. It glowed as if it were a giant version of the Echo tattoo on his face, but instead of binding the powers in a human it bound them in the very Earth itself. It amplified his own abilities. The rush of power was intense, his mind sailed up on it, he could feel the very life force of the planet and the uncountable living things on it. For a moment he felt what it was like to be a god. But then he concentrated and brought his mind back to the present. The power was so alluring, so intoxicating and so dangerous. Even more so than his own Echo abilities.

He finally understood that this ritual was Echo power use on a planetary scale, something so pregnant with awesome power, it was beyond the abilities of any normal Echo to control. He would be swept away by the power and consumed by it. Finally he realised how terribly foolish the arrogance of the Honourable Brotherhood had been. They did not merely wish to control the outcomes of a petty election. They wished to become gods themselves.

"And now you understand." The voice shocked him out of his contemplation. He opened his eyes slowly, suddenly fearful of what he would see.

Standing in the centre of the brightly glowing spiral was a single figure. The figure appeared to be silhouetted, or else formed entirely out of darkness. Yet despite that, Aries could tell that the unknown stranger was male. *Is this the Wyld Hunt itself?*

"I am but merely one aspect of the Hunt, Aurelian."

The shock at hearing his true name rocked Aries. The figure quietly chuckled. It was not a happy sound.

"You are shocked at your own name, and I thought it was daemons who feared to be called by their true names."

Aries continued reciting the mantra Simon had told him, but in in his head he thought: *Who are you?*

"Do you not recognise me, Aurelian?"

Again with that name, and his voice so familiar. It must be trickery.

"There is no trickery, Aurelian. You know who I am."

Aries felt a growing sense of recognition, and as he did so features began to be visible on the shadow man. As each element appeared, Aries felt a growing sense of dread and familiarity.

Overlord save me! It cannot be?

"The Overlord is not here, Aurelian, it is only us."

As the last few features came into view Aries knew with certainty who the Hunt was.

"That is right, Aurelian. Do you not recognise your own father?"

His eyes went wide and the shock caused him to skip a beat in the mantra. It was true! The man who had emerged from the shadow was the image of his long dead father, Memnon, Duke of Metropolis.

"You are an illusion to fool me. My father is dead!"

"No, not dead, not quite. You see, the Hunt saved me. When the end came I became one with it, after all I was its Avatar."

"LIES!" Aries felt the rage, loss and confusion all bubble to the surface. "YOU ARE DEAD!"

His father — no, the image of his father — smiled sadly. "Whether you care to believe it or not, it is true, and now you seek to kill me all over again. Why?"

"You have to be stopped! The killing must end."

"The killing will end, when Charles is dead. Do you deny that those foolish men deserved to die? Do you deny that they brought their doom on themselves?"

Aries felt the confusion overwhelm him. He had been prepared for anything, but not this. His father's words rang true. The Honourable Brotherhood had deserved to die. They had brought their doom on themselves with their meddling and plotting and pathetic scheming.

"I…"

"And yet here you are, son, about to banish me back into the hell that is the Wyld. You would do that to your own father?"

He was torn. The living embodiment of the Wyld Hunt stood before him and it was his father. How could he destroy his own father? How could he banish him to the Wyld? He was transfixed by the decision. His father's voice broke the spell.

"Will you take my hand? We have to much to talk about."

Aries found himself reaching out. When their fingers touched there was a bright white electric bang. Aries was thrown across the room, slamming into the wall with incredible force. When he opened his eyes the entire world was swimming. His father was walking towards him, out of the spiral.

Memnon crouched down in front on Aries.

"Thank you for releasing me, son. For that small act of kindness I will give you a head start."

"Head start… I do not understand, father?"

His father smiled. The smile was inhumanly wide and his face began to transform and distort, becoming the stuff of nightmares. His — its voice had become inhuman. It was as if thousands of people were all whispering as one.

"Oh yes, you see we are the Hunt, Aurelian. All of us and we need to hunt, the chase, it sustains us. So you had best run." Its voice briefly became that of Memnon, once more. "Run, son. Run!"

Aries staggered to his feet, looked at the Hunt which was growing and fading to shadow once more and turned and stumbled away. He picked up pace and by the time he had descended the stairs he was running at full tilt as he hit the streets. Behind him he heard the howling of a million hounds. He clapped his hands over his ears, but it was no good. The voice was inside his head.

Aries ran.

*   *   *

Aries ran down the nameless street in Whitetemple as fast as he could. He risked a glance behind him and almost stumbled in shock. One by one all the lights behind him were being snuffed out, plunging everything into pitch darkness. He could hear the howling of hundreds of dogs emanating from the darkness. *I am the prey and they are the predators. The Hunt chases me.* Despite his terror, despite the fact that his heart was beating an uncontrolled tempo, from somewhere deep inside him Aries found a core of resolve.

The Hunt cannot have me! I will not go down like those others. I. AM. NOT. PREY! The last thoughts had such power behind them that for a moment the voices were silenced. *I have to confront this, I have to stand and fight somewhere, but where?* The answer came to him instantaneously. *Clarice's mansion. It has to be. Only Simon can help me defeat the Hunt.*

It was dangerous, and despite his best efforts he would be putting all of them at terrible risk. But what else could he do? His choices were almost nil.

He burst out of an alleyway onto a main road in Whitetemple and paused looking around from the middle of the road recovering his breath and trying to get his bearings. The local people stared at him as if he were mad — he realised that in many ways he was. He briefly thought about trying to get help, but there was nothing they could do and he would at worst only endanger them too. He sighted the Wall looming over the district which he knew was to the North. He turned Westward on the street and ran as hard as he could.

He had not run far when he reached the entrance to Whitetemple tube station. He pushed his way past startled commuters and ran down the stairs skipping two or three at a time. He vaulted the ticket barriers and continued on towards the Westbound platform. He looked at the information display, it showed a train in two minutes. It seemed like an eternity, but what else could he do?

Then looking back up the stairs he saw it. It was as if the light were sucked out of each person walking down the stairs, they became living silhouettes. Tendrils of darkness reached out and as each touched a light it was extinguished. Their footsteps became matched in lock-step. The people heading the other way appeared completely unaware of the approaching darkness and walked into it heedlessly. Accompanying the darkness was the building whispers of an uncountable multitude of voices. They spoke one word, "Run!". Panic almost overwhelmed him.

Aries felt his eyes widen and his heart race faster. The Hunt was getting closer by the second. He had only moments before it reached him on the platform. Unconsciously, he began backing down the platform, away from the darkness, but there was nowhere to go. When the darkness reached him he would be dead. They were going to catch him here, all his attempts to stop the Hunt would have been for nought. He had failed.

Then he felt the wind on his face, and the screeching of the approaching train. He felt the tiniest flutter of hope. The train roared onto the platform, the bright lights in the carriage scouring Aries. The train rapidly slowed and Aries ran to the door and pounded on it, willing it to open sooner. The darkness got closer, it was on the platform now. The lights around it were being stretched and distorted as if it were a gravity well.

And still the doors had not opened. Aries turned his head and summoned a burst of Wyld. Plasma streamed from his eyes and tore the door open. He threw himself onto the train, heedless of the scalding hot twisted metal and liquid glass. He was only distantly aware of the screams of other passengers as they in turn sought to escape this mad Echo.

The other train doors opened and closed briefly and the train began to pull out of the station. *Thank the Overlord for these cheap automated trains on the Lower lines.* As the train began to pull out of the station, he stood and looked out. The darkness was on the platform. A monolithic wall of the purest absence of light. Then suddenly, as if in unison, uncountable yellow eyes opened, all of them staring at him. Aries screamed and stumbled backwards, slamming into the far side of the carriage.

Despite the train's increasing speed he ran as fast as he could towards the front of it. Anything to escape the eyes. The faces of the other passengers were distorted in fear and incomprehension. Aries' brain was unable to process what he saw. They were all alien to him — unreal and without substance.

The train rattled down the Lower Underground tunnels, heading Westward. John tried to focus on the information display. Everything swam before his eyes, but he could make out that this line would take him north through Overlord Station, then west across the Strip and then on to North Soho. From there he would be as close as he could get to Hampstead. He had no idea how he was going to penetrate the exclusive enclave, but somehow he would manage it. He collapsed into the seat opposite the display.

The train passed through Overlord Station without incident. For a brief moment Aries felt a sliver of hope. He looked down at his hands. They were shaking terribly and every part of his body felt like it was made of lead. He heard a voice, "Are you ok?"

He looked up at the man leaning over him to thank him for his kindness, but the words died unsaid in his throat. The man's face stretched and distorted, his mouth grew and grew becoming impossibly wide and his eyes glowed a sickly yellow. Without thinking Aries pulled his gun and pointed it at the man.

"GET AWAY FROM ME!"

The nightmare figure staggered back and Aries once more climbed to his feet. He fired his gun into the air and shouted, "ALL OF YOU STAY AWAY FROM ME! YOU CANNOT HAVE ME!" The world swam in front of his eyes. Everything was blurry and unclear. Roaring in frustration, Aries turned and continued staggering forward in the train.

As the train pulled into the Strip he saw a group of frightened passengers run onto the platform. *What are they frightened of?* He thought to himself, uncomprehending. They ran over to two dark blue uniformed men, that even through his fog Aries could tell were Metropolice. The passengers were gesturing towards him. Aries was confused, but as they began to walk purposefully towards him drawing their guns he knew he was in trouble. If they reached him or stopped the train the Hunt would have him. Their eyes were a matching yellow!

He looked down at his gun. The indicator flashed red. It was empty. With frustration he hurled it at them and then once more summoned the Wyld. His mind ached, everything felt like it was taking place underwater, but he pushed through it, though the strain caused sweat to pour down his face. He concentrated on the platform and it began to bubble and boil, a terrible heat haze rose above the melting concrete and steel. The two police officers were forced to retreat from the fierce heat.

Finally the doors on the train closed and it began to move. Aries was alone on the carriage now. He could taste blood in his mouth and he slid down the door, passing out for a few moments. When he came round, he saw the train was close to Soho station.

So close! I might make it yet.

Then he heard the door at the far end of the carriage open. A figure of pure darkness stepped through. Behind it the darkness spread like a foul corruption through the structure of the carriage, veins of pulsing darkness spread and divided, each time growing ever longer. The figure walked slowly towards Aries, and though all he could see of it was its glowing yellow eyes he could nonetheless tell that it was smiling.

When it spoke it was the voice of a thousand screams:

"You are caught. You cannot escape. It is time to die... son."

With each word the weight in his limbs magnified, until the last word, which was spoken in a single human voice. The voice of his father. Suddenly he found an untapped reserve of strength.

"NO!" Aries stood and pulled on the emergency brakes. The outside of the tunnel was lit up by the sparks as the brakes slammed into the side of the maglev tracks. He turned and once more unleashed his Echo abilities on the door, instantly vaporising it. Heedless of the still moving train, Aries threw himself out into the tunnel.

He landed hard and felt the concrete grind away at his side and left leg. He screamed with the pain — all memory of his mental control exercises gone. He stood and began to half-run and half-hobble down the path at the side of the tunnel. Despite an almost overwhelming urge to look behind, he kept his focus directly ahead. He bit down on the inside of his cheek, the pain giving him some clarity.

After running down an endless path he reached the station platform. There was a wall of armoured riot police on the platform, blocking his path. Almost incoherent with fear, adrenaline and rage, Aries unconsciously summoned the Wyld and unleashed a ball of coherent energy. He had intended to aim it further away from the police officers but his control was slipping and it exploded too close to the line of men. The shock wave brutally threw them back. He ran through the badly-wounded police without stopping. He would deal with the consequences later. If he survived. He ripped a comm unit from the belt of one of the policemen as he passed.

Moments later he emerged into the cool air of the street and ran to the North. He pulled out the comm unit he had stolen and called Clarice as he ran. Her face appeared on the screen, and seeing his expression and still-glowing eyes she was obviously shaken.

"Clarice I need you to send Six to pick me up from the corner of Compton and Standish now!" Without waiting for a reply he threw the comm away and concentrated on the running.

By the time he reached the rendezvous point, Six was already waiting in the grav car. Aries pulled open the back door and threw himself in. He just had time to shout, "Get me back to the mansion, now!" before he passed out.

*   *   *

Aries' return to the mansion was a blur, he kept fading in and out of consciousness. Present throughout it all was the incessant whispering of the many voices of the Hunt which felt like they were burrowing through the soft material of his brain. He could feel the itching in his head.

When the car did land it was not gentle. A full storm was blowing, tearing smaller branches from the trees and whipping up the fallen leaves and detritus. Six pulled Aries out of the car and they struggled through the wind towards the front door. A peal of thunder erupted overhead. The deafening power of the shock wave threw both of them to the ground, but they scrambled to their feet and kept moving. The wind picked up the gravel in tiny twisters and pelted them both with it. John felt it cut his face and hands.

Finally they staggered to the relative safety of the doorway which immediately opened and they gratefully passed through. Clarice, Simon and Dexter rushed over to them. Six vanished into the house. Clarice embraced John, then pulled back and examined him. He noticed that his blood was on her left cheek and dress.

"You look awful, John. What happened?"

It took him a few moments to find his voice, and when he did speak it was cracked and raw. "I failed. I tried to banish the Hunt, but it knew me! It was my father!"

Dexter and Simon looked confused. Clarice's eyes grew wide.

"Your father? But your father is dead."

"He... he summoned the Hunt and was consumed by it."

"Samael's blade! That is why it made me pick you. That is why... oh... oh! What did I do?" She brought her hand to her face and her eyes welled up with tears. "Oh! Oh! I am so sorry, John. I did not know!"

Aries reached out gently and touched her bloody cheek with the back of his hand. "None of us knew. This... this thing is far more clever than any of us thought. But it is now after me. It has chased me all the way here, toying with me, playing with me. Simon," he turned to Clarice's brother-in-law, "do you know of any way we can stop it now?"

Simon's brow furrowed as he thought. He quickly replied, "Yes! Perhaps in my library." Dexter meanwhile had a curiously vacant look, as if what he was hearing was not real.

Clarice looked confused, "Your library? Where?"

"Here! In this house."

"What are you talking about, Simon?"

"Come... follow me!"

Simon ran off across the hallway into the study. The study where John had first met Clarice. They followed. Without pausing, Simon ran to the fireplace and reached inside the right edge.

"A long time ago, before I met you Clarice, I had a private sanctum built. I built a fully soundproofed, Wyld Shielded, EM-shielded safe room as my private, inviolate sanctuary. I was paranoid that someone would break in, so I made it as secure as possible. It is safer than any bank vault and more secure than any prison."

A rectangular section of the floor hinged up from one of the short sides, revealing a staircase descending into the darkness.

"It is still here! Come. There may be something down there that could help."

Simon led the way, the others following closely behind. Clarice supported John as he walked. Beneath the study was a large library, and from a glance at their spines all the books here were about history, the Disciples, Echo abilities and the occult.

"By the Hammer of the Overlord!" exclaimed Dexter. They all spun to face him. He was looking at the corner of the room. Slumped in the corner was a body. The body of Charles Hamilton-Jones. The top of his head had been blown off and the wall behind him was sprayed with an ugly mixture of dried blood and brain matter. A pistol lay in his limp right hand by his side.

From the state of the body, Aries guessed he had been here this whole time. *Under my very feet as I first met Clarice!* Simon ran over to the body. "Charlie!"

Clarice and John joined him. Clarice's face was a mask of confusion. "I don't understand. How can he be here? Why is he here?"

Simon, now crouched, rocked back on his heels. "Oh no. I think I know. You see when I built this place, it was to be my occult sanctuary. I worked tirelessly in its preparation to ensure it was warded, sealed and protected. It was to be an impregnable fortress. You see I was paranoid that I would be attacked, or spied on, or my books would be stolen. Charlie, he knew about it. I had shown it to him once before... before the Asylum... when I was drunk. I wanted to get his opinion about whether I should show it to you, Clarice. But we argued and I never showed him how to open the exit from the inside. It just did not come up."

Aries completed the train of thought for him. "Charles came here, hoping it would provide protection from the Wyld Hunt, and it did, but it left him trapped, facing a slow death from starvation here. And if he did escape he would be caught by the Hunt. He must have taken his own life in desperation."

Clarice gently took Charles' dead left hand in hers. Her voice was soft and emotional as she said, "You stupid, stupid man, Charles."

A distant peal of thunder brought Aries' mind back to the present. "Simon, we still need to stop the Wyld Hunt. Can you do it?"

Simon stood once more and moved to the bookcase.

"Yes, I just need to find a specific book." He scanned the books and then exclaimed a startled, "Oh!"

"What?"

"It is not here! The book! It's gone! He must have taken it!"

"Isoke's balls! Everyone look for it! Simon — what does it look like?"

"It is about this thick," he said indicating a hand span, "with a dark brown cover. It is leather bound, very heavy. The title is *'The Writings of the Akonites'*."

"The Writings of the Akonites... I have heard that name before. Where have I seen it?" With unexpected crystal clarity Aries remembered seeing it on the desk of Sir James Villiers-Cavanaugh. "Samael's blade! Sir James has it! Somehow, I do not know how, he got hold of the book!"

Simon's eyes grew wide. "Then we are doomed! Without that book, I do not know how to stop the Hunt!"

Aries, like everyone else in the room, felt a physical blow as all hope was snuffed out. He abruptly felt dizzy and staggered to the wall and slowly collapsed.

Simon, still in shock from the news muttered, "The Hunt cannot get us in here... at least I don't think it can, but we cannot leave. Ever!"

Clarice crawled over to Aries. "I am so sorry, John." He looked deep into her eyes,

"I... we both did stupid things. I tried so hard, but it was always ahead of me. We were outsmarted, by the Hunt, and by Sir James. We have been beaten."

The silence in the room was oppressive. No one said anything, but they all knew that the situation was hopeless. The Hunt had won. Either they remained here till they starved or they went out and surrendered to the Hunt. In all his years of running from his former life, Aries had never felt so low.

Suddenly the silence was shattered.

"No!" Everyone looked around at the source of the voice. It was Dexter, who was standing. "No!" he repeated, "This is not your fault. This is Charles' fault. This is the Honourable Brotherhood's fault. This is my fault! It has to end!"

"What are you talking about, Cassian?"

"I thought I could escape the consequences of my actions. You, Aries, were a man of your word, you were going to let me escape even if that meant damning yourself. Well now we're all trapped and it's because of me and because of him!" He pointed at Charles' corpse. "I will not let it end like this."

Dexter kneeled down and with visible effort he picked up the corpse of Charles in his arms. He was not a strong man and the exertion was clear on his face.

Aries stood. "What are you doing?"

"What I should have done in the beginning. We all thought we could run away and hide from the Hunt. But we were the architects of our own destruction. There never was any hiding." Dexter turned and started up the stairs. "Simon, open the damned door!"

Simon looked at Aries and Clarice, who nodded. He sought the secret catch and released it, once more revealing the entrance way. They heard Dexter's sharp intake of breath and hurried over.

The top of the stairway was filled with absolute blackness. The Hunt was here.

Cassian Dexter turned to Aries, "Don't let that bastard, Sir James, win?"

"I won't."

Dexter took a deep breath and began to climb the stairs with the body of Charles.

"The Hunt is over! You have me and here is Charles! You won! You bloody won!" He disappeared into the blackness with a shout.

For what felt an eternity they stood there, waiting for... something to happen, their breaths held.

Have we won? Have we defeated the Hunt? Aries was wound too tightly to say the words they were all thinking aloud. Despite himself, he found himself praying to the Overlord. *Overlord guide us through this dark place and protect us from the forces of vengeance.*

It was agonising, but abruptly the darkness folded in on itself, shrinking down to the form of a man with glowing yellow eyes. The shadow figure spoke and Aries felt a terrible weight inside himself. Its voice was filled with cruel humour.

"The Hunt is not quite over. Aurelian, it is time for you to come with me." The Hunt's voice seemed to have physical form, twisting and distorting reality around it.

Clarice pushed herself in front of Aries.

"You. Cannot. Have. Him. The Hunt is over! You have what you were ordered to take, and now I banish you. Return to your darkness and stay there."

The shadow figure chuckled. "Is this what you want, son?"

The tension was palpable. Aries' throat was dry and he struggled to make himself heard.

"It is."

Again there was silence. They could feel the white hot heat of vengeance from the shadow figure.

"Very well then. You may remain here. For now." The last two words were filled with finality and Aries knew with absolute certainty that he had not seen the last of the Wyld Hunt.

The shadow figure seemed to explode and the staircase was awash with light.

Clarice turned to Aries and Simon, tears streaming down her face. "Is it over? Is it gone?"

Simon cautiously advanced up the stairs. "Something like the Wyld Hunt can never truly be defeated, merely appeased, but I think so. I think so!"

They all three ascended into the light. Aries was still in shock, almost unwilling to believe it, but it was true. The voices were gone. He knew that the Hunt had been banished, for now. Before he knew what he was doing, he turned and embraced Clarice, pulling her body tight against him. All too soon he broke the embrace as cold, hard reality hit home. The Hunt might be gone, but he was not safe yet. Clarice looked at him curiously.

"It is not over. Not while Sir James has that book. He has to be stopped. I have no choice, after all the Agency is still looking to kill me."

"But… now? Can you not wait? You are tired, injured and a mess." He was tempted to wait. The door to the study opened and Six entered.

"Miss Clarice, there is something on the WeaveNet you should see." Six activated the projection. It was on a news feed. The scrolling headlines made them all take pause.

"London Agency Commander Sir James Villiers-Cavanaugh issues arrest warrant for the Deputy Governor. The Deputy Governor has sought protection from London Metropolice Commissioner Tanaka. Tense stand-off between Agency and London Metropolice. Commissioner Tanaka describes events as 'an attempted coup'. Fears of a new civil war."

John felt the full weight of responsibility hit him.

"That answers that question. I have to go now, before he has time to strike at us all again. Before he destroys everything." *Time to take the fight to him.*

Clarice nodded, her demeanour now all business. "How can we help?"

"First you can get me a whole handful of pain killers and stims, and then I need you to do a few things for me. I have a promise to Dexter to honour."

20

Steel Year 2425.10.10 (S-Time). Day Ten, Morning.

Lovelace's arrival at the mansion shocked Aries. The transformation from near-corpse to fully healed was remarkable. Lovelace had to admit, Clarice's doctors had done an amazing job. Under their skilled hands and the nanobots, he was already feeling almost as good as new. Aside from a slight tenderness around his neck he was otherwise in perfect shape.

"Bloody hells, Lovelace! It is damn good to see you." The two men embraced.

Aries, however, looked like shit. Battered and bruised, his eye sockets were so dark they were almost black and his eyes were blood-shot and slightly glowing. The short blond hair did not suit him either. His eyes had gained a haunted cast and he looked exhausted. He was wearing a short black leather jacket and dark blue jeans. He worried at his chipped fingernails.

"Isoke's balls, John! You look like bloody death. I thought I was the one who almost just got killed?"

Aries gave a sad weak smile.

"I could not believe it when Clarice told me you were on the way. I asked her to look after you… I never thought… wow. Look, are you still going to go after Clarice?"

"Not at the moment. It's complicated."

Now Aries genuinely laughed. "That it is."

"So, I heard the Wyld Hunt is gone?"

"For now, but if we do not stop Sir James it is only a matter of time before it returns. Seriously Tarus, since you have been out, everything has exploded."

"I heard. I saw the pictures. Villiers-Cavanaugh has Tanaka and the Deputy Governor besieged in the Judgement Tower. Things out there are tense, the Metropolice are squaring off against the Agency with the Astro Marine Corps waiting on the sidelines. I've never seen it this bad. Not since the Civil War. The Commander's gone insane. He needs to be stopped."

"I agree, and we are the people who have to stop him."

"John, do I need to remind you that you've a bloody Termination Order out on you! How are you going to get close enough to Sir James to strike?"

"I have a plan, and I need your help. How good are you with sniper rifles?"

"You know I served as a sniper during my stint in Tactical with the Metropolice — back before I became a detective, right? Why, what are you thinking?"

"Given your recent history, how you would you like to get a bit of turnabout?"

Lovelace smiled revealing his teeth.

"I'd like that a lot."

"Good. Now to make this happen I am going to need the help of some of your Metropolice friends. From my side, do you think I could call on Tynes?"

"He's a good tactical agent and I think he'd side with us, but it'd be too risky to let him know what you are planning. But he won't go against you."

"That is what I thought. I know I can count on Linsbury to help us get close. With the help Kari and Clarice can give us there is only one more call I need to make."

"Oh? Who?"

"Denver."

"Denver — the Governor's son and owner of Methadrine? Why the bloody hells would you call him?"

"I'll need the media ready, and nobody gets their attention like Denver."

Lovelace, despite himself, nodded.

"Overlord! You've got the balls of a Disciple, John. Colour me intrigued, what do you have planned?"

*   *   *

Aries looked down at his hands. The painkillers and stims had helped, they were barely shaking now. Lovelace had been unable to hide his shock when he had seen Aries. *I guess I just had not thought about how strung out I was. Still, no matter. This is going to happen, now.* He finished putting on the tactical armour and checked the magazines in his DarkStorm M91 autorifle and Aralyte Terminator autopistol. If everything went to plan, he would not need the added protection, but Lovelace had insisted.

Aries sat in the back of the unmarked London Metropolice grav plane holding position in the turbulent clouds behind the Stealth Tower. Across from him sat Lovelace, similarly dressed, though he was assembling a huge sniper rifle. The two Agents were going armed for war. To his left sat Kari, her face curiously placid as she focused on interacting with the Weave, the digital reality that infused everything in London. Linsbury had provided them with the latest Agency security codes and let them know where Sir James was.

According to Linsbury, Sir James was close to events in a Mobile Command Centre outside the Judgement Tower in Tyburn Square. He wanted to be on scene to take advantage of the publicity when he finally got Tanaka and the Deputy Governor. Aries hoped Linsbury's help would be enough to get him in front of the Commander. *Now if the other pieces fall into place as hoped we should be good.*

Aries realised he felt no excitement, no nerves. Just a clarity of thought. He had faced down the Wyld Hunt. Twice. The Commander held no power over him. The last mental thresholds had fallen and now all that was left was cold determination. *Sir James will be stopped, at any cost. This is it. Everything gets decided here and now.*

Aries smiled and felt at peace.

*   *   *

Aries had dropped Lovelace off atop the Necropolis near the Commander's Mobile Command Centre outside the Judgement Tower. Judgement Tower itself was controlled by Commissioner Tanaka and her forces. Lovelace hit the ground running, covering the distance with an economy of movement that was a calculated trade-off between stealth and speed. Hypervate, a reaction-improving stim, flowed through his system along with a dose of Fury, the pain-suppressant combat drug.

I don't have long. He scanned the rooftop, his eyes alert to the smallest movement. *There!* He saw the tell-tale shimmer of a sniper in poly-mimetic armour. At any significant distance the sniper would be essentially invisible, but Lovelace was less than fifteen metres away. From here Lovelace could see the sniper had an outstanding view over Tyburn Square and the Tower of Judgement.

The Pure slowed his approach and quietly vaulted the last set of ventilation units. He charged his shock gloves and stormed the remaining distance in less than a quarter second. The sniper barely had time to react before Lovelace's huge fist smashed down into his spine, the capacitors in the knuckles discharging as soon as they made contact. The sniper spasmed and went still. Lovelace grabbed the rifle and smashed it on the low wall. He then expertly removed the sniper's sidearm and knife and hog-tied him.

Next!

Lovelace raised his binoculars and scanned the buildings surrounding Tyburn Square. The only other suitable vantage point was on the Temple of the Overlord. Aries and Lovelace had confirmed that Shield were running a so-called 'Quarter-Second Bubble' around the Commander, the theory being that the outermost security personnel could issue a quarter-second warning should the Commander be threatened or the situation change critically. A quarter of a second did not sound like much, but Lovelace knew it was more than enough.

He crouch-jogged along the roof to the nearest point to the Temple and pulled out his own sniper rifle and attached a grapple and line via a specialised barrel attachment. He quickly aimed and fired, the gauss-accelerated grapple slamming into the Temple just below the lip of the wall and embedding itself with an electromagnetic solvent.

Lovelace pulled out a slide mechanism and in one clean move – and regardless of the height – leapt over the edge of the Necropolis and connected with the wire. He silently slid across the gap in seconds. He climbed over the wall and again scanned for the sniper.

I see him! He spotted the air of distortion where the sniper was, and moved in. Just before he reached the sniper though he paused. The sniper was too cool. Either he was dead, or… Lovelace spun and brought up his armoured wrist guards.

He came face to face with the sniper primed to strike with his combat knife. The sniper had been attempting to launch his own sneak attack. *He must have seen me on the other roof! Damn!*

The sniper struck and Lovelace parried, his drug-enhanced reflexes making everything feel terribly slow. The impact against his own blade was almost stunning in its own right. The sniper, without pause, flipped the knife in his hand to point downward and slashed low and fast at Lovelace's knee joints.

He is fast!

Lovelace was faster and jumped up, the blade swishing harmlessly below his feet. The Pure used his momentum to smash his hands down on the sniper's head. The impact was massive and Lovelace heard several vertebrae make popping noises in the sniper's neck as he went down. He checked the sniper's pulse. It was still there but weak. Lovelace chuckled to himself, he had not had a chance to charge his gloves. He quickly restrained the sniper, whispered, "Sorry mate. I'll be sure to call the ambulance once this is all over." and moved over to the edge and took up position.

He was just in time, too.

Through the scope he saw the grav plane land and Aries emerge. Linsbury was there to meet John. Lovelace turned his comm onto the correct frequency to overhear their conversation as the two of them walked confidently towards the Agency perimeter security and the Mobile Command Centre, parked beyond.

"Good to see you, John."

"You too, Paul. Thanks for doing this."

"Don't thank me yet. Let's see how we get on, eh?"

Seeing who was approaching, the tactical agents on duty raised their weapons. Lovelace target-marked all five of the agents. He did not want to have to kill them, but if this failed, he would do what he needed to. From here he could read their name tags. Lovelace saw something that made him smile. *Thank you, Tattooed Man!*

Linsbury raised his hands. Aries slung his rifle, his posture relaxed as if merely out for an afternoon stroll. It was Linsbury who spoke first.

"We are here to arrest the Commander."

"I'm sorry, Captain, but we can't let you do that. We have orders to shoot him —" He indicated Aries, "on sight."

The fact that Aries was still alive was a good sign.

"Sergeant… Tynes, you know me. You all know me. I have been in the Agency since the end of the Civil War. Since before you all joined. You know I serve justice and peace and I think I have earned your trust. Well, believe me when I say that if this does not end here with the arrest of the Commander than we are facing the very real threat of another Civil War. The Commander's actions have gone beyond any duty. He is out of control. This is not about justice, this is about his personal power. We all swore a sacred oath to defend the Steel Alliance from all enemies, both foreign and domestic. Well, they don't make us swear those oaths lightly. The Commander has become the enemy, and that means it is time for you to decide which is more important to you: your honour and duty, or the Commander."

Lovelace could see the tactical agents' resolve waver.

"Sergeant Tynes. You know Agent Aries is no enemy of the state. Let him through to finish this, or millions of people — whole worlds — will burn to satisfy the Commander's lust for power. Is that what you want?"

Linsbury's words hung in the air. The tension was unbearable. Lovelace deactivated the safety on his sniper rifle. *Just in case.* Tynes was quiet, his eyes narrowed, while he made his decision.

Finally, he spoke.

"Stand down men. Let them through." Lovelace's sigh of relief came out as a low whistle.

Linsbury turned to Aries, "Take it from here, John." Aries nodded and walked through the tactical marines. Lovelace switched the magazine on his sniper rifle for a specially marked one. Aries' procession through the Agency camp was dramatic. The agents all stopped what they were doing and turned to watch him calmly walk over to the armoured truck, fitted out as the Mobile Command Centre.

He stopped outside. When he spoke, his voice carried clearly across the camp. Each word played crisp and clear over the comm connection.

"Villiers-Cavanaugh. Step out of the Command Centre, you are under arrest for treason."

The door opened and Sir James emerged. His face was stony. In contrast, when he spoke, each word was bitten off.

"Aries! You should be dead. Kill this renegade!"

No one moved to obey the Commander's orders. Villiers-Cavanaugh's eyes narrowed and he scanned the crowd.

"Fine. Snipers, take him out!"

Nothing happened.

"Your snipers send their apologies, Commander. They had an urgent appointment with Agent Lovelace."

A nervous tic developed in the Commander's lower left eyelid. Before he could speak, Aries continued, "Sir James Villiers-Cavanaugh, I am arresting you for the Act of Treason under the powers invested me by the Steel Alliance Accord. If you have the right to Legal Counsel, you have the right to remain silent. If you attempt to escape you will be stopped by any means necessary. Do you understand?"

"You. Can't. Arrest. Me! By Divine Mandate, I am the Commander, and you are a bloody pathetic renegade."

Aries' voice was quiet, controlled and powerful.

"No sir. I am an Agent and a servant of the law."

Lovelace saw Sir James' face twist up and his eyes begin to glow as he summoned the Wyld. Lovelace pulled the trigger on his sniper rifle and the Commander collapsed bonelessly to the floor.

Aries stepped forward, kneeled down and took the Commander's pulse. He looked up, roughly in Lovelace's direction and gave him the thumbs up signal. Lovelace felt a wave of relief flow through him.

Isoke's balls! The tranquilliser round worked! Thank the Overlord for that!

Lovelace packed up his sniper rifle, checked his rappel rig and launched himself off the Temple, rapidly descending towards the square and his partner and the unconscious Commander.

*   *   *

Aries and Lovelace stepped through the Agency cordon and marched the Commander into Tyburn Square in handcuffs. The Commander's feet dragged along the ground, the tranquilliser had rendered him barely conscious. He was drooling. Two familiar dark-suited Shield agents approached them. Both were holding their sidearms, ready to spring into action.

It was crew-cut who spoke.

"Agent Lovelace. Hand the Commander and this wanted fugitive —" indicating Aries "over to us now."

Lovelace smiled.

"No."

"I don't think you understand the gravity of the situation, Agent Lovelace. If you comply now we are willing to overlook your collusion with a known felon."

Lovelace's smile grew broader.

"No. The Commander is under arrest and he is coming with me."

Both Shield agents raised their pistols. Aries tensed for the imminent fight. Then another voice spoke out from behind the two Shield agents.

"You heard Agent Lovelace. The Commander has been placed under arrest, and *Agent* Aries is under my personal protection."

The Shield agents rotated and came face to face with Commissioner Tanaka, and a solid wall of fully-armed tactical police. From behind them came the noise of hundreds of engines revving in sync.

To their credit, the Shield agents did not back down easily.

"This is an Agency matter, Madame Commissioner. Your assistance is not required here."

Tanaka's face was placid. She raised her right index finger and the electronic beeping of at least twenty autorifles having their safeties disengaged was sharp in the air. Her point made, she smiled and reached into her jacket pocket and pulled out a comm. The tension was palpable in the air.

She walked over to the two Shield agents and presented it to them.

"That is an arrest warrant for the Commander and an official order rescinding the *illegally authorised* Termination Order against Agent Aries, signed by myself, Deputy Governor Vargas and... Governor Sagacious. Furthermore, it has been authorised by the office of the Aegis of the Agency on Mars. Gentlemen, do not make a mistake you will regret for a very, very brief moment. There has been enough bloodshed over this man—" she indicated the Commander, "don't you think?"

Crew-cut slowly holstered his pistol and examined the warrant and orders very carefully. Finally, he nodded his head and said to his bald partner, "Everything is in order." He then turned to Commissioner Tanaka, "Everything is in order, Madame Commissioner." His partner also holstered his weapon.

Aries and Lovelace marched the barely-conscious Sir James up to the Commissioner. Aries and Lovelace swapped a look, Aries nodded to Lovelace to take the lead. *After all, until this is all over, he is the only one of us who is actually an Agent.* Lovelace cleared his throat.

"Madame Commissioner, I formally turn the custody of Sir James Villiers-Cavanaugh over to yourself under the authority of the Governor." They passed the Commander over to two tactical officers who had slung their rifles and picked him up.

Commander Tanaka completed the formality, "Agent Lovelace, I acknowledge the transfer of custody of Sir James Villiers-Cavanaugh." Then she smiled brightly. "I think, however that you should accompany him and I to the entrance of the Tower of Judgement. There is something you might like to see."

What can it be?

They walked with the Commissioner out past the crowd of Agents and Metropolice that had formed there, and into Tyburn Square. Arranged outside was a mass of reporters and Metropolice, and many, many police bikes and cars. *Denver did his work well, it looks like every media source in the Accord is here!* Behind the police lines were thousands of ordinary people. The air was filled with grav planes. As they appeared the police ground vehicles all began to rev their engines in sync. The noise was incredible, the bass reverberation physically shook the ground.

Both Aries and Lovelace had to shield their eyes from the glare. Tanaka walked over to a rapidly prepared stage. She raised her hands for quiet and immediately the revving stopped. The silence that replaced it was all the more absolute for the contrast.

"Today we have taken into custody Sir James Villiers-Cavanaugh, Commander of the London Agency Division, on charges including, but not limited to, treason, murder, attempted murder and corruption. This is a dark day for London, that one so trusted with ensuring the peace and security of this mighty city should fall so low. Yet out of the darkness comes light. If it were not for the unswerving dedication to the law of two of his own Agents, the Commander would never have been foiled. I wish to take this time to formally commend the selfless actions of Agent John Aries and Agent Tarus 'Lovelace' Arken Karazhja. Their actions do much to clear the Agency of the tarnish caused by Commander Villiers-Cavanaugh and I think we all owe them a debt of gratitude."

Once more all the Metropolice ground vehicles revved their engines. They were invited onto the stage and shook hands with the Commissioner. Aries could see Lovelace was as uncomfortable with the media attention as he was, but they both gritted their teeth and bared it. *It is the price we have to pay if we want to see justice done, I guess.*

Still, their relief was palpable when they were shown off the stage while the Commissioner began to field the many questions being thrown at her by the press.

"I have to hand it to her, she sure knows how to handle publicity."

Lovelace nodded and said in return, "I am sure this will not do anything to hurt her own chances at becoming the new Governor."

Aries looked back at Tanaka on the stage. She commanded the space with confidence.

"I think I am okay with that."

Lovelace snorted.

"Yeah, me too."

As they pushed their way through the crowd, many people and Metropolice took the opportunity to pat them on the shoulders and back. Finally they broke through. Aries cast a glance back at the Temple of the Overlord. Highpriest-Keeper Malachi was standing on the balcony watching them. When he saw that he had been spotted by Aries he raised his hand in a silent, mock, salute. *Things are not over between us, Malachi. I may not be able to arrest you now, but I will get you, you murdering sack of slime.*

Lovelace's voice brought his attention back to their immediate surroundings. "Looks like we won't have to walk."

Six, the butler, stood in front of Clarice's grav car. As they approached he nodded and opened the rear door for them. Both Agents climbed in. Clarice and Simon were waiting for them inside the roomy interior. Clarice was smiling.

"Well done, boys. I thought you could do with a lift... and maybe a drink?"

They sank into the facing seats. Lovelace was the first to speak. "Blood hells, yes!" Aries merely smiled and leaned back, relaxing. He looked out the window at the city as the car rose into the air. He felt Clarice's hand squeeze his knee and he looked around. She mouthed, "Well done." and handed him a drink.

Aloud she said, "To the downfall of Sir James Villiers-Cavanaugh and the Honourable Brotherhood and to a victory for you and for justice."

They all drank deep. Still, behind the smiles Aries wondered if it had all been worth it. *Those men schemed so hard to gain power and in the end all they got was a dismal death while they corrupted everything around them, including me. I almost died, and so did Lovelace. If Clarice had not upset their plans and become the Avatar of the Hunt first I can only imagine what the consequences would have been. But because of that action many people died.* He realised that he was too tired to think clearly, *Questions for another day, after I've had a drink, a shower and a long sleep.*

21

Steel Year 2425.10.16 (S-Time). Several days later, Morning.

Lovelace and Aries sat in the café. They were still awaiting the formal reinstatement of Aries to the Agency, but while the necessary bureaucracy rolled at its own pace, Aries had sensibly taken the time to recover. His hair was back to its normal dark brown colour and he looked rested and well.

Both were sipping their coffees.

"Tarus, a while back you said you knew there was more to me than I was telling and I said that I could not tell you then."

"I remember."

"I think I am ready to tell you about it now. But, that is only if you want me to. Knowing the truth about me might make it dangerous for you. My secret has got people killed. Is that what you still want?"

"Yes."

"Okay." Aries took a deep breath. "I was not always John Aries. In fact I've been known by many different names, but the one I was originally born with was Aurelian Favian-DeVir. I was the son of Duke Memnon Favian-DeVir, ruler of the worlds of Metropolis, Hammer, Kyriakos and many others. I was a prince of a dying dynasty, and... my father was partly responsible for causing the Civil War."

Aries told him of Ariadne, of the death of his brother, of the riots, the revolts and the revolutions, and finally he told him about his father and the Wyld Hunt.

"You see, that was why the Wyld Hunt made Clarice choose me for the investigation. But that is also why I spent most of my life on the run. The crimes my father committed, and my status as the last surviving Favian-DeVir mean that the entire Federate Combine would go to almost any lengths to see me dead. As long as I am alive, I am a threat to their very existence and a link to the past. Even though I was not directly responsible, my hands are stained with the blood of tyranny. So now I tell you and I leave it to your conscience what you do with that information."

It was a lot to take in. He had known that Aries had a hidden background, but he had never suspected the true scale. His partner was the son of one of the most infamous nobles known to history, a man whose excesses provided one of the triggers that spun the entire Steel Alliance into the Civil War. Hundreds of millions of people died in the Civil War. Entire worlds were wiped out, and at times it had been unclear if interstellar society itself would survive. Many of Lovelace's own family had died in the Civil War.

"You understand now why I could not tell you? The risk, alone, that the Federate Combine's SSG secret police would find me was too great."

Lovelace looked at his partner with different eyes. He could see Aries awaiting a reaction.

"Why did you become an Agent?"

"Truth? The truth is that I was looking for a way to vindicate myself, to try and atone for the sins of my family. Truth is, I was looking for a heroic death."

"And now?"

"Now I just want to have an ordinary life. Somewhere along the way I realised that I wanted to try and make the world a better place, but that I also just wanted to live."

Lovelace nodded. He could see Aries was still nervously awaiting some sign of a reaction. Finally, Lovelace let out a long slow breath.

"I understand. Thank you for trusting me enough to tell me. Who else knows?"

"I think you deserved at least that much, partner. Just Clarice, she worked it out. Dexter knew, but he is gone now."

Slowly Lovelace smiled. "Your secret is safe with me. Bloody hells though, Aries! When you do mysterious pasts you don't do them by halves do you?"

Aries smiled, the relief clear on his face. He looked as if a great burden had lifted from his shoulders.

"Are you okay that your face has been transmitted all over the Accord and beyond — even as far as the Federate Combine? After all, Tanaka made arresting Sir James into a major press event."

"I think so… I've had major cosmetic surgery to change my appearance, hopefully it was enough. Either way I will keep looking over my shoulder for when the SSG do come knocking." Aries did not look convinced that he was safe.

"I've got your back now too, John."

"Thanks."

"No problem. It is a shame Malachi got away, but with Dexter gone the last evidence linking him to the murder of Highpriestess-Keeper Neteri is gone."

"True, but I am going to keep a close eye on him. Sooner or later he will make a mistake."

"Let's bloody hope so. Which reminds me: have you pieced together what happened to Charles?"

"I think so. I think after he summoned the Wyld Hunt he fled first to Hampstead Asylum and tried to see Simon. When they would not let him in, he went to his building in Lower Bricktown, only for some reason he did not make it and landed in Vauxhall. The Hunt messes with your mind. From there he ran to The Souk where he tried to throw the Hunt off his trail with the scav he killed. After that he finally made it to his Lower Bricktown building, realised that the Commander had already been there and taken the book, and panicked. Somehow, I still do not know exactly how, he made it back to his mansion in East Hampstead and entered Simon's secret vault there. Once there he quickly discovered that there was nothing there that could help him. He panicked, realising he had trapped himself and chose to take his own life rather than let the Hunt have him."

"A pathetic end."

"I guess."

"Oh that reminds me, Nigel Massey de Sargon's Aegis Foundation file came in. It turns out he was a photokinetic. I guess being able to manipulate light was no help at all when being chased down by the Hunt."

Aries chuckled, "I guess not."

"And now you know the truth about Clarice?"

"It is complicated. I love her, that much is certain. She understands me like nobody else... since my wife Ariadne, and she knows the truth about me. But things are complex. Her husband has just died, she has rediscovered her brother-in-law, and I learned the truth about my father and the Hunt's involvement with my own life. Frankly, it is going to take time to see how things play out. I hope we can figure it out, but we have such different lives. I just do not know yet."

Lovelace nodded, then smiled.

"Well if you are going to mope, I at least have some good news."

"Oh?"

"After everything that happened, I realised that I had kind of been brooding about my past with the Metropolice and then the Agency. Anyway, there might be someone in my life too."

"Who?"

"It's early days, so I'd rather not share details yet, just that with that and hearing your 'troubles' I think I can put my bad old days behind me."

It was Aries' turn to smile.

"Good man!"

"Thanks."

Aries reached into his pocket and pulled out a flyer.

"That reminds me, Simon is having his first art exhibition this evening. Would you like to join Clarice and I?"

Lovelace picked up the flyer and examined it carefully. He chuckled.

"After all this, Simon finally gets to be an artist. I guess there is some justice in the universe. Sure, I would love to come and I will find out if…my friend… is free." Lovelace changed the subject once more, "Any word on you and the Agency?"

"Linsbury says it will take a while yet, but he is confident that the inquiry will clear me of all charges and reinstate me."

"Good news, partner. It has not been the same without you."

"What about you? I heard some rumours about you and some mercenary pit fighter?"

"You heard about that? Yes, it is true. I made a promise in return for a favour. We have not yet arranged the fight, but it will be soon."

"Well, when it happens I will be there, partner."

Lovelace smiled and leaned back.

"Thanks. Aries, is being your partner going to mean every case is like this?"

"Probably." Lovelace chuckled.

"Fair enough. I think I need better medical cover."

Aries laughed. With the air cleared, the two men continued drinking their coffees in a comfortable silence.

Aries and Lovelace will return in The Firestorm Conspiracy!

Lovelace stars in Dead Angels, a prequel set before the events of The Wyld Hunt when Lovelace was still in the London Metropolice. Dead Angels is available now in ebook from www.Delta14.com.

We proudly present a sample here:

Dead Angels sample

Lovelace ignored him and proceeded over to the body. He gently kneeled down and looked up at the one remaining Patrol Officer on the pier.

"Who found the body?"

"Local fisherman." Lovelace did not want to think about the kind of fish you would hook here. "He's over there." Lovelace glanced in the direction and was pleased to see the emaciated man was already giving a statement to Sark. *Using his initiative. Good boy. He's a junior detective but he's already ten the times the police officer that Revere will ever be. Shame he got partnered with me, I guess.*

"Anyone else touch the body?"

"Just me, an EMT and these two folks from the Coroner's Office. Fisherman said he never touched her, but I think you can assume he checked for valuables."

Lovelace nodded and peeled open the plastic sheeting wrapped around the body, steeling himself as he did so. A body left for a prolonged period of time in the river was never a pleasant sight.

"Oh!" He gasped as he revealed her.

Lying there was a beautiful girl. Her pale skin was flawless and in the early morning light appeared to have an ethereal glow. Her long blond hair hung around her head like a halo. But what most stood out was that she was dressed as an angel, a lesser servant of the Overlord. With beautiful feathered, white wings spread wide and a simple gold circlet resting on her forehead. She looked like she was sleeping.

But then the hard truth slowly emerged. He could see the hair at the side and back of her head was matted. Her skin was too pale, bloodless. Pulling on forensic gloves he gently took her head in his hands and rotated it so he could see the back of her head. There, impossible to miss, was a nasty wound. The skull was smashed in. There was no doubt in Lovelace's mind that this was the cause of death.

Gently, he lowered her head once more and began a careful examination of her body. No pockets were visible in the costume and she did not seem to be carrying any identification. Then he spotted something unusual that immediately drew his full attention. Something that shocked him and brought back unwanted memories.

Tattooed on the inside of her lower right forearm were two Kapaethjan word glyphs. Kapaethjan was the language of the Pure homeworld and one that most Pures — including Lovelace — spoke.

Though hundreds of tattoos covered his own alabaster-white skin, it was highly unusual to see Kapaethjan tattoos on a human. Many Pures would treat it as an affront to their honour.

Could get a person into a lot of trouble. Could get a person killed.

They were more than just tattoos to a Pure, they were the skein of their lives. From the Kindred and Caste that all Pures had, to any major life events, such as duels of honour, or achievements. When naked, to another Pure, Lovelace's life was an open book. His tattoos were a tapestry telling of his birth and upbringing in London as part of the Warrior Caste, of his Ascension to adulthood and becoming one of the Truthsayer Kindred. It went to tell of his joining the London Metropolice. It told of the mortal duels he had fought, of the lives he had taken, the loves he had lost, his victories and his defeats.

But these tattoos told no such story, but were still potentially significant. They were the word-characters for «Serenity» and «Unity». They were in the softer, intimate form of Kapaethjan, the script of lovers and poets.

One other detail attracted his attention, a small amber glow pulsed at her wrist. *She has a Nanetic Bio-Status Unit implant.* He looked up at the Coroner.

"I need you to pull her information from her Nanetic Bio-Status Unit for me when you get her body back to the morgue. We need an identification."

"Of course, Detective."

An 'NBSU' was an expensive bit of kit. Lovelace had one as did most members of the London Metropolice and Agency, but for a civilian to have one spoke of significant wealth. *She must be from a corporate family in Uptown.*

He checked her hands. Her nails were slightly chipped, but with no signs of calluses on her fingers or palm. There was no indication of any of the childhood or adolescent illnesses endemic to the lower strata of society. Lovelace would also have put money on her having received genetic tailoring — genesculpting — probably in-vitro or even inherited. Either way it meant that there would be people looking for her.

He slowly stood. Looking down at her body he could not shake the feeling that despite the fact she was dead, the poor girl was in peace. He motioned to the Coroner to take the body.

What happened to you? How did you die? He thought again of the tattoos, And how did you live?

About the Author

Gunnar Roxen is the pen name for the detective fiction of Gobion Rowlands. "Gunnar Roxen is a work of fiction. Half-English, half-Swedish Gunnar grew up in the forested heartlands of Sweden. Raised with the myths and sagas, he grew up with the sense of freedom learned while tracking elk in the northern forests. In the UK he gained his passion for exploring. Old train stations, abandoned hospitals, and crumbling films sets were fertile hunting grounds for his imagination. In another life Gunnar has been a games designer, serial entrepreneur, an activist, a science communicator and a whole lot of trouble. Gunnar lives in Oxford with his wonderful wife and two cats."

Blog: http://gunnarroxen.com

Google+: http://gplus.to/GunnarRoxen

Facebook: http://facebook.com/GunnarRoxen

Twitter: http://twitter.com/GunnarRoxen

Thank you to the following lovely folks for tolerating my first drafts of the Wyld Hunt and providing really useful feedback and reality checks: Hannah Rowlands, Marjorie McGuirk, David McGuirk, Fiona O'Grady, Jen Lynch, Nairn McCrudden, Cat Tobin, Tom Ford, Andreas Blom, Rick Ward, Gunilla Ward, Joe Robbins, Antonia Mansell-Long, Matt Harvey, Paola Sassi and the late, lamented Paul Chamberlain. Special thanks to Marjorie & David McGuirk, and Mack & Janice Pearsall and all my friends in the wonderful city of Asheville, NC.

Thanks also to all the many inhabitants of the Broken Shield universe over the years but especially Dr Tom Ford, Sam Morris, Ian Roberts, David Willock, Jonathan Miller, Jonathan Sharland, Ben Britz and Dr Sachin Suchak.

Also thanks to the following cafés for their tolerance of a first time novelist tapping away in the corner: *The Battery Park Book Exchange*, Asheville, North Carolina, USA; *Oxfork Café*, Oxford, UK; *Combibos Café*, Oxford, UK; *Café du Jour*, Bristol, UK and the *Gerard Bar* at the RSA, London, UK. Support your local independent cafés!

This book would have been impossible without the feedback, advice and unfailing support of my wonderful wife, Hannah and my wonderful family. Jag älskar dig! Thank you all! I hope I did you proud :)

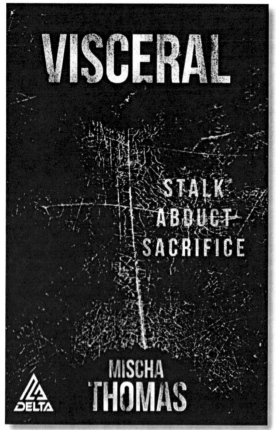

Delta14 Publishing

Bringing you the best Science Fiction, Fantasy, Horror and the Weird.

www.delta14.com

Email: hq@delta14.com
Twitter: @Delta14HQ
Facebook: www.facebook.com/Delta14Publishing

Lightning Source UK Ltd.
Milton Keynes UK
UKOW04f0726081013

218631UK00001B/15/P